Like Ants Under the Door

Robert Faulk

Book Four in the Five-Book Series:

The Songs of War

Like Ants Under the Door

Brutality beyond belief, sacrifice beyond understanding, suffering without hope

The Russian Front 1941–45

Robert Faulk

Galleon Publishing, Moncton, Canada
www.galleonbooks.ca

ISBN
    Print book: 978-1-7780781-3-2
    ebook: 978-1-7780781-4-9

GALLEON

CONTENTS

Prologue

Born on a farm in rural Canada, I grew up like most Canadian farm boys, unprotected from life's experiences and learning practical lessons that would keep me alive. I had already learned the four most important rules of survival in my environment before I went to school. First, don't walk on thin ice and 'hope' it will hold. Second, water will not run uphill. Third, although any fool can see that the sun goes around the earth, it doesn't. And fourth, never lie to my mother or Missus Wilson.

I spent my early years in a two-room school polishing the valuable skills I had learned living in lumber camps, on construction sites, and on the farm. I studied engineering, leaving university a year before graduation to work in my father's construction and lumbering business.

A few years later, under pressure from those in my household who had to listen to me hoot and howl country and western songs, I took singing lessons—no, not the cowboy music that I loved, but opera—sissy music sung by effeminate men. But the unimaginable happened—I learned to love opera and the people involved—and following a few twists and turns in our life, our family lived in Germany from 1973 to 1980, where I studied opera and voice. Seriously... I did that, and my wife and three children, whose sanity I now question, encouraged me.

The time was thirty years after WW2, and most of the German people I met who were old enough had memories of those terrible years burned into their brains. They voluntarily told me their stories, probably because I was a Canadian, and, at the time, no one but the Russian hockey team considered Canadians a threat. I regrettably didn't write them down, but most were so dramatic that they stuck. As I age and short-term memory fades, I remember more of the long-term stuff.

◇◇◇◇◇◇◇◇◇◇◇◇◇◇◇◇◇◇◇◇◇◇◇◇◇◇◇◇◇◇◇◇◇◇◇◇◇

On one memorable occasion, I think it was the summer of 1981, while driving on a Landstrasse, a country road through the black forest south of Stuttgart, looking for a construction site that had a machine I wanted to buy, I spotted a beautiful Percheron horse pulling a plow and a bearded man walking behind it. I stopped and watched them until the man stopped the horse at the end of the furrow, put a bucket under the horse's nose, and sat down. He opened a bag lying on the ground, unwrapped a bundle, sat down with his legs crossed and picked up a beer and a thick piece of Butterbrot. I dismounted from my BMW and walked up the hill.

"Na, dass ist ein wunderbares Pferd," I said, "Mein Vater hatte ein Percheron...ihre Name war 'Queen'...'Koenigen' auf Deutsch."

I had knocked down two birds with one stone. I had earned his respect when I recognized the horse's breed, and it was a fair bet the horse's name would be something to do with royalty.

He stuck out his hand, "Es freut mich." and pointed to his horse. "Zufälligerweise, heisst er 'Koenig,' und du sprichst Prussischer Deutsch aber du bist ein Auslander. Niederlander?" I had been right about the horse's name...king was close enough, and his first guess was that I wasn't a Prussian...Prussians were tolerated in Bayern, but only a few were welcome. I said, "Kanadier," and he smiled, his animosity gone.

Most Percherons are called either 'king' or 'queen,' especially if they are the only horses in the barn. Dad's horse was coincidentally named 'Queen,' and she was a black Percheron. It had been a safe bet that Hans's well-endowed Percheron was named king, or König.

I walked over to König, rubbed his neck and gave him the half-eaten apple I had brought from the car. Horses have strong jaws and impressive teeth, and the only safe way to give them an apple is to put it on your flat hand and let the horse pick it up with its lips. The man I will call Hans smiled, and I knew I had earned a couple of hours with him—maybe more if he played chess.

Hans had been in the Waffen SS and showed me the tattoo under his arm. All SS members had their blood type tattooed there. He had commanded tanks from the beginning of the war to the end, First a panzer III, and finally a squadron of panthers. He had survived Stalingrad, fought at Kursk, the largest tank battle the world has ever seen, and the Americans took him prisoner at the Elbe River a few days before the war officially ended.

We talked until I had to go and look at the Cat 215 excavator, but we met later at a nearby Gaststätte, where we ate the best Schweineshaxen und Sauerkraut I have ever eaten and played chess until they closed. This man was my fictional Klaus—you will meet him in this book— and he is also a main character in the last book, Kindersoldat.

The historical framework I used in this book and this series is as accurate as I can establish, but the characters who lived and died in this series are fictional but typical. None of the stories are factual in their details, but I have attempted to embody the spirit of my friends' unique experiences as related to me.

Chapter One

4–6 March 1941

The Wehrmacht wants You

"...young men are resisting conscription and refusing military service. They are the pioneers of a warless world."

Albert Einstein

On the morning of the fifth of March, 1941, Johann Finke became the first violin in the Bielefeld Opera orchestra, fulfilling his grandest dream. The war had played a part by drying up the competition pool, and the former concertmaster had moved up the ladder to a more prestigious orchestra for the same reason. At thirty, Johann was young to lead the string section, but he felt confident that he could do it.

When Musikdirektor Hofmann shook Johann's hand, congratulated him and shooed him out of his office, Johann's first impulse was to go home to celebrate with his wife, Barbara. But his new job meant that he had work that couldn't wait. He walked to his studio without touching his feet on the floor.

Johann tried for half an hour to practice a Wagner passage that had always plagued him, but his excitement wouldn't let him concentrate. It was almost ten when he gave up, put his violin in its open case and headed for the theatre cafeteria, the *Menza*. It was half-full, and every person in the room stood and clapped when he came through the door. Two sopranos each took an arm and led him to a table. He sat down, and a *Hereforder Pils*, a cup of coffee, and a piece of *Strudel* appeared.

"Speech! Speech!" shouted the crowd, and Johann got to his feet. The room became silent, and he asked, "Are the beer and *Strudel* paid for?" A strong contingent yelled, "*Jawohl!*" and Johann said, "In that case, I am telling you that I believe in hard work and discipline..." His crowd looked at one another and nodded. "...Not for me, for you! It's my job to criticize." The room laughed, with a few remarks thrown in.

◇◇◇◇◇◇◇◇◇◇◇◇◇◇◇◇◇◇◇◇◇◇◇◇◇◇◇◇◇

The following day, still on a high after sharing the news with his family, Johann was in his studio tuning his violin when someone knocked on the door. He said, while he stroked the last string, twisting the knob until the pitch was correct, "Come in…it isn't locked."

The second series of knocks was louder, more insistent. Johann laid the violin carefully on the piano bench, stepped to the door and pushed the handle down. His smile faded, then died.

A young soldier, ramrod straight, an envelope in his left hand, saluted with his right arm stretched toward a distant star. "*Heil Hitler!*" He asked in a loud voice, "*Name bitte?*"

Johann couldn't breathe; he had to lock his knees to keep them from collapsing. The soldier lowered his arm and waited.

When Johann found a breath, his voice broke, "*Ich heisse Johann Finke.*" Every beat of his heart drove a stake deeper in his soul. He abruptly fell from the pedestal he had been on for the past twenty-four hours.

The soldier handed Johann the letter, saluted, turned on his heel and marched down the hall.

Johann used both hands to hold the letter as he stared at the eagle on the *Bundeswehr* letterhead. He read the blurred words as the soldier's heels clicked on the brass-edged stair treads that led down to the main stage door. The door's brass hinges squeaked; it closed with a solid thud and a rattle from a loose windowpane. Johann reread the letter—the words were the same.

"The *Kriegsministerium Deutschland* hereby orders you to report to the training facility in Würzburg no later than 15:00h Monday, 20 March 1941." The department of defence orders then instructed him on what he must take with him and what was *Verboten*. The letter itself gave him free passage on the train.

Johann slid the violin to the side and sat on the piano bench, sweat beading on his forehead. From this day on, he belonged to the German army, the *Wehrmacht*.

He could run away, but where? He fought back the thought—

2

Hitler's army had swift and nasty methods to deal with *Verweigeren*, those who refused to serve. Only a fool would test the Nazi resolve.

He looked at the letter again. Life as he knew it was over.

Slowly packing his violin and bow in the beautiful case his father had given him, then laying it on the piano, Johann slipped his arms into the sleeves of his heavy woollen coat and wound the long scarf his mother Maria had knit for him around his neck. He picked up the violin case and walked out the door, softly closing it behind him. He felt the need to empty his stomach, and a lump grew in his chest.

At the office of *Städtischer Musikdirektor* Hans Hofmann, the man he had worked under for the last year, he passed the letter to his boss and friend, knowing it wasn't the first such letter the state music direktor had seen. Hans skimmed the single page. He raised his eyes to meet Johann's and put the letter in Johann's hand.

"I'll call Rudolph-August, and we'll try to sort this out!" The desperation in his tone articulated the hopelessness of it. The Oetker family had a great deal of power, but little sympathy for those who shirked their duty to the *Reich*.

Johann waved the good intentions off. "No, there is no point in fighting this." He tried to magnify a faint hope. "The war won't last more than a few months." He sat down on a chair, unwrapped the scarf and stared at the floor. "How am I going to tell Barbara?" He said it mostly to himself, but then looked up. "Hans, you know I'll make a shitty soldier. What good is a soldier who can't kill a man?"

Hans put his hand on Johann's shoulder, squeezed it with his strong fingers. "I'm afraid it may be easier than you think."

◇◇◇◇◇◇◇◇◇◇◇◇◇◇◇◇◇◇◇◇◇◇◇◇◇◇◇◇◇◇◇◇

Johann had married Barbara when he was still a student in the conservatory at Frankfurt. She became pregnant with their first child, a girl, and they named her Lisa, after Barbara's mother. A scant year later, they had another child, this time a boy. He came into the world kicking and screaming—a harbinger of things to come. Within days he became his mother's little boy, and the bond astounded Johann. Barbara named him Thomas after her father, who had died in the Great War. For months Thomas screamed and kicked at Johann, refusing to allow his father to touch him, not allowing anyone but Barbara to hold him.

Most nights, Johann sat in the children's room playing the violin, sometimes singing gypsy songs he had learned from his mother. Lisa and Thomas listened raptly without making a sound, saving many miles of walking the floor with screaming babies. Lisa became hooked on the violin, but Thomas kept his musical talents hidden.

Johann and Barbara had discussed the possibility of Wehrmacht conscription, but the reality was more devastating than Johann could have imagined. He dreaded telling his family that the Wehrmacht wanted to make a soldier out of him.

Johann stopped at the theatre Menza to procrastinate with his colleagues and feel sorry for himself over a beer. Fifteen minutes after he had taken off his coat and sat down, the word had spread through the opera house, and the small canteen quickly filled with friends. As with most bad news, they sympathized, proposed preposterous alternatives to obeying the Führer's orders, joked about how to use a fiddle in a fight, and drank beer. Finally, one after another, he and his friends ran out of things to say. They shook hands, embraced, reiterated their sympathies and trickled off home or to rehearsals, thanking God that it was Johann who had been summoned and not them. Three hours and more than a couple of beers after the *Wehrmacht* had confiscated his soul, there was nowhere to go but home.

◇◇◇◇◇◇◇◇◇◇◇◇◇◇◇◇◇◇◇◇◇◇◇◇◇◇◇◇◇◇◇◇◇

Bielefeld, a city of close to a hundred thousand people, could be more like a village when it came to gossip. When Johann reached home, unlocked the door and stepped over the threshold, Barbara leapt at him and wrapped her long arms around his neck. She was slightly taller than he was, and when she rested her chin on his shoulder, she pressed her face against his, her blond hair falling on his face. He could feel the wet on her cheek and regretted not having shaved. She didn't relax the pressure until he pushed her gently away so he could close the door. When he turned back to her, she sobbed loudly and flung her arms around his neck again. He walked her into the living room, where she let go, looked straight at him, pulled her hair back over her shoulders and swallowed her grief in a long gasp.

"Where are the children?" Johann had expected their usual onslaught when he opened the door.

Barbara managed to gain a modicum of control and simultaneously spoke, gasped, and sobbed. "I took…them…to…the neighbours."

Johann admired how different his beautiful wife was from other women he'd met. Her personality had no hint of stoic Prussian nature, but she was the strongest person he knew. From a small town in southern Germany, her open Bavarian character barely tolerated the arrogant, self-pitying Prussians she met.

"When…" she sobbed, wiping her nose with her sleeve… "do you have…to go?" She dried the tears on her face with the back of her hand. "We've…got a lot to do." Barbara shook her head, flopping her long hair back from her face. She pushed it behind her left ear and waited for him to speak.

Surprised that she was already preparing her mind for his going to war, Johann decided that she was right—acceptance came first, but action helped the process. It was time to get started.

"While I'm gone, you should go to live in Detmold, so my parents can be near you and the children. Number one, we will need to register the family in the Detmold *Bürgeramt* as soon as we've found an apartment. Number two, I won't make much money, and Dad can find an apartment for you there—Detmold is cheaper rent than in Bielefeld.…"

Barbara put her arms around Johann and pulled his face close to hers. "I can't do this right now. I need more than a hug."

Johann, frustrated, said, "But, we don't have…"

"Yes, I know. Your father called me right after Hans called him and told me you were conscripted. Theo has already found an apartment for us with a doctor friend of his. We can move in next week if you can get it ready. Hans said that you didn't need to worry about playing in the orchestra."

Johann stepped back. He hadn't told a soul about his conscription, except those at the gathering in the opera house. He walked across the living room, nodding his head, thinking, trying to decide whether he should be angry. Yes, it was logical that Hans would have called his best friend, and it was also logical that his father would have called Barbara, expecting that she would already know. Once on the line, he had to tell her.

His finger pointed at a moving target. "Good, that's good...I can get the *Wohnung* ready. We will need men and a truck to move the furniture...I will call some friends in the opera house. We'll find a *Lastwagen* somewhere to haul the furniture." He tried to be constructive and cheerful, but the thought of all the work he had to do in such a short time overwhelmed him.

She looked at him with a tiny smile, crossed her hands in front of her dress. "That's all taken care of, *Liebling*. Theo and Hans did that too."

He laid both hands on her shoulders and looked into her eyes. "How? I only received the letter a few hours ago!"

Eyes twinkling, she laughed. "I have very dear friends in high places. Hans and Theo arranged everything while you were avoiding me at the canteen." Barbara took his hand, pulled him out of the living room and down the hall. Johann waved his other hand in frustration, but his mood changed when she pulled him into the bedroom.

<hr>

For the next two weeks, Barbara was sexually insatiable, but Johann didn't complain; he didn't refuse her no matter where or when she crooked her finger. Consequently, much of the time, he walked around with a foolish grin on his face. The children spent many nights with Theo and Maria, leaving Johann and Barbara to their intimacies.

Theo joined the Nazi party, and a job for Barbara was his reward. She would work in the railway station, keeping track of travellers in and out of the *Bahnhof*. Theo specified that the job couldn't begin until after Johann left for war and officially became a Nazi.

Barbara and Johann spent the days walking and talking, holding hands like new lovers and making love as often as time allowed. As the twentieth of March approached, they clung ever more desperately to one another.

With assistance from the prop crew at the Bielefeld Opera House and a truck borrowed from the Detmold Theatre, the move to Detmold went smoothly despite copious quantities of beer and laughter. Barbara went to the local citizen's registration office, the *Bürgeramt*, to unregister the family. The next day, armed with the *Abmeldungschein* she had gotten in Bielefeld, she registered the family in the Detmold

Bürgeramt and got an *anmeldungschein* for her effort. Maria arranged for her grandchildren to attend school on Leopoldstrasse, a five-minute walk from their new home, and Johann built kitchen cupboards and installed a new sink in the small bathroom. The only bathtub in the building was in the cellar—a huge porcelain tub in the centre of a spacious room. A small, coal-fired heater supplied warmth and hot water to the room but had to be lit well before bath time.

The property owner, a medical doctor friend of Theo and Maria's, occupied the upper apartment, and he offered to buy enough coal to fill the bins if Johann would shovel it into them.

Johann showed Thomas how to start the fire in the coal furnace, keep it burning, and regulate the draft to give enough heat without ruining the tile heater upstairs. Barbara caught them discussing it in front of the furnace and put a stop to it. She insisted that Johann show her the technique, and in the end, handled the poker and coal shovel as well as Johann did. Despite Thomas's excellent arguments for tending the fire, his mother barred him from touching the furnace.

Upstairs was the heating system's heart, a tile heater, the *Kachelofen,* a beautiful tile box situated in the junction of the four equal rooms that comprised their living space. It would be necessary to walk through the two front rooms to get to the back rooms, so Barbara allocated a back room for Lisa and Thomas. She furnished the living room with an oak-framed couch and two matching chairs. The kitchen, adjacent to the living room, was large enough to hold the massive oak dining room furniture she had inherited from her grandparents.

In exchange for rent, it was Barbara's job every Saturday, rain or shine, to clean the stairs, the sidewalk to the street and the sidewalk in front of the house. Every week, she washed the coal smoke off all the windows in both apartments. Herr Doktor Baumgärtner and his wife assured Johann that they were happy to have Barbara and the children in the house.

❖❖❖❖❖❖❖❖❖❖❖❖❖❖❖❖❖❖❖❖❖

Despite Johann's willing it to, time refused to stop, and March twentieth arrived with time's intrinsic precision. Well-wishers surrounded Johann and Barbara on the *Bahnhof* platform. Barbara cried as she held Johann, kissed him and let him go so his father could hug him.

Theo hugged his only son then held him at arm's length as he said, "The army demands only one thing, son, complete obedience. Work hard, do what you are told, and most importantly, keep your political opinions to yourself!" Johann smiled. He wasn't good at keeping his beliefs bottled up.

Lisa kissed her father, hugged him while tears flowed down her cheeks. Thomas hugged him hard as the train stopped beside the platform, and Barbara gently pulled him away. Thomas desperately tried to hold back his tears, but they burst forth in a torrent when he let go of his father.

Johann kissed Barbara again, then stepped on the train, barely getting through the closing door. No tears came, and a sense of excitement sneaked through his grief, despite his efforts to keep it away. He hurried to his compartment. As he watched them disappear behind the accelerating train, his heart ached for his family...grief smothered the flicker of excitement under a blanket of sadness.

◇◇◇

Dozens of soldiers rode the night train to Würzburg, mostly in second class, where Johann sat. A young sergeant sitting across from Johann in his compartment wanted to talk.

"I'm going to guess and say that you are on your way to basic training. Am I right?"

"Is it that obvious?" Johann imagined that it was.

"I'm afraid so." The soldier smiled. "Young men on this train are either soldiers or prospective soldiers. I finished my basic training six months ago." He extended his hand, and Johann took it. "My name is Jürgen Schäfer."

Johann shook his hand. "I'm Johann Finke." He doubted the young man could say anything that would help, but he asked anyway. "Do you have any advice?"

The young man put his elbows on his knees and leaned toward Johann. "It's actually not that bad once you get through the first few days. At first, the officers try to impress you with their toughness, but it doesn't take long to figure out that they're not so tough if you work hard. If you ask for help, they'll give it to you."

Johann nodded, then asked, "Where are you going now?"

"I was on leave at home in Kassel, and I'm going for my specialist training with the Sixth Army. I will command a squad of anti-tank specialists."

Johann had no idea what to expect, nor where he would be assigned. He asked, "Do you think I could get into the Sixth Army?"

"Certainly...they need good men. They'd just started looking for recruits to build the new Sixth Army when I finished basic. I jumped at the chance. They've been in Belgium and France; they're a truly professional army that knows how to fight. Listen, I worked hard and showed initiative, and I could have gotten whatever assignment I chose—anything from the infantry to tanks, to *Einsatzgruppe*."

"*Einsatzgruppe?*"

"Yes, not many people know about them because they don't advertise. But barracks talk says they're nasty bastards that take care of things most real soldiers wouldn't do—not a very nice crew." He smiled, looked Johann over. "I doubt you would qualify."

Johann chose not to sound offended. "What do you mean by that?"

"I mean that if you have a weak stomach or a hint of morals, they don't want you. I didn't ask, but I'm sure they wouldn't accept me." He laughed self-consciously; Johann detected something more than embarrassment. "They selected a few from my group—the bad actors that no one else wanted." The uneasy laugh ended quickly, and Johann decided to avoid the 'nasty bastards' and try the Sixth Army.

◇◇◇◇◇◇◇◇◇◇◇◇◇◇◇◇◇◇◇◇◇◇◇◇◇◇◇◇◇◇◇◇◇

The train pulled into the platform in Würzburg, and the young sergeant led Johann to the last truck in a line of *Lastwagen* from the training base in the mountains. After they shook hands and said goodbye, Johann threw his suitcase to a soldier about his age and climbed into the steel box. He sat beside the suitcase-catcher, and the man offered his hand, saying, "Frederick Wolanski." His firm grip was meant to intimidate, but Johann gave as good as he got.

"Johann Finke."

"You're a good man, Finke." Wolanski laughed, showing his perfect teeth and shaking his numb hand. Frederick could have been the model for the blonde Aryan soldier pictured on every Nazi recruiting poster.

Over the forty-minute ride to the base, Johann discovered that Frederick liked to talk—mostly about himself. He had risen in the

Nazi Party as a leader and organizer of Nazi Youth groups, and like Johann, he was entering the *Wehrmacht* late, at thirty-two. But unlike Johann, Frederick was a volunteer and planned to make the army his career. He was married to Siergruna, his childhood sweetheart, and had a daughter the same age as Johann's Lisa.

Frederick's Polish-German father had immigrated to Germany in 1931 to join the National Socialists in their fight against the Communists. Hitler's fanatical views fit perfectly into Herr Wolanski's concept of the world...he believed that Bolsheviks and Jews were locked in a conspiracy to take over the world, and Hitler's Nazi Party was the only hope to stop them.

Frederick's father had risen quickly in the party, and by 1939 he was a top bureaucrat in the interior ministry. Johann could tell that Frederick was immensely proud of his father, who, without finishing school, had reached an assistant ministerial position. He then shared his father's belief that a Jewish Communist conspiracy had caused the 1929-30 collapse of the world financial system, citing a document, the 'Protocols of Zion,' that he said proved communists, particularly Bolsheviks, would provide the government authority the Jews would need to carry out their nefarious plan to dominate the entire financial world.

By the time the Lastwagen pulled into the army base and stopped in a flat courtyard, Johann vowed to avoid Frederick's political opinions.

It took the rest of the day to finish indoctrination, and, when it was over, Frederick Wolanski had, by default, adopted Johann as his friend. Johann didn't resist... He also needed a friend, and Frederick's was the only offer he had.

Frederick and Johann sat opposite one another at the end of a long table, eating *Schweineshaxen und Sauerkraut*, Johann's favourite meal, and Frederick, who seemed to abhor silence, said, "I'm sick of playing soldier with children; I want to see some action!"

"I'm not a real soldier like you are. I don't think I could kill a man." Johann reluctantly talked as he chopped his peeled potatoes into small pieces and laid the juicy sauerkraut over them. "Do you think I could get a job doing something else—maybe a medic?"

Frederick didn't seem interested in his meal. He leaned back, adopted a fatherly tone as he said, "No, you will have to do what they tell you." He leaned toward Johann and grinned, almost joyfully. "I don't have that problem—I can't wait to kill our enemies!" Suddenly embarrassed at his eagerness, he explained, "The Third Reich must save the world from the mess the Bolsheviks and Jews have created, and the Reich must have *Lebensraum*—room to expand." He leaned ahead again, spoke softly, his words intended only for Johann. "Listen, if we allow them to continue to pollute the world with their communist ideas and mongrel progeny, the world economy will never recover! Give them a year or two, and they will destroy all that Hitler has accomplished! We must attack Russia sooner or later."

Johann shook his head, put his fork down. "I don't believe that; it's all propaganda, aimed at ignorant, simple minds. People are the same, no matter where or how they live or worship. Russia is our friend... Hitler signed a non-aggression treaty with Russia before we invaded Poland and underscored it again a few weeks ago." Johann felt uncomfortable, disgusted that Frederick had drawn him into a political discussion. He grabbed the edges of his tin plate and started to get up. He looked down the lines of benches for a free space, but there was none.

Frederick put his hand on Johann's arm. "Hey, I was just spouting the party line—I guess it's a habit now. And Hitler won't attack Russia on my account. We're in the *Wehrmacht*...regular soldiers can't even join the party, let alone have a political opinion. But it doesn't hurt to swim with the current. Don't take things so seriously, or you won't survive here. Idealists aren't welcome in the Wehrmacht!"

Johann sat down. He decided that Frederick had few close friends, but the acquaintances who knew him likely avoided him. He felt sorry for Frederick.

Frederick went on, "I want to go into the *SD*, the *Spezial Einsatzgruppe*. Since I worked for the Gestapo teaching *Hitler Jugend*, I will get preference."

"Go wherever you want to, but don't talk that *Scheisse* around me. Those imaginary conspiracy accusations are nothing but blatant propaganda lies, and I don't want to hear them!" Johann held him in his gaze until Frederick looked away.

Frederick laughed without humour. "When the instructors here finish with you, you'll get over your squeamish liberal ideas."

Johann picked up his fork, loaded it with potato and sauerkraut. "I call it treating others as humans like me, and it's not open for debate." He dumped the forkful of food in his mouth, chewed it a couple of times and swallowed half of it. He pointed his fork at Frederick, still chewing.

"My morality is not negotiable."

It took a week of running, lifting, climbing and shouting before the platoon touched a rifle. When the time came, the excited recruits sat through a two-hour lecture and film on the *Karabiner* rifle—how it worked, how to disassemble the action, how to clean it, and how to safely handle a gun.

The lecture over, the sergeant led the men to a table at the back of the room where a young soldier was taking *Mauser Karabiner 98K* rifles out of wooden crates and laying them on a table. The sergeant instructed his charges to pick out a gun and a maintenance kit. When his turn came, Johann stepped out of line and asked the young soldier taking them out of the boxes if he could give him a breather. The soldier gladly accepted the offer and went for a smoke. While the sergeant watched, Johann looked at every rifle before he laid it on the table, and set two aside as rejects. When he finally found what he was looking for, he leaned it against the wall behind him. He dug another out of the box, laid it on the table, and the next recruit picked it up as though it were his newborn child.

When every man had a rifle, Johann had lain three more rejections aside. The sergeant picked up each reject, looked at it, looked at Johann and nodded.

Sergeant Janzen gave his men the rest of the afternoon to get acquainted with their rifles, and Johann asked if he could take his rifle to the gunsmith's shop. Janzen smiled and said, "Go ahead... Günter won't let you do anything to hurt it."

A veteran of the Great War, Günter the regiment gunsmith sat Johann down at a workbench opposite him. The man knew the *Mauser Karabiner 98K* rifle like he knew his own hand and helped Johann fit the previous model *Mauser Gewehr 98* sights to the *98K*. The sights were identical to the ones on the gun Johann's grandfather had given him.

Johann's talents were not restricted to music. Following the Great War, his grandfather had predicted another war in his lifetime and had become a senior member of the local shooting club. He wanted to keep his skills sharp—just in case. When Johann was fourteen, he began shooting with his grandfather, the best sniper shot in his regiment and certainly the best shot in the gun club. Since receiving his *Meisterschuss* certificate, Johann had spent four hours a week at the range, teaching members and honing his skill.

Johann spent the rest of the afternoon working on the rifle. He "cleaned up" the bolt and slides, filed the front site so that the tip of it showed a dot of bright steel and oiled the now-perfect fit of the bolt.

When Johann returned to the barracks, the platoon had gotten tired of sliding their rifles' bolts back and forth and were playing cards.

The following day, when the soon-to-be soldiers lay down to fire their first shot, Johann was satisfied that his *Karabiner 98K* was as smooth as his *Gewehr 98* at home. He slipped the single bullet that Sergeant Janzen had entrusted to him into the chamber, pulled the butt of the rifle to his shoulder, slid the bolt ahead and fired in one motion. A hole appeared at the intersection of crossed lines in a ten-centimetre circle two hundred metres downrange—ten centimetres above the cross and one centimetre to the right. Johann pulled the rear site ramp back one notch, turned the ramp a half-turn to the left, spit on his finger, wetted the front sight, and took a second bullet from the sergeant. He loaded and fired, again in one smooth motion. A hole appeared in the exact centre of the target.

"You've done this before." Master Sergeant Janzen passed him a five-shot clip. "Try a few more."

Johann loaded the magazine, put five holes in the centre of the target in five seconds, three of them touching one another. The sergeant snapped his fingers and pointed at Johann's rifle. Before handing it to the sergeant, Johann took a white rag he had commandeered from the gunsmith and wiped a trace of gun oil from the freshly-polished laminated walnut stock.

Master Sergeant Janzen slid the bolt back and forth, looked at the ramped rear sight, the filed front post. "You've changed the site to the old *Gewehr 98*... Where did you get it?"

"Günter has a few in a box—he said there are older soldiers who prefer the *Gewehr* sight."

"Okay, Finke, I want every rifle in your platoon fixed up just like this one—except for the sight, of course. Teach the men how to make their action as smooth as yours. I'll let you demonstrate using my rifle." He slid the bolt back and forth a few more times and reluctantly gave Johann's rifle back to him. "But put one of those sights on my rifle..." Janzen smiled... "I'm one of those old soldiers."

From that point, Johann's military career path turned a corner. Basic training was an opportunity to sharpen skills he already had, and he took whatever time Janzen would give him to help those who had started in a worse place. By the end of the first two weeks, he had taught the forty men in his barracks how to "tidy up" their weapons, how to satisfy even the most stringent inspection, and how to survive the Master Sergeant.

When training was over, the group was a mature fighting unit, the pride of Janzen, a fifty-year-old Swedish career soldier who made moulding men from boys his life's work. He was responsible for teaching his charges the lessons of survival and maximum usefulness on the battlefield. In his final speech to the graduating class, he declared the platoon the best he had trained. They were the first words of outright praise the men had heard from him, and a few would have wiped tears from their eyes if the sergeant had let them.

Through osmosis, Johann had become the Alpha leader of the pack.

Master Sergeant Janzen walked with Johann to the Menza, where the platoon would celebrate clearing the first hurdle.

"I hear you're going into the Sixth Army. You've made a good choice—good officers, and the Sixth is Wehrmacht—no SS units. Do you know what you want to do? No? Good. You should think about a Jäger Company, maybe in a panzer battalion."

Johann nodded. "Okay. How do I apply?"

Janzen didn't look sideways or change expression. "Colonel Stieff, First panzer Division, is expecting you. He wants your men to form a new platoon. You will go to your new home when you return from leave." He stopped, touched his cap. "I called in a favour—don't make me look bad!" Johann saluted, and Sergeant Janzen walked to where his corporal was lining up another truckload of recruits.

When Johann told his comrades the platoon would stay together and work as specialists in a tank battalion, they whooped and threw their hats in the air. They went home for two weeks before the real training began.

◇◇◇

Frederick accompanied Johann to Detmold, where his wife Siegruna and daughter Angela would meet him at the station. In one of Frederick's early marathon conversations, he had divulged that his family was living on his father's farm, 20 kilometres southeast of Berlin. She was only there a week when she pleaded to move as far from Frederick's father as possible.

In a letter, Johann asked his father to find Frederick's family an apartment in Detmold, and Theo promptly found one a short walk from Barbara.

Frederick's daughter quickly became friends with Lisa, and Barbara's letters of their antics together filled Johann with a longing to see his family. Barbara wrote that Lisa had insisted on teaching Angela to sing and play a few simple pieces on the piano, and Angela tried, but Barbara held out no hope that the girl would be a musician. The girls slept together on weekends, and every day they walked to and from school together.

Barbara's letters told a different story about Siegruna. She tried to get close to her, but Siegruna pulled back whenever the conversation became intimate. She requested that Barbara use formal pronouns when they spoke, insisting that she did not deserve a close friend of Barbara's status. The only partial exception was the girls, and even then, she spoke of Lisa as though Angela were not worthy of her. Oddly, Barbara said that she sensed Siegruna becoming more depressed and nervous as the day approached when her husband would arrive. Siegruna developed a twitch over her left eye that Barbara tried to ignore. She asked Johann to talk to Frederick.

Barbara, never one to dwell on a problem, switched smoothly to her anticipation of the day when Johann would come home on leave. Her letters became more and more excited as the day approached. Barbara told Johann that she had learned to whistle and that it had become a happy habit. She unconsciously whistled while working in

15

the crowded train station—and people laughed at her, but she didn't mind.

◇◇◇◇◇◇◇◇◇◇◇◇◇◇◇◇◇◇◇◇◇◇

Johann waited until they changed trains at Kassel, and he and Frederick were the only passengers in their compartment.

"I haven't seen you reading letters. Doesn't Siegruna write to you?" Green fields flowed past Johann's window; cattle ripped the spring grass off at the root, and leafy grain stalks, not yet stiff, waved in the breeze.

"I asked her not to write. I'm too busy to read letters, and even if she did write, I have no time to answer."

"Does she know you're coming?" Johann watched Frederick, knowing that Barbara had told Siegruna.

"Yeah, I sent her a note about a week ago when I found out what train I would be on."

Johann decided to try another approach.

"You said that your father and your wife don't get along. I suppose he misses Siegruna and his grandchild now that they are gone."

Frederick laughed; Johann detected a note of regret in the laugh. "Hell, no...my father hates kids! Angela got on his nerves. The son of a bitch beat her because she wouldn't shut up, but Siegruna ambushed him with a pickaxe handle—she fucking near killed him! He got out of the hospital a few days later and beat the shit out of her. Siegruna and Angela slept in the barn after that, and I had to get them out before my father killed my kid! I can tell you from experience that Siegruna can take a lot of shit, but I couldn't trust him around Angela..."

Johann hadn't heard the story when Theo was looking for an apartment for them. "I can see why she would want to leave." Johann watched a team of horses pulling a heavy wagon up a hill. They disappeared behind the train, and he turned to Frederick.

"Do you love Siegruna?"

"Yeah, when I'm home, but I like a strange one once in a while, even if I have to pay for it." He shook his hand in a lewd expression. "Oh yeah, you get what you pay for!"

Johann went back to his window-gazing. He began planning how he would handle Frederick if he needed to.

CHAPTER TWO

Rescue the weak and the needy... Psalm 82

"Men are afraid that women will laugh at them. Women are afraid that men will kill them."

Margaret Atwood

THE TRAIN ROLLED TO A STOP at the Detmold Bahnhof platform on Sunday, 25 May, two months after Johann's tearful departure, and the welcome he received was no less emotional. Barbara cried and pulled Johann's neck so hard it hurt. Lisa and Thomas clung to both of them, laughing and competing to see who could hug tighter, until Theo and Maria finally convinced the children to let their parents say hello.

Barbara kissed Johann passionately, and their embarrassed children giggled and turned away. When the kiss was over, in his periphery, Johann saw Frederick and Siegruna embrace. Frederick's hand gripped Siegruna's breast, and when he squeezed, she winced. Johann fought the urge to interfere.

Angela waited until her father let go of her mother, then approached him slowly with her head down. He stepped over to greet his daughter, but she turned away when he tried to kiss her. He awkwardly hugged her, and although Angela put her arms around her father, there was no affection in the gesture.

The families walked together to the station's exit. Once outside the station, Johann and anyone within ten metres would have heard Frederick say, "Now where's this new house Theo found for you, Siegruna? All I need is a bed and a woman!" He then patted his wife's bottom and winked at Johann.

Siegruna lowered her head, her face red. "Yes, you must be tired, Liebling." Angela walked a step behind, gaze fixed on her feet.

Frederick turned to Johann, said loud enough that a dozen people turned and stared, "How about looking after Angela for an hour or so while Siegruna and I get reacquainted?"

Barbara focused a concerned look on her husband, then said to Frederick and Siegruna, "Of course… she can stay for the whole afternoon. Mittagessen is almost ready, and I made an *Eintopf* large enough for both families if you would care to join us."

"Thanks, but no." Frederick pulled Siegruna crudely against him. "I've got something better than Eintopf in mind!"

Siegruna put her hand on Barbara's arm and kept her voice down, targeting only Barbara. "It's all right, Barbara…I'll come over in a couple of hours to get Angela." The group split at the intersection of their respective streets, Frederick and Siegruna walking down Wiesenstrasse to their house, the Finke family continuing to Mühlenstrasse 45.

Theo and Maria hung back with the children while Johann and Barbara continued ahead, holding hands and laughing like children. Lisa and Thomas skipped over the sidewalk while Angela stood to the side, watching them jump from one block to the other without stepping on a crack. Eventually, she joined them, and they reached the house without making a mistake.

◇◇◇◇◇◇◇◇◇◇◇◇◇◇◇◇◇◇◇◇◇◇◇◇◇◇◇◇◇◇◇◇◇◇◇◇

The casserole was one of Thomas's many favourites, and he wolfed it down in less than five minutes. Eisbein und Sauerkraut was Johann's favourite too, but he took his time, enjoying the meal with his family. Thomas wiggled in his chair as he waited for the strawberry dessert his grandmother and Theo had brought. Maria whipped the cream, skimmed off the top of the milk, folded in a bit of sugar she had scrounged from somewhere, then spread the whipped cream over the berries.

Sitting next to Lisa, Angela quietly picked at her food and looked wistfully around the table. When Barbara smiled at her, the little girl's sad eyes brightened, and she curled the corners of her mouth slightly upward. Barbara smiled again, showed her perfect teeth, then laughed—the musical laugh Johann loved so much. Angela laughed with her and began to eat.

"Will you play chess with me after we eat?" Thomas looked hopefully at his father.

18

Johann winked at Barbara. "I've thought of nothing else for two months!"

When Maria put a bowl of berries in front of Thomas, he grinned from ear to ear and picked up his spoon. Johann pinned it to the table, shook his head, and didn't release it until everyone had a bowl of berries in front of them. Thomas shouted, "*Guten Appetit*," and pushed his spoon into the bowl.

After dessert, Johann kissed Lisa's cheek before heading to Thomas's bedroom, where Thomas had the chessboard set up.

As he passed her, Johann whispered in Lisa's ear, "Will you play the violin for me after I've beaten your brother at chess?"

"Yes! Maria has taught me most of the Mendelssohn concerto. But first, she's going to give me a lesson." She looked pointedly at her grandmother, and Maria nodded. Since she was two, Lisa had spoken like an adult, using nuances that amazed her parents and grandparents. Sometimes it was difficult not to laugh at the complicated phrasing she used.

Both the grandchildren addressed their grandparents using first names, perhaps because Theo had not allowed anyone to call him *Opa*. When Lisa first began to talk, he had introduced himself to her as Theo. If her *Opa* were Theo, then she reasoned that her *Oma* was Maria. Thomas naturally followed her lead when he learned to talk. They introduced them to others as *Oma* and *Opa*, but they were Maria and Theo within the family. Maria liked it that way. She thought of the children as her friends.

◇◇◇◇◇◇◇◇◇◇◇◇◇◇◇◇◇◇◇◇◇◇◇◇◇◇◇◇◇◇◇◇◇◇

The chess game lasted a lot longer than Johann had anticipated; his chess was rusty from the two-month hiatus, and the quality of Thomas's game caught him off-guard. Theo played chess with Thomas twice a week, and Theo was a good teacher. Delighted that he had come so close to beating his father, Thomas smiled confidently as he walked beside him to the living room, where Lisa finished her lesson with an arpeggio from the Mendelssohn concerto.

"I'll bet I can beat you before you leave for the war again!" Thomas could barely contain himself as they waited for Maria to finish her constructive criticism of Lisa's playing.

Johann laughed, said, "I guarantee that you will beat me someday, but probably not in the next two weeks."

"I thought you were going to be home for weeks and weeks!" Thomas almost burst into tears, but he held them back. Lisa gave her brother a reproachful look that sent him to the kitchen where his mother worked on a plum *Torte*.

Lisa played most of Mendelssohn's masterpiece on a new-to-her full-sized violin that Theo had found, and the sound she produced was glorious. She omitted the most difficult passages—Maria had taught her how to 'cheat' her way around them—and Johann was thrilled with the result. Angela sat on the sofa, listening, her knees up to her chin, her fingers locked in front of them.

Johann applauded his daughter, turned to his mother. "Mother, I can't believe what you've done in two months...Lisa is becoming a virtuoso!" He quickly left the room, returned a few minutes later with his violin. Lisa and Maria laughed at his enthusiasm as he tuned his instrument to match Lisa's.

A quiet knock on the door disturbed the tuning. Johann laid the violin on the sofa and went to answer the door, but Barbara cut him off in the foyer, opening the door before he could reach it. Siegruna stood on the stone step, her cheek swollen and black, blood caked in her hair. Johann took Siegruna's arm; she cringed, favouring her foot. He half-carried her into the house.

"My God, Siegruna, what happened?" Angela hugged her mother, buried her face in her mother's blouse. Johann helped Siegruna into the living room and to the sofa.

"I fell down the stairs..." she looked at Barbara... "Frederick drank too much, and I couldn't wake him, so I came here."

Barbara looked at Johann and shook her head.

Johann knelt down to speak directly to Siegruna. "You've got to go to the hospital! Our landlord is a doctor and has a car. I'll go upstairs and get him." Johann started for the door.

"No, I can't go to the hospital!" She grasped Barbara's hand, looked from her to Johann and back to Barbara. "Please, I don't need a doctor! If you help me get cleaned up, and I soak my foot in hot water, I'll be fine." She tried to stand, cried out and fell back on the sofa.

Johann looked at Barbara, and when she nodded he turned and ran up the stairs two at a time.

When he returned with Doctor Baumgärtner, Barbara had already cleaned the wounds on Siegruna's face and scalp. The doctor knelt in front of Siegruna and opened his bag. He gently lifted her foot and tested it in various directions, diagnosing it as sprained, not broken. He removed her stocking and bound the foot tightly. He checked Barbara's work cleaning the head wound, pulled a jar of ointment from the black bag, and gently applied it to the badly swollen cheek. He gave the bottle to Siegruna and told her to apply a thin coat twice a day until the swelling went down. Then he sat beside her and said gently, "Tell me what happened to you, Siegruna."

Siegruna hung her head and said nothing. Barbara waited, then said, "Siegruna told us she fell down the stairs."

Doctor Baumgärtner put his hand on Siegruna's arm and quietly but insistently asked, "Siegruna, you must tell me what really happened. I've treated wounds like these before—I know you didn't fall down the stairs."

She looked down, spoke so quietly Johann could barely make out her words. "He only hits me when he drinks too much..." Her voice rose... "It's my fault—I shouldn't have bought the schnapps for him!" She became agitated, crying, her voice loud. "Please don't tell him I told you! He might hurt Angela to hurt me."

"Siegruna, I must report this to the police." Doctor Baumgärtner held her hand. "You and your daughter must stay here with us until the police arrest Frederick. Do you understand?"

"No! No! I can't do that! The police can't arrest Frederick...how would we live?" Siegruna stood up, staggered with the pain. "I want to go home now!" She beckoned to her distressed daughter. "Come... Angela, we must go home. Let me lean on your shoulder." Angela reluctantly went to her mother's side, but Doctor Baumgärtner took Angela's place.

"I will drive you home." He dug his keys from his pocket, and Johann opened the door, then supported her as they walked down the stone steps. Doctor Baumgärtner left to get the car.

Johann said, "Siegruna, I'll be there tomorrow morning when

Frederick wakes up. If he wakes during the night, don't say anything to make him angry."

She looked at him and said nothing. The car stopped in front of them, and Johann helped her get in the rear seat. Angela got in the other side. He watched the Mercedes leave the curb, then returned to the living room where Lisa was waiting, grim thoughts turning over in his mind...

This was a problem only he could solve.

◇◇◇◇◇◇◇◇◇◇◇◇◇◇◇◇◇◇◇◇◇◇◇◇◇◇◇◇◇◇◇

The ends of Johann's fingers hadn't touched a string since leaving Detmold two months before, long enough that they became red and sore after half an hour.

"I'm sorry, Lisa, my fingers are telling me to stop." He blew on them to cool the burning sensation.

"That's okay, Vati. It's time for us to go to Maria and Theo's house anyway."

Maria smiled at Johann, put her hands on his shoulders and spoke softly in his ear.

"Theo and I have paid for your dinner at the Detmolder Hof, and the children will spend the night with us. It's our anniversary present."

"I don't know what to say, Mother. Thank you very much." He whispered, "Thanks for reminding me about our anniversary; I must admit I had forgotten." Johann touched his mother's hand affectionately and kissed her cheek.

Theo came into the living room from the kitchen where he and Barbara had prepared coffee and Torte. He wiped his hands on his white apron and said, "Barbara and I have a plum torte hot out of the oven. Is anyone interested?"

Lisa put her violin in its case, slammed it shut, and headed for the kitchen. Maria followed on her heels, and Johann went to the bedroom to put his violin away. He arrived in the kitchen just as the family sat down.

The only vacant chair was next to Theo, who sat at the head of the table. Johann said nothing, but he felt a little strange, like an intruder. Maria noticed his expression, as mothers are wont to do, and spoke to Theo.

"Theo, Johann sits there—you should change places with him!"

Theo, flustered, stood and began to gather his plate and cutlery.

"I'm sorry, Johann, but since you left, I've become so used to sitting here that I guess it's automatic." His face reddened. "Please forgive me."

Johann gestured for his father to return to the seat. "Dad, I'm just happy to be home; it doesn't matter to me where I sit. The war will be over soon, and you should sit there until we are a permanent family again." Theo put his cutlery on the table and sat down; Johann felt a dark cloud pass over him as he pulled out the chair next to his father. Maria took Johann's hand under the table and squeezed it.

Maria said to Lisa, who was sitting across from her.

"Lisa, would you say a prayer of thanks for the blessings we have?"

The family joined hands around the table, and Lisa paused before beginning. When the children recited the usual prayer of thanks for the meal, it was from memory, and if the hot *Kuchen* were already on the plates, they rattled it off so fast the words blurred together. It was the same ritual at every meal.

This time, Lisa began thoughtfully and reverently. "Thank you, God, for my father and mother, for Theo and Maria, and for my brother. Thank you for the family I love so very much. I thank you too for the meal that Theo and Mother have cooked.

"But God, if you don't mind my saying so, I don't like your war! If you control everything like the priest says you do, I want you to stop it as soon as you can. Please don't kill my daddy...don't kill any more daddies. I want him home with us so we can play the violin together and so he can play chess with Thomas. Please, God, make the governments stop the war. Amen."

The amen echoed around the table.

The milk, fake coffee, and Kuchen disappeared in fifteen minutes, and the men left to clean up the basement. Johann, Thomas, and Theo spent the next two hours there, with Thomas sweeping the coal room while Johann, the tallest of the crew, cleaned the light fixtures in the ceilings and washed the whitewashed brick arches that grew out of the massive stone walls of the old house.

Theo focussed on the bathing room. He took the water heater apart and cleaned the small pipes that ran through it. Small chunks of burning coal created the heat, and every month soot would clog the area between the tubes. Theo had an identical setup in his home at Gartenstrasse 18, and he made short work of cleaning this one.

Curved red legs supported the white porcelain bathtub that stood in the centre of the dark-red marble floor. The whitewashed brick walls curved up and out of the marble in a graceful parabolic curve. The curve began at a short stub wall and became an elliptical arched ceiling, meeting in the middle of the room over the tub. Johann thought that it was the most beautiful room he had ever seen.

Theo cleaned every crack and cranny of the black wooden door and oiled the hinges and latch.

The work in the cellar complete, the family gathered in the living room, and Barbara put their *Lili Marlen* recording on the phonograph. Lala Anderson's poignant voice filled the room, accompanied by the German Army Chorus. When it was over, everyone clapped, asking for more. At the end of the fourth playing, the adults sang the last verse while Lisa and Thomas marched around the room.

Wenn sich die späten Nebel drehen,
Werd' ich bei der Laterne steh'n,
Wie einst, Lili Marlen?
Wie einst, Lili Marlen.

When the last note of the bugle died, Lisa said, "I don't understand. Mutti... What happened to the soldier?"

Johann looked at Barbara. She fought tears, so he answered Lisa's question.

"He came back home and met Lili Marlen under the lamp post, as he had before the war."

"Oh." Lisa smiled. "Maybe you and Mutti will meet under the lamp post in front of our house when the war is over."

Barbara smiled, touched Lisa's hair. "Yes, that's our plan." Barbara left for the bedroom to powder her nose, and Maria took the children to the kitchen for a last piece of *Kuchen.*

Finally, Kuchen eaten, Theo and Maria gathered the children. Barbara met them at the front door, dressed for dinner at the Detmolder Hof. Johann came out of the bedroom in the same suit he had worn at his wedding, with a thread-worn white shirt and a wrinkled black tie.

"You look as though someone you hate died, and I'm forcing you to go to his funeral!" Barbara then said sweetly, "Why don't you take off the jacket and put on your tartan vest?"

Johann turned around, and two minutes later was back in the entrance dressed in his tartan vest with the white shirt open.

"How about this?" he asked the question hopefully.

Barbara squinted. "It's all right, but I think you should wear a tie, just not the black one—there's a red one in the *Schrank*, hanging on the inside of the door."

Johann turned around and returned with a red necktie under the vest.

"Okay, how's this?" He felt more hopeful.

"I think you should put on your tweed jacket—and only fasten the top button."

"Yes, dear." He turned, headed for the bedroom again.

Barbara and the rest of the family waited for five minutes, but Johann didn't show up. Barbara excused herself and went to check on his progress. When she entered the room, Johann was fastening the last button on his army blouse.

"You're not going to the restaurant in that, are you?" Barbara was more than just curious.

"Yes, I am." Johann smiled, said, "You are not permitted to redesign the Wehrmacht uniform, and our reservation was for five minutes ago!"

He offered Barbara his arm, and she laughed as she laid her hand on it. Then she kissed him. "Am I forgiven?"

"Not yet; that's something you have to earn. I'll let you know when you've paid your debt." He grinned impishly.

Barbara and Johann followed Theo, Maria and the children up *Langestrasse* to the Detmolder Hof. They walked hand in hand, Barbara humming Lili Marlen. She stopped humming and asked, "Do you think the soldier's spirit could actually join his love under the streetlight after he was dead...I mean...do you think she would know he was there?"

Johann stopped. He took her shoulders in his hands, locked his eyes on hers.

"I am *not* going to die! But...if I do, promise me that we will meet under that lamp?" He smiled, pointed to a nearby streetlamp, and kissed her on the cheek.

Barbara's eyes glistened. "Don't laugh at me, Johann...I'm frightened! I can't lose you!"

In the middle of the sidewalk, under the streetlamp, they held one another long enough that they forced several groups of people to take to the street.

When Barbara finally let Johann go, they hugged the embarrassed children, then continued arm in arm to the hotel.

◇◇◇◇◇◇◇◇◇◇◇◇◇◇◇◇◇◇◇◇◇◇◇◇◇◇◇◇◇◇◇

Everything was perfect. Johann hadn't eaten a Jägerschnitzel in months, and despite rationing, the hotel dining room managed to stretch it to three courses. The waiter sensed his customer's mood and left them alone until Johann signalled that they were ready for more food or wine. A pianist played a small grand piano, neatly modulating through the popular songs of the day.

They drank a bottle of French red wine and talked about their friends—some gone to war, others still performing in the Bielefeld opera house.

Twice, when their meal was over, as they enjoyed a cup of genuine coffee, a small group of people came to their table to thank Johann for his service to their country. Embarrassed, he stood up, shook hands and thanked them.

The pianist modulated from the popular songs he had been playing into a soprano aria from Lehar's operetta, The Merry Widow. As he began 'Vilja,' Barbara put her hand over Johann's and leaned over to him. "I write to Juliette every month...she is singing all over Germany..." Barbara paused, scanned the room for prying ears, then said softly, "...and she's taking terrible risks." She squeezed Johann's hand.

Johann looked around the now emptying dining room. "And Peter? Is he still singing?"

"Concerts and oratorios in France and Belgium...he seems quite busy."

Johann spoke softly, "He's involved with the same people as Juliette?"

Barbara nodded. "I think so, but she is careful what she says in her letters, and I never ask questions. Every time she writes, she complains that he is doing too much singing. She wants him home with Nina."

When the last course was finished, the dishes cleared, and they were drinking their second cup of coffee, Barbara asked, "Do you know where they are sending you?"

"Master Sergeant Janzen has arranged for most of the platoon to go into the Sixth Army, to a Jäger scouting unit. We will work with artillery and panzers."

"Is that dangerous?"

War is, by definition, dangerous."

"Johann…" Barbara looked deep into his eyes…

There was no use in lying or sugarcoating anything. Many soldiers had already died, and many more would die. Johann took her hand.

"I don't know that scouting is more dangerous than sitting in a panzer or an aircraft or fighting in the infantry. What I know is, I'm in excellent physical shape; I was one of the best close combat fighters in our platoon, and I am the best shot, thanks to Opa." Johann paused, his eyes not leaving Barbara's.

"Barbara, I love you, and I will try to survive, but I can't give you any assurances. Bullets and cannon shells are indiscriminate, and luck is more important than skill. In war, survival is winning; winning takes confidence; confidence comes from training. I'm not afraid of dying. That fear in itself would raise the likelihood of it happening."

Barbara tried to let go of his hand; Johann held tight. She said, "But… can't you find something safer? For me? You could be a medic, or drive people around…or…"

"*Liebling,* I can't choose where I fit in the army. I'm thankful Sergeant Janzen has arranged for me to go to officers' school, but the reality is that he thought of the *Wehrmacht* by putting me where he thinks I will be most effective. The army does what is best for the army, not what is best for the individual. Basic training is a winnowing process, separating men according to their talents. I suspect that officers' training pulls that string a little further."

Barbara's eyes glistened. "You are not a soldier; you are a musician. The army has a band, don't they?"

Johann shook his head. "I don't want to play in the *Wehrmacht* band. That's no guarantee that I wouldn't have to fight, but it would guarantee that I would be no good at fighting." He took her hand in both of his. "If I want the best chance of survival, I must be the best at my job. Lazy, fearful, badly trained soldiers are nothing but cannon fodder—sacrificial diversions so the talented fighters can be more effective. The Wehrmacht does not sacrifice its brightest and best!"

Barbara smiled through tears. "I believe you, Johann, and I know you will do your best to return to me. Your intentions are good, perhaps too good, and that's my fear. Will you kill a man before he kills you? Will you shoot him in the back?... or will you give him a fighting chance?"

The pianist began a medley of popular excerpts from 'Carmen' as the waiter arrived with a tray of chocolate truffles and pastries and a fresh carafe of coffee. Barbara discreetly dabbed her tears with a pretty lace handkerchief, chose a truffle and a puffed pastry with cream filling. Johann went with fresh *Kaffee* and a piece of *Apfel Torte*.

◇◇◇◇◇◇◇◇◇◇◇◇◇◇◇◇◇◇◇◇◇◇◇◇◇◇◇◇◇◇◇◇◇◇◇

Late in May, the Detmold sun was still well above the roofs at seven-thirty, and tonight the temperature was unseasonably warm. Barbara and Johann walked home arm-in-arm, enjoying the evening sun. Johann sweated in his uniform, and Barbara confirmed what he suspected.

"You'll need to have a bath when we get home," Barbara said as they walked side by side on the narrow sidewalk. "I won't let you in my bed smelling like that!"

Johann laughed. "I don't smell anything..." He pretended to be hurt... "I had a bath a couple of days ago, and Sergeant Janzen told us that we have to get used to going a few weeks without water to bathe in."

"We have lots of water at home, and I'll wash your back if you're good."

"Is that all...just my back?"

She ran ahead of him, looking back and laughing. He tried to catch up to her, but when he got close, she put on a burst of speed and beat him to the stone steps that led to the front door. Barbara opened the door, pulled him in, and probed his mouth with her tongue as she kissed him. She let him go and pointed at the cellar door.

"Get clean...I'll bring your housecoat down. Leave your clothes on the floor."

As Johann stumbled down the steps into the cellar, he suddenly remembered that it had been Barbara's idea to have the men clean it. He'd heard her ask Theo to pay special attention to the bathing room... he hoped he knew why.

In under a minute the fire was going and the tub half full of hot water in another ten. He eased himself in, gasping as the water reached his genitals. From there, it was easier. He took a cake of soap from the little wire basket hanging on the edge of the tub.

The latch on the oak door clicked, and a couple of seconds later Barbara was beside the tub, dressed in a white bathrobe that he recognized as his. She held a nightdress in her hand and draped it over the chair near the tub.

"Can I be of assistance, Herr Finke?"

"No, I can handle this job by myself...I'm still working on the first layer." He quickly began washing, but before he had finished the first leg, Barbara folded a towel on the floor, got down on her knees and took the soap and washcloth from him. With a small bar of soap buried in her hand, she assisted with cleaning the crucial parts.

Johann laughed nervously. "Too much of that and you won't have any fun tonight!" The laugh stuttered; he sucked in his breath noisily. Barbara moved higher up his body and began washing his chest, then his back. She soaped his hair, rinsed everything and pulled the plug.

Johann waited for the water to drain while Barbara used a handle-less cup to rinse the soap from his body.

"Hey, that water's cold," he yelped. Barbara filled the cup, splashed it in his face. He cried out and tried to get to his feet, but she pushed him down in the slippery tub.

"Not yet!" She laughed, filled the cup again. Four cups of water later, she said, "Okay, you can stand up." He obeyed and stood there while she washed the substantial ring from the tub.

"You can sit down again." Barbara reinserted the drain plug, mixed hot and cold, tested, and opened the taps wide open. The water flowed in torrents, filling the tub rapidly. She turned off the water and then, in one fluid motion, dropped the housecoat on the floor and stepped into the tub with her feet beside his hips. Her naked body towering over him, Johann's breath growled deep in his throat. She took his hand and placed it in her triangle.

◇◇◇◇◇◇◇◇◇◇◇◇◇◇◇◇◇◇◇◇◇◇◇◇◇◇◇◇◇◇◇◇◇◇

The water gurgled out of the tub; the exhausted lovers dried one another, then worked their way to the bedroom. They slept on one side of the double bed, entwined in one another's arms.

Within minutes, Johann was sleeping soundly. Barbara couldn't sleep despite, or perhaps because of her feeling of intense happiness. She gently unwound Johann's arm, slipped out of bed and opened the heavy black curtains. Looking at the carpet of stars through the large window, Barbara was at peace, her body relaxed for the first time in two months. She slipped into bed, wrapped her legs around Johann and kissed his cheek. But he didn't waken—his breathing was deep and slow, the sleep of children and the innocent.

◇◇◇◇◇◇◇◇◇◇◇◇◇◇◇◇◇◇◇◇◇◇◇◇◇◇◇◇◇◇◇◇◇◇

Johann stirred when the sun streamed into the room. Without waking Barbara, he quietly dressed in his spare uniform and went to the cellar.

He had set up a workroom before going to war and quickly found the oilstone he used to sharpen Barbara's knives and his set of 'Zwei Kirschen' wood chisels. Johann's grandfather had given him a long heavy knife that he had made from a car spring, and he took it out of its leather scabbard, stroking the edge on the oiled stone, moving it in small deliberate circles as his grandfather had taught him. He tested the knife by shaving the fine hairs on the back of his hand, wiped the oil off the blade and buckled the leather handle in the scabbard. The smell of *Ersatz* Kaffee drifted downstairs, and when Johann came up from the cellar, Barbara was in the kitchen.

He wrapped his arms around her, kissing her neck from behind. She wiggled around and kissed him on the mouth. She said, "I love you, Liebling," and pushed her breasts against his chest. "But right now, I'm hungry for food." She wriggled loose, took four eggs out of the boiling water, cooled them under the tap before putting them in a dish on the table. "Why are you dressed in your uniform?"

"I promised Siegruna I would talk to Frederick this morning." Johann had answered without looking at her.

30

She pressed on. "Why do you need your uniform to do that?"

"Because I want to make a point."

Barbara sat down across the table from Johann and took her time buttering a *Brötchen* she had torn apart.

Her tone even, she asked, "What are you going to do?"

"I am going to explain, in a way he will understand, that if he hurts Siegruna again, I will hurt him."

Barbara's hand shook as she slowly spread marmalade on the bun.

"What if he tells you to go to hell, or he fights you?"

"Then I will have to deal with that, but he still wants to be my friend, and he won't want to ruin that." Johann smiled at her. "We've trained together—Frederick knows what I can do."

Barbara knew that Johann was not a violent man, but he was physically intimidating—he had a muscular, one-metre-eighty-five frame and the agility of a cat. When he was young, his grandfather, a hero of the Great War, had taught Johann how to defend himself, and the Wehrmacht had honed those skills. Barbara knew Johann's strength... she found it sexy to own that part of him.

"Please don't kill him! I know he deserves it, but we can't lose you! Siegruna is welcome here for as long as she wants to stay, and Theo and I will protect her if you aren't around. She has other options, and if she doesn't take them, you shouldn't take responsibility for her!"

Johann laughed. "No, Liebling, I won't kill him. We know one another well enough that he will listen to me." Johann finished his first egg and cracked the second. "Frederick needs to make an adjustment for his own good. I won't have to hurt him—he is basically a coward. Frederick avoided fighting me in 'hand-to-hand' training, and despite the sergeant's efforts to pair him with his equal or better, he always found a way to get out of it. Trust me in this—Frederick will understand me when I tell him he is not to harm his family—he just needs a little guidance."

"Maybe I should go with you." Barbara chopped at her eggs, already in small pieces and covered with ground pepper and butter.

"No, that would embarrass him, and he may think he has to fight for his pride. I'll invite him outside where we will have privacy, and I won't humiliate him. I don't intend to punish him—I'll just give him a little advice."

Johann went around the table to kiss Barbara. "I'll be back in an hour."

She returned the peck on the cheek, and he left for Wiesenstrasse.

<hr>

Johann lifted the heavy Wolenski doorknocker and released it without adding any velocity. The weight was enough to cause a loud clank as it hit the bronze striker plate. The door opened almost immediately, and Frederick stood in the opening, dressed sloppily in his wrinkled uniform.

"Frederick, let's go for a walk. I have something I want to discuss with you in private." He stood still on the top step.

Frederick answered nervously, tentatively. "Sure...that sounds uh... serious. I would like to talk to you too...just, uh...wait a second; I'll tell Siegruna where I'm going. She's in bed resting a sore foot... fell down the stairs last night."

Johann waited inside the doorway until Frederick joined him there. Outside, on the sidewalk, moving away from the house, Johann walked slightly ahead of him. They went toward the Bahnhof.

Johann looked straight ahead as he talked. "Frederick, stop the bull-shit. I know Siegruna didn't hurt her foot falling down the stairs...she came to us for help after you went to sleep." He paused, but Frederick didn't comment. "I don't know how she walked on that foot!"

Frederick was silent for a moment; Johann watched his face change from nervousness to self-righteous anger. He growled ominously, "Like hell she didn't fall down the stairs..." He pulled Johann's shoulder back. "What did the lying bitch tell you?" Frederick stepped in front of Johann, blocking his way.

Johann stopped, grabbed Frederick's wrinkled shirt with his left hand and twisted it in his fingers. "She fell down the stairs... that's what she told us, but we are not stupid. Doctor Baumgärtner wanted to call the police, and I agreed, but Siegruna wouldn't let him!"

Frederick couldn't hold Johann's gaze; his eyes dropped, and he half-heartedly tried to pry Johann's hand from his shirt.

Johann tightened his grip, then released it. "I want you to listen carefully! If you harm Siegruna or Angela again, I won't call the po-lice—I will hurt you...badly!" Johann spoke the next words softly, choosing them carefully. "If you want any chance of being a father again, do not underestimate me...do you understand?"

Frederick breathed deeply—his shoulders rose and fell. When he lifted his head, Johann let his shirt go. Frederick, relieved, said, "I think that's clear enough, and I promise that I won't hurt her again. It's the schnapps, and I promise not to get wasted again while I'm home." He looked at the knife hanging from Johann's belt, then raised his eyes to meet Johann's.

"I hate who I am. You know, I don't ever *want* to hurt Siegruna... I always feel like shit afterwards, and I know she hates me for it. She only stays for my paycheck!" He paused, turned away from Johann, then turned back to face him, eyes narrowed, speaking as though he had a new thought. "Have you got a thing for her?"

Johann reached for Frederick's shirt again, thought better of it and dropped his hand.

"You know that isn't true." He stared at Frederick. "I just met your wife." Frederick dropped his eyes. "I wouldn't let you treat your dog like you treat her, and if you abuse her or your daughter..."

"Okay, okay, I get it, man...that's enough!"

Johann waved his arms in frustration. "Why in hell can't you lay off the booze and enjoy the few days you still have with your family?" He put his finger on Frederick's chest, started to say more but turned and walked away in the direction of his house.

Frederick caught up to him.

"Listen, just so you know, I've never touched Angela and I never would!" Frederick said it far too loudly. "I would never have hurt Siegruna either if it hadn't been for the damned schnapps!" He put his hand on Johann's shoulder. "Johann, believe me, I feel terrible about this whole thing." He pulled his hand down, turned away, then back to Johann. "I made breakfast for Siegruna to make it up to her, and I'll make it up to you and Barbara, if you'll let me."

Johann pulled Frederick's hand away. "All right, Frederick, but getting breakfast for Siegruna doesn't compensate for what you did to her." He pointed at Frederick's chest as he said emphatically, "I'll see how it goes from here."

Johann turned to go, then turned back before Frederick had turned for home.

"Barbara and I will come by tonight to check on Siegruna, and we'll bring supper. Siegruna is in no shape to cook. Lisa and Thomas will come with us, and they can play with Angela while we talk. Will that work for you and Siegruna?"

Johann had met a few men like Frederick in basic training—deceitful, brutal when fighting weaker men, and clever. He knew that what little friendship he had for Frederick was over but decided not to tell him. Frederick now represented all that Johann was beginning to hate about the Nazi party.

Frederick smiled like a child who had lied and gotten away with it. "Yeah, that would be great! I'll help Siegruna today... You'll see... everything will be fine! Thanks, Johann." Frederick looked thoughtful, then grabbed Johann's hand. "I needed this!" He pumped Johann's arm up and down, pulled him to his chest and hugged him.

Johann let go of Frederick's hand, then turned toward home without saying anything, but on his way back to Mühlenstrasse 45 Johann decided he would never turn his back on Frederick.

When Johann told her about his confrontation with Frederick, Barbara shook her head. She said, "I will never understand men if I live forever."

Barbara looked down at Johann's shoes—he went to the bench beside the door and removed them. When he returned, he said, "He is not a man; he is an animal. Dying for the fatherland would be a good idea for him!"

The evening with Siegruna and Frederick went well. They acted like two lovebirds and Frederick treated her like a queen, waiting on her every wish, checking with Johann after each act of kindness. Angela played outside with Lisa and Thomas while their parents played *Doppelkopf* in the living room. Everything was as normal as the milk and cookies.

Outside, on their way home in the spectacular evening light, Barbara talked while the children hopped from one paving block to another. "Frederick seemed to be a perfect gentleman with Angela... Are you sure he won't change?"

Johann tried to hide his disappointment in Barbara's comment. "No matter how tame a wolf appears, he will kill you if you give him the opportunity." He removed his coat and put it over Barbara's shoulders. The evening was cooling off. "Frederick is a dangerous man, and the sooner he leaves here, the better."

<hr>

The two-week furlough was over much too soon for everyone. Every day, Johann felt Barbara's closeness become something more, making the inevitable parting harder. At the Bahnhof, when Barbara held Johann, tears flowing down her cheeks onto his uniform, she whispered, "Don't let me lose my Johann. You must come back."

Johann could barely speak. He whispered, "Under the lamppost," let her go, and picked up his bag.

The children wailed in protest as he and Frederick climbed aboard the train. Maria and Theo stood to the side, Maria wiping her eyes with a handkerchief. Even Siegruna stood with tears in her eyes as Angela gave her father a hug. As Siegruna waved goodbye to Johann, she mouthed, "Thank you!" Frederick saw it, looked at Johann with an expression that could have meant anything, then stepped onto the train. Johann blew kisses to the children, then followed Frederick to their second-class compartment.

Chapter Three

8 June 1941

Übung macht den Meister

(Practice makes the Master)

JOHANN AND FREDERICK SPOKE LITTLE as the train worked its way through the heart of Germany. Johann, beside the window, studied the trees standing at exact intervals, planted in ruler-straight lines. He watched perfectly rectangular fields pass the window, tiny green seedlings poking through the brown earth in perfectly straight rows. Johann thought of his country, worshipping at the altar of Ordnung. He remembered the plans he and Barbara had made before an obsessed Hitler decided to organize Europe under an oppressive blanket of order and perfection.

He wiped his cheek with the grey-blue sleeve of his uniform—his eyes focused somewhere between the green and brown landscape and the window glass. His mind drifted back to Barbara, Lisa, and Thomas. The separation had driven him closer to them, and he couldn't let himself believe that he would die before he saw them again. But his intense sense of logic told him his optimism, based on nothing, would not stop a random bullet or a cannon shell. He tried to picture fighting for his life, and it seemed impossible that he could kill a man, depriving a family of their loving father or son.

When the train stopped in Stuttgart, Johann's destination, Frederick stepped into the corridor while Johann pulled his bag off the overhead shelf. Frederick was bound for Munich and his Einsatzgruppe training, an hour farther south. Johann avoided Frederick's open arms and shook hands with him. Frederick, embarrassed, stepped back into the compartment, and Johann hurried toward the exit and immediately found a sign indicating where the Sixth Army was gathering their new recruits.

A young private sitting at a temporary table asked him his name, looked on a list and instructed another private to show him to a bench under a canvas-covered frame in the rear of a Lastwagen. Fifteen minutes later, the seats on both sides full, the driver started the engine. The vehicle rode like the truck it was, jostled and jarred its load over rough gravel roads for an hour before reaching a large camp of tents and long wooden buildings that suddenly appeared in the middle of the Black Forest. A sign announced they were entering the *6ᵗᵉ Armee Schwartzwald übungsplatz*. One of the young men chatting in the canvas-covered truck bed, a veteran of the Sixth Army's French campaign, clearly enjoyed the mesmerizing effect his war stories had. Most of the new recruits listened in awe as he told his version of fighting the helpless British and French, pushing them into the sea at Dunkirk.

"We will teach you how to fight like tigers and survive," he said confidently, "and you will learn to do things you didn't think you could ever do! It's our job to separate the cannon fodder from the real soldiers!"

Johann noted the single grey stripe around his collar, the standard decoration of an enlisted man at the bottom of the rank pole.

◇◇◇◇◇◇◇◇◇◇◇◇◇◇◇◇◇◇◇◇◇◇◇◇◇◇◇◇◇◇◇◇

Johann had assumed that basic training was over—no more running, climbing, beating one another up in hand-to-hand combat training... but he painfully learned that he was wrong. The morning five-kilometre run, rain or shine, worked up a soldier's appetite for breakfast, and another five kilometres after Abendessen assured a sound sleep. The routine was as unvarying as brushing his teeth.

A week after beginning officers' training, Johann, so tired he could hardly lift the pencil, spent three evenings trying to stay awake long enough to tell Barbara what was happening to him. He kept a triangular *Gummi* eraser on the little table beside the thin sheet of paper the Bundeswehr gave every enlisted man. Every soldier writing home walked the tightrope of what would get past the censors, and an eraser was an integral tool for correcting momentary lapses into the truth. How to tell Barbara what he experienced every day without distressing her—how to fill the single permitted page with information disguised as triviality, and phrase it so that a clever censor would accept it, was a political exercise worthy of a sly Nürnberg lawyer. He reread the letter, almost worn through in places by the eraser.

> "Liebling
>
> I said goodbye to Frederick at the Stuttgart platform, and I can't say I was sad to do it. A rat is a rat and cannot be anything else. I believe that Siegruna is better off when he is far from her.
>
> We got out of the Lastwagen that took us to the camp, marched to our quarters and had minutes to eat. It took an hour to get our rifle (Somehow, my platoon's rifles had found their way here) and a pack full of the necessities, and then we ran five kilometres before darkness and fatigue put an end to it. Every day since then has started and ended with a five-kilometre run carrying rifles and packs.
>
> I will apparently be an officer if I do well in officer school. I am now commanding a platoon of sixty men, and I will be a sergeant when my training is over."

Here, the paper's surface was rough from multiple erasings—he had written of his tactics classes, a no-no for the censors. General Nehring, commander of the Eighteenth panzer Regiment, was their enthusiastic instructor, and Johann's excitement had filled the page before he realized that not a word of it would pass.

Nehring was not a fan of setting up fortresses. He had begun his discourse with a description of the French Foreign Legion's philosophy of forts and fixed positions and then turned to the Americas and the Spanish and Mexican wars against the Apache Nation.

The Apaches had successfully fought with arrows and spears against Spanish muskets in Sonora—with outdated guns against the Mexicans—and against modern repeater rifles when they fought the American Army. The Apache losses were minuscule compared to the contemporary armies of the time, and the tactic they used was given a name. The Spanish called it *Guerilla*, a small war, and Nehring called it *Asymmetrisch Krieg*, a war fought against a larger and more powerful foe.

The Spanish had invented their version when fighting Napoleon, and the Apache Indians had used it against the occupying forces in North America. Cochise, chief of the Apache tribe, and Geronimo, his lieutenant, drove the Spanish out, then forced the Mexicans to a stalemate. In the end, even the American army had to accept a peace they didn't want.

The Apache's glory days left them with a reputation as the finest soldiers the world had ever seen. Nehring described the Apache tactic as *Schlagundlauf*, hit and run. He taught his class how the Apache successfully implemented it and the difficulty that a modern army would face defending against it.

Johann erased most of the page and thought for a long time. In the end, he decided to leave the letter for the next evening. One more try at writing the words he wanted to say was all the paper would stand and was more than he could face tonight.

On the third day, Johann found the energy to try again. His muscles were adapting, and the evening run had left him on a high.

"My mornings are devoted to theoretical war—how a model war is fought on paper—what should be the result if nothing outside the model interferes. Experts speak on successful and unsuccessful battle tactics. This morning the subject was the purposeful sacrifice of men to reach an objective, and our tactical discussion centred on the appropriateness of surrender. When presented with a virtually hopeless situation, I was shocked at how many officers supported fighting to the last man! I found myself one of a small minority when I disagreed with that choice. I defended the idea of an organized withdrawal, saving as many men and as much material as I could.

The general who led the discussion told us that our positions were less important than whether we could justify them. I watched him closely, and he took notes whenever a view was expressed."

Johann reread the letter and put it away before the barracks' lights went out. He lay there, considering the concept of killing men who were strangers and sacrificing men he knew as friends, all a part of a grand scheme to help his side force its will on other people. On people who spoke a different language or worshipped another God. He tried to find the right in what he was learning to do and went to sleep without a resolution.

The following day, a new sheet of paper lay on the foot of his bed; he folded it and hid it under his pillow roll. When the evening run was over, he began the second page of his letter.

"I am charged with getting every one of the sixty men under my command home alive…"

Johann wrote the words jammed together and as small as he thought would be legible. He had to leave room for the sweetness aching in his heart, but he wanted Barbara to know that survival was his objective.

"We are officially First Platoon of First Jäger Company, but unofficially we are "Die Musiker," something the men grabbed when I found a violin and played for them. We are specialists in scouting and night action."

Done with writing about army life, Johann's words of affection poured onto the page and up the margin before he finally signed off with a painfully inadequate expression of his love. He folded the letter, then opened it, read it one last time before giving it to the mail carrier. He wanted to write more, but he wouldn't get another sheet of paper for three days.

◇◇◇◇◇◇◇◇◇◇◇◇◇◇◇◇◇◇◇◇◇◇◇◇◇◇◇◇◇◇◇◇

A week into his life as Sergeant in command of First Platoon, First Jäger Company, Johann's company commander, *Leutnant* Kohl, gave him a package of papers and a briefing for the First Platoon's initial training exercise. They must attack and take a heavily defended position at the foot of a steep hill, surrounded by dense forest. Johann listened to the briefing, looked at the general description, and opened his mouth to ask a question. The leutnant smiled and dismissed him with a salute.

Johann went to his barracks to study the map and aerial photographs. A narrow swamp covered with what appeared to be impenetrable brush protected the defenders from below, and a steep hill rose behind them, too steep to climb or descend without climbing gear. The contour map and aerial photograph showed the slope as a partly forested escarpment that rose thirty metres in fifteen horizontal metres—with trees and brush hiding the defenders from observers and guns above them. He made a mental note that this worked both ways—attackers at the top of the slope would be invisible to those at the defenders' camp. The aerial photograph didn't show gun positions. Johann's men would have to find them.

Leutnant Kohl's orders gave Johann twenty-four hours to take the position, and he must plan the attack using First Platoon's own intelligence forces.

◇◇◇◇◇◇◇◇◇◇◇◇◇◇◇◇◇◇◇◇◇◇◇◇◇◇◇◇◇◇◇◇◇◇◇◇◇◇

Johann's platoon, fascinated with Nehring's description of Apache warriors, nicknamed their scouts after Nehring's famous North American Indians. Ian Kempner, formerly an engineering student from Heidelberg University, became *Cochise*, "made of oak," chief of the Chihuicahui Apache Nation. Wilhelm Neumann, the son of a wealthy farmer near Stuttgart and a philosophy student, became *Geronimo*, "one who yawns," a charismatic war leader of the same Apache nation. Nehring considered Cochise and Geronimo to be the best guerilla fighters of all time.

Johann ordered his scouts to reconnoitre the enemy positions, and they returned an hour after dark. The platoon gathered around them to hear their report.

Cochise spoke first. "Four machine guns guard the corners of the clearing, and there's a rifleman every two metres along the perimeter that doesn't face the escarpment or the swamp. There are two sentries at the top of the cliff and four more, two at each end of the camp, about two hundred metres outside the perimeter. It's impenetrable without serious casualties."

"Exactly where are the sentries?" asked Johann, bending over the map with a flashlight.

Cochise pointed out the sentries' locations on the aerial photograph.

"Okay, Ian, let's look at one thing at a time. Do you think you can neutralize the sentries without alarming the camp?"

Ian looked at his partner, and Wilhelm nodded. He turned back to Johann and said, "Yes, sir. If we can have two men for each sentry. Ten men should do it, but we want to pick them."

Johann felt like a child playing a game. He tried to tell himself this was a rehearsal for a time when men would die, and kept his tone level when he said, "Then we agree? If we attack before dawn, and,

42

if everything goes perfectly, it can be done." Cochise and Geronimo nodded, said, "Yes, sir," and Johann felt a twinge of something like responsibility.

"Okay," Johann turned to the men gathered around him. "Cochise and Geronimo will pick out the men they want.

Johann turned to his excited men and raised his voice. "They want to teach us humility—we aren't supposed to win. But the Apaches defeated powerful modern armies using their brains and stealth. In other words, they were sneaky bastards who didn't play fair! I don't intend to play fair either. Are you with me?"

The men said, "Yes, sir," with an energetic whisper. Embarrassed at the platoon's eagerness to follow him, Johann felt his face burn and was glad for the darkness.

◇◇◇◇◇◇◇◇◇◇◇◇◇◇◇◇◇◇◇◇◇◇◇◇◇◇◇◇◇◇◇

Johann and the scouts could not see that the 'enemy' consisted of fifty seasoned veterans of the Polish and French campaigns who knew when to expect the attack. It was essentially an ambush, set up to teach the raw recruits a lesson on their first exercise.

Johann began his instructions believing there was no more than a slight chance of success. The Wehrmacht would not make it easy for a platoon of new recruits; there had to be a lesson in this. This had to be a trap, and his men were the mice.

"Ian, Wilhelm, if you two Indians can take out the sentries before they sound the alarm, Corporal Gronert's squad will take care of the machine guns. I will accompany Gronert. We'll do it quietly if we can, but we'll have to use grenades if we're discovered." He turned to the Corporal. "You will attack the guns on the east side at precisely ten minutes after four—you won't have to worry about sentries." He glanced at Ian, and Ian grinned. "I will take half your squad and take out the other two guns." He turned back to his Geronimo and Cochise. "That gives you ten minutes to take out the sentries. Is that enough time?"

"Yes, sir!" Ian and Wilhelm staggered their reply.

Johann spoke to the rest of his men. "Second squad will take out the riflemen at the same time we take the machine guns, one man for each target. I expect at least one of them to see you coming, but if the alarm hasn't been sounded by then, everyone will storm the camp as quietly as they can. Use knives. They know the rules…show them the knife before they see you, and they're dead." Johann hoped they would follow the rules, but they would want to win as badly as he would. "No one is to fire his rifle unless he is discovered, and a shot will be the signal to attack using rifles and bayonets." He let his eyes wander from one man to another. "Is every man clear on what he has to do?"

"Yes, sir," repeated itself as Johann focused on one man after another. The platoon had practised sneaking up on one another until most of them were nervous wrecks. It had become a game in basic training, and Johann had carried on with it. He had nothing to measure their skill against, but, in the dark, he would rather be the hunter.

"We are two kilometres from the camp. We will move forward a thousand metres at oh-three-thirty. If you have a question, ask it before then. Once we move up, there will be no talking. Walk silently, do your job right, and do it on time! It is for sure they know we're coming, and they will be alert. Do not underestimate your enemy! He will get some of us— whether you are one of those is up to you."

Johann looked at his watch. "We begin the attack at precisely oh-four-hundred—I have twenty-two hundred hours and ten minutes…." He held his wrist up and counted, "five, four, three, two, one…now!" He looked around the group. "Is everyone clear on what he has to do?" The squad leaders nodded, and men Johann couldn't see murmured their agreement in the darkness. "Okay, let's get everything ready— then we will sleep for a couple of hours."

◇◇◇◇◇◇◇◇◇◇◇◇◇◇◇◇◇◇◇◇◇◇◇◇◇◇◇◇◇◇

First Platoon had worked out the equipment they needed to move silently and invisibly, and every man carried it in his pack. The Jäger attackers covered their boots with oversized heavy wool socks—their soles covered with sewn-on soft leather. They blackened their faces with burnt cork, covered their shiny buttons and all metallic surfaces on guns, knives and bayonets with dull black boot polish, and then they pulled knitted black ski masks over their heads.

At precisely oh-four-hundred, twelve silent attackers eliminated the sentries, and ten minutes later a twelve-man squad took out the four machine guns. The third squad took care of the riflemen, and sixty soldiers moved silently into their objective, found their targets, and took them prisoner without firing a shot. The action took three minutes; the camp was theirs, and they forced the embarrassed leutnant commanding the base to announce their accomplishment over the camp radio.

◇◇◇◇◇◇◇◇◇◇◇◇◇◇◇◇◇◇◇◇◇◇◇◇◇◇◇◇◇◇◇◇◇

First panzer Division's new commander, Colonel Stieff, was furious when his field telephone awakened him at dawn, but he staggered across the room and picked it up. He didn't hide his annoyance when he answered "Stieff" in a clipped voice. There was a short period of silence, increasing his frustration.

"*Oberst* Stieff, we have a problem." The unidentified caller waited. Colonel Stieff hated his captain's habit of withholding information. The captain seemed to enjoy the feeling of power that came from possessing knowledge yet undiscovered by the object of his torment. Those unfortunate people forced to deal with him felt a genuine hatred toward him, and his chances of stepping on the next rung of the promotion ladder were slight to nil.

"What is the problem, captain?" the colonel asked impatiently.

The captain didn't try to hide a hint of disdain in his voice. "The Finke Platoon took the objective."

The colonel raised his eyebrows. He had put his best lieutenant in charge of the defence and given him the best men he had, hand-picked by Leutnant Schröder. They were supposed to teach this naive Jäger Company how much they had to learn.

"How many men did they lose?" To take the objective, Sergeant Finke would have sacrificed at least half of his men, and that would still be enough to teach him a lesson.

"None, sir," the captain answered, and Colonel Stieff was sure from the tone of his voice that the captain had a smirk of satisfaction on his face.

"Finke's platoon?" Colonel Stieff was losing patience. "They couldn't have taken the objective without losing a man!"

Captain Karloff's tone made it clear to his colonel that he was enjoying himself. "Sir, there were no casualties among the attackers—that would be Finke's platoon. However, the defenders—that would be the veteran platoon led by..."

45

Yes, yes, I know who they are... I'm the one who picked them. Go on... How many men did they lose?"

"Uh... All of them, sir, killed or captured."

Colonel Stieff's brain froze for a moment, and he said nothing. Then he smiled. Perhaps he had something in this platoon, and particularly in this sergeant. He would test them again in a few days.

"Thank you, Captain." Stieff hung up the telephone and went back to sleep.

◇◇◇◇◇◇◇◇◇◇◇◇◇◇◇◇◇◇◇◇◇◇◇◇◇◇◇◇◇◇◇

Two days later, Colonel Stieff personally asked Johann's First Platoon to destroy a fixed artillery position, bypassing his captain. He gave them two tanks to help with the heavy lifting and was surprised when Johann decided not to use what he called "the noisy monsters."

Johann's platoon overran the position and destroyed twelve theoretical guns in a night action that lasted five minutes. Two of Johann's men made critical mistakes, and four men theoretically died, but Colonel Stieff was still delighted at the success. Captain Karloff was more than a little miffed when he found out the colonel had bypassed him with the operation assignment.

◇◇◇◇◇◇◇◇◇◇◇◇◇◇◇◇◇◇◇◇◇◇◇◇◇◇◇◇◇◇◇

The mortality rate was unacceptable to Johann, and he spent two hours analyzing mistakes with his men. Johann quickly dismissed every excuse, forced his men to face the facts until they found solutions. He added remarks to the meticulous notes he kept, as he had when learning new violin pieces. By the time the music he made with his violin reached performance standards, Johann's scores looked like a hen with dirty feet had walked all over them—the same was true of the log he had started when he began officers' school.

When the meeting was over, and he was alone in the darkness of the barracks, looking up at the ceiling he couldn't see, Johann vowed that when live bullets started flying, none of his men would die of stupid mistakes. He felt a heavy load on his shoulders—he had sixty lives in his imperfect hands.

Chapter Four

22 June–December 1941

Barbarossa

The impact of treachery is proportional to the depth of trust.

BARBARA PUT A BOWL OF STRAWBERRIES, honey and fresh milk in front of wide-eyed Thomas and Lisa as she said, "...When you've eaten your *Grünkohl*..."

Somehow, Oma Maria found special treats for them every Tuesday and Saturday when she prepared dinner for the family and gave Lisa her violin lesson. Despite rationing, she had her little cart loaded with food that had almost disappeared in wartime Germany. Barbara wiped her hands on her apron, and sat down opposite Maria, a letter in her hand.

"I got a letter from Johann this morning." Barbara held the letter by one corner and waved it in front of her mother-in-law. "He wrote a whole page just for me!"

Maria laughed. "Barbara, that's wonderful. Can I read it? The family parts? Unless..."

"I will read the family parts as soon as Lisa and Thomas finish their Mittagessen."

Thomas, his eyes on the dessert, shovelled his Grünkohl as though he hadn't eaten in a month. Lisa picked at a small piece, finally screwing up her face as she put it in her mouth. She immediately spit it on the side of her plate.

Grünkohl was, according to parents, an edible green plant that every German child in wartime knew tasted like spoiled grass. According to those parents, it was an excellent source of vitamins, but as soon as the plate landed on the table, the battle began. Parents tried to hide the taste with greasy chunks of *Mettwurst,* principally pork fat, whose primary virtue was that its strong taste covered the flavour of just about anything. Its primary drawback was that it tasted almost as bad as whatever taste it was intended to hide.

"It's better with lots of vinegar." Maria dripped some on Lisa's greens. Lisa stirred it in and tried a minuscule piece.

"I can still taste it!" She screwed up her face.

"Try it with a piece of Mettwurst." Barbara cut one of Lisa's Mettwurst slices into four small pieces.

"They're still too big." Lisa took the knife and fork from her mother and cut the smallest piece in two. She used her knife to cut a tiny speck of green from the Grünkohl, placed it delicately on the tiny piece of sausage and speared it with her fork. Lisa stared at it for a few seconds, then plugged her nose and put it in her mouth. She gagged, spit it on her plate, and started to cry.

"I don't care about the strawberries if you will read *Vati's* letter. But I can't eat this...this..."

Maria looked at Barbara, pleading Lisa's case with her eyes.

"That's alright, Lisa." Barbara stirred her fork through Lisa's food. You and I will eat something else." She smoothed Lisa's hair. "You can eat your strawberries."

"That's not fair! I had to clean my plate!" Thomas swallowed his last bite of strawberries. The only reason to wash his bowl and plate was to decimate the germ population.

Barbara ignored Thomas and unfolded the letter.

"The letter was dated last Friday, the twentieth...today is the twenty-fourth. I hope our army is as efficient as its postal service!"

Every morning Barbara sat on the front step, waiting for the bright young woman who delivered her mail. When there were no letters from Johann, Anna always waved and apologized; when there was a letter as happened this morning, she said, "He wrote. That means he must be alright," as she handed it to Barbara.

Barbara read the second page, the 'family' page, aloud; the first page was for her.

> *"Liebe Barbara und alle,*
>
> *I wanted to write earlier, but my paper didn't arrive until yesterday, and since then, Wilhelm has given me his sheet so I can write a longer letter. The first page is Barbara's bit."*

Thomas grinned as he put up his hand. "I want to hear Mutti's bit."

Lisa pulled Thomas's hand down. "*Vati* and *Mutti* need privacy, just like when Vati's home." Barbara smiled at Maria and went back to the letter.

"I don't know whether I told you about the violin. When we first started training, a man from the village near our camp gave it to me. He takes away our garbage and sells vegetables to the Gulaschkanone— that's what we call the field kitchen. It's a two-wheeled cart pulled by a horse if we're on flat ground, two horses if we're in the hills. We are well-fed, with an Eintopf at midday that Maria would be proud of. (I'm rambling, but an extra sheet of paper does that to a man.)

His wife teaches music in the village, and I told him that I played the violin. The next time he came to the camp, he left the violin for me. I don't know where he got it, but it's a good instrument. It is a bit rough but has a great sound and is easy to play."

Lisa interrupted, "I can't wait for Vati to come home and play the Mendelssohn concerto with me." Her voice cracked a little, but she controlled the urge to cry.

Maria put her hand on Lisa's, and Barbara continued.

"We are becoming a fighting unit, and our colonel now has confidence in us. He gives us impossible problems to solve, and we fight against theoretically much stronger forces. It's a challenge to figure out how to overcome the enemy, destroy the target, then get out without casualties! I keep a log of our practice exercises, and I study them every day. I'm always looking for ways we may have done more with less risk, and that's the reason for our training.

The men under my command are individually excellent fighters—but what pleases me most is that they are becoming an efficient team. We have become so close I can't imagine how I will react if one of them is killed in a situation I can't control, or worse, one in which I made a mistake. Our instructors tell us that it

*will happen—that we will make mistakes and get others
killed. But they also tell us we must keep fighting. I
don't see how I could do that, but the veterans say that
I will get used to it.*

Barbara put the letter on the table in front of her. "How can they ask my husband, the kindest warmest man in the world, to do this?

Theo sat with his hands folded, fingers intertwined, head down. "In the Great War, I watched good men desperately and savagely kill other good men. The whole point of training is to teach a man to kill quickly, without thinking, before the enemy kills him. My greatest fear is that Johann will be good at it and learn to enjoy it."

"Is Vati going to kill someone? Is he going to do something bad?" Thomas asked innocently. His grandfather realized his mistake and tried to fix the damage.

"I meant that your father will be good at being a soldier...I'm afraid he will forget about his music."

Thomas searched his young mind for a solution. "Why doesn't he run away? He could come home, couldn't he?"

Theo grabbed the crumb. "If he has to run, he will. He wants nothing more than to come back to you and Lisa. But right now, he has to be a soldier so he can protect his family."

Maria tousled Thomas's hair, and Barbara waited. She decided not to read the next paragraph and skipped to the bottom of the page. She cleared her throat before she began.

*"I miss everyone more than I can say with words. Lisa,
I want you to keep working on the Mendelssohn, but I
have found another composer you might like. His name
is Antonin Dvorak. Ask Maria to find a copy of his violin
concerto, and I will play it with you when I get back.*

*Thomas, I want you to concentrate on your schoolwork,
but take time to play some soccer. I am in excellent
shape, and I'm looking forward to playing with you.
We have a soccer ball here, and I'm practicing, so
watch out. My chess is not so good now, but I will find
someone to play with, so don't count on beating me!*

I love you all so much it hurts, and, like you, I want

this war to be over. Germany is not at war with any
country near where I am, so I may not have to fight at
all. Russia is near here, and there are rumours that we
may practice war games with them.

The rest is for Mutti, so remember that I love you more
than I love my life, and I will be home soon. I must go
to bed now so I can dream of my children. Remember,
Lieblinge, the war is almost over."

"He called me sweetheart!" Thomas stood up, pretending to be disgusted. "I hope Gunther doesn't find out." He forgot to excuse himself, stopped at the kitchen door and said, "I'm going to play soccer with Gunther."

Barbara opened her mouth, but Theo was there first.

"I'm sorry I can't play chess with you today, Thomas; I have to work at the theatre."

Thomas had leaned ahead, ready to run, realized his mistake and turned to his grandfather. "I forgot...I'll stay here...I would rather play chess with you than kick a ball around the field with Gunther."

Theo stood and went to Thomas. "It's a beautiful day, and I really do have work to do. Gunther's house is on the way. We can walk together."

Barbara gave Theo a sympathetic look, and Theo winked at her with the eye Thomas couldn't see.

After Thomas and Theo left, Maria turned to Barbara and pointed to the letter.

"May I hear the paragraph you skipped?"

"Johann is afraid he will make a mistake that will get him and his men killed."

"Read it to me."

Barbara read:

"Our Jäger Company is trained to fight behind enemy
lines. We are through our training, and all of our
exercises were scouting for tank formations, setting up
ambushes, and destroying enemy artillery positions. Most
of the maneuvers involve hand-to-hand fighting, mostly
at night, and I am scared that I won't be able to do it
when the man I'm fighting is also fighting for his life.

My fear is not so much of death, but I am terrified that when the battle begins, I will not be able to kill, and my inability or hesitation will get my men killed...I can't live with that!

Winning depends upon killing the enemy before he sees us. They must die before they can raise the alarm and before they can fire their gun. We will almost always be outnumbered, and surprise is all we've got.

What if I don't kill my target? What if he cries out or shoots me because I hesitated? Everything depends on every man doing his job, but I can't picture myself killing a man with a knife or a bayonet!"

Barbara lowered the letter, tears falling on it as she laid it on the table.

"He is going to die, Maria. I can feel it."

Maria leaned over Barbara, put her arms around her and spoke softly in her ear.

"In war, all men learn to kill—he will do it when he must. The tragedy is that it may break his heart!"

Barbara put her hand on Maria's arm, spoke softly, as Maria had, "I don't care how many men he has to kill, as long as he comes back to me. If his heart is sick, I will heal him."

◇◇◇◇◇◇◇◇◇◇◇◇◇◇◇◇◇◇◇◇◇◇

That night, as always, Barbara listened to the news on the *Volksempfänger.* When Hitler was elected Chancellor in 1933, he had made the radio available to every German. It was cheap at 76 Reichmarks, and, encouraged by Hitler and the Nazi party, most households bought one.

By law, businesses closed their doors during Hitler's speeches. The Nazi government was the only approved source of news of any kind, all of it created and filtered by Goebbels' *Reichsministerium für Volksaufklärung und Propaganda.* And on the evening of June 23 1941, it was illegal and punishable by death to listen to foreign radio stations.

Barbara hated the radio, hated the Nazi-biased information, and hated Hitler's ranting speeches. But it was the only contact she had with Johann's Sixth Army, and she forced herself to listen. She sat in her armchair, knitting a pair of mittens for Thomas, waiting for the start of the evening news broadcast. The evening report began with military music, followed by the abrupt announcement that German forces had attacked Russia along a two-thousand-kilometre front, and Barbara dropped her knitting.

The radio's aggressive male voice first explained that Russia's communist ideology threatened Germany's efforts to save the world. Then the voice began a rational justification of the German people's need for *Lebensraum,* defined as room to expand Nazi ideology—space not being utilized by people who were worthy of it.

The stern, assertive news voice of the *Reichsrundfunkgesellschaft,* the only radio station approved by Goebbels' Propaganda Ministerium, announced jubilantly that German forces were already fifty kilometres inside Russian territory. The attack was only two days old, and the Sixth Army was already fighting its way across Ukraine!

"Lebensraum? You make my Johann kill people for *Lebensraum?"* Barbara shouted at the radio, "You only want my husband to steal land from Jews and Bolsheviks so you can give it to your bastard friends. You can't have my Johann!"

Barbara sat heavily on the sofa, feeling the need to smash something, when a small, sweet voice came out of the darkness. "It's all right, Mutti." Lisa stepped lightly over to her mother's side and began rubbing her back. "Daddy will be alright."

Barbara sobbed into a soft cushion.

◇◇◇◇◇◇◇◇◇◇◇◇◇◇◇◇◇◇◇◇◇◇◇◇◇◇◇◇◇◇◇◇◇◇

June 21: Johann and his men moved from the Alps' beginnings to the Carpathian Mountains foothills in southern Hungary, where Johann assumed he would participate in more war games. During the night of the twenty-first, the Sixth Army loaded him and his men into Lastwagen and drove through the mountains until, in the grey predawn light, they crossed the border into Russia. Wilhelm pointed at a roadside sign and an open barricade—and two dead Russian soldiers beside it. "It doesn't look like we're here to play war games."

Johann didn't answer for a few minutes. His men were silent, waiting for him. He finally said, "I don't understand what is happening, but if Hitler is attacking Russia, we are going to be here for a long time."

They followed Sixth Army tanks and didn't hear a shot fired all day.

The silence continued when they stopped to set up camp; the night was ominously quiet.

An hour before daylight, the world around Johann exploded. Shells landed in the forest where his platoon had dug trenches the night before, filling the air with shrapnel and wood splinters. Barrage after barrage rolled over them, moving through the camp to where five Mark IV tanks of the First panzer Division sat under the trees. One of the tanks took a direct hit just as the engine started, and it instantly caught fire. The only man who attempted to get out of the tank burned to death before he could crawl over the lip of the hatch. Johann and his horrified men watched the soldier writhe, heard his screams over the explosions as flames devoured his body. In seconds, it was over—the man was mercifully dead. But the men in the trench didn't let their eyes leave the man's inert body as flames consumed it.

All the officers ran to the First panzer Division command centre, and Johann arrived with Colonel Stieff. The first words the colonel said to Johann were: "Can you find those guns?" He commanded more than questioned. Stieff was a veteran of the French campaign, and Johann could sense his excitement. Johann's own heart pumped so fast he felt sick.

"Yes, sir, I can find them." He knew from the scream of the shells over his head where he should look for them. "Before I came here, I took the liberty to send out Ian and Wilhelm. They will pinpoint the location—the guns are close; the shells are falling almost vertically; probably howitzers."

As part of their training, Johann's platoon had experienced barrages from near and far, from large calibre guns and small calibre field pieces. They all sounded different, and the effect when they struck had a signature that Johann had learned to read.

Stieff said, "Good work! We're going to withdraw between the hills. Find and destroy those guns!"

"We'll get them, sir." The colonel's lips formed the word to begin his next question, but Johann interrupted before he got that far. "One hour, sir. If you don't hear from me or if they don't stop firing in an hour, you had better send someone else."

The low cloud ceiling, darkness, and the morning fog hanging below the tops of the hills ruled out airstrikes for Colonel Stieff, but it would all help Johann. The colonel was stuck until First Company eliminated the guns—the tanks needed to be underway again before the Russians could organize their defences. Stieff smiled at Johann.

"Son, I know the excitement you feel right now, but don't be a dead hero!" He put his hand on Johann's shoulder. His barely one-metre-fifty height forced him to reach up. "This is only the beginning, and I will need you many times before this is over. Stay calm, remember your training, and be sure you are ready before you attack. Doing it right is always better than doing it fast. If you can't do it, we'll wait for the Luftwaffe or the artillery."

Johann smiled down at him, uncomfortable with the thirty-centimetre difference. "Sir, I have no intention of dying. If we can't take them out, I will send the coordinates." He trotted off to join his men, adrenalin rushing through his veins, fear pushed out of the part of his brain where logic should reign. He told himself it would be like playing solo in front of a full house.

Shells crashed down on the withdrawing Germans as Johann and his men left the camp. They ran toward the guns until they were clear of the explosions and then waited for Cochise and Geronimo, who arrived in minutes.

Ian's hands shook, whether from excitement or fear; Johann couldn't tell. "The Russian spotters are dead, and twelve guns are ten minutes away. They don't have a perimeter, and they don't have sandbags around the guns. There are only enough men to fire the guns and carry ammunition, and most of them aren't carrying rifles. We can go around behind and take all of them at once; no sweat!"

◇◇◇◇◇◇◇◇◇◇◇◇◇◇◇◇◇◇◇◇◇◇◇◇◇◇◇◇◇◇◇◇◇◇◇◇◇◇

When they reached the guns, the flashes lit the night around them, and the noise hit Johann like a wall. He sent five men to each artillery piece and five men to the trucks where the Russians stored the ammunition. Johann's men were within thirty metres of their enemy when the first Russian dove for his rifle, ten metres away. Minutes later, half the Russians were dead, and the others were prisoners. Johann had killed his first man with his rifle and shot and wounded another. He felt nothing as the Russians still alive threw up their hands.

Johann's mind struggled to keep up. None of the exercises had gone this well, and none had passed so quickly. His men took their targets in a matter of seconds, as fast as they could run the thirty metres to them. Every man knew his job, did it with precision and without any apparent emotion.

When they had silenced the Russian artillery, they loaded explosive charges into the gun's breaches and barrels; the cannons would be useless with shattered beaches and barrels. They packed explosives in the boxes of shells in the Russian trucks and wired everything to blow up at once. The explosions shook the ground as Johann and his men marched their prisoners down the road. Wilhelm smiled at his boss.

"Do you suppose it will always be this easy? Are the Russians really this stupid?"

Johann wasn't smiling. "Don't get cocky; Hitler caught Stalin napping once—he won't do it again. Russians are like us—they will get tired of dying."

The Sixth Army fought its way east, pushing the surprised, ill-equipped and poorly-trained Russian Army ahead of them. Johann's platoon became better at their job, and Stieff used them often. They became ruthless destroyers of the primitive Russian tanks, often catching the unwary crews parked at night, sleeping in their tanks or close by in shallow dugouts with their infantry. The infantry guarding the tanks became the first victims, followed closely by the tanks and their crews.

A month after capturing their first prisoners, Johann's platoon, arriving at daylight, brought fifty dejected Russian soldiers back to the camp.

"Take them to the prisoners' compound," Johann directed Wilhelm, then turned to report directly to Colonel Stieff. The colonel kept his tent close to where the men lived, and the entire side where Stieff sat on a cloth chair was open to the July sun.

"More prisoners, Johann?" The colonel spoke before Johann reached him.

"Yes, sir. We captured fifty infantry and tank crew. We thought about driving the tanks back here, but they didn't look like anything you would want."

"You destroyed them?"

"Yes, sir."

"Sit down, Johann. I've intended to talk to you about the prisoners, but the time was never right. I must do it now." The colonel motioned Johann to a canvas chair beside him.

Johann thought he knew what was coming. He waited while Colonel Stieff lit a cigar.

"The problem, my young sergeant…." He stood up and inhaled, and Johann moved to stand up. The colonel gently pushed him back in the chair…"is that you and your men have captured over two hundred Russian soldiers; only one other platoon has captured as many as eight." He puffed on the cigar, blew the smoke away from Johann. "Tell me why that is."

"Sir," Johann cleared his throat to get a few seconds to think—it didn't do any good. "Sir, I don't know."

"Then, I will tell you." Colonel Stieff flicked a long ash from his cigar, put his hands together and said, "They are shooting the Russians you would take prisoner. It's much easier for them and for me. I have ten men looking after the Russians you have brought back—a waste of good soldiers."

"But sir, we can't shoot them in cold blood… Sir, I won't order my men to do it, and they wouldn't do it if I did."

Stieff leaned toward Johann, making him uncomfortable. "Sergeant Finke, would you rather be shot, or would you prefer to starve to death?"

"Neither, if I have a choice. I have a wife and two children, and I want to see them again."

"The Russians you capture have no choice. If you bring them to me, they are taken to the Einsatzgruppe, and those bastards work them to death. They don't feed them, and they work them like donkeys, and, under those circumstances, no man lives very long."

Johann had heard such rumours but had dismissed them.

"That can't be true, sir. Germany treats war prisoners well, much better than the Russians do!"

Colonel Stieff took one last puff, pinched the glow off his cigar and put it in his pocket.

"Johann, don't bring me any more prisoners. It will be better for them and better for you and me." Johann understood but didn't want to admit it. He couldn't imagine murdering a helpless man. He stood up to face his colonel.

Colonel Stieff straightened his arms against the side of his legs. He raised his voice, and the outcome was not what he obviously intended—the combination of short stature and high-pitched voice was comical.

"I am giving you an order that was given to me!" He lowered the pitch, but the apparent effort ruined the intended effect. "Don't bring any more prisoners to this camp!"

Johann left the tent, confused and depressed, and met Wilhelm and Ian on their way back from the prisoners' compound.

As they walked, Johann announced, "We can't bring any more prisoners back to the camp."

"What happened?" Wilhelm was too intelligent, and they had been together too long for him to miss Johann's mood.

"Colonel Stieff ordered me not to bring any more prisoners back to the camp!" He waved his arms toward the prisoners' compound. "The 'Einsatzgruppe' works them to death and doesn't feed them."

Ian and Wilhelm walked silently, one on each side of Johann.

"Well, if we can't bring them back, what do we do with them?" Wilhelm paused, then went on. "We could take their guns and let them go." It was more of a question than a solution.

Ian answered. "We can't do that, and we all know it." He stopped walking; Wilhelm and Johann stopped beside him. Johann looked around for witnesses—Ian went on, frustrated. "I've heard rumours that the Einsatzgruppe are forcing the prisoners to work on the roads and do God knows what else..."

Johann let his eyes wander as he spoke. The conversation was becoming dangerous. "Yes, that's true...Stieff told me...but we knew that, didn't we?"

"Was he the one who told you that they don't feed them? They work them all the daylight every day until they drop; then they shoot them... Did he tell you that?" Ian's voice rose in volume and pitch. Johann considered telling him to shut up but decided to say nothing.

Wilhelm kicked the dirt. "I've heard they do worse than that, and I believe it's true." Wilhelm at least kept his voice down.

Johann started walking, purposefully keeping his thoughts to himself. He tried to work out how to avoid shooting prisoners, but his logical mind hit a wall as soon as he went there. He would prefer to bring them back to a worse fate, as long as he didn't know for sure. But Stieff had ruined that.

"I know a man in the Einsatzgruppe, and he's a murdering bastard with no pity!" He thought of Frederick joyfully shooting helpless prisoners, and the picture fit. They stopped outside their tent, and Johann searched for listeners. When he was satisfied there were none within earshot, he said, "Stieff is right—we can't bring them back here. They would be better off dead than…." He stopped talking.

◇◇◇◇◇◇◇◇◇◇◇◇◇◇◇◇◇◇◇◇◇◇◇◇◇◇◇◇◇◇

A week later, the First panzer Division of the Southern Sixth Army camped on the Ukraine Steppes with no enemy in sight. They waited for the Romanians on their southern flank and the Sixth Army fighting north of them to catch up. The well-trained Romanians had German equipment, but with rugged terrain to negotiate they took many casualties from snipers and artillery, slowing their progress.

While waiting, Johann and his men settled into the relaxed pace of camp life until, a month into the wait, Stieff asked the Jäger officers to join him for coffee.

Stieff stood up, and every man reluctantly put down his cup of genuine coffee, the first they had tasted in six months.

"This little break has been the calm before the storm. We are going into Kharkiv soon, and we will fight from city to city after that. I want the Jäger companies ready to fight in the cities, house-to-house, hand-to-hand."

The officers looked at one another. Leutnant Kohl, First Jäger Company's commander, spoke first, "We are trained to fight at night, using stealth to overrun enemy positions before they know we're coming. We will need to work out tactics and train our men." Stieff nodded but remained silent. Kohl added, "We will need time and help from someone who knows how to do this."

Stieff paced behind his rivetted officers. Finally, he stopped and spoke. Those with their backs to him turned in their chair. "I can't guarantee anything, but you could have two weeks here, and perhaps a

59

few weeks after that before we reach a city. Somewhere in this army we have men who know how to fight in the streets—I will find them, and they will help you train your men."

The officers gathered outside when the meeting ended. They grumbled about being in a panzer Division, untrained for city fighting, and then sat down to work out the tactical problems they would face.

Lieutenant Kohl leaned back in a canvas chair and looked at the officers he commanded. He was younger than Johann, dark-skinned, with coal-black hair. In addition, his dark eyes and oversize nose belied his loud claim to be from a Bayern village, descended from a long line of pure-blood Aryan Germans. Wilhelm had a theory that a gypsy rooster had jumped the fence when his father wasn't looking.

Kohl said, "Let's hear what you think. How do we do this?"

Johann began the conversation by stating the obvious. "We need machine pistols. A rifle is no good at close quarters."

Wilhelm said, "We have a few Russian *Papa* machine guns, and they're a lot better than our machine pistols. The Papa is more reliable, uses our standard nine-millimetre pistol ammunition, and it's one tough gun! Until we can confiscate enough Papas, we should train our men with rifles, bayonets, grenades, and knives. No point in wishing for what the German army doesn't have...better a reliable rifle than a machine pistol that jams if you hold it wrong."

Kohl let the men argue the merits of MP40 machine pistols, Russian Papas, and rifles until they had exhausted the possibilities without a consensus, then changed the topic to girls, and finally to cigarettes by bumming one from Wilhelm.

◇◇◇◇◇◇◇◇◇◇◇◇◇◇◇◇◇◇◇◇◇◇◇◇◇◇◇◇◇◇◇◇◇◇◇◇

A barn and an abandoned house became the training ground for the Jäger housebreakers, and they were in service day and night. Leutnant Kohl pitted unit against unit, and Johann's First Platoon, using rifles and bayonets, consistently came out on top.

The house had eight rooms in two storeys, five with doors. The barn, attached to the house and accessed by a door from the kitchen, had a high loft split by a wall with a door in it. Two sets of stairs connected the loft to the ground. The barn's main floor was cluttered with cattle stanchions, two box stalls, and a small room at the end farthest from the house. A large double door beside the room swung open to the outside.

The arrangement covered many scenarios, from breaking into an occupied room to an all-out gunfight in the barn at night. Kohl's men could invent deadly games faster than they could execute them. Night in the windowless barn was Johann's squad's favourite playground.

Two weeks later, they packed their tents and began walking toward Kharkiv.

Colonel Stieff's First panzer Division spent the summer and fall of 1941 advancing to the city's southern outskirts, then setting up winter camp to wait for spring. Johann's platoon did nothing but scout for First panzer's tanks and artillery, seeing little action. They didn't fire a shot and so didn't have to resolve the prisoner dilemma. The Sixth Army infantry took Kharkiv without Stieff's help, and he ordered his men to stay out of the city.

◇◇◇◇◇◇◇◇◇◇◇◇◇◇◇◇◇◇◇◇◇◇◇◇◇◇◇◇◇◇◇◇◇

"Why do you suppose we trained to break down doors?" Wilhelm and Ian sat just far enough away from a roaring fire to keep their clothes from smoking. Wilhelm seemed in a particularly sour mood. "The regular infantry took Kharkiv while we were sitting here toasting our *Wurst*. Not that I'm complaining—it's excellent *Wurst*." He pulled his stick back from the fire and examined the *Bratwurst* stuck on the end of it.

Johann wrapped his hands around his knees and stared at the flames, mesmerized by the flickering fire. "Most Ukrainian people hate the Russians more than they hate Germans. They make things hard for the Russians and easy for us—maybe our regulars didn't need help."

"And now they get their reward..." Ian's sarcastic tone wasn't lost on Johann.

"Do I detect bitterness?" Johann took his eyes from the flames and looked at Ian.

"Officers are the last to hear." Ian lay back on his elbow. "The Einsatzgruppe followed the regulars into the city. They murdered half the people in the villages around Kharkiv, stole all their food, and now they're working on Kharkiv."

"Half? That's *Quatch!* I won't believe that until I see it for myself!"

61

Johann stood up, picked up a dry stick and threw it into the raging fire. Other soldiers surrounding the fire did the same, and those downwind moved upwind to get away from the sparks.

Ian countered, "I can find you a couple of guys from the regulars who helped cover a mass grave. They trucked the victims there, the Einsatzgruppe shot them, and the regulars covered them with dirt!"

"Ian, this is not something I want to talk about. It's camp talk, and it's dangerous—even if we had what you call proof." Johann left the circle and walked back to the cold tent. It was dark, and Wilhelm surprised him at the entrance.

"The way I look at it is this..." Wilhelm held the flap open... "If it is true, our men had nothing to do with it. We have our business to do, and we should stay out of the Einsatzgruppe's way."

Johann lit the kerosene lantern and dug out his paper and pencil. "Wilhelm, think about this. The Einsatzgruppe is part of the German Army, and so are we. Whatever they do, they do in the name of Germany, and we are Germans. We all work for the same man. If that bullshit were true, wouldn't we be responsible? Aren't we the soldiers who take the towns they destroy?" Johann sat down, laid the paper in front of him and fiddled with the pencil. "Perhaps that's why we didn't go to Kharkiv—Stieff would never send us anywhere near those bastards." He tried to sound as though he believed it to be true.

◇◇◇◇◇◇◇◇◇◇◇◇◇◇◇◇◇◇◇◇◇◇◇◇◇◇◇◇◇◇◇◇◇◇◇◇◇◇

Every week, Johann wrote a letter to his family, most of the time on a single piece of paper. Occasionally, a second sheet appeared on his bed, a gift from one of his men who had no one to read his letters.

As always, the tricky part of writing from the fighting front was telling the truth. Johann suspected that some version of Ian's bleak picture was accurate—his country was pillaging and plundering the Russian countryside as its soldiers marched across the vast land—and he was aware that his growing certainty of it bordered on treason. He wanted to shout his frustration from the rooftops, but even minor deviations from Goebell's propaganda invited severe punishment. If they even smelled his suspicions, the ubiquitous Gestapo spies would deal with him.

"30 November 1941

Liebling

We are camped on the Steppes, near a city I can't name. We hear rumours that the city's people are starving, mainly because the Russian Army destroyed their crops so the German Army wouldn't have them. We have plenty to eat, however, so don't worry.

The Einsatzgruppe, the force that Frederick joined, follows us as a 'clean-up' crew. I have sent two hundred prisoners behind the lines to them. There is a lot of work on the roads and other less pleasant jobs, and occasionally we see Russian prisoners working in the perpetual mud. It looks like the lucky ones are sent to Germany to work in the factories."

Johann was using paper too fast. He tried to write smaller.

"There is slimy, slippery mud everywhere, sometimes halfway to our knees. The roads are nearly impassable for anything with wheels, and tracked vehicles break everything from tracks to transmissions and final drive gears. To make it worse, last night, the temperature froze the mud hard, and this morning nothing with tracks could move. The slime between track segments froze solid, making it impossible to turn them. Vehicles sitting in the mud froze to the ground. To thaw them out, we burn old tires close to the panzers. But even then, we won't have half our tanks in usable condition if the Russians attack today. Fortunately, the Bolsheviks appear to hate the mud as much as we do.

I lost a man yesterday, the first one since we came to Russia. He was helping with a demag we use for scouting—that's a vehicle with tracks on the rear and wheels on the front. It was stuck in the mud, and he slid under the spinning tracks, cutting off both his legs. He bled to death before we could help him.

There is so much more I would like to say, but for many reasons, I can't. I miss you and the children, and of course, Theo and Maria. Tell everyone not to worry—the Russian bear is in hibernation. We have tired him out, and he will rest for a while, probably until spring."

Johann only had room for a few lines of sweetness, but he was depressed and didn't feel like sweetness anyway. He wanted to be home, not writing with a piece of lead on a sheet of manufactured paper. He could see no chance to see his family for a long time; the Russians had proven that they would fight to the death, and Russia had almost three times as many Russians as Germany had Germans. Russian soldiers had learned that to surrender was to die, often slowly, and so if they could pull the trigger, they fired their gun until they ran out of bullets or stopped breathing. Some kept a bullet in their pocket so they could kill themselves rather than surrender.

Truckload after truckload of Einsatzgruppe soldiers arrived; their destination, a small city of tents separating them from the regular Sixth Army. They set up a perimeter isolating themselves from the regular army.

Johann, Wilhelm and Ian had nothing to do but watch the trucks fill the small town of tents.

Wilhelm said, "I don't see any horns or forked tails."

He didn't laugh, so Johann assumed sarcasm as he pointed toward the camp. "I want to talk to one of them—just one will do. Find a way to get him to our tent."

Ian said, "Are you sure you want to know what they've been up to?"

"Just make friends with one of them and bring him here for a beer—if we don't have enough, I'll give him mine."

Wilhelm smacked his lips. "Beer sounds good to me."

A week later, Wilhelm reported that it was impossible to talk to any member of the *Einsatzgruppe,* let alone get one out of their compound.

"I guess that means they're up to no good." Johann couldn't get his brain around the rumoured mass murder of civilians. "But… Maybe there's a saner explanation."

Ian looked at Johann as a parent would a foolish child. "The explanation is simple. If you look for them, there are many insane people in the world. Our insane Führer hired the lunatic Himmler to put all the crazy soldiers to work for the Einsatzgruppe and the SS!"

Johann searched his mind for a suitable *reparté* and decided the best thing to do was end the conversation. He said to Ian as he watched a convoy of Lastwagen approached the Einsatzgruppe gate. "If you don't shut up, you are going to get us all killed."

Chapter Five

March–April 1942

Juliette

"Courage is the price that life exacts for granting peace."
Amelia Earhart

THEO BANGED THE KNOCKER on Barbara's door at the start of *Mittagspause,* and Barbara opened it. Wiping her hands on her apron, she stepped aside, but Theo stayed on the doorstep.

"Barbara, I have good news." His beard wiggled when he smiled and talked at the same time, and his eyes twinkled. "I have hired a guest to sing Nedda in the upcoming production of *Bajazzo.* She's arriving this afternoon: your friend, Juliette Durand.

"*The* Juliette Durand? My Juliette?"

"The same." Theo pointed at a car parked in front of the house. "I need you to pick her up; she arrives at three, and I have a rehearsal. I've booked two rooms for her and her manager at the Detmolder Hof."

"I would love to, Theo!" Barbara kissed his cheek. "I can't wait to see her!"

"No need to drive me back to the theatre—I need the exercise." He dropped the keys to the car in her hand.

Barbara watched Theo walk up the street, so happy she wanted to scream it out to the world. She had met Juliette in October 1939, when Barbara and her family had lived in Bielefeld. Juliette had sung *Mimi,* and Johann had escorted her. Juliette and Barbara had immediately clicked and had become close friends through an endless exchange of letters.

After reading a love letter from Johann, Barbara was still high, and Theo's news sent her over the top!

Barbara sang as she fed Thomas and Lisa, then shooed them out the door. There was still an hour before Juliette arrived, but she wanted to spend half of that getting ready.

The train stopped within thirty seconds of the scheduled time, and Juliette stepped from a first-class car onto the platform. Barbara recognized Juliette's manager, Marcel. He carried a small suitcase, set it down beside Juliette, and left to get what Barbara assumed would be the real baggage.

Juliette lifted her head and immediately recognized her friend.

"Barbara!" she shrieked, throwing her arms around her. "I'm so happy to see you!" Barbara returned the hug and then held Juliette at arm's length.

"Johann's father, Theo, told me you were singing for him. He is rehearsing, and it's my job to get you to the hotel."

"I'm singing for Johann's *father*?"

"Theo is the Detmold theatre's music direktor. The children and I moved to Detmold when Johann was conscripted..." A cloud swept across Barbara's face.

"Barbara, I can't imagine Johann as a soldier; I cried when I read your letter."

"He's a sergeant, a platoon commander in the army, and right now he's in Russia."

Barbara smiled; the cloud disappeared. "If you believe Herr Goebbels, the war will soon be over. I pray for that every day."

Marcel arrived with a cart piled high with suitcases and hatboxes, and Barbara and Juliette walked ahead of him to the car, chattering as though they were neighbours who had just met on the stairs.

Barbara chuckled when Marcel only had enough room left in the old Mercedes' back seat to squeeze himself in. She asked Juliette, "How long are you staying?"

"The premiere is a week from Saturday, but we will probably be here until after the last performance on the twenty-first of March."

Barbara ground second gear as she pulled onto Paulinenstrasse, but she shifted smoothly into third as the speed built. "I hope Theo doesn't give you too much to do...I look forward to seeing you as much as I can while you're here."

Juliette was gazing out her side window at the historic *Fachwerk* buildings, her mind obviously elsewhere. She snapped out of it and turned back to Barbara. "I plan on making you and your children sick of me if that's okay with you."

Maria arrived at the house to look after the children at four. Barbara had a shift at the station until midnight, and, as usual, Maria fed the children and put them to bed before she went home.

People came and went, and Barbara took their names and addresses. It was surprising how many regular travellers she knew personally; she waved them past and noted their arrival or departure in her ledger. The heavy traffic ended at six-thirty.

At a quarter to seven, Juliette tapped her on the shoulder. She and Marcel had approached while Barbara had her head down, deep in thought.

Juliette pointed at the ledger. "Who needs all those names and arrival times?"

"No one… at least no one has ever taken any of the ledgers away or come to look at them."

Marcel scratched his head. "So…why do you collect such information?"

"Because they pay me." Barbara laughed. "Why are you here asking me silly questions?"

"We're not here to ask silly questions… we're here to meet a girl-friend of mine." Juliette caught Barbara's happiness.

Barbara tried to sound stern. "I must record her arrival before you take her out of the station!"

Juliette smiled, but her mood had changed, and Barbara thought she knew why. Johann had told Barbara of Juliette's Jew-smuggling ways, and her letters had reinforced what Barbara knew.

The train from Kassel stopped at exactly 19:02, the time on the schedule. Juliette and Marcel met two women as they stepped off the train, one a strapping *Brunhilda* figure, the other a woman who could have been a starving child. They came to Barbara's table at the exit, Juliette in the lead.

"*Ausweiss bitte.*" Barbara used her official voice. Juliette opened her passport. Brunhilda passed two identification papers to Barbara, and Marcel watched over Barbara's shoulder as she changed the names and addresses on the travel information. He touched Barbara's shoulder, and Juliette mouthed a "thank you" when her charges walked past.

Two hours later, Barbara ticked off the Brunhilda arrival entry when she caught the return train to Kassel.

◇◇◇◇◇◇◇◇◇◇◇◇◇◇◇◇◇◇◇◇◇◇◇◇◇◇◇◇◇◇◇◇◇◇

The next morning, mostly to satisfy her curiosity, Barbara walked to Gartenstrasse 18. She entered through the unlocked main door, tapped on the kitchen door, opened it and walked in. Maria sat at the table, a cup of ersatz coffee in front of her.

"Do you have another cup in the pot?" Barbara pointed at the pot sitting on a dishtowel next to Maria.

"Help yourself. I made enough for Yvonne in case she got up, but she's still sleeping." Maria looked tired.

Barbara poured a cup full. She added honey and enough milk to change the colour slightly. "Yvonne? Is she the other woman I saw at the train station?"

"Yes, the woman with her brought her here from Poland. Yvonne will stay with us until she is well enough to go to Belgium with Juliette and Marcel."

"I saw her documents, and she is Belgian. Why didn't she go directly there?"

Maria played with her cup, apparently trying to decide what to say. Finally, Barbara said, "I know that Juliette has smuggled Jews out of Germany. Last year, when we lived in Bielefeld, Johann helped her get a Jewish woman and her husband to the train station. In her letters, she says things that tell me she's still doing it."

Maria looked at the cup of *Ersatz* she was fiddling with. "I thought I knew Germany. I've lived in Detmold all my life, and I'm as old as *Externsteine*, but right now, I believe that my country is wrong. Hitler has made us the most hated nation on earth, and he is killing his own people! He's taken Johann away from us; he may even kill him—and for what? *Lebensraum?*"

Maria was visibly distraught, a one-hundred-eighty degree change from Tuesday.

Barbara asked, "Did you listen to Goebbels' speech last night?"

Maria raised her head. "No, I can't stand the sound of his voice! What now? What does Hitler want from us now?"

"He wants everyone to be ready to fight to the 'end' for the father-

70

land, and by that he means we should be prepared to die for him. Many Germans actually believe we should kill every Jew, Romani, and any person in Europe who can't work. He claims the unemployment rate is virtually zero... But when the unemployed are forced to work in camps, who would dare admit to being unemployed?"

Maria looked out the window. "My worst fear is that you and the children won't make it through this... Sometimes I hardly sleep. British bombers have destroyed half the cities in the Ruhr valley, and almost every night, they pass overhead on their way to destroy another target. It takes an *hour* for them to pass, Barbara, and all that time, the china rattles in the cupboards." She released a tense breath, then peeked through the living room door toward the front bedroom. She shook her head sadly. "Yvonne has information about a concentration camp in Poland. It's called *Auschwitz;* it's near Krakow."

Barbara had heard the rumours. "Do you think that's true?"

Maria looked at Barbara as she would a naïve child. "We have concentration camps filled with Jews and Romani in Germany. Many Detmold citizens have disappeared—where are they? I know people, all Jews, who are no longer here, and there is no forwarding address at the *Burgeramt.* These people just disappear into thin air! In Germany? You and I know that is impossible!"

Barbara stood up. "But to just... murder them? We would know if that were true; how could the government hide that?"

Maria turned her head to look in the direction of Johann's bedroom. "Yvonne was tortured and scheduled to die, but she escaped. The Polish and German underground got her here, and Juliette must take her to Belgium. Somehow, someone will get her to the British so she can tell her story. Juliette's father and the people he works for believe that if the world's newspapers print the truth, the German people will rise up against Hitler. The Wehrmacht would never fire on German citizens, and Hitler's generals would then force him to negotiate an end to this horror!"

Barbara looked out the window onto Gartenstrasse. The new leaves on the golden rain tree across the street were still tiny yellow spots on the branches. She looked beyond the tree, beyond the houses across the street... "Maybe Yvonne's story will be the excuse the Allies will use to destroy us."

"Am I too late for breakfast?" The heavily French-accented German came from the door to the living room. Barbara audibly gasped when she saw the emaciated form standing there. She had been shocked at the train station, but a heavy coat, wool leggings, and a wide-brimmed hat had concealed the worst. Now Yvonne wore a light blouse and skirt, short stockings, and simple leather shoes. The bones in her hands, wrists, and legs were covered by nothing but a thin layer of skin.

Maria went to the sink to fill a pot with water and eggs, then filled the kettle to make tea. "I will put a few eggs in a pot, and we can all eat something. I picked up some fresh *Brötchen* at the bakery."

Yvonne sat beside Barbara, offered her hand, and Barbara shook it. It felt like shaking hands with a skeleton. Yvonne couldn't help but notice Barbara's astonishment.

"I am so thin, no?"

Barbara tried hard to avoid Yvonne's sad, sunken eyes.

"I…I…I'm sorry, but I don't know what to say. I am happy to meet you. My name is Barbara Finke, and I'm married to Maria's son, Johann."

Yvonne looked at her hands, then at Barbara. "I am a Jew, and I was in Auschwitz. I got not much food… It was not good there…" She stopped, looking for words. Barbara and Maria waited.

When Yvonne began again, she spoke her battered German in a determined flow. "I lived in France, and the Pétain, the Vichy traitors, took me from my home and gave me to the SS. German soldiers put me in a cow train with many other Jews. We had no food or water until we reached Auschwitz, in Poland. Some died. They left the dead on the train. The children… *Mon Dieu!* The guards took them from their mothers and killed them with gas. And they only kept the people who could work. Children, old people and anyone who couldn't work… gas."

She said it as though she were reciting a poem in school. Barbara felt a lump growing in her throat…she couldn't speak.

"Can I have a glass of milk?" Yvonne looked at Maria as though she didn't expect to get it.

Maria filled in a blank for Barbara. "Last night, Yvonne told us they kill people in rooms filled with poison gas." She set a glass of milk in front of Yvonne, put a plate covered with Brötchen, and a piece of butter on a small stone slab on the table. She went back to the counter for a plate of Wurst and cheese.

"They kill people just because they can't work?" Barbara almost shouted her question.

Yvonne sipped her milk, relishing it, then spoke softly to the window. "No, not just for that. They kill some because they misbehave or because they are sick. But they kill the small children because they arrive in the camp." Yvonne sipped the glass of milk as though she wanted it to last forever.

"Oh my God..." Barbara put her hands in front of her face and began to cry. She pulled a handkerchief out of her purse and blew her nose.

Yvonne said quietly, "I'm sorry I upset you, Barbara; my story doesn't bother me so much anymore. I guess I am used to telling it... no?"

"You're sorry? My country starved you—they tried to kill you. I apologize to you!"

Yvonne shook her head. "I not blame you for what Nazis do to me. You help me—you fight them—*oui?*"

"The Nazis are our government..." Maria took a bun out of the basket... "and we will pay for what they do in our name. I want to think that most of Germany does not agree with what Hitler stands for, but those who don't are silent because they like the prosperity he has brought us...or they are afraid. Through silence, the German people have allowed evil to grow until it has overpowered what is good!" She ripped the bun into two pieces. "And the world will punish us for what that evil does!"

Barbara said, "Then you believe that the war is already lost." Barbara ladled honey on the bun and gave it to Yvonne. "If the Allies find out about these camps, they won't stop when they reach our borders—they will treat us like the criminals we are."

Yvonne took the bun, licked the honey, and brightened noticeably. "I find very strange you are so, how you say...*fataliste?*"

"Yes, I guess I am." Maria looked at Yvonne. "How will it get worse? Where does it stop now that our government is setting up murder factories?"

Yvonne pulled one of the eggs out of a bowl that Maria put on the table. She banged the side of it on the edge of her plate and began to peel off the broken shell. "Yes, that is very bad, much worse than you think. But do not forget about Juliette, and Theo, and you...*Non?* Many take much chances to bring me here!"

Yvonne chopped the egg into small pieces, covered it with butter, then laid a piece of cheese over half of the bun. It took her five minutes to eat it, and no one spoke until Yvonne announced, "I cannot eat more," and pushed the plate aside.

Barbara asked, "Yvonne, do I understand that you still have hope?"

Yvonne smiled like a little girl, embarrassed. "I always hope, and, most times I was not—how you say—*découragée* in the camp. I met many friends there." Barbara shook her head, as though it would help her understand. She asked, "Aren't you afraid of what might happen to you...to all of us?"

Yvonne played with her knife on her plate, watched the tip of it drawing circles. "I am sometimes so much afraid I get sick. If soldiers come, I kill myself." She looked up at Maria. "You understand my intention?"

"Yes, I do, but you are safe here."

"I was safe in my home, in France, with my husband. The Pétain broke down the door, said my husband belong to *Maquis*, shoot him dead, drag me to a *camion*... how you say, *camion?*"

"I understand." Barbara's curiosity boiled over her anger. "Was your husband in the Résistance?"

"*Mais non!* My husband was teacher. He teached school in our *village.*" Yvonne pronounced village in French, quickly looked at Maria to see if she understood. "He was very, how you say...*tranquille* man, but, Jew."

Yvonne stood up. "I am *fatigué*. May I sleep for some time?"

"Of course, my dear. You can do whatever you want. You need a lot of rest and food, lots of food." Maria looked at the pile of food still on the table. "You must try to eat more."

"I am sorry. I will do better when I am not so, *fatigué, oui?*"

Yvonne walked lightly through the living room, gently closed the door to her bedroom.

Barbara stood up. "I need to go home to think about this. I believe Yvonne. Surely, when the world hears her story, they will know that all of Germany is a prison. Surely they will stop bombing our homes and find a way to kill Hitler!"

Maria made a point of changing the topic. "Do you want to bring the children here on Saturday? Marcel and Juliette will have Mittagessen with us, and I can't leave Yvonne alone."

"I will bring the children, and we will go through the market to buy meat and vegetables. But we must not talk about what Yvonne's been through in front of the children."

"Of course, but no need to bring food. We have enough."

◇◇◇◇◇◇◇◇◇◇◇◇◇◇◇◇◇◇◇◇◇◇◇◇◇◇◇◇◇◇

Juliette and Barbara got together every day until Juliette's final performance on 21 March. The next day, Barbara said a tearful goodbye to Juliette, now like a sister to her. Yvonne looked healthy enough, but still very thin. The weight gain had gone on her face and hands, filling the gaps between the bones so that Yvonne now had a striking appearance. Her spindly legs, intentionally hidden behind a long skirt and wool stockings had gained a little muscle. But the importance of remaining in hiding meant she could only take infrequent walks with Maria in the *Palais Garten,* just around the corner from Gartenstrasse 18.

Maria and Barbara waved at the train until it disappeared. As they left the train station, Barbara took Maria's arm. "I pray Juliette will make it!" She was so frightened for her friend that she felt ill.

Maria tightened her hand on Barbara's wrist. "Juliette is not new to this game, but I do worry. She is the bravest person I know, and brave people tend to die young. Worse than her courage, she is carrying a vendetta for the Nazis, and that makes her reckless."

"What is the vendetta about?" Barbara was surprised that Juliette hadn't mentioned it to her.

"When Theo asked her father for some kind of proof that he wasn't walking into a Gestapo trap, Jacques finally had to tell Theo the truth about her hatred for the Nazis." She pulled Barbara's arm so that they walked almost touching heads and said softly, "Peter's mother is Jewish, and on *Kristallnacht,* Juliette and Peter visited his grandparents who lived in Munich. They were there to announce their engagement. The

SD broke down the door, killed Peter's grandparents and the Jewish neighbours who had come to the apartment to warn them. They took Peter to Dachau."

"In front of Juliette?" Barbara shivered involuntarily. "That must have been horrible!"

"It is worse than that, much worse." Maria spoke so softly Barbara had to lean her head so that her ear was next to Maria's mouth.

"A brute of a man stayed behind when the others left, and he raped Juliette." Maria said the phrase carefully, as though the words were fragile.

Barbara couldn't speak—she sobbed when she tried.

Chapter Six

24 March 1942

Lessons in School

"Give me a child until he is seven, and I will show you the man."

Aristotle

Tuesday morning, Juliette had arrived safely in Brussels with Yvonne. Maria's butcher friend had a pork hock and fresh sauerkraut ready for her when she stopped on her way to see her grandchildren. Despite the terrible details of Auschwitz that Yvonne had recounted during her time at Gartenstrasse 18, Maria still found joy in the day. The weather was bright and warm for March, a perfect spring day, far away from war.

Maria hummed to herself as she towed her bouncing cart over the cracks between sidewalk bricks. Anticipating her afternoon with Lisa, she stopped at Nägel's bakery, where Frau Nägel went behind the counter and brought out a fresh-baked strudel she had saved for her. Maria said, "Danke schön!" and Frau Nägel answered as she always did, with a musical "Bitte schön!" as Maria went out the door.

Working in the kitchen and watching for Maria through the kitchen window, Barbara reached the door in time to help her pull the cart up the steps into the house. She closed the door while Maria took the cart to the kitchen.

Barbara said, as she walked from the foyer to the kitchen, "I hope you only shopped for yourself and Theo. We have enough, and you shouldn't use your ration stamps for us."

"That's all right, dear. I just picked up a nice pork hock for the children, and Herr Strang had some fresh cream for the strawberries he found for me."

Barbara smiled. She knew that Herr Strang somehow found the

meat and cream without using Maria's ration cards. His wife was Maria's close friend.

Barbara helped Maria unload the cart onto the kitchen table. "And I see you found a nice Strudel. Frau Nägel told me this morning that she didn't have one!"

Maria laughed at Barbara's faked consternation. "Now, you know Frau Nägel plays in my little string quartet, and she always has something nice for me."

Barbara pulled her clay pot down from a high shelf. "I will soak the pot and get the pork hocks ready; you can help Lisa with her violin when she gets home...she should be here any minute now."

Maria was in the living room sorting through Lisa's music when the front door swung open, hit the wall with a bang, and Thomas shouted, "Is Theo here yet? I learned a new opening in school, and he hasn't got a chance!" He rounded the corner into the kitchen.

"Thomas, you didn't close the door," Barbara yelled, but Thomas was already in the kitchen.

"Lisa's right behind me. She can close it." Thomas was bouncing off the walls, high as a kite on spring sunshine.

"No. You go and close the door." Barbara tried to sound stern. "Maria brought something special for you today."

"I'm home!" Lisa yelled from the front hall.

Thomas gave his mother an "I told you so" look and pinched some raw sauerkraut from the clay pot.

"I simply must have some help with my bowing!" said Lisa as she came into the kitchen. "I don't have time to help set the table; that's what little brothers are for." She was gone when Thomas made a rude sound with his lips.

Lisa bounced into the living room and over to Maria. "My bowing is terrible; I really, really need help!" Lisa pulled on Maria's arm, lifted her up from the sofa. Maria knew it couldn't be that bad, but Lisa's standards rose more rapidly than she could progress. She hugged Lisa, and the little girl took her violin out of the case.

"Daddy will be home soon, and I've got to learn the Mendelssohn so we can play it together!" She was as excited as a little girl can be.

Four years before the war, Maria had played a public performance of the forbidden concerto with the Bielefeld Opera orchestra, conducted by the opera house's Jewish music director. The Nazi government fired him shortly afterward, along with the theatre manager, who was also Jewish. The Mendelssohn concert gave the Nazis the excuse they wanted, and the talented musicians left Germany at the last opportunity to do so. The Jewish composer's music had been verboten before and since then, but Maria still played the concerto privately, and she continued using it as a teaching tool for Lisa. Maria played the orchestra part on the piano, skipping the most difficult passages until Lisa's virtuosic skill improved. Lisa screwed up her face whenever Maria left out one of the difficult sections and secretly worked on them. Her goal was to have the concerto perfected when her father came home.

Maria solved the violin-bowing problem quickly by lowering Lisa's elbow and slightly adjusting her wrist movement. In ten minutes, the bow was moving square to the strings through its entire length, and the sound from the old Italian instrument was glorious again. Maria gave Lisa a few exercises to do while she went to talk to Barbara, but as she turned to leave the room, Lisa suddenly spoke.

"Oh, Maria, I forgot to tell you that I've been invited to Angela's birthday party! Isn't that fantastisch?" Lisa loved modern words that adults seldom used, and fantastisch had a fashionable ring to it. The invitation to her friend's birthday party was special because Angela and her mother had become part of the Finke family.

"Lisa, that's wonderful! Is Thomas invited too?"

Lisa wrinkled her nose and squinted. "No, it's only for girls...besides, he's too young!"

Maria smiled wisely. "That's okay. He would probably rather play chess with Theo."

◇◇◇◇◇◇◇◇◇◇◇◇◇◇◇◇◇◇◇◇◇◇◇◇◇◇◇◇◇◇◇◇◇

Theo arrived quietly, hanging up the coat he didn't need on this uncommonly warm day. He went straight to the kitchen and pinched a bit of raw sauerkraut from a bowl.

"Like grandfather, like grandson." Barbara kissed Theo on the cheek. "And speaking of your grandson, Thomas is going to beat you today."

Theo chuckled. "He can wish, but wishes don't make winners."

Thomas's chess was improving to the point where Theo occasionally lost a game to him. On those occasions, Thomas always apologized, afraid that Theo wouldn't play anymore if he became too victorious. But Theo never purposely let him win and didn't give him any quarter by letting him reconsider a move; Thomas earned his wins. That only heightened Thomas's desire to win, and he set regularly beating his grandfather as his life's next success benchmark.

"No chess until we finish eating!" Barbara cut them off as Thomas tried to pull his grandfather to his room and the chessboard.

"Oh, Mutti, I'll beat him real quick. It'll only take a few minutes!" Thomas pulled, and Theo resisted just a little, giving Barbara time.

"No." Barbara stepped into the kitchen doorway with her hands on the frame, blocking Thomas's way. "The food will be on the table in a few minutes, and I don't want you two in the middle of a game. You have to wash up and wait in the living room."

Barbara smiled, stepped aside, and Theo took Thomas by the shoulder, steering him out of the kitchen and down the hall.

Barbara called after them. "Maria brought something special for us!"

"Alright…" Thomas shrugged and looked up at Theo. They went to Thomas's bedroom sink and washed their hands. Theo saw that the board was set up with white on Thomas's side.

"I need to play white to do my new opening."

"Why don't you move, and I'll see what I can do." Theo put his finger on his lips in a ssh.

Thomas moved his knight, and the game was on.

Half an hour later, Lisa passed the door on her way to the bathroom. "You're in big trouble if you don't go to the table right now!"

Theo smiled, hooked Thomas's king with his knight, said, "Checkmate!" and stood up.

Thomas stared at the board. Theo rubbed the top of his grandson's head affectionately, then turned him around to face the kitchen.

"You can study that later. It's time to eat our Mittagessen."

A dejected Thomas began the six-metre journey to the kitchen, but he arrived laughing with Theo pushing him to his seat. Everyone sat down at their usual places, and Maria set plates down in front of them. When Maria cooked, everyone at the table knew never to touch a plate because she always heated them in the oven. They sat with their hands in their laps, smiling and chattering happily while Theo found a ladle.

"Oh man, this is my favourite meal!" Thomas knew this particular pot...and then he saw the strawberries in a large bowl on the counter with a glass bowl of whipped cream next to it. "Strawberries!"

"Strawberries and cream!" squealed Lisa. "That's my favourite!"

"No strawberries until you've eaten your meal!" Barbara's effort to sound strict fell somewhat short, and Lisa smiled at her mother.

Theo served Lisa first, and she stopped him with one small ladle, insisting that he take half the meat back to the pot. The small piece that remained was still more than Lisa wanted, but she would get away with eating half. Thomas would finish it off.

When everyone's plate was full, the family joined hands and thanked God for the beautiful meal. Before the "amen," Lisa thanked God for caring for her daddy. All loudly echoed her amen.

The table became silent as everyone concentrated on eating. A few minutes into the meal, Thomas's face suddenly clouded over, and he dropped his fork.

Barbara had observed the growing agitation in Thomas and immediately asked, "What's the matter, Thomas? You're not upset because of the chess game, are you?"

"No, that's alright." He paused, and Barbara waited. Finally, he blurted out, "Dieter's Mutti is gone."

No one said a word, and the sounds of cutlery and eating stopped. Dieter's father, Joachin, was a mechanic in the Luftwaffe and Dieter's mother worked in a bakeshop. Both were well-liked by their friends, who included Maria and Theo. Half of Detmold knew that Anna's grandfather had been Jewish, but no one had ever mentioned it.

"Where is Dieter now?" Barbara was concerned that the boy would suffer the same fate as his mother.

"He has to live with his Tante Gretchen from now on." Thomas's expression was almost unreadable, but Maria knew better. She pressed the boy further. "How did they find out Anna is Jewish?" Thomas looked into his Oma's eyes. He was such an open and honest boy that he could never hide anything from Maria.

"Dieter is our group leader now, and he told something." Everyone looked around the table. Thomas and Dieter were in the Pimpfe, the first step on the ladder to the Hitler Jugend. "Dieter told important information about his mother!" Thomas cried out. "And they took her away!"

"What important information?" Maria walked around the table and turned Thomas's chair so that he faced her. She knelt in front of him, her eyes level with his.

Thomas said, "Seine Mutti ist eine Judin!" much too loudly, with an expression of distaste that was very close to loathing.

"Dieter proved it, and he got the Fatherland Security Medal!" Maria stood up, looked at Barbara, then at Thomas as though he had suddenly become a stranger. Thomas went on, "I wish I knew a Jew so I could get a medal!"

Barbara tried to hide her shock by turning away but had to turn back. As she stared at Thomas, she suddenly didn't recognize her little boy. She turned to Maria, then Theo. Her expression asked, "What do I do?" Theo dropped his eyes and, almost imperceptibly, shook his head.

Maria looked from Barbara to Thomas, fear and disappointment in her eyes. She went to the counter to prepare the strawberries in a room full of silence. The silence remained while the family ate their strawberries.

When Thomas asked Theo to play chess, his Opa said he had work to do and left for the theatre. Barbara and Maria stood on the top step, watching him walk up Mühlenstrasse. His long stride gone, Barbara sadly watched him shuffle along with his head down—suddenly an old man.

When Theo left without giving Thomas his usual hug, Thomas went to his room, and Barbara waited only a minute before she followed him. She found him practicing a new opening on the chessboard. She sat on the bed and tried to decide how far she should go—she missed Johann.

"Theo has something important to do at the theatre," she began, not sure where she was going.

Thomas looked at the floor. "Theo doesn't like me anymore because I don't like Jews. He didn't give me a hug." Thomas looked up at his mother. "He didn't even say goodbye. He never forgets to give me a hug and say goodbye!" Barbara put her arms around her son and turned his face so that she could look into his eyes.

"Thomas, please listen to me! Your Opa loves you. He is disappointed right now, but he will play chess with you again. Theo will always love you." Barbara gripped Thomas's chin, brought her face close to his so that their breath mingled. His lifeless eyes broke her heart, and she let his chin go without saying what she had intended. He dropped his head and spoke so softly she could barely hear the words.

"If I promise to like Jews, will he play chess with me again?" Thomas twisted his lowered head toward his mother, and the pain she saw there started her tears.

"You don't know very many Jews..." Barbara put her hand on his back and rubbed between his shoulders. "How do you know whether you like them or not?" He didn't squirm away as he usually did. She smiled and wiped her wet eyes. "If you want, you can have a friend over this afternoon."

"I don't want to!" Thomas shook his shoulders, threw himself on the bed, rolled onto his back and looked at the ceiling. Barbara stood up and left the room. She would have given anything to read his confused mind—to see how at one moment he could be a little boy filled with hate for people he didn't know, and the next, a sensitive little angel. She was terrified of losing him to the Nazis.

Barbara returned to the kitchen, where Maria looked up as she wiped the kitchen table with a damp rag. Barbara looked back toward Thomas's bedroom. "What are we going to do with him?" Maria walked over to the sink, dropped the rag and leaned on the counter. Barbara picked it up, rinsed it with water from the tap.

Maria put her hand on Barbara's shoulder. "If Lisa is to be on time for the birthday party, we've got to get going." She turned away and called out, "Lisa, come...we have to go now!" Barbara went to the front hall, found Lisa's spring coat and held the jacket out while Lisa slid her arms in the holes. Barbara and Maria donned their coats and walked down the steps, following the happy little girl bounding along ahead of them. She ran all the way to Wiesenstrasse, holding the bundled present she had made for her friend tight in her hand. She waited impatiently at the intersection for Barbara and Maria.

They turned right and walked a block further to the two-storey house where Angela and Siegruna lived.

Maria had woven Lisa's brown hair into two perfect braids, and they tossed as she ran up the steps. Before Barbara could catch her, Lisa banged the knocker hard on the door. Angela immediately opened it. Her hair was exactly the same as Lisa's, and they squealed as they touched one another's braids and ran into the house. As they passed, Siegruna put out her hand to Barbara. Barbara took it between hers and said, "Hopefully, you'll survive the afternoon!" Barbara had suffered through Lisa's birthday party only a month before.

"I've got the afternoon free if you need help." Barbara gestured in the direction of the squeals coming from the living room. "Honestly, I can help with the party if you like."

"No, no, it's alright. Lila Weber's mother is in the kitchen getting the sweets ready, and she's an old hand at this. Everything is under control." Siegruna swept a long arm through the air and looked skyward. "The afternoon will soon be over!" she laughed.

Maria waited on the sidewalk, waved to Siegruna as she closed the door. Barbara returned to her side, and they began the ten-minute journey to Mühlenstrasse 45. Barbara slowed to prolong the journey.

"What can I do about Thomas?" She was desperate, a mother at the end of her rope. "God, I wish Johann could be here!"

Maria took Barbara's arm and pulled her close. "At the moment, you can do nothing...don't say or do anything. You can only love him and set an example. You can never say anything!" She stopped and took both Barbara's shoulders in her hands, looked deep in her eyes and anxiously reiterated her warning, "Listen to me! Say nothing to that boy...nothing!" She turned away, then back to Barbara. "Those little angels got Dieter's mother into Dachau or Auschwitz, or some other horrible place. Remember, when you talk to your son, you are talking to the Gestapo!"

In less than fifteen minutes, they walked up the steps to number 45. Thomas ran to the door and confronted his mother.

"Can Gunther come over for the afternoon?"

Barbara immediately regretted her offer of a friend to play, but she couldn't say no. Gunther was a rough, aggressive young man with a mean streak, but Thomas seemed to enjoy manipulating him. He lived only a block up the street and, when Barbara reluctantly agreed, Thomas was off like a shot.

Barbara shook her head and laughed nervously. "Sometimes, I think he plays us all."

Maria shook her head. "That's why I think we will all survive this, but Barbara, you must be careful."

CHAPTER SEVEN

MARCH–JUNE 1942

The Barankovo Mousetrap

"The only certainty in war is human suffering, uncertain costs, and unintended consequences."

Barack Obama

SPRING IN UKRAINE BEGINS IN MARCH with melting snow, sleet, rain, mud, and water. The rich earth becomes gritless slime, slippery as the legendary eel, and a step forward rewards the stepper with half the progress it should. The mud sucks on a man's boots. If they aren't laced tightly, the boot doesn't necessarily follow the raised foot.

Tracked vehicles travelling on roads leave ruts that make the road useless for anything else. But if heavy tanks and half-tracks take to the fields, they run the risk of bogging down in a morass of unpredictable depth. The dilemma inevitably results in tanks buried to the top of their tracks, tanks travelling on the roads with wheeled vehicles, and, inevitably, pandemonium.

A Lastwagen on the road ahead of Johann's First Platoon, trying to keep its wheels on the ridges between the ruts the tracked vehicles made, slipped sideways—the driver cut his wheels hard, trying to steer back onto the higher, firmer ground. But the truck ploughed ahead without turning, the sideways front wheels pushing mud over its bumper until, finally, it stopped.

While a squadron of panzer III tanks waited, a half-track backed up to the mired Lastwagen, men attached a cable, and, with a meter of slack in it, the *demag* surged forward. When its six tonnes accelerated, the moving weight yanked against the suddenly taut cable with enough momentum to snap it. The half-track and the Lastwagen swung across the road, pointing in opposite directions, both with their front ends buried in the ditch, their muddy carcasses blocking all progress.

The first in a squadron of waiting panzers became impatient, turned off the road, crossed the ditch with his charges following him. They were on their way to face Russian tanks on the Donets River and had no time to waste. Farther back, infantry followed, some in Lastwagen, most slogging through the mud. Officers drove in *Kubelwagen*—small, light, four-man vehicles that clawed their way forward better than anything else with wheels.

The straggling convoy filled the road. Vehicles were chained together, three in a line, with tire chains on the Lastwagens and a demag half-track pulling the train. Johann's light Kubelwagen drove behind the panzers on what was left of the road, keeping its tires on the muddy ridges while his men picked their way along the road shoulder, trying to stay out of water-filled holes of unknown depth.

The frustrated commander of a panzer squadron took his charges across the ditch to drive on the adjacent field, leaving a gap in the line. Ian closed it by driving up to the crosswise Lastwagen, and the string of vehicles followed the noisy little Kubelwagen until it pulled over to the shoulder and stopped moving. Johann, Ian and Wilhelm dismounted to join their men standing in a line on the narrow strip of sod at the road's edge. The soldiers had already set up a betting pool on how far the *panzer IIIs* would get in the soft field.

The tank squadron drove ahead, rationally staggering their tread marks to keep from following in the shallow ruts left by the panzer ahead of them. Water squeezed out of the tough sod, leaving a new set of tracks, but the intertwined plant roots carried the tank.

Unfortunately, the lead tank slowed when it encountered a drainage ditch, then stopped when the front of its treads broke through the sod at the edge of the water. The front of the tank slowly sank as it slid into the ditch. The gunner was too late when he tried to swing his turret—the gun's muzzle speared into the mud. Its gun buried, its rump in the air, the panzer's driver tried to drive ahead out of the ditch. He applied full power, and the spinning treads pulled dirt, water and rocks out from under them until the tank was sitting firmly on its belly. Water flowed over the top of its tracks, and the driver shut off the engine. A moment of silence ensued before a loud snap announced the fracture of the turret's turning circle. Johann guessed the load the front of the tank had put on its gun barrel had pried the turret out of its track. The front of the panzer sank, and the crew bailed out.

A second panzer tried to cross the ditch thirty metres downstream and met the same fate, although its commander had learned from the first panzer's mistake and turned his gun around before trying to cross. The three remaining tanks stopped, and Johann and his men watched the commanders of all five tanks meet at a small log bridge, confer while gesturing energetically, then reach a consensus that a tank on the other side of the ditch could pull the stuck tanks out. One of the tanks would have to cross the little bridge first, and the lead tank of the three drew the short straw.

Johann and Wilhelm found a dry place on the edge of the road, pulled out their *Zeltbahn* groundsheets and sat down, and thirty men followed their sergeant's lead. It didn't take long for the betting to become serious, and the odds settled at two to one that the bridge would collapse. Johann had been surprised often enough with what the Russians could do with nothing that he bet all the money he had that the bridge, designed for horse and wagon, would hold the twenty-three-tonne tank.

The panzer commander screamed at his driver from the open hatch, loud enough that Johann and his men could hear him plainly. He yelled, *"Voll Gaz geben!"* and the tank went through three gears at full throttle before it reached the bridge. When the front of the treads hit the first log, the wood disappeared into the mud. The tank lifted a little, crushed the second log, then crossed the bridge without a creak or groan from the structure. Johann put out his hand, and the men who had bet against him filled it with Reichmarks.

The last two tanks crossed the bridge uneventfully, and while the commander of the panzer stuck with its gun barrel in the mud walked across the field toward Johann, the first tank to cross the bridge backed up to his boss's buried panzer III. Two men unwound a cable and had it hooked to the swamped tank when the leutnant reached Johann. Johann returned his salute.

"Sergeant, we need your men to help us dig out our tanks."

"Yes, sir, you certainly do." Johann's men were already cleaning and folding their groundsheets. "We will need tools... Perhaps in one of these Lastwagen." He motioned to the line of trucks, creeping forward again, dragging one another through the mud. The half-track and Lastwagen at the head of the line were moving again.

"Bring what you can find, but send half your men right away. Every panzer carries two shovels."

Wilhelm took ten men, slipped and slid across the ditch onto the sod in the field. Johann let a truck pass him, looked in the back and called to a soldier sitting in it, "We need shovels, timbers, chains, and tools to dig those tanks out. Where do we find them?"

The soldier jumped from the slowly moving truck and waited for two more to pass. He struck gold in the next group. They were filled with timbers, axes, saws, hoes, and shovels—equipment intended to dig defensive trenches. One of the trucks had a dozen buckets of 9 mm chain.

Johann confiscated the loads from the willing caretakers, enlisted them to help with the tanks, and ordered them to park the trucks at a bulge in the narrow road.

An hour later, twenty square timbers lay on the sod beside the immobile tanks, and twenty men dug in shifts. It took another hour to lay the beams across the stuck tanks' treads and chain them to the track segments.

The tank squadron commander, Leutnant Klaus, signalled the panzer III tied to the front of his now almost mud-free tank to go forward—gently. The driver didn't understand 'gently' in the same way Leutnant Klaus did, and he nailed the throttle. The cable was only slightly slack, but a metre at full throttle was enough; the parting of a 19 mm steel cable resulted in a sound that could be heard for half a kilometre. It snapped at the end fastened to the immobile tank, and fifteen metres of steel snake whipped around the towing panzer, cutting one of the digging crew almost in two at his belt buckle, spraying blood and pieces of flesh for ten metres. His legs squirmed a little, his hands grabbed the sod, and then he relaxed in death, eyes and mouth wide open in an expression of surprise.

Johann was not used to machines in the way that Wilhelm was. Wilhelm grew up on a modern farm and had warned Johann and his men of this possibility—prompting them to move well clear.

"Carry him to the road." The frustrated leutnant waved his arms, and four men carried the bloody mess through the mud. He turned to Johann. "Have your men get the cable off the back of the other tank and hook it up."

Johann made eye contact with the leutnant while Wilhelm took two men to get the cable. The look of disgust on Klaus's face shocked Johann back to work, and without saying a word, Johann pretended to supervise Wilhelm's supervision of the cable hookup.

While his men fastened the panzers together, Johann stared at the puddle of blood and excrement on the grass. Wilhelm shouted for the second time, "Johann, climb up on the tank and tell that driver to put the transmission in neutral. Better yet, tell him to shut off the fucking engine!" Johann looked at Klaus's back as the leutnant walked past on his way to supervise the digging around the second stuck tank. He looked back at Johann, and Johann climbed up on the tank as instructed.

The driver, shaken and crying, followed Johann's instruction to shut off the engine.

Johann tried to make his voice kind. "Can you drive, or should I find someone else?"

"Don't tell the leutnant that I was crying," the driver pleaded. "He will make me fight in the infantry… I don't want to walk in the mud."

Johann ignored him. "Don't start the engine until I tell you. Corporal Neumann will instruct you when it's time to pull. Do what he tells you—do *exactly* what he tells you!"

Wilhelm left the towing tank and stood with his men, well back from the tanks. Leutnant Klaus, almost a head shorter than Johann, stood beside him. Neither man spoke when Wilhelm, crouched in the buried tank's turret with his head out of the hatch, coached the towing driver to tighten the towline, creeping the tank forward until the cable was taut. Ian coached his driver to ease ahead, and the tank crept forward, pulling the timbers chained to the tracks under it. The gun's barrel climbed out of the mud and the turret settled into its groove with a clunk. The tank moved ahead until the first timber was buried. Wilhelm called a halt.

Both tanks shut off their engines while men threw new wooden beams under the front of Ian's tank and removed the chains from the timbers that were now entirely buried under it. They moved a safe distance away, and the tanks drove ahead another five metres. The panzer was high and almost dry.

It took another hour to free the second tank, and then Johann and his men helped gather up the timbers and chains they could find and dig out of the mud. They loaded them in the Lastwagen and continued the journey to their new digs. Johann let Ian and Wilhelm fill the Kubelwagen with exhausted men and walked with his men. He didn't join in the colourful discussion of the young soldier's gory death.

Tents up, fires lit, and bellies full, the Jäger soldiers played skat or threw dice. Johann had a sheet of paper, a pencil, and the intent, but couldn't find the will to write to Barbara. The day had exhausted the last fleck of optimism he could find, and he didn't want to put his mood on paper. He spent the time before sleep searching his fading memory for pictures of his wife and children.

◇◇◇◇◇◇◇◇◇◇◇◇◇◇◇◇◇◇◇◇◇◇◇◇◇◇◇◇◇◇◇◇◇◇◇◇

The mud didn't begin to dry until the middle of April, but with dryness came hope. The camp became filled with fresh recruits, new artillery, and modern panzer IV tanks. Stukas flew low over them almost every day, wagging their wings in greeting. Although a reasonable person would know that the pilots couldn't see or hear them, the men cheered and waved. Every man had all the Wurst and beer they wanted, and when combined with the effect of spring sunshine and a winning attitude, they became a happy horde of invaders.

Johann and his men sat on what passed in Ukraine for a hill. They lay back on the grass with an extra ration of beer, watching puffy clouds drift across the peaceful sky. Two Stukas flew over them in close formation, heading east at less than a hundred feet. They turned while still short of the Russian lines and flew south, into the sun.

Johann shaded his eyes, followed the aircraft until they became black dots. "We had a couple of days in *Offizierschule* on a tactic called *Schwerpunkt*. The attacking force uses a ruse to get the enemy to concentrate a large force on a small area, feints a retreat, then encircles him in a pocket." Johann picked his teeth with a sliver of wood, a habit that irritated Wilhelm and Ian. Wilhelm made a face, and Johann put the sliver in his shirt pocket. "General Heinz Guderian wrote a book about it and other ways to use armoured vehicles. He called the book *Achtung! panzer!* and I read a few paragraphs from it every night."

"What's so interesting about it?" Wilhelm chewed on a piece of soft green alder wood, a habit that irritated Johann and Ian.

"He came to the *Schule* and talked about setting a trap at a *Schwerpunkt,* tempting the enemy to it, then encircling him. It works like this:

"Our army retreats on a short piece of the line, so the Russians will think we are weak at that point. They charge ahead, thinking they can flank us—we withdraw the centre but hold solid at both ends. We intentionally bait the enemy into creating a deep bulge in the line."

Using his finger and a patch of dirt, Johann drew a teardrop-shaped bulge in the middle of a line.

"As an engineer, I don't like the sound of that," Ian interjected. "I like straight lines; fluidity makes me nervous."

Johann understood Ian's perspective, but the artist in him saw elegance in the trap. "The bulge is intentional; its shape is controlled by the defending army. We keep our air force away except to stop their air force from attacking our tanks and men until it's time to spring the trap."

"Okay, but when do we fight back? It sounds like *we* are backing into a trap, not them." Ian shook his head.

"Look..." Johann traced the lines he had drawn. "This is a drop of water hanging from the edge of a leaf. The top of the drop, where it joins the leaf, is narrow, and the bottom of the drop is the Schwerpunkt. That's where we've set up our real defence... And we stop their advance there." Wilhelm smiled; Johann spoke directly to him. "Now, we shut the door, something like when the drop falls and seals the top, and the enemy is trapped inside it."

Johann pulled the wooden sliver out of his pocket and slid it between two of his front teeth. "Then we call in the Stukas and the artillery. The men in the pocket have nowhere to go—we squeeze them into a smaller and smaller area until they have to surrender or die."

"So, why are you mentioning this now?" Ian looked away from Johann and made a face when Johann pulled the blood-stained sliver from his mouth.

"Because Stieff told me not to worry about the Russians advancing at Izyum. They are just south of us, and we could stop them, but our forces are withdrawing. Remember the Russian tanks we saw on the other side of the Donets? They're on this side now, and they think we are weak at that point. They're sending everything they've got across the river... They're going to push the bulge back."

Johann pulled the bloody stick out of the joint between two back teeth and looked at it. He found a piece of Wurst stuck to the point, licked it off, and Wilhelm feigned throwing up his meal. Johann smiled like a cat. "We will be busy in a few days, so we had better enjoy the sunshine while we can."

◇◇◇◇◇◇◇◇◇◇◇◇◇◇◇◇◇◇◇◇◇◇◇◇◇◇◇◇◇◇◇◇◇◇◇

As Johann predicted, the Germans put up a lacklustre defence, retreating ten kilometres, and the Russians took the bait. Like mice nibbling at the cheese in a mousetrap, they chased the Germans, thinking they were winning. Johann's platoon scouted along the Russian line with orders not to engage the enemy. They were to find out where the main Russian front was growing and keep battle headquarters informed. Johann reported a Russian buildup on the other side of the Donets River, but the intelligence officer seemed indifferent. There were over a dozen key and temporary bridges across the river, and Johann assumed that the Luftwaffe would simply blow them up to stop the Russian counterattack, but two weeks passed, and the bridges remained.

Johann and his platoon watched from a ridge as, at 06:30 on May 12, unopposed Russians crossed the river on two new floating bridges. Over the next few days, part of the Russian forces in the now significant bulge south of Izyum broke out and raced north to meet the army crossing the bridges under General Timoshenko. Johann retreated, along with most of the German Sixth Army.

Johann's scouts called in artillery strikes, then moved back when the barrage ended, and the Russians attacked. German artillery hammered them again. When they ceased firing, Johann's Platoon helped move the guns farther back and reset them. The guns pounded the Russians from the new position, and thousands of Russian soldiers died, but when the guns stopped, the Russians attacked with renewed strength. The Germans moved their guns back yet again. panzers positioned to protect the guns did not attempt to advance—the only gear they used was reverse.

Johann tried to relate what was happening to the trap he had studied. He contented himself that he hadn't lost any men, and the enemy was taking terrible casualties for every metre they advanced. The Fourth panzer Corps, the outfit Johann's men now worked for, had not lost a tank or gun. Johann felt he was witnessing history, and if he survived, he wanted to remember it.

The German anti-aircraft guns moved, stopped to shoot, then moved again, skillfully targeting the otherwise unrestricted Russian air force—outdated aircraft against accurate anti-aircraft fire, a deadly combination. The Sixth Army slowly withdrew, convincingly feigning a retreat that wasn't quite a rout. Stieff devoted Johann's company to keeping track of the advancing Russians, with orders to do no more than that.

Johann nervously watched his army backpedal until, on the morning of May 14, they were fifteen kilometres southwest of the Donets River bridges. The day dawned bright and clear, except for an overcast of Luftwaffe aircraft flying east to meet the Russian air force. By sundown of the fifteenth, the Russian air force in the area had ceased to exist, and Stieff ordered Johann's Jäger fighters to go to work, using stealth and darkness to strike terror into the Russian tank and artillery crews. They worked the edges of the Russian camps, silently killing sentries and guards, and in the three days between the sixteenth and nineteenth of May, Johann and his platoon had killed twice their number without losing a man. No Russian who saw them lived to tell about it.

During daylight hours, camouflaged and hidden in copses and ditches, Johann and his men watched Stuka dive-bombers and ground-attack aircraft destroy the Russian armour, leaving the infantry defenceless. At night, the nervous Russians had to deal with German Jäger forces. Johanne's men made sure rest was a luxury few Russian soldiers enjoyed until it was eternal.

When the Russians finally realized what was happening and reversed the traffic on the Donets bridges, the German Luftwaffe destroyed the only escape route. The Sixth Army surrounded the Russians in a ring of steel and men, and the slaughter began.

On the twenty-fifth of May, Johann's platoon joined an infantry battalion, waiting for the inevitable Russian attempt to counterattack and blast their way out. But the Russians attacked without tanks or artillery; Johann's men, equipped with MG-42 machine guns, the feared 'Hitler's saw,' so named because of the ripping sound it made, mowed them down like wheat. It took German infantry, panzers and artillery thirty minutes to kill or wound every one of the thousands of attacking soldiers.

When the battle was over, Johann walked among the dead and dying, sick to his stomach, marvelling at the power of modern weapons when applied without mercy. He ordered his men to help the wounded Russians until Sixth Army Lastwagen arrived to take them away.

"Will they kill them?" Wilhelm leaned on the barrel of his loaded rifle, the butt on the ground.

Johann waved to the other side of the field. "If they wanted to kill them, why wouldn't they kill them here?" The roar of a bulldozer carried over the cries of the wounded. Johann watched soldiers check for signs of life before the burial crew laid the dead Russians in a trench dug by the machine. He stepped around a moaning young man trying to hold his insides in a hole in his abdomen. A German medic laid him on his back, pressed a square bandage on the wound, and then put the young man's hand on it. Johann looked up at Wilhelm. "Stieff told me they need slaves to work in Germany..." He looked across the battlefield as he said, "And that may mean prisoners are now an asset."

Three days after the attempted breakout ended, a combination of air and ground attacks had annihilated any remaining tanks and infantry that tried to break out. At the post-battle-assessment briefing, Johann and his men applauded when Stieff announced that the "mousetrap" had netted the Sixth Army two hundred forty thousand prisoners and two hundred seventy-five thousand Russian casualties. The price for the Germans was twenty thousand dead, wounded, and missing. None of Johann's group was among them.

The Sixth Army celebrated for two days. Johann and his men ate and drank too much, and during a break in the celebration, drunk on victory and German beer, Johann found the mood to write home.

Liebe Barbara und Alle.

Today, we are drunk. We are drunk on beer and victory, celebrating our greatest triumph over the Russians. We have killed or captured an entire army—over five hundred thousand men! It was the best day of my life!

I didn't lose a man, and the entire 6th Army only lost twenty thousand; nothing when compared with the Russian losses.

We trapped the Russians, who were too optimistic to see it coming. They interpreted a planned withdrawal as a retreat and chased us into a trap, where we annihilated them! We proved the German superiority so convincingly that I doubt our enemy will have the will to fight much longer! Such a magnificent victory means the war cannot go on. The Russians fight with junk—even their rifles are inferior. Indeed, we've heard rumours that several Russian soldiers sometimes share a single gun!

Our Luftwaffe waited to attack their antiquated air force until the third day, and we wiped them out—their air force is no more. I don't see how they can keep fighting.

There are rumours that we will be in Moscow before the snow flies, and I don't see why not. Stalingrad is not far from here, and the oil fields are not far from there; our commanders say we will smash the armies protecting them, and then we will run the Russians out of fuel. Our soldiers are cutting their supply lines as I write this letter, and everyone says we will be home for Christmas!

I must go to bed now. Celebrate with me, Liebling, and be joyful, for I will be home soon! My head hurts from celebrating, and we will be back on patrol tomorrow.

Deine, Johann

Barbara read the letter and cried. She showed it to Maria and Theo as the children played *Gummi* on the street with their friends. Their laughter as they jumped over the rubber band stretched between them carried through the open window.

"We have lost him, haven't we?" Barbara watched the children doing 'doubles,' but didn't really see them.

Theo passed the letter to Maria. He had read it twice, trying to find the son he had sent to war. "Johann is not lost; he only appears to enjoy the war. In his heart, he hopes the victory means the war is over, and he will come home soon. When he says…" Theo looked at the letter in Maria's hand… "It was the best day of my life…" he is overjoyed that the battle is over, and he is alive. War does that to men… Success against other men is an aphrodisiac, and such a victory means he is invincible."

Theo put his arm around Barbara. "You haven't lost him."

"But he didn't say he loved me…" She looked at the letter Maria was holding. "There is no sweetness."

Maria put the letter on the table and held Barbara. She couldn't hold back her tears.

Chapter Eight

July 1942

Folly

Given circumstance and point of view, the words Idiot and Genius can be equally appropriate when referring to the same person.

Johann knew something was up when, on June 14, Colonel Stieff called his Jäger officers into his command tent—the Jäger Companies were always the first to engage the enemy. They scouted the terrain a few days ahead of the regular army, clarifying enemy positions already mapped using aerial reconnaissance, locating enemy armour and artillery hidden in forests or camouflaged in plain sight, a Russian specialty. First Jäger Company had been idle since Barvenkovo and had a severe case of camp fever. Johann and Leutnant Kohl entered the tent with a sense of excitement; they had had enough of playing cards and drinking beer.

Johann saluted, Stieff returned it and waved him to a canvas chair. The leutnant sat beside him, offered Johann a cigarette, which he gladly accepted, and took one out for himself. Johann flipped his lighter open, lit Kohl's cigarette, then his own. They both inhaled, blew smoke upward, leaned back and crossed their legs. The tent had a blue haze just above Stieff's head when he leaned against the map table and began his briefing.

"I have good news. We are going to finish off the Russians this summer."

Johann picked a bit of tobacco off his tongue, looked for somewhere to put it. Kohl put a tin cup/ashtray in front of his nose. "I can live with that," he said to himself, put the cigarette in his mouth and inhaled. Stieff waited while the men in the tent got their comments over with.

"In a few days, we will begin advancing toward the Caucasian oil fields as part of the Southern Army under Field Marshall Von Reichenau; the operation is called *Fall Blau*. We will move toward the Volga with the Fourth panzer Army."

Johann understood as well as any man in the tent the importance of fuel and oil to an armour war. Stieff waited for questions, and Johann started to stand up. He found himself looking at the top of Stieff's head and sat down.

"If we take the oil fields and cut off the Russian supply, how long can they last?"

"That's irrelevant to us. More importantly, Hitler admits that our forces will come to a standstill in three months without the Russian oil. The Russians can last a long time with oil from the east and American oil shipped through Murmansk and Vladivostok. In other words, the army that has the oil wins the war!"

Johann spoke before his brain was done thinking. "What I hear from you is, 'Case Blue' is 'do or die' for us, but not necessarily for them." He tapped the ash off his cigarette into his cupped hand. "That doesn't sound so good."

Stieff tapped the ash off his cigarette into an ashtray on the table, turned back to face his men. He ignored Johann and his comment.

"The Southern Army is immense and well equipped. On the other hand, the Russians have used the winter to re-equip their armies, but they started with nothing. Our Southern Army will crush them in a few months, depending on the weather."

Kohl asked, "So, when do we start?"

"The Jäger companies begin scouting tonight; the rest of you move out on the twenty-eighth."

The meeting went on, mainly with questions about supply logistics. Russian Partisan forces were beginning to affect rail traffic, down to an average of only eighty-five percent utilization. Lastwagen could replace that, but as they moved farther from Germany, the line would become longer, easier to sabotage, and more truck convoys meant more targets for the Russian Air Force.

The Colonel addressed the problem before anyone asked the question. "We will do what we can to avoid a supply problem and hope that the Führer has planned a solution to it."

Johann left the meeting with a mixture of confidence and trepidation. The supply question seemed the most relevant, but he hadn't seen evidence of a problem so far. His soldiers had everything they needed, up to and including beer and paper to write home. Asked for, it was delivered. He had a dozen extra sheets of paper with the Wehrmacht eagle on the top of the page. That had to be a good sign.

When Johann's platoon began scouting the Russian positions, they were excited to the point of recklessness, and Johann decided to fix that. When they got back to camp after the first night mission, Johann instigated a training update before going out on their next mission, planned for two days down the road. The following day, he took his platoon for a run.

The rain cascaded down; lightning streaked through the clouds, splitting air molecules with crashes that made conversation nearly impossible. That didn't keep Wilhelm from trying, and he out-shouted the almost-continuous thunder.

"Do you think running in the rain is a good way to build morale, or are you trying to kill the weak ones before we go into battle?"

"Wilhelm, I didn't hear a thing you said, but the answer to the question is that you should shut up and save your energy. There are a couple of hills ahead, and you will need the breath you're wasting!"

Johann trotted with a brand new *Ppsh 41,* a Russian machine gun, over his shoulder; Wilhelm carried a special edition *Gewehr 98* sniper rifle; Ian had a *Papa* identical to Johann's slung across his back. Strung out in a double column behind them—sixty men carried various combinations of rifles, packs, and *Papas.* Four MG-42 machine gun crews, loaded with extra weight, fought to keep up. In the infantry, it took four men to make a machine gun crew, sometimes five. But in Johann's platoon, three men carried the barrel, magazine, tripod, and ammunition for the heavy machine gun.

They grumbled, and Johann said, "Yes, the new MG-42 is heavy, but we can't leave it behind—I fought too hard to get them." The winter refit had added many pounds to the load his men carried.

The half-drowned platoon arrived at the tent compound as the sun rose high over the flat steppes. The storm had moved on, leaving their tents sitting in puddles.

Johann said, "There's no time to change into dry clothes—ditch the packs and bring your *Papas*—we're going to the street-fighting range." Johann and Wilhelm looked into their tent: everything on the floor was either floating or covered with water.

"*Scheisse*—I hate the rain worse than I hate the Russians!" Wilhelm waded into the tent, lifted his duffle bag out of a puddle, looked for a dry place to put it, then dropped it back in the water. "I want to get this damned war over with!"

For three hours, broken by breakfast delivered from the cook wagon, Ian's squad fought Wilhelm's to a standstill in a row of houses. Johann had the men change sides and wondered at the skill the men exhibited. Aggressor or defender, they could fight as either and win.

Two weeks of abuse later, a confident, capable platoon took to the battlefield.

◇◇◇◇◇◇◇◇◇◇◇◇◇◇◇◇◇◇◇◇◇◇◇◇◇◇◇◇◇◇

A year before the *Fall Blau* mission, Johann had heard rumours of a new Russian 'super' tank—faster and more maneuverable than the panzer IV, with a superb 76 mm gun mounted on a super-quick turret. According to the rumours, the new Russian T-34 design could do everything but drive on water and was impregnable to all but the heaviest German anti-tank weapons.

Rumours flew through the tank corps that the Russians had thousands of T-34s lined up waiting to destroy the inferior German tanks. Wehrmacht Intelligence reported that aerial photographs showed only the usual Russian *Schrott,* junk, little more than meat tins, facing the Sixth Army. Stieff decided to send his best scouts to find the truth.

Late in the afternoon of June 20, Johann took ten men in two demag half-tracks on their first deep penetration of the Russian lines since the mud season. When it was as dark as it would get, they left the half-tracks in an abandoned barn close to the Russian lines and continued on foot. They moved quickly, stayed low, crouched in moon-shadows as much as they could. When they moved ahead using field drainage ditches for cover, the tall hay left only their black heads visible, and only when they stretched their necks to look around, like gophers checking on their enemies. Johann considered the muddy ditch bottoms a small price for the cover they afforded.

Aerial photographs showed guns and tanks all along the expected battle line, but no T-34s. If they were there, Stieff had to know where they were so he could hit them with his artillery. The Russians didn't have a tank that would live through a direct hit from an eighty-eight-millimetre shell.

The night was not as dark as Johann would have liked; the moon was in its first quarter, and the stars were bright. There was little moisture in the dry air. It would be easy to find the Russians, but if their sentries were alert, it would be risky to get close enough to find and identify their tanks.

Half an hour into their journey, slithering from ditch to ditch, they reached the edge of the Russian camp on the photograph. It was the usual maze of holes in the ground where Russian soldiers spent most of their time, even in winter blizzards, and a few rough buildings and tents that housed the officers. Rows of artillery stretched for kilometres in both directions, separated by two hundred to five hundred metres of what Johann knew would be minefields and tank traps. The Russians had spent the winter digging ditches, strewing mines in random but logical patterns between them. Russian tanks crouched in rows, ready for the assault, but on close inspection, it was evident that they weren't the main body. There were no guards close to the tanks, and there were no tell-tracks to show they had recently moved. They were the same ineffective *Fleischdosen,* meat tins that Johann and his men had fought until now, and there were no crews. He decided to explore the nearby woods and farms.

The only forests in the area were along the banks of creeks and ditches flowing into the Don River, and Johann led his men to the edge of a promising stream located east from the camp. The forest was dark and thick overhead, with mature spruce trees preventing the sun from encouraging anything to grow on the forest floor.

In every opening where harvest roads cut through them, T-34s were parked two abreast, covered with tree branches and painted canvas. The crews lived in holes strewn over the surrounding forest floor.

Johann sent Wilhelm and Ian to work their way through the woods parallel to the tanks. They found gaps in the guarded perimeter, moved undetected to examine the tanks, then reported to Johann.

"Those are the new T-34s we've heard about. There are close to a hundred in this area." Wilhelm looked back through the trees. "*Sheisse!* They look better built than anything we've got. It looks as though Mercedes is building tanks for the Russians!"

Johann took his men southeast and found two more creeks, their gently-sloped banks covered with trees. Before daylight, they had documented over three hundred hidden T-34s.

The darkness was yielding to the light when the demags started with a puff of black smoke. Johann forbade his men to use the radio and ordered his drivers to get them back to Stieff's headquarters as fast as they could safely do it in the morning twilight—they arrived as the sun's rim peeked over the edge of the world.

Johann saluted and sat down before his commanding officer ordered him to.

"Are you certain those were T-34s?" Stieff asked. "How could they produce so many so quickly, and then somehow get them here without us knowing?"

"Yes, sir, T-34s, and if they perform as well as they look, we have a problem."

◇◇◇◇◇◇◇◇◇◇◇◇◇◇◇◇◇◇◇◇◇◇◇◇◇◇◇◇◇◇◇◇◇◇

The Sixth Army moved out a week later, split along two lines, one stretching north, and the other to the east, forming a soft 'V.' A swarm of Stukas flew over the centre of the 'V' an hour after artillery set up the night before began pounding the Russian camp. The Stukas concentrated on the strips of trees growing along the creeks.

From his demag, Johann watched fighters drop out of a cloudless sky onto a line of trees. Protesting against the turbulence induced by the many protrusions a Stuka is blessed with, the fear-inducing *Jericho-Trumpet* sirens fastened to the landing gear, and the dive brakes sticking out of the wings, the sound of bloody murder put the fear of God into targets on the ground. Simultaneously, all that paraphernalia served the primary purpose of limiting the Stukas' diving speed so they wouldn't lose their wings as they plummeted vertically through a wall of turbulence. Johann spoke to battle command through the magic of his microphone. "The Stukas are on target; those trees are full of Russian panzers." Sixth Army intelligence confirmed receipt, and Johann lifted his binoculars to see what the surviving tanks would do.

He found it difficult to believe that anything could crawl out of those flattened forests, but groups of tanks fanned out like ants as the aircraft pounded them mercilessly, first with bombs, and then when they tried to flee with their infantry, with 20 mm cannons. StuG III tank destroyers waited for them, hidden in ditches. The barrels of their 75 mm guns, mounted low between their tracks, were barely visible above the long grass. Using their low profile to conceal their movements, the strange creatures fired out of the muddy drains they had crawled into the night before. They knew where their enemy would come from and had set up a field of fire guaranteed to decimate what Russian armour the Stukas missed.

As the German panzer IV tanks and StuG III tank destroyers moved onto the tank battlefield, the Sixth Army's artillery and the Luftwaffe turned their attention to the Russian camp and artillery installations, driving the infantry into their holes.

At the end of the first day, the Russian Thirty-Eighth Army abandoned the camp and retreated southeast down the Don River, fighting a rear-guard action as they attempted to break out of the Sixth Army's semicircle. When they had devastated the Russian artillery and infantry, the German Sixth Army gave the survivors no time to set up an effective defence. They destroyed the bridges over the Don, cutting off any escape to the east.

◇◇◇◇◇◇◇◇◇◇◇◇◇◇◇◇◇◇◇◇◇◇◇◇◇◇◇◇◇◇◇◇◇◇◇◇

Johann's platoon fought within the First Jäger Company, assisting the XXIV panzer Corps, chasing the Russian armour and artillery down the Don River toward Voronezh. The Twenty-Fourth's assignment was to contain the Russians but let them run deeper into the trap. They were not to attack unless the cornered Russians tried to break out.

On the first day, five T-34 tanks and a company of infantry tried to break out of a pocket forming along the river. First Jäger Company kept them busy, using machine guns, mortars, and grenades to halt the infantry giving the tank destroyers time to set up a semicircle ambush. Johann's platoon held, then withdrew, and the eager Russians chased their anticipated victims into the trap. Johann's platoon targeted the infantry in a murderous cross-fire, while the T-34s became meat in the tank destroyers' grinder.

On the second day, a group of four tanks tried a different tactic. They zigged and zagged their way uphill toward Johann and his men, the T-34s' cannons and machine guns firing madly at First Platoon's gun and mortar positions. Two hundred infantry ran behind the tanks, and Johann's platoon retreated before the onslaught. Again, the Russians ran headlong into a pocket of StuG IIIs. But this time the T-34s were too close for the StuGs to be fully effective—the range and speed of movement of the T-34s exceeded the agility of the turretless StuGs, and it turned out to be nearly impossible for the destroyer's gunners to put their sight on the fast-moving tanks.

The Russian infantry were not so lucky. The zigzagging tanks moved too fast and erratically for men on foot, and Johann's men, who'd re-treated to ditches, sprayed them with machine-gun fire and mortar shells.

Three Russian tanks slowed to allow their beleaguered infantry to catch up, then drove at Johann's platoon, avoiding driving a straight line for more than a few seconds, and the infantry fired from behind them. In the ditches, with nowhere to run, the knot in Johann's stom-ach told him he had waited too long to withdraw. He yelled and beck-oned to Wilhelm and Ian—time was running out—they had minutes to work out a strategy.

"Scatter along this ditch and stay down until they're on top of us. The T-34s must turn to cross the ditch at a right angle, or they'll slide into it. When they turn, stay low so their machine guns can't get you. Move the MG-42s to the ends of the ditch, so they have the infantry in a crossfire. Those who have rifles should fix their bayonets."

The tanks moved slower now that they needed the infantry to pro-tect them. The destroyers fired as fast as they could load and sight, and struck one of the T-34's tracks, stopping it. Now a stationary target, a second shell hit it, skewing the turret, and the crew opened the hatches. The exhausted infantry, running with full packs and heavy rifles, had faded to fifty metres behind the tanks, trying desperately to keep the remaining zigzagging tanks between them and Johann's platoon's over-whelming fire. If they turned and ran, they faced certain death; their only chance was to reach the ditch behind the tanks and kill Johann's men. Everywhere Johann looked, Russian soldiers fell or threw themselves to the ground.

A T-34 blew up when a destroyer's shell struck its fuel tank, and the last two Russian tanks turned to square up at the ditch, barely thirty metres from it. Without the tanks' protection, the MG-42s had the Russian infantry in the crossfire Johann had anticipated. They streamed steel bullets through the grass growing over the edge of the ditch. The last fifty Russian infantry either fell or lay down, one of the two T-34s took a direct hit on its soft side, and the last tank stopped before reaching Johann's position, leaving its engine idling. Twenty of his men surrounded the T-34 while Ian and Wilhelm's squads surrounded the surrendering infantry.

With the StuGs waiting, the Russian tank had no intention of moving away from the shelter of the German soldiers. Johann jumped on the tank, placed a grenade on the turret hatch cover and jumped off. When it exploded, the clang was loud outside, and Johann could only imagine how loud it was inside the turret, but no one tried to come out.

While Johann and his men discussed firing machine guns through the slits, the tank suddenly drove toward the ditch, and Johann waved his men to wait. A StuG fired a shell into the ground in front of it. The T-34 stopped moving, but the hatches remained shut.

"How much fuel do these things hold?" Johann stood beside the stopped T-34 with Ian.

"We can't wait that long."

Johann watched a StuG III work its way behind the tank, stopping two hundred metres from it. Two more StuGs drove toward the tank from the sides and stopped with the Russian crew looking down their gun barrels.

"They have no way out." Ian pointed to a slit where the driver was looking at him. "We've got him, and I'm sure Colonel Stieff will find a good use for a brand new Russian tank."

The tank remained still, its idling engine the only sound. Johann looked around, trying to find a reason for the tank commander to hope. The Russian infantry unit that had started the action lay in a wide strip of bodies leading from the river. Fewer than half were alive, and most of those were wounded. Jäger Company's men rounded up those who could walk, and German medics dealt with the injured who had a hope of surviving.

Johann decided to call the commander's bluff.

"Wilhelm, climb up on that tank and show the commander we mean business—we can't sit around here all day."

Wilhelm jumped up onto the front-sloped armour and calmly walked up to the top of the turret. He tapped the hatch with the butt of his *Papa* machine gun, then stuck its barrel in an open gun port. He didn't fire. A crewmember tried to close the port, but the gun's barrel held it open.

"*Sdat'sya ili umerat!*" Surrender or die! Those were the Russian words taught to every German officer in Russia, and Wilhelm said it as though he meant it.

A voice shouted something from inside the turret, and the latch scraped and clanked. The cover opened just enough to let two hands exit. They lifted it cautiously until it was wide open. One after another, four crew members crawled out of the tank and stood with their hands behind their heads. Johann turned to Wilhelm and his prisoners.

"Let's get this tank moving."

Wilhelm looked at his men, waiting for orders. "I have someone who flunked out of panzer school. I'll see if anyone knows how to shoot the gun."

Johann shook his head. "Just a driver. You can ride in the turret, but don't touch the gun."

Ian joined Johann and jerked his head toward the prisoners and wounded. "I'll take Wilhelm's prisoners with the others." Then, as an afterthought… "I lost two men; one wounded, the other one is dead."

Johann looked at Wilhelm, working his way into the turret hatch. "Wilhelm has three wounded, but two of them can still walk and shoot; I guess that means we won."

Johann took a few minutes to adjust his mind to the casualties, then covered the Russian tank with Ian's dead soldier's body and the wounded; he didn't want a Stuka to ruin Colonel Stieff's surprise.

◇◇◇◇◇◇◇◇◇◇◇◇◇◇◇◇◇◇◇◇◇◇◇◇◇◇◇◇

Johann hadn't written home since a week before the action on the Don

River. He decided to remedy that omission and sat down on a flat stump beside a Russian foxhole he had expropriated. He dug out his pencil and a piece of official paper and tried to think.

He said to Wilhelm, "I have to admit, not only do the Russians build good tanks, but they also know how to dig a good foxhole." He rolled the pencil between his fingers, stared at the paper and waited for Wilhelm to answer. He didn't. Johann wrote, "*Liebe Barbara,*" and stared at a tree. Then he remembered and wrote, "*und Lisa und Thomas.*"

Wilhelm laughed. "If you don't want to tell them our platoon destroyed twelve tanks and twenty-three pieces of artillery, you could tell them we captured a brand new Russian tank! You could also tell them that we helped the Sixth Army kill two-hundred-thousand Russians and take the rest of the Thirty-Eighth Russian Army prisoner! If that's not enough, then I guess we'll just have to try harder from now on." He lay back on the groundsheet and locked his fingers behind his head.

Johann looked at Wilhelm as though he had lost his mind. "I can't tell her that—Barbara thinks I'm fighting a humane war, without killing anyone."

Wilhelm laughed. "Then, for sure, don't tell her we're having a good time!"

"*Are* we having a good time?"

Johann wrote, "I miss you and the children," then put the end of the pencil in his mouth and bit the wood back from the tip. He looked for a flat rock to sharpen the lead.

"I've never had a better week." Wilhelm looked skyward. "It is fun to win... For sure, it's a lot more fun than losing!"

Johann found the rock he was looking for and rubbed the lead gently on its flat side. "Yes, it's all about winning, isn't it?" He had to force his hand to stop shaking.

Wilhelm used his hat to block the sun. "I think it's all about being the one who survives. When I see a Russian die, I don't hate him—I can't hate a man who is that brave—I'm just glad it's him and not me."

Johann pressed a little too hard, and the lead broke. "Scheisse!" He pulled his hand back to throw the pencil, didn't, pulled out his grandfather's knife and whittled the wood back. He sharpened the lead, but, with the blade's last stroke, accidentally broke it again. He looked at Wilhelm.

"It's about the excitement of winning the ultimate game—kill the other guy before he kills you—isn't it?"

Wilhelm sat up and took the pencil from Johann. "Yes, there's that too, but it isn't that way for the Russians. They fight for their families first, then for their lives, and lastly, for their country—this is no game for them. I'm afraid our cruelty and bestiality have created a nation of fanatics, and they will not stop until they've ravaged Germany and our families as we've destroyed their country and murdered their wives and kids."

Wilhelm set about carving a neat point, his hands as steady as Johann's had been when he used to play the violin. "We are now in a position where we must pound them into the ground until they are either dead or without a will to fight. Otherwise, we will lose everything."

Johann took the pencil from Wilhelm. "Thanks a lot! Now I don't know what to write. I can't tell her I'm having fun, and I wish she were here. And I can't tell her the Russians are coming, but not to worry because Wilhelm and I will save her by killing all the Russians. I kill Russians because I must—before they kill me! But I don't hate them."

"I pity anyone who gets on *your* hate list." Wilhelm lay back again. "Tell Barbara you're sitting on a stump talking about the war we're winning and wishing you were home." He focused his eyes on the bright edge of a dark cloud. "You could lie and tell her we'll be home for Christmas."

"Don't get cocky, Wilhelm. The Russians are learning fast, and there are a lot of them."

Johann wrote smaller with the sharp pencil. He said nothing about the battle or the tank they had captured. Instead, he told Barbara how he valued Wilhelm's friendship and how hard his men worked to survive.

He wrote, "My men have become a fearsome bunch of soldiers—if anyone survives this war, we will," hoping to give some comfort to Barbara.

He remembered his parents just before he put the letter away and added a greeting to them. But no matter how many combinations of words he thought up, it came out as an afterthought. He put the folded sheet in the envelope—he hadn't filled the page.

Wilhelm was nodding off when Johann said, "I'm proud of what we've done. We are the best platoon in the Sixth Army and maybe as good as any in the entire Wehrmacht."

Wilhelm reluctantly pushed his hat back from covering his eyes.

"What have we done that's so outstanding?" He waited while Johann thought, then interrupted before Johann got the planned response out of his mouth. "What is it that makes us the best platoon in the Sixth Army?"

Johann changed his planned response. "You disagree with me?"

Looking sideways at Johann, Wilhelm smiled but didn't say anything.

"Okay, smartass, which platoon do you think is better?

"At what?" Wilhelm pulled his hat over his eyes.

"At fighting Russians... Isn't that what we do?"

"So far, we've lost twelve men out of sixty. How many more do you think will die, lose a limb or walk with a limp? How many will babble like a child for the rest of their lives? I've lost count of the Russian men who won't see their homes again because of us. On top of that, all those men had fathers and mothers, siblings, friends. We *have* made a huge hole in our planet." His hat slid down over his nose, and he pushed it back up without looking at Johann. "I guess we probably did the most damage of any platoon relative to the number of men we have." He lifted his hat enough to peek at Johann. "Is that why you think we're the best platoon in the Sixth Army?"

"Our orders are our orders...we have no option but to obey." Johann found himself shaking Barbara's letter for emphasis, and a flood of guilt forced him to stop talking. He tried to hold his right hand still but had to grasp it with his other hand.

Wilhelm watched Johann's struggle to quiet his hand. "Well, then I guess we are the best platoon in the Sixth Army, but not in the entire Wehrmacht. The Einsatzgruppen would have several platoons that have killed more people than we have."

"What they do is evil...."

"They have the same orders we do. The only difference is that their victims are Jews, Bolsheviks, and prisoners instead of Russian soldiers carrying guns. Our victims are as helpless as theirs, or at least we try to set it up that way."

"No. What the Einsatzgruppe does is murder!" Johann said it with a little more fervour than he intended. He instinctively looked around to see if anyone else had heard him.

Wilhelm spoke softly. "We try to make what we do into murder, and they try to say what they do isn't murder, but the only real difference is in your point of view. Now, let me go to sleep—we may have to murder some more Russians tonight. Hopefully, they will not see us coming, and we can kill them before they have a chance to defend themselves."

Chapter Nine

When you think things can't get worse, they usually do.

They sent forth men to battle,
But no such men return;
And home, to claim their welcome,
Come ashes in an urn.

Aeschylus, Agamemnon.

Stalingrad sits between the Volga River, which flows south past the city's eastern edge, and the Don River, running parallel to the Volga sixty-five kilometres to the west. The German Sixth Army stopped at the Don's west bank to set up a base from which to attack Joseph Stalin's namesake. The Wehrmacht constructed supply depots and extended resupply chains from Germany to fill them.

On the twenty-third of August, the Luftwaffe attacked Stalingrad with a thousand tons of incendiaries and high explosive bombs. In the ensuing three days, most of Stalingrad became a rubble field.

Sitting outside their tents, waiting for the word to advance, Johann and his men watched the firestorm on the eastern horizon. Ian's voice penetrated the steady rumble of exploding bombs.

"How can anything survive in that?" Though ten kilometres away, the sound of bombs bursting and buildings disintegrating was loud and continuous; and the fires on the eastern horizon revealed that hell had found a fissure and was rising to the surface to search for victims.

Ian said, "This should make the fight a lot easier for us!"

Wilhelm looked at Ian as though he were lecturing a child. "You know, the British are bombing our cities, and it looks just like this! The Americans are in the war now, and they will double or triple what the British can do. What we are doing here is giving them justification to do it!"

As Wilhelm spoke, a tongue of flame surged above the line. Ian, staring at the fire rising out of the horizon, said, "I suppose I should thank you for reminding me."

Johann silently thanked God that Detmold was too small to have any tactical value. The only industry was a clock factory, and the city was far away from militarily vital road and railway facilities.

Despite Johann's infrequent letters, Barbara wrote every week, concentrating her message on the children and the agony of separation. In February, she had written that Juliette Durand, a soprano Johann had met when he played in the Bielefeld opera orchestra, had visited Detmold and sung a successful *Nedda* in *I Pagliacci*.

Johann had helped Juliette get a Jewish woman and her husband to the train station, and from there, Juliette had smuggled them out of Germany. Johann translated Barbara's letter to mean that Juliette had successfully pulled off another heroic adventure. He decided he had to revise his opinion of sopranos.

In April, Barbara had written that Juliette had lost her husband, Peter—*an accident while working in France*—she wrote. Johann tried to read her code but couldn't decipher what had happened to Peter. The only thing that was certain for Johann was that Peter's death had not been an accident.

Otherwise, Detmold was a boring place to weather the storms of war; certainly, Stalingrad was not.

◇◇◇◇◇◇◇◇◇◇◇◇◇◇◇◇◇◇◇◇◇◇◇◇◇◇◇◇◇◇◇◇

First Jäger Company joined the Sixteenth panzer Corps for their attack against the northern edge of Stalingrad. As they moved unopposed into the area surrounding Gumrak airport, the squadron of panzer IIIs and IVs Johann's Company was charged to protect surged ahead, outdistancing the scouts.

With no intelligence and a bad feeling about what they were facing, Johann wasn't surprised when a shell struck a panzer III behind his platoon, disabling one of its tracks—and then a direct hit blew its turret in the air. A second panzer III took two hits on its front armour, then one on a track. The men inside bailed out and ran.

"That's an auto-loader, probably two. My guess is two anti-aircraft guns." Johann spoke to his radioman sitting behind him in the demag half-track. "Tell headquarters that we have guns shooting at our panzers. Range, five hundred metres—they're hidden between buildings and impossible to hit with artillery."

A second battery opened up on the panzer IIIs advancing on Johann's left, and two of them stopped in their tracks. One of them burned with no apparent survivors, and the other drove off its track, spun sideways and stopped. Four men poured of the hatches. In a burst, several shells landed among the infantry, killing and wounding at least a dozen men before they found cover.

"Tell Headquarters that we must withdraw and assess the situation!" The man repeated the words into his microphone, and headquarters immediately responded with an order to withdraw at Johann's discretion.

◇◇◇◇◇◇◇◇◇◇◇◇◇◇◇◇◇◇◇◇◇◇◇◇◇◇◇◇◇◇◇

Johann's driver set some kind of speed record getting the demag back to Sixteenth's battle command, and Johann arrived in time to join a group of the Sixteenth's officers. As the officer in charge of the forward scouting unit, Johann identified a dozen anti-aircraft gun positions around the airport and along the city's western edge using recent aerial photographs. Their fields of fire overlapped, taking bypassing them out of the discussion. The airport was a primary objective—the battle orders were clear.

Generalmajor Günther von Angern looked at Johann, then at his officers standing around a table. When he spoke, he got the undivided attention his rank demanded.

"The aerial reconnaissance report—the one we should have had yesterday—shows that those guns are on trailers, hidden in bunkers between buildings. *Um Gottes Willen,* this report barely mentions them!" He stared pointedly at his intelligence officer, who wisely said nothing. "It is now too late for our bombers to take them out until the weather clears, there's no time to set up artillery, and I doubt they could drop their shells in there anyway."

He concentrated on Johann. "Colonel Stieff speaks highly of you. He says that this kind of thing is your specialty...so, tell me about those guns and how you would take them out without losing my panzers!"

Johann nodded, looked at the map, the aerial photograph, then at the generalmajor.

115

"Sir, those look like auto-loading 37 mm anti-aircraft guns…a very effective gun against tanks at short range. I doubt those particular guns have armour-piercing ammunition, but they can still take out a tank, and they can do a lot of damage against infantry. But, in my opinion, a frontal assault is not a good idea."

"Yes, Sergeant, I think that's obvious. Tell us what you would do."

Johann looked at Leutnant Kohl, who nodded. Johann said confidently, "I believe that a platoon of Jäger soldiers could flank them, but we need to know what we are facing. We can scout one of the installations tonight, and I will tell you before midnight whether and how we can take them out."

The general folded his notes, said, "If you think you can take those guns out, do it. Report back to me only if you can't, and I will get some Stukas to take care of them when the weather clears." The men at the table returned the general's salute, turned, and left.

◇◇◇◇◇◇◇◇◇◇◇◇◇◇◇◇◇◇◇◇◇◇◇◇◇◇◇◇◇◇

Six hours before daylight, Wilhelm and Ian appeared out of the darkness. Rain falling from thick clouds had blocked all light, giving them the cover they needed to locate the guns and the infantry protecting them.

Ian said, "Two and three storey buildings surround the guns. The only guards are a dozen soldiers who like to sit in windows and smoke." Ian pulled on a Russian cigarette he had picked out of a dead Russian's pocket. "The Russians seem to learn slowly."

"There is one other item we should discuss." Wilhelm looked to Ian for support, but Ian looked at his feet.

Johann said, "Okay, what's the problem we have to discuss? I have no authority to discuss a pay raise." Johann smiled, and Wilhelm looked at the sky as if trying to guess how long the rain would last.

Ian broke the silence. "They're all women…teenagers, I'd say."

"*Women?* Women killed thirty men and blew up four tanks?"

"Yes, women, but more like girls. And you can assume that they hate us." Ian waved a hand in a gesture of helplessness. "I didn't sign on to kill girls!"

"Maybe they'll surrender if we ask them nicely." Wilhelm grinned, then shrugged.

Johann ignored the comment. He wasn't sure he could kill a woman with a knife, and he decided that most of his men would have the same problem. A stealth attack on the women was out of the question—Johann's men had to force them to surrender.

"First, we need to get into those buildings and eliminate the outer perimeter. Once we have that secured, we can use those positions to fire down on the guns—maybe we can even use a couple of those damned *panzerfausts* we've been dragging around. We'll attack them from behind and the flanks simultaneously... If we surround them, they'll surrender."

They gathered around the detailed map that Ian had drawn. He had noted every window and roof position that faced the guns.

Johann looked at his battle-hardened men. They were eager for a fight—but not against women who reminded them of their wives and daughters....

"All right, we need Ian's squad to clear and occupy the buildings, and then Wilhelm and I will take out the guns. Wilhelm will flank them with half the squad, and I will take the other half and attack from behind."

"What about our panzers?" A leutnant commanding four panzer IIIs assigned to help Johann pointed at his rides. He outranked Johann, but his boss had put Johann in charge.

"I want your panzers to shell the targets from the front at a safe distance, but don't miss long—that's where we will be. You will damage a few buildings, but you won't damage the guns unless something falls on them. The point is to get their attention."

Johann put his finger on the map. "We will come in from the rear and the flanks. When I fire a flare, stop firing, or you will hit us!" He straightened up. "It only matters that you fire, not that you hit the guns. They are thirty-seven-millimetre flak guns on wheels, firing from a bunker—a small, well-protected target. We need a distraction, nothing more... So don't risk your tanks."

The panzer IIIs began firing two hours before dawn, while Ian and his crew worked their way into the buildings overlooking the guns' positions. Gun flashes and grenade explosions from the upper floors announced the battle for the high ground, and less than ten minutes into the attack, panzerfaust shells, designed to take out a tank, rained down on the flak guns' position. Johann waited until Wilhelm's unit was in place, then fired a flare...the panzers ceased firing, and Johann moved his men out from behind buildings two blocks from the gun. Simultaneously, Wilhelm's men moved down parallel streets, converging on the guns' makeshift bunkers. The four-woman gun crews and a dozen soldiers faced simultaneous attacks by an overwhelming force, from the flanks and rear.

Wilhelm's unit had already eliminated half the soldiers guarding the guns when Johann and his men reached the bunker. Johann found himself facing a Russian soldier who had obviously run out of ammunition. The young woman held her rifle in front of her, bayonet fixed, determined to skewer him. She screamed as she thrust at him. He easily side-stepped her bayonet, and her momentum carried her to him. He pushed her back against the wall of sandbags.

"*Sdat'sya ili umeret!*" Johann shouted while he tried to hold her squirming body. But she wouldn't quit—she broke free and swung the barrel of her rifle at his head. He ducked and tried to grab the gun but missed it.

She screamed, "*Ya vybirayu smert!*" and before he could stop her, she flipped the rifle, put the butt at his feet and impaled herself on the bayonet. She gasped, fell against Johann, and, after eternal seconds, died. Johann laid her small body on the ground. The girl didn't look old enough to be out of school, and a vision of Lisa flashed in his mind.

The last defender threw herself on her own grenade.

Every one of the eight women had died defending the guns, three by their own hand. Johann's men had won the battle. They had even prevented the crews from 'spiking' the guns. The operation was a complete success, but there was no celebration.

Wilhelm stood with Johann, watching men pile up bodies on the side of the street. He said, "If Stalingrad is defended by soldiers like these, we had better go home before they really get mad!" His voice had a catch in it, and his smile was sad. "When you kill them with a bomb or an artillery shell, you can tell yourself they could have run away, or it was just bad luck—but this...?" They watched a Wehrmacht soldier throw a girl's body on the pile.

Johann put his hand on his corporal's shoulder. "Everyone will fight to the death if they believe that death, or worse than death, is inevitable... In that, women are not different from men." He looked far away as he said, "We haven't got enough bullets to kill them all."

It was dusk, two and a half months after the German army had taken out thirty-seven anti-aircraft/anti-tank guns, all manned by women. Aided by two panzer IV tanks, Johann and his men chased a group of Russian soldiers to a warehouse on the corner of two intersecting streets. The once-mighty Sixty-Second Soviet Army was twenty percent of its original size, trapped in a thousand yards of desolate land between the German Sixth Army and Stalin's declaration that, for the Sixty-Second, "there is no land east of the Volga!" With nowhere to go, the Russians resolved to "win, or die where they stood." And they fortified buildings where they could carry out their promise.

The Russians fought using what they called a "hugging" tactic—fighting close to the Germans, hampering their ability to use artillery and Stukas without hitting their own men. The battle for Stalingrad had become spread out, hand-to-hand, a war of personal contact, fought to the death. No quarter was asked, and none was given by either side.

Johann and his men dropped to the ground or stepped into doorways as rockets launched from the warehouse struck the panzers, turning them into smoking hulks. Four men crawled out of the hatches, but Russian machine guns firing from the warehouse roof and a dozen windows cut them down. Johann and his men withdrew to wait for total darkness before trying to take the building. He sent his scouts to reconnoitre the area around the three-storey building and spread his men out, well back from the Russian machine-guns' field of fire.

Leutnant Kohl was dead, and Johann commanded what was left of First Jäger Company, now reduced to less than platoon strength. Casualties inflicted by an intelligent, elusive Russian army had reduced the original company strength of over two hundred men to sixty-five, and many of those men were walking wounded. The Sixth Army fought a different foe than the one they had defeated on the Don River.

It was late November.

Darkness fell quickly, leaving a cold light rain to blanket all sources of light except the fires burning the last remnants of flammable material in the demolished buildings. With the coming of night, the sounds of war died to a few isolated explosions, the occasional burst of machine-gun fire, and, infrequently, to a single shot or a cry of pain.

Ian and Wilhelm returned. While his men watched the street, Johann crouched with his scouts behind what was left of a wall. All three men would have traded their gun for a cigarette, but to light one was to invite a sniper's bullet. Ian cradled his *Papa*—the light from a fire across the street flickered in his eyes.

"The building is full of Russians; I'm guessing more than a hundred of them." Ian noted the number as though it were normal to take on odds of two to one. "We can get into it from the rear building. There's a narrow alley there, and only the roof and two windows overlook it. The roof on the adjacent building is about the same height, so it's possible to jump across the gap. Also, two windows face one another, and we could take that route too."

Johann knelt on one knee with Ian and Wilhelm, memorizing Ian's neat layout plan by the light of a nearby fire. The situation was a variation of many they had encountered. It took only a few minutes for them to formulate a plan and another five minutes to come up with a couple of alternatives should things go wrong.

Plans complete, Johann waited while Ian and Wilhelm went through the details with the men, then took over.

"I don't want to attack until just before daylight tomorrow morning. Tonight, I want Ian and Wilhelm to check out the building next door... see who is in it, find out what we can do with the Russians on the roof without alarming those inside. There will be no room for mistakes. Keep everything simple; take one step at a time."

Ian and Wilhelm nodded, took three men with them, and Johann followed ten minutes later. He left ten men and two MG-42 machine guns to cover the building's entrance with overlapping fire from the other side of the street.

As Johann approached the rear building, a small stone landed in front of him. He looked up but could see nothing but blackness. He had no doubt that Ian had dropped the stone; *Cochise* could sneak up on a black cat at midnight in a coal mine. The pre-arranged signal meant everything was clear, and Johann entered the building ahead of his men, blessing the soft boots they always wore on night missions. Felt glued to the soles made walking soundless, and their blackened faces, clothing, and weapons made them invisible on a black night—to everyone but Ian.

"The building is secure." The sound of Wilhelm's voice from the darkness sent a shock through Johann, and he barely controlled the urge to yelp. He stepped toward the sound of Wilhelm's voice but didn't see him until the distance between them was less than six feet.

Johann said to him, "You two are more like cats than men." Wilhelm might have smiled, but Johann couldn't see enough to be sure.

"I want to go to the roof." Johann spoke as softly as he could with his heart in his mouth. Wilhelm turned around, said, "Wait here," and disappeared.

Johann gathered his men together in what was a massive room. Artillery or bombs had blown out most of one wall, but the concrete floor was still intact. As his night vision sharpened, he could pick out the black forms of most of his men and four still forms lying on the floor. First Jäger Company's only surviving officer, other than Ian and Wilhelm, was young Sergeant Gronert, and Johann stood next to him.

"Gronert, sir... We're all here."

Johann spoke to him quietly. "I want you to leave half your men to guard the entrance and set alarm traps. Bring the rest of them to the second floor."

It took the sergeant five minutes to organize his men, and then he followed Johann and Wilhelm up the stairs. Johann stepped around a Russian, lying on the halfway landing with his head pointing backwards, then stepped aside to avoid a window. Wilhelm said, "Look out the window, but don't show yourself." He said it quietly as he jerked his thumb around the frame.

After rolling the dead Russian aside, Johann carefully peeked around the frame. He could see a shadow outlined in the candle-lighted window of the warehouse next door, barely a metre and a half from him. A Russian soldier slept, leaning against the window frame, his machine gun on his lap. Johann pulled back, said, "We'll take care of him later."

Johann and Wilhelm left the sergeant and his men on the second floor and climbed a steep, narrow stairway to the roof. At the top of the roof stairs, Johann slithered behind Wilhelm over a thirty-centimetres-high coaming that supported the roof hatch. They found Ian lying on a small pile of rubble—once part of the building's flat roof. Two dead Russians lay in a pool of blood a metre from him. He said nothing to Wilhelm and Johann as they crept up beside him.

A low perimeter wall sheltered them from the other warehouse's roof, a metre below them and a little over two metres away. Johann cautiously peeked over it to where Ian pointed his finger. He stared at the dark space until he could see two fixed machine guns, two anti-tank guns, and eight men. Johann lowered himself, looked at Ian, raised eight fingers—and Ian nodded. Johann raised his head again, verified that he had missed nothing, then pointed to the stairs. They quietly worked their way down to the second floor.

"We will need ten men to clear the roof," Johann said it so softly he barely heard himself, "We'll use knives."

Wilhelm pulled out his pocket watch. "When do we go?"

"At five." Johann held up five fingers and looked at his watch. "It's two minutes past midnight...now." Wilhelm set his watch. Johann went on, "We will sleep in two shifts. If anyone snores, wake him." He grinned at Wilhelm.

The night passed slowly for Johann. He couldn't sleep, so he didn't rouse Ian and Wilhelm for their shift, only waking them at five. If anything, the darkness seemed to press harder as they gathered seven men. Ian went to the roof to see that nothing had changed and returned with a paper drawing of the Russians' positions. Johann noted the locations of Russian soldiers and their guns—they were only on three sides of the roof, and none occupied the side facing them. Ian reported that most, if not all the Russians were asleep.

"We will jump across one at a time, and each man will take a Russian. When we are all in position, I will whistle, and we must kill our targets immediately." Johann got a nod from each man.

The soft boots made no sound as Johann and his men jumped

across to the warehouse wall and stepped down onto the roof. The men with the targets farthest away jumped first, and Johann jumped last. Every man stood silently behind his victim until Johann whistled. And then the only sounds were dying men kicking their feet.

Ian and Wilhelm readied ropes for the descent to the armed windows, and the sergeant followed Johann back across the gap. They gathered the men; Johann updated them and outlined the attack.

"The roof is ours, and the eight men we left there will take out the top floor as soon as we enter the building on the ground floor. Ian and Wilhelm will take out the two men guarding the windows above the entrance." Johann looked at the intent black faces around him, repeated the same speech he had made a dozen times. "Do not make a sound—someone will eventually discover us and raise the alarm—until then, use only knives, rifle butts and bayonets."

The main door was gone, removed by a bomb blast, and the man assigned to guard the opening was snoozing when Johann's sharp knife found him. The dying man let go of his machine gun and wrapped his fingers around his throat in a vain attempt to stop the flow of blood. Johann caught the *Papa* with one hand, dragged the man out the doorway with the other. He died kicking his feet in a pool of blood.

Johann stepped back to look up at the windows—Ian and Wilhelm hung on ropes over the glassless holes, ready to drop on the soldiers who guarded them. Johann waved, stepped over the body and up two steps into the building to where a dim kerosene lantern on a small three-legged table lit the hallway.

Sergeant Gronert and his men crept behind Johann. He passed an open door on each side of the short passage and stopped outside a third open door at the end of the hallway. Sergeant Gronert took one man to the door on the left and motioned two others to the right. He nodded, and they disappeared. Johann heard a scuffle through the right-hand door but no sound from the left. The four men reappeared, the sergeant nodded. Johann looked around the third doorframe and found what he guessed to be thirty men, most sleeping on the floor, scattered around a large room. Two men at the other end of the room—Johann assumed they were the guards—played a dice game in the light of two candles.

Johann backed into one of the secured rooms. The men followed him.

"The shooting has to start now." Johann patted his *Papa*. "It's a big room with about thirty men. Only two are awake, and they are playing cards. We will split the room. How many were born in an odd year?" About half of the men waved their hands. "You take the right side, everyone else the left...and everyone remain in the middle of the room and hold your fire until the Russians see us."

The men zippered into a line. Johann stepped forward quickly, as quietly as he could. He reached the men playing dice, shot them before they realized why he was there, then swung his *Papa* to cut down a group of men trying to get to their feet. The room filled with noise—a Russian fired his weapon, killing one of Johann's men before a German *Papa* cut him down.

Johann ran to a stairway, emptied his machine gun into a crowd of soldiers coming down them. While he changed his magazine, two men with fresh magazines took his place. In five seconds, they filled the stairwell with dead and dying Russians. A grenade bounced down the stairs, but one of Johann's men kicked it across the room into a group of dead Russians. It exploded as Johann hit the floor, then, from his knees, he emptied his gun at the Russian soldiers who tried to follow the grenade.

Everything became quiet. Johann waved his hand at his men, and they stood still, listening. He pointed at the ceiling, at the sound of Russian boots. He walked under the sound, aimed his *Papa* upward. His men followed his example, and when most of them had picked a spot, Johann pulled the trigger. The room exploded with a stuttering sound, followed by screams in the room above. Johann signalled for silence, loaded a fresh magazine and picked out the sound of a man crawling. His men found new targets, fired, and again the room exploded, but with fewer screams. Johann signalled for silence. Nothing moved; they had caught on.

"Up the stairs," whispered Johann, just loud enough for the men close to him to hear. Sergeant Gronert beat him to the first step, shot two Russians coming down the stairs, and a hail of bullets met him when he stepped over the bodies on the landing. As Gronert fell, Johann counted to three, threw a grenade around the corner onto the floor above, and heard it bounce, a Russian curse cut off by the explosion. Stepping over Sergeant Gronert's body, his squad followed him up the stairs.

Ian and his men entered the room from the stairs to the third floor, and men with fresh magazines replaced men who had fired theirs until finally, the Russians stopped firing. A single Russian soldier stood up, raised his hands, and Ian put a bullet into his broad forehead.

Johann looked around and saw that they had lost two more men; a third was wounded in the leg.

"Get the bodies away from the windows and man the Russian machine guns." Johann turned to Ian. "Get the rest of our men outside, prop a few Russians up where they can be seen. Their comrades will be here at dawn."

<hr>

Dawn came with little foreplay, changing from blackness to grey light in less than ten minutes. A cold rain fell in torrents.

Russian soldiers came out of the mist, sheltering in doorways as they made their way to the warehouse. Johann's men waited for their boss to fire—he stood beside a window, peeking around the frame. A German soldier next to him held a Russian body up behind a German MG-42 that had changed hands for the second time—a second man held the ammunition belt ready to feed it into the gun.

A familiar sound rose above the pounding rain—a T-34 drove into the street and rumbled toward the warehouse; fifty Russian soldiers ran behind it, oblivious of the German MG-42 they had passed. Wilhelm tracked the tank from the roof with the Russian anti-tank gun. When the tank was close to the building, Johann fired, choosing precisely the right time for Wilhelm to hit the top of the tank's turret; Wilhelm's shell peeled back the thin steel and exploded inside. Immediately the T-34 stopped, smoke belching out of the hole where the turret had been. The German MG-42s set up in the street and the machine guns in the warehouse came alive at the same instant, and the soldiers caught in the killing field between them died where they stood.

Chapter Ten

21 November 1942

Rattenkrieg

Only fools and children tell the truth.

S TIEFF LOOKED UP FROM AN ORNATE RUSSIAN DESK. "General Paulus has a problem." He sat on an equally ornate chair of the same vintage, his feet dangling a few centimetres from the floor. "And he's made it our problem."

"Of course, sir..." Johann smartly saluted his colonel and sat down... "That's how the Wehrmacht works." In Stalingrad, the colonel took the salute more as an attempt to humiliate him than standard protocol.

Colonel Stieff stood up and pushed the chair away as he asked Johann, "'Of course,' means you believe Paulus has a problem, or 'of course' means you think he wants us to solve it?"

"'Of course,' means I believe that Paulus has a problem, and, 'of course' means I think you want *me* to solve it...sir."

"Stop the 'sir'... That could become a habit, and a sniper might take you seriously."

"Better you than me...sir." Johann smiled, just a little.

"You've lost ten men in the past week, and you can smile?" Stieff leaned against his desk. "Do you know what the Russians are doing on the other side of the Volga?"

"Yes, sir, they are building parking lots and filling them with T-34s, tank destroyers, artillery, and many thousands of men."

"Correct." He crossed his arms. "They will attack us, but not directly across the river. They will cross the Volga above and below the city and move around Stalingrad in a pincer. The Russians might be slow learners, but we've repeated the lesson enough times that the student has surpassed the teacher!"

Stieff slapped the desk. "You and I know it, General Paulus knows it, but the Führer does not!" He looked away, eyes settling on a spot on the floor in the corner of the small room.

"If we stay here, we will not be rescued. There are no German armies close enough to help us...and from where I sit, that's how Hitler wants it." Despite his effort to hide it, Stieff's look of desperation was pathetic.

Johann shrugged. "It doesn't matter now—I have lost hope of getting back to my family. When we killed the women—no, girls, not yet women—defending their city using little anti-aircraft guns against our tanks, I stopped writing home. I don't want to think about a time when my little girl will have to die for Germany."

Johann turned around in his chair so that he could look directly into Stieff's eyes. "My Company has killed four or five times their number of Russians...no, I'm wrong, we've killed a lot more than that!" He put up his hand to prevent his colonel from interrupting. "Yes, I've lost ten men in a week, but we've killed over a hundred—and yet—every damned night, hundreds of Russians cross the river to join their comrades fighting against us. We are fighting professional soldiers, but we are also fighting women and old men, and they never quit! I don't believe we can win—no, that's wrong too—I know we will lose, and I don't believe I will ever see Germany or my children again."

He waited, but Stieff was silent. Johann shrugged his shoulders. "I guess Stalingrad is as good a place to die as any...."

Stieff lowered his eyes to the edge of his desk. He said, "We do what we have to," and returned his gaze to Johann. "You've given up; you've already got one foot in your grave. Don't you think it's a little early for that?"

"There is no point in trying to deal with things we can't change." Johann slouched in his chair—it was not designed for comfort. "So, let's get back to why I'm here. Who do you want me to kill?"

Colonel Stieff stood, thoughtfully walked along the edge of the desk, guiding his path with his fingers on the exquisite walnut edge.

"Hitler has forbidden us to withdraw, intentionally forcing us into a position where our only escape involves pushing the Russian Army east, across the Volga. If we can somehow perform that miracle, he can say we took Stalingrad. With the Russians attacking our flanks and closing the pincer to the west. Death or a Russian prison are our only options."

"So, you want me to chase the Russian Army across the Volga. Do I have to do it alone, or could I have a little help?" Johann didn't intend to laugh, and he certainly regretted the sarcasm in it. But the absurdity of the idea tickled something, perhaps his sense of reason. "And, of course, you want that done by morning." He laughed again, louder, less sarcastically.

Stieff's expression adapted the grimness of a man who knew the end was near, but his eyes betrayed a softness that carried pity.

"Do you know the story of Pavlov's house—the actual story, not the rumours?"

"I know, sir, that a stupid general ordered our army to move on, to bypass it. The *Dummkopf* left Sergeant Pavlov and a dozen men in a big indestructible building. Pavlov held on for weeks, giving his comrades time to fill the building with soldiers and guns. I've seen Pavlov's House, and it *is* impregnable, even using tanks. Bombs and shells just shift the rubble around. And the Russians mined the ground around the building so infantry and tanks can't get near it. That building can't be taken or destroyed without losing half a Division!"

Colonel Stieff leaned against the desk, picked up a pencil, flipped it across his hand through his fingers, and then looked at Johann.

"The key to taking fortresses like Pavlov's House is the same today as it was two hundred years ago: cut off their supply of food, water and ammunition. In this case, those supplies are coming through the sewers...we must make them too dangerous for the Russians. Cut off their supplies, put bombs and tripwires in the sewers—make them terrified to flush a toilet!"

Johann looked up at his boss from his uncomfortable chair. Stieff, at 150 centimetres, preferred to have his officers seated—standing was a 'no-no.' "So, you want me to cut off the supply routes to the fort and starve them out?" He looked down at his hands, then back at Stieff. "They can live forever without food—those men are not like us."

"I was thinking more of water, ammunition and reinforcements— we can wear them down in a few weeks."

<hr>

Johann began his assignment as he had started every mission since training, learning everything he could about the enemy's positions. He sent his scouts underground to measure all the sewers large enough to crawl through, and then Ian drew maps of over ten square kilometres of them. Johann and Wilhelm allocated common names of German streets and towns to main sewer lines and intersections. Map distances were typical steps for a man bent over in a confined space so anyone with a map could accurately locate intersections in the pitch black of a sewer by counting steps.

Every man drilled the map's features into his head. Once in the sewers, every soldier in the company knew exactly where he was. They knew the quickest way out and the exact route the hunt would follow. They also knew where the booby traps were because they had placed them there.

A week after completing the map, First Platoon ambushed two groups of Russians transporting supplies. There were about fifteen men in each group, including four or five soldiers. The remainder were civilians forced or willing to carry the supplies. The armed soldiers were there as much to guarantee that the "volunteers" delivered the goods to the intended recipients as to defend the column. Both groups carried kerosene lanterns and flashlights, and their chatter could be heard bouncing off the brick-walled interior of the sewers from a thousand metres. It was pitifully easy to ambush them—too easy, and Johann expected the Russians to fix that problem.

◇◇◇◇◇◇◇◇◇◇◇◇◇◇◇◇◇◇◇◇◇◇◇◇◇◇◇◇◇◇◇◇◇◇

Two weeks later, Colonel Stieff saluted and began talking before Johann could return it.

"I have some reinforcements for you—I need you to train them so they can train others. That way, we can eventually control all the sewers and get rid of all of those damned fortresses."

Johann sat in the uncomfortable chair and looked at his boss. "Okay, what's the problem—I get replacements all the time. And what do you mean by 'others?'"

"They are SD, specifically, *Einsatzgruppen.*"

Stieff waited; at first, Johann was too shocked to say what he felt. He paused, thought of sugar-coating his response but gave up the idea.

"My men won't fight alongside those bastards... If we go into the sewers with them, they won't come out!"

"Your men have no choice. We have thousands of these *'bastards,'* and there is no 'mopping-up' for them to do now that we and the Russians are stalemated."

"So cold-blooded murder is called 'mopping-up' now?" Johann shook his head. "I don't give a shit what you or anyone else says—there are too many rumours to ignore. If you send me *Einsatzgruppen,* I can't guarantee anything."

"I am ordering you to take them into the sewers and train them!"

Johann waited, cooling his temper. He stood up, saluted smartly. "Yes, sir! Will there be anything else, sir?"

"They will arrive at your place of business tonight...try not to kill them right away—that would make me look bad."

◇◇◇◇◇◇◇◇◇◇◇◇◇◇◇◇◇◇◇◇◇◇◇◇◇◇◇◇◇◇

The new additions arrived in the early morning, just before the grey pre-dawn twilight, and Frederick was one of the *Einsatzgruppe* soldiers assigned to Jäger Company. Johann hadn't seen him since going home on leave almost eighteen months ago...a lifetime on the Russian Front.

"*Schöne Grüsse, Frederick!*" Johann used the neutral greeting that said nothing or everything, wrapped his arms around him in a man's hug and let him go.

"*Na, wie geht's?*" Frederick answered with the standard greeting that required no answer. "Man, you've changed! You're not a musician any-more—you really *are* a soldier!"

"I was a soldier the last time you saw me."

"No, you were still a musician. You hadn't killed anyone, and that changes a man. You've killed many men since then—I can see it in your eyes."

"And you... How many?"

Frederick shrugged and spread his hands. "No idea."

Frederick had a war-weary look, the mark of every professional soldier, but his eyes had an added darkness that could be anything or nothing.

◇◇◇◇◇◇◇◇◇◇◇◇◇◇◇◇◇◇◇◇◇◇◇◇◇◇◇◇◇◇

Johann and Frederick spent most of the day talking about their wives and children in Detmold and the safety of living in such a small town. But eventually, as the strangeness wore off, the conversation became more personal.

"In the end, I wonder if having a family back home makes any difference now." Frederick rubbed his finger on the rough hemp of the bale of rope he was sitting on. "Siegruna hardly ever answers my letters. Tell me, how do you and Barbara get along? Does she write to you?"

Johann, surprised, laughed self-consciously. "I guess we get along alright. We don't argue much since I learned to agree with her, and now…well, I can't expect her to write if I don't."

"No, I mean something more personal. I don't understand Siegruna…I can't figure out what she wants from me." Frederick looked at his fingers as he tried to pry the strands of rope apart for no good reason.

Johann looked at something far away. "Perhaps she doesn't trust you."

Frederick slapped Johann on the back, "Shit, I don't care if she trusts me—I just want her to act like she loves me…you know…I want her to tell me when she wants a little something. Siegruna seems to dread it. I can get what she gives me for fifty marks. I wouldn't be surprised if she hopes I'll be killed!" He spoke far too loudly for the situation.

Johann hung his head, pulled his grandfather's knife out of its scabbard, and absentmindedly tested the edge with his thumb. It would give a decent shave.

"Maybe she doesn't like sex with a man who beats her," Johann replied, almost under his breath. He regretted saying it and looked at Frederick for a reaction but couldn't see one. He tried to smooth the water, just in case. "Siegruna seemed happy when we left Detmold." He smiled at Frederick, hoping he would change course and talk about something else.

"Yeah, she was happy, but I wasn't. Does Barbara love you, Johann?"

Johann put his head down and flipped the knife at the floor, sticking it into the soft wood. He considered going outside, but he would be breaking his own rule.

"Yes, she does. My problem is the opposite of yours."

"Well, either she's missing something other women have, or she hates me." He screwed up his face.

"I don't think it has anything to do with that." Johann, embarrassed, wanted to end the conversation, but he was in too deep. "It's more likely that she's afraid of you." He kept his voice low.

"What do you mean? Afraid of me? I haven't hit her since that time you straightened me out! And when I go home again, I won't hit her unless she really needs it...and despite what you think, I would never hit my kid!" Frederick spoke loudly and looked at Johann with a puzzled expression. Johann cringed—Frederick's volume in the quiet room felt like shouting.

Johann pulled the knife out of the wooden floor, keeping his head down to hide his awkwardness. He spoke softly so the men wouldn't hear.

"I don't know what to tell you, Frederick. What you are doing to Siegruna isn't making love to her; it's attacking her." He lifted his head with the knife in his hand. "I don't want to talk about this anymore. We've got a war to fight, and our wives are years away... There is a good chance that I won't ever see Barbara, and you won't see Siegruna again."

Johann's voice had risen. Jäger Company soldiers had been deep in quiet conversation with Einsatzgruppe soldiers before the wife-beating conversation distracted them.

Frederick said nothing, and the conversation between the soldiers resumed. As Johann listened to the men talk, he became increasingly agitated at what he overheard: a few of his men were trying to get the new recruits to confirm rumours of murdered civilians. Finally, Johann stood up, said to Frederick in a voice that was far louder than he intended, "We've all heard that Einsatzgruppe soldiers are killing civilians and Russian prisoners behind our lines! No bullshit, just facts... Is it true?"

Conversation stopped—all eyes were on Frederick. A few of Johann's men believed they knew the answer and, until now, had avoided speaking of it. But for the rest, the implication of rumours that German soldiers were shooting women and children and burying them in ditches was too horrific to accept. A confession from Frederick would fill that gap.

Frederick laughed nervously, stood up and looked at his SD comrades, then at Johann. "We follow the Führer's orders...we eliminate Jews and Bolshevik bureaucrats, and sometimes we eliminate some of the prisoners. We can't feed all of Russia, can we?

Silence greeted his question. The other Einsatzgruppe soldiers hung their heads, but Frederick ploughed on, louder than ever.

"We are doing what is best for Germany! We need room to expand... Lebensraum...you know... *Deutschland über Alle! Heil Hitler!*" He clicked his heels and saluted with a stiff arm.

Johann's face betrayed the shock he felt, but he still held a faint desperate hope that Frederick was joking or exaggerating. He said, "The Wehrmacht doesn't use that salute. You're in a Wehrmacht unit—use that salute when you're around me!"

Frederick laughed and saluted with his fingers together against his forehead. "Man, where have you been for the last two years?"

"How many?" Johann looked down at the floor. He flipped the knife hard into the wooden boards. His target was a small knot in a pine board, chewed to pieces by the knife. The blade buried itself in the soft wood.

Frederick hesitated, shrugged, and spoke too quickly. "All of them."

"All of them? What does that mean?" Johann wiggled the knife from side to side to loosen it, then pulled it out of the floor.

"As far as I know, we killed every Jew and every Bolshevik Communist bureaucrat in every town you took. Your Sixth Army even helped us sometimes, at least until General Reichenau died last January—he was twice the man Paulus is! Paulus doesn't have the stomach to serve a man like Hitler!"

Johann squeezed the handle of the knife until his knuckles turned white. When he looked at Frederick, his weathered face was a mixture of devastation and disbelief. Johann stood up, sheathed the knife, turned away from Frederick and walked to the centre of the room. Half of the men stood or sat with their heads hung; a few looked at Johann sympathetically. Most had feelings for or against Jews, but every one of them had empathy for unarmed men, women, and children. Johann wanted to think that none of his men would qualify for Himmler's *SS* Einsatzgruppe.

From rumours he had heard, Johann had expected something bad, even horrible, but nothing like the magnitude of Frederick's admission. This explained why the Russian villagers who had first welcomed them, or at least tolerated their intrusion, had turned against them as they progressed farther and farther into their homeland. And when it became unambiguous that the Einsatzgruppen would get Hitler's Lebensraum by exterminating the people who lived there, the farmers had burned their crops rather than let German soldiers eat them. Some burned their houses rather than let German soldiers sleep in them.

The beginning of the invasion process was the destruction of the Russian Army, the only defence the people had. And then the death squads had killed the Bolsheviks and Jews, helped by Russian citizens who shared the Nazi viewpoint. When the massacre expanded to include women and children, it became too much for the most fervent Russian Jew-hater, and they had turned their animosity toward the Nazis.

Until Stalingrad, the German plan had been flawlessly executed. But there, the Russian Army had informed Hitler that the Russian bear was not yet dead—it was gathering strength and was hungry for Nazi flesh.

Johann and his men turned away from the eight Einsatzgruppe sitting close together, and the conversation stopped. Standing in the middle of the room, Johann asked the question his men needed to know. "Do regular Wehrmacht soldiers take part?"

Without a trace of remorse, Frederick explained, "At first, the main army helped us with transport and logistics. Sometimes we used their Lastwagen to take the prisoners to the holes; sometimes, they dug the holes, but they always left before the shooting started. General Reichenau chose appropriate units and forced them to cooperate. But as far as I know, Wehrmacht soldiers didn't see anyone killed, and they were sworn to secrecy anyway. That fucker Paulus changed everything. He took his men and equipment away, and I got blisters from shovelling dirt!" He opened his hands to show his calluses.

Johann looked at his men; the expression on their faces told him what to say. "It's easy to understand why units like ours are not taking part." He paused; Frederick raised his eyebrows. When Johann spoke again, it was with ice in his voice, "You and your kind would be the ones in the holes!"

Frederick smiled at Johann as an adult would smile at a child who didn't understand that the meat on their plate was once a live animal.

Johann now knew for certain the fate of the Jews the SS and SD had removed from Bielefeld—people who had disappeared, sent to 'work' camps. Hitler's *"Arbeit Macht Frei"* took on a new meaning, and every man in his Company was now connecting dots.

In the ensuing silence, the distant sound of artillery fire from what they knew were Russian guns underscored each man's effort to deal with the inescapable. The Russians were in the final stages of surrounding the city—they were at the gates, and the Sixth Army's fate was a simple matter of time. Johann and his men understood what the Russians would do to them if they surrendered. Frederick's confessions had limited each man's options to one—if he had the courage to do it.

✧✧✧✧✧✧✧✧✧✧✧✧✧✧✧✧✧✧✧✧✧✧✧

The coming darkness was the harbinger of another game of cat and mouse in the sewers. Johann suspected that the underground war would test Frederick's men's nerves in a way that a member of the *Einsatzgruppe* could never imagine. They had likely never fought in the dark, or for that matter, against a well-armed and experienced foe. Johann decided to keep them close, apprehensive of the Einsatzgruppe soldiers' reaction to the deadly combination of darkness, claustrophobia, machine guns and grenades.

"A fight in the sewers is frightening to any soldier…." Johann said to the eight men in the *Einsatzgruppe*. He looked from one of them to another as he spoke… "And you must do exactly as we say! The darkness is complete. You will not see the faintest shadow. You will become disoriented—even up and down will be a problem. No matter how smart you think you are, all of you will have problems with direction and balance. And no matter what happens, you must not make a sound!"

The SD men looked knowingly at one another and were patronizing Johann with smiles when he said, "Now, we must get everything ready. There will be no discussion about the equipment—you will do as you are told."

Men who knew when and how to use them carried the only lights; the remainder left all sources of fire or light in their quarters with their cigarettes. They would take two flashlights into the sewers, one for each end of the line.

It took several hours to outfit the new members of the Company, darken their faces with burnt cork and cover their weapons with boot

136

polish. Each of them got a pair of soft boots to deaden their footfall and a Russian *Papa* machine gun. Johann tried to help Frederick with his preparations, but Frederick insisted on doing everything his own way. He assured Johann that his German MP40 machine pistol was superior to "that Russian shit" and wouldn't fail—Johann shrugged and checked him for rattles.

Johann ordered the SD soldiers to zipper between his regular Company soldiers, making a total of seventeen men. There was no time to teach them the maps, and he didn't want any of them to get lost and start shooting at ghosts. Suppressing a bad feeling about the mission, he left twenty-four men to guard the warehouse, with instructions to contact Colonel Stieff if he didn't return.

The days of a Stalingrad winter are short, and it was less than a month to the shortest day of the year. At five o'clock, it was almost dark, with a clear star-filled sky and no moon. The entry point was a manhole Wilhelm had named *Kassel Platz*, five blocks from the abandoned warehouse that had been Johann's mens' home for the past few weeks and three blocks from *Pavlov's Haus*. The journey through the streets had taken an hour, zigzagging from corner to corner, covering each other as they ran. The platoon included a machine gun crew carrying an MG-42 and three thousand rounds in ammo belts. The ammunition carried into the sewers would last two and a half minutes at the full-fire rate, long enough to kill everything in the narrow space in front of them.

When they reached *Kassel Platz*, they changed to their soft-soled footwear.

Previously, Johann and his men had ambushed sewer supply convoys, and none of them had heard or seen anything until hell broke loose. The mêlées had lasted less than a minute, and no one who lived had seen a German. Wilhelm and Ian had laid traps, trip wires that triggered grenades and landmines, and Johann's men had surprised the Russians four times in two weeks. They hadn't seen a Russian in the sewer for over a week.

One man carried a steel bar designed to lift manhole covers. Without the bar, it was nearly impossible to pry the tight-fitting disc out of its rim, but with it the cover at *Kassel Platz* lifted smoothly out of its frame. Johann climbed soundlessly down the ladder and stopped on the rung just above the sewer's roof to listen. A few seconds later, he lowered himself to the ledge beside the flowing drainage water, looked down each of the three branches, and strained his eyes to see a sign of life. He spent a full minute listening, then clicked his tongue, a sound that could have been a bursting bubble or a ripple touching the sewer's wall.

Johann's men climbed down the ladder until the last man, the one who had removed the cover, silently replaced it, no small feat considering he had to fit a twenty-five-kilogram piece of cast iron into a steel ring without making a sound. When closed, the cover shut out all light, and when the man reached the bottom rung, Johann guided his foot to the ledge. The second-last man was an Einsatzgruppe soldier, and he was already breathing hard.

Ian waited until every man was in his place in the line and clear of the intersection, then rigged two grenades to trip wires at the bottom of the manhole.

Johann put Wilhelm at the front of the squad—he would lead eight Einsatzgruppe soldiers and eight Jäger zippered together behind him. Johann had decided to put Frederick ahead of him and behind Wilhelm. Ian would be the last man in the line, and the three-man machine gun crew was in the middle.

Wilhelm, a big man, had grown up on a farm in Bayern but had majored in philosophy at university. Hitler, who considered philosophy irrelevant, had conscripted him. His father, an avid hunter and angler and a veteran of the Great War, had used the family cat to teach young Wilhelm how to stalk prey as soon as he could walk, and at two, he could track the cat at night with the lights off and the drapes drawn shut. Predictably, the cat became a nervous wreck, and Wilhelm learned to be quiet and deadly, especially in the darkness his father taught him to love. For that reason, Johann wanted Frederick where Wilhelm could reach him.

Ian, Johann's Cochise, was intelligent and sneaky. His upbringing had not included violence of any kind, and he looked like he should be an accountant. In fact, his father was a pastor, and Ian was an engineer. Ian was of medium height and build and had a jolly round face. His brown eyes, set far apart, had a softness in them that was an illusion. Ian had a thoughtful engineer's mind, but when action was required, he was mercilessly efficient.

Touch was the only practical form of interaction in the sewers. The darkness complicated communication, evolving the exchange of information into an abbreviated sensory language. Each man kept track of the one in front of him by occasionally touching his back or arm; a quick hard nudge meant danger, a yank on the arm meant "Get down!" The squad's movement was deliberately slow, especially with eight frightened and excited men in their midst who were armed to the teeth.

They crouched under the low arched ceiling, picking their way along the narrow walkway on the side of the three-metre-wide sewer. They would stay on the main line until they passed Pavlov's House, crawl two more blocks, and exit at the mouth of a narrow alleyway.

Pavlov's House was a thousand paces ahead, and Johann's plan would simplify the journey but make it more dangerous. They took a new route and used random manholes to enter and leave the sewer system each night. They always travelled past Pavlov's House to set traps and check for traffic to and from the fortress, creating a limit to the possible variations, but they approached from a different direction each night. Johann's sense of caution rebelled against using the main sewer for so long, but the side sewers were small, sometimes forcing a man to crawl on his belly. The rookies would fold in those close quarters.

Johann's anxiety sharpened the sixth sense that had so far kept him alive, and it was screaming at him.

Wilhelm crept along the wall; Johann heard nothing out of place, not even Frederick, who was so close he accidentally bumped his shoulder from time to time. Only the faint sound of his own breathing, heartbeat, and blood roaring through his head broke the silence.

◇◇◇◇◇◇◇◇◇◇◇◇◇◇◇◇◇◇◇◇◇◇◇◇◇◇◇◇◇◇◇◇◇

Johann almost screamed when he heard a hard-soled boot scrape the bricks behind him, and his senses told him the boot was at *Kassel Platz*, a hundred paces behind him. He tapped Frederick twice on the back, stopped dead, and pushed his shoulders down—the signal to lie flat.

Wilhelm was already hugging the ledge when Frederick reached ahead to tap him. Johann slipped into a hundred and fifty millimetres of cold, filthy water and worked his way back down the line, feeling for the machine-gun crew.

He met them as he passed the second SD soldier and waited for them to set up in the water—something they had rehearsed a dozen times. As they silently readied the machine gun, he slid into the water behind them. The tripod was just tall enough to keep the barrel and action out of the water. The gunner lay behind the breach, half-floating, the ammunition feeder crouched on his knees beside him. The rest of the squad lay on the ledge, out of the line of fire.

◇◇◇◇◇◇◇◇◇◇◇◇◇◇◇◇◇◇◇◇◇◇◇◇◇◇◇◇◇◇◇◇◇◇◇◇◇

When the hard-soled boot dragged on the rough bricks, Ian was the closest man to it. Without a sound, he pushed the man ahead of him down and reached forward to make sure that the next Jäger soldier had done the same to his charge. He turned back toward the boot-scrape and dropped to the floor as he lifted his *Papa,* his finger ready to cock the bolt and flick the safety off.

Johann strained to see in the direction of the sound, and although the distance was over eighty metres, he could make out an area of faint light in the dimensionless total darkness. Johann surmised that the only thing that would do that was light from above—an open manhole cover. His platoon hadn't left that cover open. The opening let in just enough starlight that Johann could pick out faint shapes… They had to be Russian hunters, and they had to be hunting Germans.

Johann knew they had only seconds. He tapped the gunner and feeder on the shoulders and dropped onto the gunner's legs to prevent the recoil from moving the man backward. He hoped everyone was flat on the bricks. The machine gunner opened the breach, the ammo-feeder slid the end of the belt across it, and the gunner snapped it closed. Ian and every Jäger soldier cocked their Papa and flipped the safety off.

When Johann's gunner pulled the trigger, Ian leaned against the wall and opened fire. The SS Einsatz soldier behind Ian fired past him, hitting the wall a few feet in front of Ian's face in a flash of fire and sparks. The deafening hail of steel bullets, half of them ricocheting off

140

the arched-brick sewer walls, blew what could only be unlit Molotov cocktails to pieces as the hot bullets and sparks lit the gasoline. A Russian fell or stepped on Ian's tripwire, and two grenades erupted with a roar, and then everything went quiet.

Seconds passed, and then bullets whizzed past Johann's prone body, coming from behind him, followed by the staccato sound of machine guns. The sound came from Russian Papas—Johann had led his men into an ambush. He squirmed around until he could see the flames bursting out of the Russian gun barrels and the forms of men lit up by the flashes. Lifting his Papa high enough that he wouldn't hit his men, he pulled the trigger and held it down until the gun clicked on the empty chamber.

Frederick picked that second to get on his knees so he could shoot—Johann dropped his gun and reached out to grab Frederick's shoulder. Before he could pull him down, a blow on his raised arm threw it sideways, and he fell back into the water, his arm numb. Frederick took hits from his own men, who were firing wildly up the sewer from behind him. Wilhelm pushed Frederick's falling body into the water and opened fire at the Einsatzgruppe soldiers from the floor, emptying his magazine.

A second of silence was followed by the sound of men standing up. Johann opened his mouth to stop them, but a Russian voice screamed, *Fashistkaya krysa...idi k chertu!* The words were cut off by the sound of another burst of machine-gun bullets coming from the same direction. Johann and all but two of the Jäger made it to the floor, but the last SS Einsatz butchers joined the Devil. Johann and his men had heard the expression before. If a Russian used those words, the German who heard them usually died from a Russian bullet. It meant, "Go to hell, fascist rats!"

Johann and Wilhelm fired from their position in the water, emptying fresh magazines. The sewer was suddenly quiet. Johann waited, listened for breathing, movement, a cry of pain. When he was satisfied that the battle was over, he spoke to Wilhelm.

"Turn on a light so we can see the damage."

Wilhelm pulled the flashlight out of his pocket and shone it back in the sewer. Four Jäger stood up, but the Einsatz men lying on the floor and in the water didn't move. Johann checked Frederick; he was dead.

"What were you doing trying to save that piece of shit?" Wilhelm shook his head as he helped Johann wrap his wounded wrist. "You're lucky to be alive!"

Johann said nothing as he wiped what he assumed to be Frederick's blood from his face.

When Wilhelm was done, he slapped Johann on the back.

The squad left eight dead Himmler SS Einsatz soldiers in the sewer and carried two dead Jäger to the next manhole, using the flashlight to guide them. They picked their way past six Russian bodies, and Johann led his men out into the starlit night. An hour later, the platoon was in their building with sentries posted.

Ian reported two men dead, one man with a graze wound, and a hole in Johann's forearm.

Wilhelm asked Johann, "What about Frederick and his men's bodies? Are we going to leave them in the sewer?"

Ian smiled as he drew on his Russian cigarette. "The sewer seems appropriate... That's where all the rats live." The cigarette tasted like shit but contained lots of nicotine. "Let the Russians find them—they will give them the respect and burial that all Einsatzgruppe soldiers deserve."

Johann sucked hard on his last German cigarette—Wilhelm toasted him, then Ian with their canteens.

Behind them, the other soldiers said nothing.

Chapter Eleven

November, December 1942

Connections

The line that separates belief from reality is a myth.

Late November always brings rain and penetrating cold to Detmold, and on the twenty-first of November 1942, rain, driven by a northeast wind, hammered against Barbara's bedroom window, waking her. Something was wrong—someone was in the room. When she switched on the light, she was alone. Nervous, frightened, a sense of urgency swept over her. She tried to dismiss the feeling that Johann was close to her and needed help. Fear for him filled her heart. She buried her face in her pillow and cried, "No, no, please, God, no!" The rain beat against the window, and the wind howled. She was sure that Johann was dead.

Barbara cried for half an hour, and little by little, the terror subsided. Peace slowly returned... She went to sleep, leaving the light on.

Barbara woke at six, still inexplicably feeling that Johann was close. She got up in the pre-dawn darkness and prepared for the day, distressed by the dilemma in her heart. She felt certain that Johann was dead. Should she tell someone? How could she tell Thomas and Lisa, Theo and Maria? What if she were wrong? She decided she wasn't sure enough to say anything.

In the living room, Barbara sat on the sofa and thought about *Lili Marlen*. She took the record out of its sheath, intending to play it, but decided it was too early. She pictured herself waiting for Johann under the lamppost on Lange Strasse—brought up the memory of Johann joking about joining her there—and cried.

It was Tuesday morning; Barbara had a lot to do, and feeling sorry for herself wasn't on the list. The first item was getting Thomas and Lisa off to school, and then, as usual on Tuesdays, Maria and Theo would come for Mittagessen. Barbara forced herself up from the sofa, put the recording back in its plain brown sleeve and slid it into its hiding place, between books of world maps.

She went to the kitchen, lit the gas stove and put a small pot on the front burner with enough water to cook eggs. She was slicing cheese when Thomas came bouncing out of his room. "Good morning, Mutti; how are you this morning?" Her son's mood forced her to smile.

"How did you sleep last night?" Barbara asked him with her back turned, aware that her eyes still glistened with tears.

"*Wunderbar!* I dreamed about Daddy...it was dark, he was in a noisy battle, but he's okay... Aren't you going to warm the Brötchen?"

"I almost forgot—thanks for reminding me." Barbara lit the oven.

The water reached a boil; she put three eggs in the pot and turned the gas as low as it would go. Stepping sideways to the sink, she put four buns in a paper bag and sprinkled it with water. She finished slicing the cheese, checked the egg timer and put the bag of Brötchen in the oven.

Lisa arrived, and Barbara sensed that her daughter was troubled. She wiped her hands on her apron as Lisa went to her place at the table without saying a word. Barbara took the paper bag full of warm buns from the oven and spoke as she dumped them in a basket bowl.

"How was your night, Lisa?" She waited, looking at Lisa expectantly until her daughter said, "Fine," and turned to look wistfully out the window.

"Lisa, what's the matter?" Lisa turned back to her. Barbara straightened her daughter's hair while she waited for more. Lisa, annoyed, shook her head, and Barbara pulled her hands away.

"Nothing's wrong, nothing at all!"

Thomas looked apprehensively at his sister but said nothing—he had figured out when to keep his mouth shut around the women in the family.

"Okay, but 'nothing' is certainly upsetting you," Barbara insisted.

"I want Daddy to come home!" She accompanied her anguished cry with a torrent of tears.

Barbara wrapped her arms around her daughter's shoulders and rested her chin on Lisa's head. "He can't come home now, but you know he loves you."

"Yes, I know he loves me, but Mutti, he hardly ever writes anymore, and I think he might be dead!" Lisa looked at her mother through her tears.

"Yes, you're right, he might be dead, but if he were dead, they would tell us." Barbara felt her mood swinging. "I believe he is alive. He is fighting for us, for our country, and we must not give up!" Barbara wrapped her arms tighter around her daughter.

Lisa, sobbing, pulled back, stood to face her mother with clenched fists. "I know there's something wrong! Stop treating me like a child!"

Barbara looked at Thomas. He wasn't at all upset.

"Thomas, are you worried about your father?"

Thomas shook his head. "No, Vati promised he would come home soon and play chess with me." He smiled and spread his hands. "Can't we have breakfast now? I'll be late for school."

Barbara put the eggs, a small piece of butter and slices of Wurst on the table. Thomas and Lisa ate quickly and left for school, and Barbara began the daily routine required to keep the family functioning smoothly. Tuesdays, Thursdays and Saturdays were free from work at the train station, and she filled them with housework and family.

An hour later, Maria arrived with her usual treats for the family and something special for the children—today, a bottle of Johnathon Zimmermann's honey to spread on fresh *Brötchen.* Following the Mittagessen at one o'clock, Theo and Thomas went to Thomas's room to play chess, while Lisa pulled Maria into the living room for her violin lesson.

"How are you today, Fräulein Lisa?" asked Maria. "You seemed very serious during the meal. In fact, Thomas was also very quiet. Is anything wrong?"

"No, we're fine. In fact, everything's fine... Vati's fine too." She passed her violin to Maria. "I just tuned it, but it isn't right... Show me what I did wrong."

Maria put the violin on the chair next to her and took both of Lisa's hands.

"Now, tell me what's wrong." Maria looked deep into Lisa's eyes, trying to read her intelligent mind.

"I'm afraid Daddy's dead!" Lisa looked down, trying to hide her tears.

"What does your mother say?"

"She said she believes he's alive, and she said he loves me. She told me to always believe in him, no matter what happens." She raised her head, watching her Oma's reaction as she said, "I felt him in my room last night, and I think something's wrong. Do you think that's possible, Maria?"

Maria was quiet for a moment, then said, "Yes, it is possible, but it's also possible that you had a wide-awake dream. You miss your daddy very much, and he has been away for almost two years. He is fighting in a horrible place, and he can't write as often as we would want. But don't let your imagination ruin even one day of your life; your father wouldn't want you to do that." Maria hugged Lisa, then let her go as she said, "Please don't tell Theo that you think your father is dead... He's sure that Johann is alive and you mustn't make him worry. Your dreams may mean something else or nothing at all. Just because you feel that your Vati is with you doesn't mean he's dead—it only means that you remember him and see him in a special way." Maria and Lisa hugged for a long moment, and then Maria picked up the violin and checked the tuning.

◇◇

As he set up the chessboard, Thomas said, "I dreamed about Vati last night."

Theo didn't say anything. He turned the chessboard around so that Thomas had the white pieces, and his grandson opened the game with the queen's gambit.

A few minutes later, Thomas said, "Vati was in trouble, but he's okay now. He fought a big battle, but he's alright."

Theo listened carefully, then moved his knight.

Thomas smiled. "I couldn't see very much. The fighting was in the dark, and there was a lot of noise. There were flashes, and Vati was lying down in the water so he wouldn't get hurt. When it was over, he went home with some other men."

Theo moved his queen.

Thomas protected his rook with his knight. He smiled at his grandfather. "I like dreaming about Vati, and I'm going to talk about him in Pimpfe today! Whenever I tell them about him, they always tell me how brave my Vati is—they say he's a hero!"

They completed their game of sacrificial attrition in silence. Thomas cornered Theo's queen, and when Theo sacrificed it, Thomas cheered, but three moves later, Theo checkmated Thomas's king with a pawn. Thomas squealed in admiration and, with Theo's help, replayed the elegant trap.

<hr>

On Tuesday, the fifteenth of December, Barbara received a letter from Johann for the first time in months. It had two pages, one typed, one signed. When everyone had finished their dinner, she gave each of the children a bowl of bread pudding and took Theo and Maria into the living room.

"I have a letter from Johann; he was wounded the same day we were all so upset. I know it seems crazy, and I can't explain it."

Maria smiled. "It seems that Thomas has a direct line to his father."

Barbara went on, "Frederick is dead. Johann said he was killed in action, but since they haven't found his body, he is listed as missing." She looked at Theo. "I will tell Siegruna...Johann said I should say that he died fighting with his unit."

Theo grunted. "When you tell her, take a bottle of champagne with you; she'll want to celebrate. She will get the war widow pension and, if she needs it, tell her I will find her a job in the theatre."

Barbara smiled. "Yes, that sounds about right, but the champagne would be a little too much."

"What about the rest of the letter? May we read it?" Maria smiled a wicked smile.

"You can have it all. Johann has stopped writing the things anyone would censor." Barbara passed page one to Maria and the typewritten page to Theo.

Theo quickly read the words on the page...about Johann gladly giving his life for the Führer and the glory of dying for the Nazi cause. His face reddened as he read, and when he reached the bottom of the page, he tore it into the smallest pieces he could pinch between his fingers. Theo stood up, shouted, "*Gottverdammte Nazis!*" went to the front door and yanked it open. He stepped outside, slamming the door behind him. Maria stared at the page she had been reading. "I've never in forty years seen Theo so upset... What was on the second page?"

"The second page was written by the Goebbels *Ministerium von Volkserklärung und Propaganda.* It sounds like the men in Stalingrad are doomed and proud to sacrifice their lives for the *Reich.* It scared me when I read it, but there was no signature at the bottom."

Maria put the first page on the sofa and went to her knees on the floor, trying to pick up the pieces of the second. She began to fit them together but gave up when Barbara took her hand.

"It's not worth it, Maria. Johann will not sacrifice himself for anything but his family!"

Chapter Twelve

20 December 1942

Major König

Stolz und Dummheit wachsen auf demselben Holz.

(Pride and stupidity are the fruit of the same tree.)

COLONEL STIEFF SAID, "General Paulus had a problem; he gave it to me, and I'm going to do my job and give it to you." The Colonel sat behind a camp table in his tent—the tent was set up in a giant warehouse that had lost its roof. The war was almost over for the Sixth Army, and they both knew that within weeks, if not days, the choice would be death or a *Gulag.*

"Sit down, Johann—I'm going to tell you a story." Johann sat in a canvas chair.

"I'm sure you are aware of the success that Russian snipers enjoy, and we both know that I can't tell you anything you don't know about the fortress called *Pavlov's haus.*"

"Yes, sir, we know that area, and we know what the snipers can do, especially Zaytsev."

Stieff stood up, increasing his height slightly. Johann looked at a rifle lying on the table, and Stieff went on, "Zaytsev occasionally visits the building—he's killed dozens of German soldiers from that building, most of them officers. He is more than an excellent shot—that man is intelligent—but more than that, he has the instincts of a fox and the cunning of a weasel. At the moment, Zaytsev is teaching snipers in the field, and he is teaching them well. They have killed hundreds of our men, and we must stop them."

Stieff stopped, and Johann waited for the same old shoe to drop. It did. "We think you and your men might be the key to breaking the chain this sniper has set up."

Johann said, "Yes... Or we might get a few more killed. Where do I find him?"

Colonel Stieff laughed sarcastically. "That's what we want you to tell us!" Stieff began to pace with his head down.

"His full name is Vassily Zaytsev. He is a ghost..." he pointed at Johann... "and you are not to try to kill him; it would be suicide to try. We have someone else for that job."

Johann made a face. "So, why are you telling me about this sniper genius? You are underestimating us—I have men who are as capable as any Russian sniper! Give us a week, and you won't have to worry about Zaytsev anymore."

Colonel Stieff stepped around the table, put his hand on Johann's shoulder and looked into his eyes, clearly patronizing him. Johann turned, and Stieff let go, then resumed his pacing—he could walk four steps before the low tent ceiling met his head. His tiny size turned his marching into a comical 'Charley Chaplin' routine. He stopped, facing Johann, hands locked behind his back. Johann stifled a laugh.

"The Russians have been using snipers to harass us since we invaded them, but it wasn't a serious problem until Zaytsev turned it into an art form." Colonel Stieff resumed his march while continuing to talk.

"In the past few months, Zaytsev and his men have started shooting officers, and it is now clear that we must train professionals to hunt professionals, adding another dimension to this *Scheiss Krieg*. Better late than never, the Bundeswehr has established the Bundeswehr *Scharfschützer* sniper school somewhere close to Berlin. Major Erwin König is the direktor."

Johann crossed his arms. "Why haven't we sent one of his trained snipers to shoot him?"

Stieff put his rear end against the edge of the table and crossed his arms. "We have...five of our best. Zaytsev killed all of them and their observers."

"Obviously, we don't know how to train snipers."

Stieff stopped talking. He didn't blink for a long time.

"It's just as obvious that you are arrogant."

Johann bulldozed on, a man with nothing to lose. "There are exceptional men, but none are immortal, and they all make mistakes. Perhaps we need a bit of arrogance—I prefer to call it confidence—to solve this problem. Whatever we're doing isn't working because mathematically, five well-trained men don't get killed trying to hunt one man, even an intelligent one with the cunning of a fox!"

"Weasel...and your insolence is the reason you aren't a colonel." A slight upward curl of Stieff's lips cut any seriousness from the remark.

Stieff said, with a hint of satisfaction, "Major König is here, waiting outside. He will tell you what he wants from you and your men."

Stieff looked at the tent flap and raised his voice. "Bring the major." A voice behind the flap said, "*Jawohl, Herr Oberst,*" and stomped away.

Less than a minute later, a man Johann assumed to be Major König entered the tent, escorted by an adjutant who closed the flap from the outside and disappeared. Johann stood up and saluted. The man touched the front of his officer's hat, then took it off and plopped it on the table. He offered his hand, pumped Johann's hand once, let it go, and interrupted Colonel Stieff before he could speak. "I'm Major König. Oberst Stieff has told me you will help me kill Zaytsev."

König pointed at the Russian rifle lying on the table, known to Johann and every German soldier who fought them but modified at the bolt and equipped with a glass sight. "That is the Mosin–Nagant sniper rifle. Pick it up and sight on something."

Johann opened the bolt to check that it wasn't loaded, slid it solidly in place and put the butt against his shoulder. The sight fell comfortably in front of his right eye. The top of the tent flap jumped back to him, blurred but distinct enough, and the crosshairs were sharply visible.

Major König pulled the flap aside, and Johann sighted on the inside corner of a brick wall. He could pick out tiny cracks in the mortar.

"All right, Major, nice rifle. What do you need from me?"

"I need you to find Zaytsev for me. Do not try to take him—that's my job...and you may keep the gun."

Johann nodded. Wilhelm would make effective use of the rifle. "We already know where he hunts—just follow the trail of bodies. Give me two days, and I will have his exact location."

<hr>

Johann gave the Russian rifle to Wilhelm, Wilhelm gave it to Ian, and the next day before dawn, Ian and Wilhelm went hunting for Zaytsev's lair. The gun's sight brightened the morning twilight, and Ian picked off two Russians sitting behind a machine gun on a roof. A few hours later, Ian and Wilhelm returned with a second Russian sniper rifle.

The next day, Major König met Johann and his scouts in their abandoned warehouse five blocks from Pavlov's House. Ian and Wilhelm now had three Russian sniper rifles. König put out his hands, and Ian passed one to him. He took a quick peek through the site and tested the trigger. "I see you've filed the trigger release. It's a little touchy, don't you think?"

"I found it in a bombed-out building, and you can blame the trigger on the previous owner. She was not very strong." He didn't smile, but Major König did.

"A woman?"

"No, a girl." Ian continued, "I like the trigger—amateurs don't shoot my gun."

"Touché, Sergeant Kempner. I see you've found another one." He picked up a second Russian rifle lying on a bale of rope. "Another girl?"

"No, an old man." Ian smiled. "I will have another tonight. We've been watching another Russian sniper, and we know where she and her partner live. Tonight will be their last."

Ian sat on a wooden plank stretched across two barrels of nails. "Zaytsev doesn't hunt alone. He uses two sets of eyes—his eyes shoot, while the other pair searches for targets and trouble."

"How do you know this?" König laid the gun carefully on a second bale of rope.

Wilhelm gestured at the rifle. "Before I killed him, I had a short chat with the Russian soldier who owned that gun. I killed his partner with a knife, and the sniper didn't want to die like that, so he told me what I needed to know. Zaytsev has a partner, a woman, and, as of yesterday, they were hunting around the tractor factory. The Russians are still building tanks there, and Zaytsev is trying to discourage us from interrupting production."

"I came from there this very morning...and of course, I didn't see Zaytsev."

Johann, whittling with his grandfather's knife, stopped for a moment and looked at König. "Perhaps that's a good thing, Major. If I were you, I wouldn't try to take him alone. If I knew where he was, I would follow him home and kill him while he slept, or better yet, call in the Stukas, if we still have a Luftwaffe."

König ignored Johann and turned to Wilhelm. "Will you take me to Zaytsev?"

"Only if Johann orders me to do it." Wilhelm looked steadily into König's eyes.

Johann clarified, "You work for me *and* Major König. You should follow his orders as though they are mine." Johann noted that with the end near, his men had lost their shyness around superior officers.

◇◇◇◇◇◇◇◇◇◇◇◇◇◇◇◇◇◇◇◇◇◇◇◇

A week later, Stieff had found a chessboard somewhere and invited Johann to play. The difference between an invitation and an order being academic, Johann showed up on time. Their meal of canned Wurst, army bread, and *Herforder Pils* beer before the game was worth the dangerous ten-block trip from Johann's warehouse to Stieff's headquarters.

Johann sat down opposite Stieff and opened with, "I have news about Major König—it's not good."

"Give it to me then."

"He's dead—Zaytsev killed him."

Stieff stood up, put the knuckles of both hands on the table and leaned toward Johann. "König?" Johann nodded. "How do you know? König is the best we've got!"

Johann corrected him. "He *was* the best we had. Ian and Wilhelm captured one of Zaytsev's snipers and his partner, and they independently verified, after a little persuasion, that Zaytsev killed König. He might have caught the reflection of König's sight, or maybe our sniper genius sneezed. In any case, Zaytsev shot him through a piece of tin from three hundred metres. One of Wilhelm's prisoners claimed he saw König's body—our Major is definitely dead."

Stieff spoke angrily, puzzling Johann. "You trust the word of a Russian prisoner? Whatever they said is a lie!"

Johann spoke softly. "I guarantee they spoke the truth. Ian and Wilhelm interrogated them independently, and their stories overlapped perfectly."

Stieff spoke far too loudly for the situation. "I want to interrogate those prisoners! Where did you take them?"

153

"Sir, our business is getting information—we know how to interrogate, and those men told the truth."

Stieff sat down, blinked tears out of his eyes and wiped them with his sleeve. "Fuck, I hate Stalingrad. And I hate Russia!" He looked at the board. "I gave you black, hoping I might win one." Stieff's voice was full of defeat as he moved the white king pawn forward two squares to e4; Johann slid his opposing pawn to e5. Stieff moved his bishop pawn to f4, wiped his face again with his sleeve and said, "Okay, while you figure out whether to accept or decline the gambit, I will tell you what's going on."

Johann had already decided to decline with Bishop to c5.

"As you know, the Russians' *Operation Uranus* began late in November, and, as of a week ago, they had sealed off all the Sixth Army's escape routes to the west. They are concentrating on our flanks north and south of the city, and they are closing the pincers on the west, leaving only one way out—across the Volga. But what's left of the Russian Sixty-Second Army is trapped between us and the river." He looked at Johann, his eyes clear, his mood back to normal.

"It's difficult to find any reason for this debacle, other than Hitler is allowing the trap to close so we will fight harder. I'm afraid he has miscalculated and is going to sacrifice the entire Sixth Army." Stieff lit a cigarette and offered one to Johann. He nodded, and Stieff lit it from his own.

"I know you've made excellent progress in eliminating the Russian supply routes, and almost all the fortresses have fallen, but it is of no use if we can't finish off the Sixty-Second and cross the river. The Russians have offered their army on a platter, but Stalin is counting on them stalemating us until their pincer forces can squeeze hard enough to force our surrender."

Johann moved his black bishop to c5, and Stieff moved his white knight to f3.

"Aha, the Classic defence," announced Johann. He leaned back when Stieff did, and asked the question every man in the Sixth Army wanted the answer to.

"Is there really no way out? Couldn't a small unit, say a small company of scouts, sneak through the Russian lines at night? Why couldn't we work out an escape route where the Sixth, at least some of them, could fight their way out!"

"Perhaps, but there are several layers of Russians, and they are expecting us to try that. And we would need authorization."

"What about the generals? Have they talked to Hitler? Why wouldn't he at least let us *try* to get out?"

Stieff spread his hands, palms up. "General Hadler warned Hitler a month ago, and he kept it up until Hitler fired him and put General Zeitsler in charge."

"And General Manstein? Is he okay with losing his most effective army?"

Stieff said, "Ah, you mean Field Marshall Von Manstein—he and Göring are Hitler's official lapdogs. Hitler actually offered to allow the Sixth Army to fight its way out, but Manstein told him that the Sixth should keep attacking. He said he would send the Don Army to rescue us, and Göring promised to set up a *Luftbrücke*—an air bridge that would supply food and ammunition to four hundred thousand men...somehow." Stieff shook his head. *"Scheiss Wahnsinn!* Even the lowest-ranked officer in the Luftwaffe knows that's impossible."

Johann went back to the chess game. "So, every Sixth Army soldier is doomed to die or spend the rest of their lives in a Russian prison. Hitler sees this as our *Götterdämmerung*. Hitler should stop listening to Wagner!"

"You've got it right—unless we can cross the Volga to the east." Colonel Stieff pulled hard on his cigarette, and Johann moved his pawn to d6.

Johann asked, "What are our chances?" as the colonel immediately moved his pawn to c3. Johann looked at it for a few minutes before he cautiously moved his knight to f6.

Johann knew he was in trouble when Stieff pushed a pawn to d4 and spoke without looking at the board.

"We are facing an enemy that knows exactly what he's doing, and he is determined to win. We are outgunned, outnumbered, and we are led by a madman in Berlin who can't accept that he could be wrong about anything. If we kill every soldier in the Russian army who is between us and the Volga River, there are half a million men, a few hundred tanks, and a thousand pieces of artillery waiting for us on the other side."

Johann, shocked to hear his commanding officer speak so bluntly, even treasonously, pushed his pawn at e5 ahead, taking white's pawn at e4 to buy time.

Colonel Stieff immediately took Johann's bishop with the white pawn on d4. "You are now a move behind, and I have many more pieces developed...it would be advisable to surrender."

"It's not so bad, although I admit that was a stupid move."

Johann made another stupid move two moves later. Stieff jumped on his pawn and said, "Check." He looked at Johann sympathetically. "Give up, Johann."

"I'm not going to surrender yet—I will find a way out." He studied the board but found nothing good—everything had him checkmate in fewer than four moves.

"Go home, Johann, and take your men with you."

Johann tipped his king and stood up.

"When it is time, I will go. Will you go with me?"

"I'm flying out tomorrow. Hitler has called me back to Army Headquarters in Berlin—I have no idea why. He calls me his *Giftzwerg*...a poisonous dwarf...it appears that I amuse him."

Johann smiled so he wouldn't laugh. Helmuth Stieff was very small, and perhaps that's why he got away with speaking his mind. And maybe Stieff was right... Hitler found him amusing.

"Johann, you are a fighter—you must fight your way out, but you must do it after the surrender, or they will hang or shoot you for desertion."

Johann grinned. "As you probably have guessed, I have an idea of how to get myself and my men out of Stalingrad. I suppose I hang onto hope like everyone else, even when the situation is hopeless. But I like to call it planning."

◇◇◇◇◇◇◇◇◇◇◇◇◇◇◇◇◇◇◇◇◇◇◇◇◇◇◇◇◇◇◇◇◇◇◇◇

Two weeks later, General Paulus surrendered the Sixth Army to the Russians. When he had confirmation, Johann gathered his men around him. It was bitterly cold in the unheated room, and there was no food or unfrozen water.

"As you all know, our orders are to put down our arms and surrender at Mamayev." He looked from one man to another. "Technically, our duty demands that we follow our commander's orders."

"Speaking of commanders, what about Oberst Stieff?" Wilhelm asked. "Wasn't he ready to run the last time you saw him?"

"He left Stalingrad over a week ago, at Hitler's request. If the Russians didn't shoot down his plane, he's in Berlin."

"How convenient... for him."

Johann looked at the faces around the room and waited for comments, but none came. He decided to address the men one at a time and turned first to Wilhelm.

"What are you thinking, Wilhelm?"

Wilhelm lifted his gaze from the floor, looked at Johann from his place on a pile of old canvas tarpaulins. "Leonidas, a Spartan commander, had three hundred men at the battle of Thermopylae; the Persians had thousands! The Persian commander offered him a chance to save himself and his men by surrendering his weapons. What do you think Leonidas's answer was?"

"Didn't the Persians wipe out the Spartans at that battle?"

"Yes, they did, but the Spartans damaged the Persian army enough that they stopped. Leonidas's answer to the Persian offer was, "Come and get them!"" Wilhelm paused. "I want to try and get back to the German lines west of here. I will follow you anywhere, including to hell... But I will not follow you to a Russian Gulag!"

"What about you, Ian?" Johann looked for doubt in his eyes.

Ian returned Johann's stare. "Knowing what our Einsatzgruppe soldiers have done, I can't believe the Russians will let us live—I'm damned sure I wouldn't! I will be going back to Germany, one way or the other. I for sure won't die in a Russian prison camp!"

Johann looked around the room, saw men nodding in agreement with Ian. He stood up, walked over to a post and leaned against it. His men, one by one, returned his steady gaze with expectations and trust. Johann had never felt the weight of command more intensely. When he broke the silence, he was uncertain about his plan.

"I've been thinking about this for a while, and there is a way out. Our chance of success is small, but..." He was trying to convince himself... "we've trained ourselves to survive while living and working in the enemy's back yard."

Johann let his eyes drift from one man to another as he spoke. "The Russians expect German soldiers to follow Hitler's orders—we do have that reputation." Johann wasn't sure what Hitler's orders were, but they certainly had nothing to do with capitulation. Johann was confident that the surrender had been Paulus's idea. "And that gives us an advantage. We are a Jäger Company...we are hunters. The darkness is ours because regular soldiers avoid fighting at night. Both sides think escape is impossible, so no one will be looking for us. If we hide during daylight hours and travel at night, I think we could make it to the German lines to the west. We have no food, and our ammunition is limited, but we have our wits and our skill."

Johann kept his eyes moving as he went on, "I want each of you to decide, and in a few minutes, I will ask for your decision." He sat down on the rope bale and waited. Before he was ready to stand up, Wilhelm stood in front of him.

"We want you to tell us your decision before you ask for ours. You know mine and Ian's, and we deserve to know yours."

Johann looked up at Wilhelm, cocked his head just a little to one side, and said, without emotion, "I'm going back to Detmold, or I will die trying."

A murmur went through the room, and every man agreed.

Johann stood up, nodded, and said, "All right then, we will go home. The first step is to get out of this damned city, and I think I've worked out how we can do that."

Chapter Thirteen

Nine times out of ten, escape is impossible.

Von Zeit zu Zeit errinert uns das Leben daran dass unsere Lebenszeit etwas sehr kostbares ist.

(From time to time, living reminds us that life is something very precious.)

After returning from losing the king's Gambit to Stieff, Johann had sent Ian and Wilhelm to look at options, and they came back with the one he was expecting. Johann had used the information to prepare the route. If the Russians forced Paulus to surrender, Johann's men had a way out.

Two weeks after Wilhelm gave Johann his report, the Russian pincers moved into the city, gripping at the Sixth Army's throat, leaving capitulation or suicide as General Paulus's only options. The Russian line, compressed as it was against the wall of the Sixth Army, was shallow—the distance through it as short as it would ever be. For First Jäger Company, it was go now, or surrender.

Thirty men, all that was left of the Company, gathered around Johann, steam from their breath mingling into an evaporating cloud as they listened to the man they had followed into hell and hoped to follow out of it.

Johann pulled out his worn map of the city and spread it out on the floor. On his knees, leaning over the map, Johann ran his finger along a strip of empty land running southeast to northwest through the centre of Stalingrad. A meandering black line indicated a small brook flowing southeast across the unused land to the Volga River.

"The sewers from the Volga run north and west, parallel to this small brook. There are swamps and trees on both sides, with places to hide during the day. The ground won't support armoured vehicles or soldier transport." He pointed to the street on the eastern side of the brook. "The sewer in that street drains a huge area to the northwest and is large enough to crawl through until we are clear of the fighting front. Since the Sixth Army has surrendered, the Russians will not be on guard for an escape, especially in that area, and, if we use the sewer during the night, we should be behind any alert soldiers by morning."

Johann looked at the faces crowded around him. Ian and Wilhelm knelt on the other side of the map, and the men jostled one another to look over their shoulders.

Wilhelm took over. "Ian and I have scouted the route to the end of the sewer. The plan is to go into the sewer tonight and go as far as we can before daylight. We will sleep in the sewer during the day, and tomorrow night we will follow the brook while it's still dark."

Johann circled an area on the map, then continued the briefing. "The rest is unknown except for what is on the map. It looks like there could be trees there—we don't know their size or how many, but we will plan to sleep under them until the following night. The Don River is close to the Volga in that area, and it will be frozen. When we cross the Don, we will find our army."

The men who couldn't see the map watched Johann. His mood went from concentration to believing in a possibility, then to optimism, and finally, to excitement. By the time Johann had finished, he had convinced himself that they could escape, and the men began chattering as they busied themselves with checking their equipment. They passed oily rags around, wiped their submachine gun's action down and checked and rechecked every magazine. They sharpened their knives and dulled their boots with fresh polish and grease. Every man checked every detail. And then they talked in low voices until darkness fell.

◇◇◇◇◇◇◇◇◇◇◇◇◇◇◇◇◇◇◇◇◇◇◇◇◇◇◇◇◇◇◇◇

Despite the cold night, the clouds were thick, and there was no light. Flurries swept over the ground, twirled to a stop, then whipped away again, their lightness making them part of the fickle wind that deflected from the broken walls of blasted buildings. Faces and guns blackened, the men put on their packs and picked up their Papas. They left the heavy MG-42 machine guns for the Russians, minus a few essential parts.

There was no chatter as they walked out of the building, worked

160

their way southwest and lifted the manhole cover at the foot of the street that Johann had told them would take them to safety. They descended into the sewer, and the last man replaced the cover behind him.

The first three hundred metres of brick-walled ancient sewer was high enough the men could walk in a crouch, but the next manhole changed everything. After the manhole, the walls of the sewer resembled a horizontal wooden barrel. There was no water, but the bottom was slimy, and the smaller diameter forced the men to crawl on their hands and knees. The pipe retained its size for two more manholes, where Johann estimated that they had travelled more than a kilometre northwest. The sewer exiting the opposite side of the manhole was smaller, but still large enough for a man to crawl on his belly. The bottom was dry, and Johann crawled up the pipe far enough that all the men would be dry before he stopped. He whispered "Rest" so softly that only Wilhelm could hear, and he passed it on. The sewer was much warmer than the air outside, the smooth, dry bottom was comfortable, and Johann waited an hour before signalling Wilhelm and moving on. They were already farther from the fighting line than Johann had expected they would get, and they were past the area that Wilhelm and Ian had scouted.

Johann crawled into a square concrete manhole and was tempted to climb the rusty steel rungs cemented in the side. They could make better time on the surface, and in the darkness they would likely be safe, but he told himself not to add even the smallest unnecessary risk. The risk would be less at the end of the line, farther from where he knew Russian soldiers watched the streets.

The wooden sewer continued for another five hundred metres before its size out of the manhole was too small to allow them to continue. Johann whispered, "It's just about dawn. We'll stay here until dark tonight." Wilhelm passed it down the line.

Sitting with Wilhelm at the bottom of the concrete manhole, Johann watched shafts of light from four bright holes in the round cast iron manhole cover creep from one side of the manhole to the other, then disappear as the round brightness faded into the darkness. The short day seemed endless in the cramped sewer, but Johann would not let himself lift the cover, and Wilhelm showed no interest in looking outside.

The holes had been invisible for an hour when Johann climbed the steel rods mortared into the brick side of the manhole. The cover resisted enough that when Johann braced his elbows against it and lifted with everything he had, it didn't move. Pulling his knife out of its sheath, Johann found a crack under the edge of the cover. The sharp tip slid a centimetre under the edge of the iron. Johann pried down gently on the handle, and just when he was going to quit for fear of bending the tip, dirt fell into the manhole. He felt the cover move, but it stopped, and he carefully withdrew the knife. He went to the other side and repeated the process. Twice more, and the manhole cover slid out of its place. Johann held his breath as, supporting it on his fingertips, he carefully slid it to the side.

He raised his head until he could see. It was snowing lightly; there was no light from the stars or the moon. He listened, heard nothing but his own breathing—not a shot nor an explosion came from the direction of the city. Johann crawled out into an empty, quiet black night.

Wilhelm followed him, then Ian followed Wilhelm. They raised themselves to a kneeling position, machine guns ready to fire. The only sound was the movement of the men's clothing and their excited breathing as they crawled out of the manhole.

The street was apparently not important enough to anyone to clear the rubble or snow—there was no possibility that a vehicle had driven down it lately, as the snow was unmarked by man or machine. The men huddled; Ian slid the cover back on the manhole and joined them. Johann noted that the falling snow was rapidly filling the traces of their presence.

"We have a major need for water." Johann pointed downhill, the direction that should take them to the small brook. "I'm not positive where we are, but if we find running water at the bottom of the hill, we are where we should be. If it's there, we will follow the brook upstream for a few kilometres until we find shelter. There will be trees along the edge of the meadow."

The men grunted or nodded in agreement. Wilhelm said, "I will lead, if you don't mind."

Johann whacked Wilhelm's shoulder. "I got you here, didn't I?"

"Anyone can follow a pipe." Johann couldn't see his face, but he knew Wilhelm was smiling. "Right now, we need my German Apache instinct. Let this Teutonic Indian show you the way."

Johann could barely see his feet and was happy to give up the lead.

The brook was where it was supposed to be, and Wilhelm found a patch of shell ice formed by an air bubble. A few taps with the butt of his *Papa* and water flowed into and under the hole. The men drank and filled their canteens. There were bilberries frozen on bushes along the brook bank, and the men spent as long as Johann would let them, picking and eating. Finally, Wilhelm whistled softly, the signal to follow, and a line of thirty men with purple-stained lips, tongues, and teeth followed him.

The brook flowed through and under an open frozen swamp, blown free of snow by icy north winds, the *Siberian Express*. Johann didn't trust the ice over the fast-running water, and Wilhelm agreed to keep to the meadow. There the wind whipped the lightly-falling snow into their tracks so fast the last man could barely see where the first man had walked.

The swamp and the creek continued for two kilometres, then abruptly ended in a thicket of short black spruce trees clinging to the steep bank. Johann and Wilhelm stopped at the edge of the dark trees, and Wilhelm said, "We are more than three kilometres from where we started, and at least five from the Volga."

"And we're clear of the Russians in Stalingrad." Johann finished the thought, nodding. He kicked a little snow from his boot. "And you think this thicket would be a good place to spend the day."

Wilhelm cradled his gun in his crossed arms. "If we go on, we could get into trouble if there's no cover when daylight comes. We might get to the German lines with one more night of walking, but it's for sure we can't get there tonight. My mother told me never to go past a chance to pee or eat because you never know how long it will be before you get another opportunity. I think this is one of those situations."

Although he wanted to go on, Johann knew Wilhelm was right. He stepped around him and pushed two small trees apart, picking his way into the thicket. Snow from the disturbed trees falling down his neck tempted him to exchange places with Wilhelm, but he decided against it. Wilhelm followed him with the rest of the men, working their way up a steep hill, searching for the end of the trees. Johann found it in five minutes. The land suddenly flattened, and the trees stopped, giving way to what looked like the edge of a field. He eased himself back into the cover of the thicket, removed his pack, and laid it on what felt like a level spot. He moved its contents around so he wouldn't break anything and sat on it with his back against a tree. The men scattered, most of them taking care of business before they too sat down. They crossed their arms on their knees, rested their heads on them, or leaned against the small trees. Most of them were asleep within minutes, all of them with a cocked and ready machine gun across his stomach or lying in the snow beside him. Two men took the first watch. Satisfied and hopeful, Johann went to sleep.

<hr>

Grey morning light and Wilhelm's hand on his shoulder woke Johann from a fitful sleep. Mist filled the air; the temperature had climbed above the freezing point, and the wind had changed. Wilhelm crouched beside him—Johann tried to get up, but the big man pressed down on his shoulder. Wilhelm tilted his head, finger to his lips in the universal quiet sign, and Johann crawled in that direction. Hidden by thick branches, he looked across a small field at a level just above the ground.

Through the fog and slowly receding darkness, Johann could see the outline of a T-34 less than thirty metres away—two men, barely visible in the grey mist, sat on the rump, eating and quietly discussing something. As Johann's eyes became used to the twilight and the fog, he saw that the tank, parked on the edge of a snow-packed road, was not alone. Dark outlines of T-34s in a line ahead and behind it dissipated into the greyness.

Wilhelm left Johann and worked his way through the trees to each man. He woke them and quietly explained the situation. No one said anything, and no one moved except Wilhelm.

Johann watched the men on the tanks through his binoculars—he guessed they were no more than eighteen. As they ate their morning ration, their chatter and laughter carried in the fog as though the Russian soldiers were in the woods with them. When Wilhelm joined him, Johann's stomach grumbled so loudly he was afraid the Russians would hear. Whatever the Russians were eating, it was better than the nothing he and his men would get.

A Russian officer shouted an order, and before the sound of his voice died, the first tank fired its engine. Within minutes, every tank pushed smoke out of its exhaust and shook the ground with its cold, rough-idling diesel engine. Infantry came out of the fog, and the tanks began moving, advancing at the walking pace of the infantry. They swung their turrets back and forth to warm the cold grease in the turning circles. Johann counted... Fifty tanks passed him.

"There's going to be a battle somewhere today." Johann watched the last tank crawl out of sight, followed by a line of service trucks towing trailers.

Wilhelm got to a crouching position. "That means the Wehrmacht can't be far away."

An hour later, as the mist lifted, the sounds of battle carried to Johann and his men. The German lines could not be more than two kilometres away—they could see dirt and smoke thrown up by Russian artillery shells.

Johann pointed toward the sound of big guns firing. "Let's find that artillery."

"Okay..." Wilhelm spoke and nodded slowly... "and what do we do with the guns when we find them?" Wilhelm showed his empty palms. "We don't have anything but our *Papas* and a few rounds of ammunition."

"They've got cannons—they'll have some explosives we can borrow." Johann grinned. He was in the mood for a fight. "We've got knives and bayonets... Come on, pussy, let's go!" He moved to step into the field, but Wilhelm pulled him back.

"Johann, please think about it... We should at least wait for darkness. In the daylight, we can't get close to those guns without them seeing us. We've survived this long—why die now and accomplish nothing?"

Wilhelm broke the end off a dry twig and thoughtfully picked his teeth to give Johann time to reconsider. There was no chance there was food between his teeth, so he stopped picking. "How about we wait for dark, kill a guard or two, rummage through their stuff, and who knows...? We may find something useful."

Wilhelm had a point; a day attack would be suicide. Johann blamed hunger for his frozen brain as he said, "Of course, you are right. We work at night, don't we?"

As the battle raged, Johann became more frustrated. He fought his urge to do something and was close to the breaking point when the big guns slowed their firing rate. He made himself as comfortable as he could...it was over eight hours until dark, and he was tired. A few minutes later, the explosions stopped.

<hr>

Johann awoke with a start. The mist had become a few scattered snowflakes, and a howling north wind promised colder weather. He could hear small arms firing, and every few minutes a minor explosion...grenades or mortars. The sun shone between fluffy fast-moving clouds. The temperature, he guessed, had dropped at least ten degrees. He looked around: Wilhelm slept in his crouch position, but nearby a few men were awake. Johann waved to Ian, standing watch at the edge of the trees, and indicated that he would take over. When Ian crept to his nest, Johann settled down to watch the field.

The sun slipped down through the trees on its way to the horizon; the wind increased to a gale from the northwest as a Siberian weather train rolled south.

Darkness brought crisp cold air and renewed artillery activity—staggered shots aimed at specific targets. The moon rose, its pale light reflecting off fresh twinkling snow, softening the hard cold night.

When Wilhelm joined him, Johann said, "Good timing...I was about to get you. Wake the men; we're going to find those guns." Wilhelm touched his hat brim and crawled to the men. When he returned, Johann was ready to go.

"So, how many guns?" Johann wanted to check his own estimate.

"Judging by the flashes, probably about ten heavy artillery pieces—eighty-eights, I think."

Johann shook his head. "I'm guessing a dozen..." He trained his binoculars on the flashes on the horizon... "But I could be wrong."

First Jäger Company hugged the trees growing along the edge of the steep bank, working their way toward the guns estimated by Wilhelm to be less than a thousand metres away. When they were close enough to count them, nine eighty-eight mm cannons were manned by thirty men. There was no infantry, and there were no sentries that they could see. The Russian Army now had a Russian-controlled Stalingrad at their backs and felt no need to protect their rear. Their objective was in front of them... First, the German Ninth Army and then, two thousand kilometres away... Berlin.

All five of the trucks and four tractors parked in the field were manufactured in America. Johann assumed the trucks nearest the guns carried ammunition. Every man in the guns' crews was busy, either firing or carrying ammunition from piles of shells near the guns; none guarded the trucks.

Johann sent Wilhelm and Ian to reconnoitre while the rest of the men waited in the black shadows created by a wall of small spruce trees on the edge of the field.

Ten minutes later, Ian reported sufficient explosive packs in one of the trucks to do the job on the guns. Wilhelm had brought one with him, and, in a few minutes, he and Ian had it figured out. They had also brought their packs filled with *Papa* ammunition, enough to carry out the attack if it lasted an hour!

The assault on the guns was routine for Jäger Company. They shot the gun crews before they could reach their weapons. Then Ian, Wilhelm and a dozen men set charges under the gun's carriages and the vehicles, lit the fuses, and ran.

Ian said as he trotted up to Johann, "Those guns won't fire again." He looked at flashes on the horizon. "I suppose our lines must be over there. All we have to do is get past the damned Russians. I thought we did that yesterday."

Wilhelm asked Johann, suddenly concerned. "You aren't planning to go over there right now, are you?"

Johann knew better than to say yes—Barbara and Wilhelm had a lot in common, and Johann knew that *"You aren't planning to wear that to the restaurant, are you?"* wasn't necessarily a question.

"No, that would be a bad idea. We have no idea what's going on, and in the darkness, we could be killed by our side as easily as we could by the Russians." Johann pointed in the direction of dark quiet, farther up the Don River to their left. "We'll head straight for the darkest spot we can find and cross the river on the ice—it's wider up there, so the current will be slower; the ice will be more reliable."

Wilhelm grunted his agreement, stood up, and led the remnants of First Jäger Company across the field at a slow jog. Johann let them trot past him, then ran behind them. They were back in business, doing what they knew.

Chapter Fourteen

February 1943

Aftermath

To be resurrected from the rumour of death is almost as joyous as the real thing.

Maria and Theo joined Barbara in her living room on Wednesday evening, February third, to hear an important announcement on the German national radio station regarding the war in Russia. Rumours that the Sixth Army had suffered complete defeat had spread like a petroleum fire, and the country braced itself.

While they waited, the regular Wednesday evening programming was supplanted by the Berlin Symphony playing the heartbreaking adagio movement of Anton Brückner's Seventh Symphony—an ominous sign.

An announcer interrupted the music, announcing for the third time that listeners should stay tuned for an important announcement. Theo turned the radio down.

"I'm afraid I have a confession to make."

Barbara, on edge, spoke sharper than she intended to. "Can't it wait, Theo?"

Theo looked at Maria. She nodded.

"We received another letter from the Bundeswehr a month ago that had Johann's name on it, but it wasn't from him. Someone else had signed his name."

"Why didn't you tell me?" Barbara was close to angry, but something told her there was more to this.

Theo looked at Maria again, then went on.

"I didn't tell you because the letter wasn't from him. It was a carbon copy of a typed letter, probably written by Goebbels' office."

"But what did it say?" Barbara tried to hurry Theo.

"It was dated 31 December and, in words attributed to Johann, said, 'We have been encircled by the treacherous Russians, but we are committed to dying for the Fatherland.' Theo waited, but Barbara didn't interrupt. He went on with the words he had memorized. 'We are prepared and content to sacrifice our lives for our glorious Führer and our Fatherland.'"

Theo looked at Maria again. "I burned the letter and didn't show it to anyone because I knew it was another lie from Goebbels' Volkserklärung und Propaganda Ministerium, and I guarantee that Johann has never seen that letter. I wasn't going to tell anyone, but I decided to tell Maria." He checked with her, she smiled. "She agreed that you didn't need to know about it. I am afraid the announcement we are expecting may change things."

Barbara couldn't hide her anger, but she didn't direct it at Theo. "Yes, of course, the letter couldn't have come from Johann! But what kind of heartless person would send such a letter? They knew that the Sixth Army was in trouble, and that letter verifies that they purposely sacrificed an entire army…thousands of men…gone…for nothing! Nothing makes sense anymore."

The music stopped again, and a different voice interrupted.

"We regret to announce that Stalingrad has fallen to the Soviets. The courageous Sixth Army has succumbed to vastly superior enemy forces and to unfavourable circumstances. Stay tuned for further information."

The adagio from Brückner's Seventh Symphony began again.

"That's it?" Barbara was furious. "A whole army—gone? How many are dead, captured? The Sixth Army has hundreds of thousands of men… Surely some of them have escaped!" She hit the radio with her fist, then picked it up over her head.

Theo grabbed the radio before Barbara smashed it on the floor, and Maria put her arms around her.

"I want my husband back! I want him to come home!" She screamed so loudly that Thomas came into the living room, followed closely by Lisa.

"Is Daddy dead?" Lisa's words overlapped Thomas's.

"We don't know." Maria took Lisa in her arms, and Theo pulled Thomas against his leg.

Barbara sobbed and collspase on the sofa. When Theo sat beside her, she pushed him away.

The light in Maria's eyes went out for a while following the announcement, but the optimism of Barbara, ten-year-old Lisa, and eight-year-old Thomas renewed her life. Barbara, convinced that Johann was alive, continued to work at the train station and check the mail every day. She documented everyone travelling to or from Detmold, although she suspected the documents went nowhere. Maria cared for the children while Barbara worked, the *Postmädchen* brought no news, and life went on.

Maria's grandchildren were her life. She gave Lisa a violin lesson every Tuesday and Saturday afternoons on a roughly-built *Ventapane* violin that Theo had found in a pawnshop. Theo gave her Johann's violin case to protect it, but kept Johann's violin, lovingly wrapped in silk material and cared for by Maria. Lisa's natural talent for music, and in particular the violin, enchanted Maria.

Lisa sang in the children's *Detmolder Schlossspatzen* choir and sang to herself wherever she went. Pitch-perfect, she couldn't understand how anyone could play or sing a sour note. Lisa sang herself to sleep every night, and when she slept over at Gartenstrasse 18, she slept in Johann's room, and she and Maria sang Brahms *Volkslieder* until Lisa couldn't keep her eyes open. As the days passed, Maria's eyes began to light up, but a dark shadow persisted behind her cheerful facade.

Tuesday morning, the sixteenth of February 1943, dawned clear, sunny, and warm; spring had come early to Detmold. The crocus blossoms were almost gone. The daffodils, Lisa's pets, were budding in Maria's garden, promising to bloom any day. As she did every Tuesday, Maria walked to Barbara's house to prepare Mittagessen for the family and give Lisa her violin lesson. They were family days—Maria did her thing, and Theo played chess with Thomas.

Maria walked briskly, her little two-wheeled cart bumping along behind her. She followed her usual route, turning left onto Hornschestrasse, past the Lippische Hof Hotel and across Paderbornerstrasse. She crossed the bridge that spanned *Am Wall,* the brook where she and Theo fed the ducks and swans that called the narrow strip of water home. Am Wall was the favourite place in Maria's world, a narrow strip of nature that wound through Detmold, populated by birds, fish, and small animals that had learned to accept humans as safe companions and providers. People walked the path every day, in all kinds of weather, spreading crumbs of bread and grain on the water. Volunteers had built tiny houses for the birds and anchored them in the middle of the slow-moving stream where their eggs would be safe from predators. Maria could identify every duck and swan. She watched them raise their families, live their lives, and then give way to a new generation.

Once over the bridge, the street name changed to Paulinenstrasse, and a block further, Theo and Maria's friend Otto Strang ran his butcher shop. Otto Strang's wife played the viola in Maria's string quartet, and the couples had become close friends. Despite rationing and his dislike of chamber music, Otto always found something special for Maria.

Otto knew Maria's Tuesday morning route well and expected her at the usual eleven o'clock. He had set aside a Mettwurst and two litres of strawberries, berries grown in Strang's private greenhouse. Otto greeted Maria while waiting on another customer, then retreated through the door to the "meat room." He took a half-litre of cream out of the cooler, carefully concealed behind jars of goose fat, the wartime substitute for butter. He put the Mettwurst, cream and strawberries in a cloth bag and waited until the bell on the door clanged, announcing that his customers had left. He went to the counter, put the bag in front of Maria, and she handed him her ration cards. He tore off what he had to, and Maria gave him a big "Danke schön" and a peck on the cheek. He had charged her only for the Mettwurst.

Young Thomas and his grandfather Theo loved *Wurst und Sauerkraut*, and the entire family loved strawberries. The whipped cream would be the *coup de grâce*, and Maria sang to herself as she pulled her little cart along the brick sidewalk and thought of her family.

Rationing made sugar almost impossible to find, but Maria had a substitute—a bottle of her brother's honey. Johnathon Zimmermann lived in nearby Holzhausen and kept bees, supplementing his small pension with the sale of honey and medicinal pollen. He had connived a system of tiny scrapers that removed pollen from the bee's legs as they entered the hive, and he had used it ostensibly to cure people of arthritis and various skin diseases. It tasted awful and caused all sorts of intestinal problems, but Maria's brother left out those details.

No bombs had fallen on Detmold. There were no factories in or near the town, and there were too few people to have any terror value. Maria walked through the narrow streets past three-hundred-year-old Tudor-style houses, still in wonder at the beauty of the black oak beam frames filled in with hand-made bricks. Two neighbouring houses on her route were the birthplaces of the German poets Grabbe and Freiligrath, and Brahms had lived and written some of his music in another of the old houses still standing there. Unfortunately, General Frederick Stroop of the SS was born on a nearby street, and Maria refused to say his name or walk on that street.

Barbara heard the clink of the brass flapper and the rustle of paper that signalled a letter dropping through the mail slot. She left the kitchen to check, wiping her hands on a towel as she looked at two envelopes in the little box that caught the mail before it fell on the floor. Barbara screamed when she saw Johann's name, in his hand, on the return corner of one of them. She threw the other letter on the sofa and tore his letter open.

A twenty-minute brisk walk, a stop at Frau Nagel's Bäckerei, and Maria bumped her little cart up the stone steps at Barbara's house. Theo had a rehearsal but promised to be there for a late Mittagessen.

Maria lifted the knocker on the solid oak door, let it drop, and Barbara suddenly swung the heavy door inward. She tackled Maria in a tight hug that almost knocked Maria off the steps.

"Maria, Johann is alive!" She waved a sheet of paper in Maria's face. "He escaped from Stalingrad!" She pointed at an unopened letter on the sofa. "I got two letters—one is from the Wehrmacht, and this one is from Johann!"

Barbara danced into the house, tears of joy flowing down her face. Maria yanked the cart over the door threshold, slammed the door and tore the letter from Barbara's hand. It was indeed Johann's letter.

Maria nervously tried to read the letter, but tears filled her eyes, and she handed it back to Barbara. "Damn it, Barbara, I can't read without my glasses! Read it to me. I must hear his words!" Maria sobbed, cried, and laughed, then finally gathered herself with a deep, noisy breath... "And don't you dare skip the sweet nothings!"

They sat on the sofa, and Barbara began slowly.

> *"Dearest Barbara,*
> *I've been told that the Wehrmacht has*
> *announced my death without consulting me."*

She put the letter on her lap and shook her head. "He doesn't take anything seriously...." She went on,

> *"Thirty of us escaped from Stalingrad and are*
> *now members of the Ninth Army. I am now the*
> *leutnant in charge of the Eighth Jäger Company,*
> *and I've given Wilhelm and Ian each a platoon."*
> *Including new recruits, I now have thirty-five men*
> *in the First Platoon and forty in the Second. Not*
> *a large Company, but new recruits arrive almost*
> *daily, and I get a leutnant's pay."*

Barbara looked at the wall and smiled wistfully. "I wonder if this means he won't have to go on missions. There must be a limit where the officers stay behind and guide the fighting from a safe distance." She turned to Maria. "Does a leutnant have to carry a gun and fight?"

Maria shrugged her shoulders, said, "No idea..." and rubbed her hands on her skirt. While Barbara pondered, Maria found her glasses in her purse, and, frustrated with Barbara's dithering, put out her hand. "I can read it now. Do you mind?"

Barbara handed her the letter. "Of course not, Maria...please, take your time... I've already read it several times."

Barbara picked up the Bundeswehr letter, dated 4 February.

"We regret to inform you that your husband is missing in action and pre-

sumed dead or captured by the Russian forces in the battle for Stalingrad."

Someone Barbara had never heard of had signed it.

Barbara got up from the sofa and pulled Maria's cart into the kitchen. She alternated between singing and laughing, and she ceremoniously dropped the Wehrmacht letter in the wastebasket on her way past. Maria got up and retrieved it.

Barbara spoke loudly from the kitchen; her voice pitched a whole tone higher than usual. "Hopefully, you've only been shopping for yourself and Theo. I've got everything we need for today's meal." It was a game they played: Maria brought something special on Tuesday, and Barbara counted on it but pretended it wasn't necessary.

Maria interrupted her reading to say, "Just a little something for the children, dear." as she always did.

<hr>

Lisa arrived home from school early and ran into the living room when she heard Maria's voice. She hugged her as though she hadn't seen her for years.

"What did you bring for us, Maria?"

Maria looked up from the letter, passed it to Lisa, tears glistening her cheeks. Lisa took it apprehensively, slowly brought it up to where she could read it. She read for a few seconds, then jumped up and down and screamed so loud it hurt Maria's ears.

"Daddy's alive!" She began crying, and then became quiet as she read the letter, wiping her eyes with her forearm. She read the single-page letter twice before putting it down. Lisa hugged Maria and said, "Maria, Vati's alive! He's really alive!"

Thomas came into the house a few minutes later, and Lisa stood in front of him before he got the door closed.

"We got a letter from Daddy! He's alive!" She held it up in front of Thomas. He took it from her, looked at it, looked at her as if she had committed blasphemy. "Of course he's alive—did you think he wasn't?" He removed his coat and dropped it on the floor, a broad smile plastered on his face. He took the letter with him, chuckling.

Theo arrived at ten after one as always, and Barbara and Thomas met him at the door. Thomas pushed the letter in front of him. "It's from Vati!" Theo's hand shook as he searched in his shirt pocket for reading glasses. He read the letter, then leaned against the doorframe.

"Thank God; he's not even injured. I barely dared to hope."

"*I* knew he was all right!" Thomas piped up, strutting back and forth.

Barbara went over to her son and leaned over to kiss him. He ducked, but she caught him.

"*You* told me he hurt his arm, but he didn't mention it in the letter." She messed his hair.

"He didn't want you to worry." Thomas pivoted to Theo. "I'm going to beat you in chess today." He pulled on Theo's arm. "I figured out a new opening, and I'm going to win for sure!"

Maria put her arms around Theo, and Thomas let him go. Theo and Maria cried tears of joy.

CHAPTER FIFTEEN

24 MARCH 1943

Mosquito!

Coincidence happens all the time; it is the unplanned synchronization of time and events that leads to an unexpected result. And it is the natural order of things.

FLIGHT LIEUTENANT GARNET STEEVES and Warrant Officer Calvin O'Rourke, RAF No 105 Squadron, started their roll on the long east/west runway at Marham in East Anglia. When Garnet had transitioned from the Blenheim night fighter to the Mosquito, it was akin to the commutation of a death sentence. The only hope a Blenheim pilot had against any German fighter was that the German would run out of ammunition or gas, preferably both. The Mosquito was a dream to fly and was so fast that the pilot could choose whether to fight or run. Either choice gave him a better chance than his enemy of returning home.

The Mark IV that Garnet flew was faster than its predecessors and carried four five-hundred-pound high explosive bombs. Two-second fuses delayed the detonation until the bomb tore a hole through the target and embedded itself into the ground beneath it. The high explosives blew upward and outward, vaporizing everything within thirty feet and knocking down walls of buildings a hundred feet away. It was the perfect bomb for Paderborn's railway yards and repair facilities, a small German industrial city two hundred miles across the English Channel.

Mowed stubble of very tough grass and weeds poked through the smooth surface of the compacted gravel runways at Marham Aerodrome, their roots tangled around small stones, holding them in their tight grasp. A goldenrod plant had died weeks ago, and slowly the roots relaxed their grip on a stone half the size of a child's fist. A botched approach had necessitated a pilot's heavy application of brakes, and a dragging wheel had dislodged the stone so that it lay in the path of Garnet and Calvin's Mosquito.

Flight Lieutenant Steeves eased the throttles forward. The Mosquito's propellers turned counter-clockwise, generating a strong 'P' force in the clockwise direction until the aircraft had its tail off the ground. Garnet offset it by combining full left rudder and more power to the starboard than the port engine to hold the plane on the centre of the runway. Three hundred feet into the takeoff run, with both engines at full throttle and the tail off the ground, the nose was slightly to the right of the centre of the runway. The pilot could not have known the consequences the slight misalignment would set in motion, or he would have corrected the minuscule imperfection.

The slight offset in Flight Lieutenant Steeves' takeoff run caused the propeller on the starboard engine to pass precisely over the loose stone, sucking it off the ground and striking it with one of its blades. The propeller's angle of attack and supersonic tip speed reduced the stone to dust, but at the cost of a tiny dent six inches from the tip. Unaware of the stone's demise and the relentless chain of events that the incident had set in motion, Garnet and Calvin continued their takeoff routine.

"Flaps 15, Airspeed ninety." Calvin read the next item on his checklist in a broad Irish accent, and Garnet noted the flap setting in the subconscious recesses of his mind. Calvin continued to read from his list until the wheels and flaps were up and locked, and the aircraft had settled into the cruise-climb that would continue to twenty thousand feet. They held that altitude until they reached land on the enemy's side of the channel, where, on the Wing Commander's signal, Garnet increased the throttle and boost on the two-stage superchargers. The squadron climbed to twenty-five thousand feet and settled on a true airspeed of three hundred twenty miles per hour.

◇◇◇◇◇◇◇◇◇◇◇◇◇◇◇◇◇◇◇◇◇◇◇◇◇◇◇◇◇◇◇◇◇◇

Garnet had flown twenty-two missions in the Mosquito and had seen two German fighters—he had ruined the first one's day before the German had seen him, and had run away from the other.

Nothing could find and catch the light wooden aircraft on low-level missions, flown at under a hundred feet, invisible to German radar. But today, flying high above Hitler's territory, the German controllers at Deelen would dispatch fighters to intercept the squadron. By the time they reached the Mosquito's altitude, Garnet and his friends would have dropped their bombs and be halfway home, going like a bat escaping from hell, and at an altitude well above the service ceiling of the German fighters.

◇◇◇◇◇◇◇◇◇◇◇◇◇◇◇◇◇◇◇◇◇◇◇◇◇◇◇◇

The twenty-four planes in the Mosquito squadron were easily observable dots in the clear March sky, with long contrails pointing to each of them. The Met briefer had promised unlimited visibility to the target and back, and typically, that meant fighters, but German radar operators were not sure the Mosquito targets were bombers. They announced, "Targets, possibly Mosquitos," and let the Deelen controllers decide whether the Luftwaffe would waste gas and time trying to catch them.

The bomber squadron changed course twice in the next ten minutes before settling on a track for Berlin.

Calvin said, "Message from home… We have fighters climbing out of Hamburg and Bremerhaven." His voice showed no alarm.

Garnet checked the oil pressure and exhaust gas temperature; everything was in the green. "It must be frustrating to watch the enemy fly higher than you can."

Calvin laughed. "Those poor Nazi pilots… War just isn't fair."

The Mosquito's Squadron Leader turned for Paderborn precisely as planned, quickly eating up ground. In today's perfect conditions, Garnet had no problem staying on station a hundred and fifty feet to the right and behind the Squadron Leader. The engines droned in harmony, perfectly synchronized, and the day was beautiful. If it hadn't been for a few flak bursts below them and the bombs in the belly of the plane, the flight would have been glorious.

As they approached Paderborn, the squadron formation changed to a staggered nose-to-tail configuration, and Calvin directed Garnet to the target. Officially, the bombing run started when Calvin opened the bomb bay doors, but precise course corrections came from Calvin five minutes before that. When he opened them, the doors' increased drag slowed the aircraft, and the turbulence caused the mosquito to rumble like a train. Calvin bent over the bombsight and waited for the crosshairs to line up over the railway yards.

When the small stone dented the propeller on the Mosquito's starboard engine, it concentrated stresses at that point, starting what the engineering lexicon calls a *fatigue cycle*. Tiny hairline cracks began at the dent then fanned out across the blade, moving in small jerks along the path of least resistance. The tip separated at the exact moment Calvin reached for the bomb release lever.

A twelve-foot three-blade propeller spinning forty revolutions a second creates a tip velocity over the speed of sound. When six inches of one blade suddenly departs, the propeller is wickedly out of balance, generating an unimaginable destructive force, giving the pilot seconds to kill the throttle before the flailing engine destroys the engine mounts and separates from the wing.

When the piece of blade separated, Garnet, without hesitating to guess which engine was self-destructing, pulled both throttles back to idle at the same time he pushed the control wheel forward and banked to the right, away from the formation and the target.

The Mosquito immediately lost three thousand horsepower, and the drag requiring that much power killed a quarter of the plane's airspeed before Garnet could get the nose down. The shallow dive he initiated to compensate for the lost propulsion kept them flying south at two hundred fifty miles per hour and descending at two thousand feet per minute—rapidly eating up real estate and altitude.

While Garnet fought the stricken aircraft, Calvin looked to the engines to find the problem and was concentrating on the starboard engine when it vibrated to a stop. Oil flowed along the cowling's surface and, while he watched, it reached the hot exhaust where it erupted into flames that trailed two feet behind the wing. Calvin turned on the fire extinguisher, and a cloud of smoke and chemical smothered the fire. Unfortunately, the fifteen-gallon oil tank was not yet empty—the hot flammable fluid still flowed toward the exhaust, and the exhaust still had enough heat to ignite it. Calvin pulled the button, but the extinguisher was empty.

The Mosquito passed through twenty-two thousand feet with its right wing on fire; Garnet and Calvin were in deep trouble—trapped in a burning aircraft with half-full fuel tanks mounted in wooden wings. The critical left engine was running smoothly—it would get the plane home, but the fire had to go, and soon.

Garnet saw a single possibility... "Close the bomb bay—I'm going to dive and see if I can blow the fire out!" Calvin flipped the switch as Garnet pushed the stick forward, and the rumbling gradually stopped.

As the speed built, the fire dwindled until it was no more than a glow. Calvin watched the airspeed grow...four-fifty...five hundred...the fire died. Calvin reported to Garnet, "Okay, it's gone," as though a piece of bird shit had just fallen off the wing.

Garnet pulled back gently on the stick. They still had four five-hundred-pound high-explosive bombs behind their seats, and the weight of them combined with the G-force of pulling out of the dive was visibly bending the wings, dangerously close to their breaking point. Garnet could feel the ailerons chafing against the twisted wing...and the strange resistance did not go away when he levelled the plane—the wings were close to failure, and the bomb load had to go.

"Drop the bombs, Calvin, or we lose a wing."

Calvin flipped the door switch, the rumbling started, and he put his thumb on the bomb release switch, waiting for the thump that would tell him the bombs would clear the open doors.

The turn and descent had taken the Mosquito south of Paderborn. A town appeared over the nose, and it had a small railway yard. Garnet said, "Hold that thought, Calvin... There's a target dead ahead." He made a slight left turn to take the Mosquito directly over the tracks. Garnet glanced at the altimeter. Nine thousand feet. At their rate of descent they would be at about seven thousand over the town.

"We're going to drop our load on the railway tracks."

Garnet lined the wounded Mosquito up to fly over the tracks, and as they disappeared under the nose, Calvin pulled the bomb release. The hairs in his bombsight were precisely on the target.

◇◇◇◇◇◇◇◇◇◇◇◇◇◇◇◇◇◇◇◇◇◇◇◇◇◇◇◇

Tuesday, 24 March 1943—Maria arrived at Barbara's house with her cart full of dinner ingredients and a present for Lisa to give to

Angela. Angela would become a teenager today, and Herr Strang had pulled a miracle: he had given Maria the bag of Lindt Swiss chocolate truffles she had in her cart, an impossible feat in wartime Germany. She dragged her cart, thumping up one stone step at a time until she reached the landing. Before she could lift the knocker, Barbara opened the door and grabbed the cart's handle.

"Let me take that." Barbara pulled it over the door threshold. "I told you we have enough, and you shouldn't use your ration stamps."

"Herr Strang and Frau Nagel never take my stamps if I'm alone."

"But you are taking a risk buying *Schwartzspeize*." Barbara towed the cart into the kitchen, and Maria followed, talking to Barbara's back.

"It's only black market if I pay for them; it's okay if they give me a gift."

"You must be careful—there are people who want to earn favour with the Gestapo, and the Gestapo has no interest in your nit-picking arguments."

"I don't know any of those miserable people, and none of them know me." Maria began to unpack the leather bag, and the chocolates came out first.

"For me?" Barbara took them out of Maria's hand before she could pull them back. "You really shouldn't have, Maria; I will get fat!"

Barbara loosened the string on the top of the beautiful white bag and rotated her body so Maria couldn't get her chocolates back.

"Those are for Lisa to give to Angela!" Maria feinted one way, reached around the other, and almost caught a string of the bag. Barbara lifted it high over her head, and Maria gave up.

"I will make a deal with you..." Barbara giggled, dancing away from Maria.

"It doesn't look like I have a choice, but if you eat them, I will tell Lisa on you."

Barbara lowered the bag, peeked inside. "There are more than a dozen chocolates in there...too many for a little girl like Angela—she will get sick." She pulled two out of the bag. Maria lunged, but Barbara put both hands over her head, one holding the chocolate duet and the other with fingers tightly around the bag.

"One for you and one for me?" Barbara smiled the kind of smile that encouraged Johann to give her what she wanted.

Maria laughed. "Alright, but for the record, you forced me to do it."

"It's a deal!"

Barbara put the bag on the table and gave one of the chocolates to Maria. They unwrapped them and reverently held up the treasure inside.

They said, "*Prost!*" together and popped the chocolates into their mouths. Moaning as the sweetness melted, they sighed when the last bit slid down their throats. Barbara looked at the bag again, but Maria whipped it away before she could strike. She took it into Lisa's bedroom and closed the door.

When Maria returned to the kitchen, Barbara was singing a Brahms song about a shepherd pleading at a maiden's door. The maid set conditions before opening it, adding another each time he promised to fulfill one. Barbara's untrained voice was beautiful and clear, proving that Lisa's musicality and perfect pitch hadn't come from only one side of the family.

"I love to hear you sing, Barbara. You make me so happy when you are happy." Maria pushed a stubborn piece of hair on Barbara's forehead back where it belonged. "Don't tell me that one chocolate did that!"

"No, but it helped!" She put her finger on her lip and pulled it down in a coquettish way. "*I* got a letter from Johann…a letter that no one but me is allowed to read."

"It's about time! I was going to write to him about that..." She looked into Barbara's beautiful big blue eyes… "But I see that I don't have to."

Thomas stormed into the house with Lisa hard on his heels. Lisa stomped her foot as soon as she arrived in the kitchen. She pointed at her brother. "Tell him he can't come to Angela's party with me!" With a devilish grin on his face, Thomas stole a strawberry. He popped it in his mouth before his mother could tell him to wash it. "She only invited *me*!"

"I'm sorry, dear, but Siegruna invited both of you." Barbara smiled at her daughter and slid the *Eintopf,* a *Szegediner goulash* dish, into the oven. It was another of Theo's and Thomas's long list of favourites.

"That's not fair!" Lisa stomped her foot again.

"I have a surprise for you to give Angela." Maria intercepted Lisa before she reached her sneering brother. Lisa stopped when Maria gave her no choice.

"What?" She looked dangerously around Maria at her brother.

"Come to your bedroom, and I will show you." She took Lisa's hand and steered her around Thomas—Lisa stuck out her tongue when she passed.

"You know, you shouldn't tease your sister like that." Barbara put the boxes of strawberries on the table and sat down. She pushed a box in front of the chair next to her, then slid a bowl between them. Thomas made a face, sat down, and began hulling strawberries.

"If she wouldn't get mad, I wouldn't tease her."

"Why would you want to go to a party with twelve screaming girls?"

Thomas shrugged as he ripped the green top off the strawberry in his hand. "Lisa wants me to stay home more than I want to, so if I stay home, she has to give me something."

Barbara lifted her son's chin with her hand and turned his head to face her.

"You are a dishonest little boy. You don't care if you ruin your sister's and Angela's party, do you?" She laughed like she knew how to win this one and let his chin go. "I'm going to tell Lisa not to give you anything, and I'm going to make you go to the party."

"Okay, how bad can it be?" Thomas chuckled, and Barbara didn't like the sound of it.

Lisa's squeal and running feet broke into the mother-son moment, and Barbara had to catch her so she wouldn't stumble past.

"Look, Mutti…look what Maria gave me to give Angela for her birthday!" She held the secret chocolates in front of Barbara. "Angela and I are going to be best friends forever and ever!" She put the bag on the table, loosened the string, dumped the wondrous treasure out of the bag, read the label and began counting them.

Barbara exchanged a worried look with Maria.

Lisa finished counting, reread the label, then put the chocolates in a pile. She carefully slid them sideways, one by one, moving her lips as she calculated.

Barbara's stomach turned as she stood up, went to the stove, and opened the oven door. She used a fork to pull out the steel grate under the Eintopf pot and removed the top with an oven mitt. When Lisa's scream split the air, Barbara had the fork in a piece of meat to gauge whether it was cooked. She grimaced as she closed the oven door, and, as Lisa yelled at Maria, took her time turning around.

"They cheated you, Maria! There are supposed to be fifteen chocolates in the bag. Look..."

She held the bag in front of Maria with her finger on a distinct *15 Stücke* written under *Lindt*.

Maria glanced at Barbara with a look that would kill; Barbara turned to the sink and filled a glass of water. Maria turned back to Lisa. "Does it really matter, *Liebling?* I'm sure someone intended to put fifteen pieces in there; maybe they got distracted and lost count."

"I'll count them again, this time out loud." Lisa slid a beautifully wrapped chocolate sideways and said, "One!" emphatically, then, "Two...."

She had gotten to eight when Barbara couldn't take anymore.

"Maria and I each ate one..." She faced her daughter with the glass of water in her hand... "We're very sorry."

"I didn't want to do it..." Maria pointed at Barbara... "It was your mother's fault—she made me eat one of the chocolates so she could eat one."

"You weren't hard to convince!" Barbara tried not to laugh, but a snort came out.

"This is serious!" Lisa stamped her foot. "You both *stole* from Angela! That's very wrong, and God may punish you."

"Well..." Barbara smiled, very close to an outright laugh. "...you don't have to tell her, or God, do you?"

"I can't believe my mother and grandmother are thieves!" Lisa picked up the chocolates one by one and put them in the bag while Maria joined Barbara in a giggling fit that became hysterical laughter.

Lisa had the last chocolate in her hand when Thomas put his hand on top of it.

"I could stay home and play with Gunther...for a price." He grinned at his sister.

"You are worse than Maria and Mutti!" Lisa threw the chocolate at her brother, missed, and Thomas picked it up from the floor. He began to unwrap it, and Lisa grabbed his arm.

"You can't eat it in front of me!" She caught his hand before he had the truffle ready to eat. He smirked his most evil and irritating smirk and headed for the living room. Lisa stuck out her tongue at his back, and he let out an embellished groan of pleasure as he put the chocolate in his mouth.

Theo arrived to find a house full of women in moods varying from laughter to tears, and to a self-satisfied little boy who was ignoring the women and practicing chess in his room. Theo returned to the living room, and Thomas followed.

"Theo, I've got a new opening. Dinner won't be ready for a while, so we can try it." Thomas pulled Theo's hand. When Theo resisted, Thomas said, "I'll tell you what happened when we get in my room."

"Don't you say a word, little man!" Barbara pulled a serving spoon out of the goulash dish in the centre of the table and shook it in his direction, spraying gravy everywhere. "We will tell him what happened, and we don't need your help!"

"Mutti and Maria stole Angela's chocolates," Lisa blurted before Maria could shush her, "and then Thomas made me give him one so he wouldn't go to Angela's party!"

"I don't need to know all the gory details." Theo laughed, turned around, steered Thomas out of the room in the direction of his chessboard.

The dinner, punctuated with snickers and smart comments about the delights of chocolate, was delicious. When Maria and Barbara were ready to leave with Lisa, Barbara brought the family together in the living room.

"Now, Lisa, tell your brother that you still love him and give him a hug." Barbara looked hopefully at Lisa. If she could get Lisa to soften, her brother might follow her lead.

"I think you're a dirty rat!" Lisa said it with as much venom as she could muster.

"And you are a sore loser!" Thomas sneered.

Maria tried to engineer a compromise. "Come on, you two, you can at least give one another a hug."

"I hate him! I would rather die than hug him!" Lisa pushed her brother.

"That's okay with me because I hate you too, and I would rather die than have you hug me!" Thomas wasn't quite as convincing as his sister was.

"I think Thomas should come and play chess with me. I've only got a few more minutes before I go back to the rehearsal." Theo, the peacemaker, steered Thomas toward his bedroom. "Lisa, you should go and enjoy your party with Angela." He pointed his finger at her.

Barbara and Maria each took one of Lisa's hands and headed for the door.

"Do you forgive your mother and Maria?" Barbara bent over and looked at her little girl's face... "Please?"

Lisa smiled. "Are they really, really, really good?" She looked from her Mutti to her Oma and didn't have to wait long for an answer.

"Scrumptious!" both women said at once. "Absolutely scrumptious!"

When they reached Siegruna's house and dropped Lisa off, the screams of little girls echoed into the street. Barbara thanked her friend Siegruna, gave her regrets that Thomas had to do homework, and returned to Maria, waiting in the street.

"I couldn't help but notice that you didn't offer to assist with the party." Maria smiled, then broke into laughter—the full-bellied laughter of a barmaid. Barbara joined her as they walked toward home. When they turned the corner onto their street, they agreed to stop before they wet their pants.

◇◇◇◇◇◇◇◇◇◇◇◇◇◇◇◇◇◇◇◇◇◇◇◇◇◇◇◇◇◇◇◇◇

Siegruna heard the aircraft just before the first bombs exploded. Her brain registered fear, then relief that the bombs had missed her house.

◇◇◇◇◇◇◇◇◇◇◇◇◇◇◇◇◇◇◇◇◇◇◇◇◇◇◇◇◇◇◇◇◇

The fourth bomb had always released a split second after the others. Garnet and Calvin were mindful of it because the plane would jump twice. The second jolt, a split second behind the first, was smaller, but Garnet guessed correctly that it was the bomb that always "hung" a little. He had mentioned it in his report to the mechanics every time

187

they returned from a mission—they put it on the non-priority section of the 'snag' sheet and assured him that they would look into it when they had the time.

Garnet's run took him along the tracks, then over the houses on the south side of the yard. They began at the railway station and followed the tracks' curve. The hung bomb hesitated less than half a second—enough time for the speed of the damaged plane to carry it two hundred feet. The bomb's erratic trajectory took it another hundred feet wide of the target, and it landed in the centre of a house on Wiesenstrasse, where twelve little girls played birthday games.

Garnet trimmed the aircraft to fly straight with one engine and then relaxed. He set the left engine's throttle at sixty percent power; the trip home would take half an hour longer; they could live with that... His worst fear was fighters.

"Jesus H Christ!" Calvin broke out of his reverie with a jolt. Two anti-aircraft shells burst a hundred metres in front of the Mosquito, and then a third exploded ten metres in front of the left engine, and the engine buried itself in an exploding cluster of shrapnel. Two more shells exploded in front of the Mosquito, close enough to punch holes in the wood-and-cloth wing structure. The death rattle in the left engine forced Garnet to shut it down. Immediately, it burst into flames, and he waited for Calvin to pull the extinguisher. When that didn't happen, Garnet reached for the knob and pulled it... The fire didn't go out, and the shuddering airframe approached the ground at a breathtaking rate.

"We're too low to get out! I'm going to ditch it!" Garnet eased the column back to kill airspeed and looked for a field. Calvin didn't answer, and when Garnet found a second to glance at him, he saw that shrapnel had blown out a piece of the canopy and almost decapitated him.

The airspeed was still over two hundred miles per hour when Garnet, heart in his throat, pointed the plane at a field about six miles away. He banked hard to the right, then left, killing airspeed and altitude. He was still going to overshoot, so he raised the nose slightly, put in full right rudder and left aileron. The aircraft stood on its left wingtip and slid downward at a frightening angle. The crossed controls quickly bled the speed, and the plane dropped like a stone. He glanced at the indicator: 110 mph.

The left wing's tanks beside the burning engine still had fuel in them. The wood surrounding them burned at a high temperature, fanned by the hurricane-force wind generated by the descending aircraft. As quickly as the burning wood used oxygen, new oxygen replaced it. The tanks rapidly approached the critical temperature required to detonate the mixture of high-octane gasoline and air. Garnet levelled the wings and began to hope that he might make it. He was less than a mile from a smooth field at least a thousand yards long... He would land without the wheels.

A thousand feet from the threshold, the tank exploded, blowing the left wing off the fuselage. A ball of fire enveloped the cockpit, and the aircraft dropped vertically, exploding as it hit the soft spring grass growing on a field east of the small farming village of Barntrup. The fireball was visible from Sergeant Jürgen Turm's elevated gun platform, and the young men who fired the gun jumped up and down, shook hands and slapped one another on the back—they had their first kill.

Chapter Sixteen

March 1943

Not The Children!

"If there ever comes a day when we can't be together, keep me in your heart. I'll stay there forever."

Winnie the Pooh

A. A. Milne

The bomb smashed through the roof, through the living room where twelve children were playing games. The wall collapsed, leaving Siegruna on the sagging kitchen floor at the edge of a hole. Her confused brain spent its last seconds trying to make sense of the cloud of dust, falling debris and bodies of children. She opened her mouth to scream, but there wasn't enough time—the bomb stopped, buried in the floor of the cellar, and its fuse detonated the explosives precisely as designed. Siegruna's home and everyone in it rose upward in a cloud of dust and debris.

<hr>

Blasts shook the house where Barbara and Maria were having a cup of tea. Theo had gone to work, and Thomas was in his room, teaching Gunther how to play chess—a formidable challenge. None of them had ever experienced a bomb blast before, and they all screamed at the same instant. The direction was unmistakable, and the last explosion brought Barbara and Maria to their feet.

Maria headed for the front door, crying out without sound. She ran down the stairs leaving the door open, then to the street, shouting, "Lisa! Lisa!" Barbara headed for Thomas's bedroom, met him and Gunther in the hall. She grabbed Thomas by the shoulders and pushed him toward the basement stairs. "Go to the cellar! Do you hear me? Go to the cellar!" She let him go and ran out the front door.

Outside, Barbara saw a huge smoke cloud rising above the train station and dared to hope. People ran down the street toward it, and emergency sirens wailed. Bomb blasts were a new experience in Detmold, and those who ran were close to panic. Maria pointed at a second cloud rising from the direction of Siegruna's house, and Barbara's heart sank. They reached the intersection of Wiesenstrasse, turned the corner, and stopped.

Thomas and Gunther caught Maria and Barbara as they rounded the corner—they hadn't followed orders.

Maria slowed to a walk, crying, reaching out for help from an unseen hand. Barbara stood still, fists clenched, her face white, her mouth wide open, screaming soundlessly. Debris littered the street... A cloud of dust was beginning to settle on everything. Siegruna's house was no longer there.

Maria shrieked, "Oh, Lisa! No!" Barbara finally screamed, breathed, gasped to fill her lungs when the sound no longer came. She fell to her knees, sobbing. Maria knelt beside her, and they rocked back and forth in one another's arms.

Gunther and Thomas stood still, paralyzed. Thomas, his face distorted, said softly, then louder, then screaming... "Verdammte Englander…Verdammte Englander…Verdammte Englander!" as he had learned in school. When his brain finally connected the nerves he needed to move his feet, he moved toward the large hole where his sister had been eating chocolates with her friends. He clenched his fists, shouted until his vocal cords could do no more... "Verdammte Englander!"

Barbara rose to her feet, went to him, knelt, and held Thomas in her arms until he stopped trying to scream. He turned away from the hole and sobbed into his mother's blouse.

Gunther stared at the crater that had been Angela's house. Thomas freed himself from his mother and screamed at Gunther, then his mother. "I told her I hated her! I wanted to hug her, but I told her I hated her!" He pushed Barbara away when she tried to comfort him. Gunther stared at him, bewildered. Thomas said, "I didn't even say goodbye!" He slumped on his knees, put his face in his hands, and cried, "I want to hug my sister!" He let out a long heart-rending wail.

All the mothers of the children at the party lived in the neighbourhood. Within minutes, they were there. Friends and neighbours came with them, wept with them, held them in their arms. But there were no words to console the mothers' unbearable grief. The wailing of broken hearts and unrestrained anger rose to a helpless God who could not undo what the bomb had done.

◇◇◇◇◇◇◇◇◇◇◇◇◇◇◇◇◇◇◇◇◇◇◇◇◇◇

For weeks, Barbara cried until there were no more tears, and then she slept. When she ate, she saw Lisa sitting at her place at the table; at night, Barbara saw Lisa going to her room; in the morning, she saw her coming into the kitchen. She heard her playing the violin in the living room, saw Lisa and Maria working on the Mendelssohn Concerto. Barbara wept for hours, until all her tears were gone.

When Thomas heard his mother crying at night, he came to her bed and lay down beside her. She held him, and he stayed until his Mutti slept.

Maria and Theo tried to help, but everything they said changed Barbara's grief to anger, and she rejected them. Barbara turned to Thomas, and, day by day, the anger subsided, but she refused to talk to anyone about Lisa's tragedy.

In early April, the pit containing Barbara's depression deepened, and although Theo and Maria tried desperately to help her out of it, she pushed their effort aside. Maria went early every morning to check on her and help Thomas get ready for school. She cleaned the house, prepared food, and made the beds. And then, if Barbara hadn't gotten up, she clattered and banged around the house until she did. Barbara barely spoke to her, but Maria made Barbara's breakfast and stayed with her until Thomas returned from school.

◇◇◇◇◇◇◇◇◇◇◇◇◇◇◇◇◇◇◇◇◇◇◇◇◇◇

Late on an April evening, Barbara, as had become her comfort, opened a bottle of Apfelschnapps and poured a water glass full, leaving it on the little table beside her bed. The strong scent of blossoms came through the open window—the apple tree was in full bloom. She lay her head back on the pillow, closed her eyes and said Lisa's name for the first time since... She said it again, louder. She tried to connect with her, feel her in the room, but Lisa's face faded.

Barbara couldn't remember the sound of her daughter's voice. She began to shake; she sobbed with her efforts to control it. She sat up, drank the schnapps in three tries. The sobs and shaking stopped.

Barbara tried to sleep, but sleep wouldn't come. An hour passed—the feeling of Lisa's presence wasn't there as it had been every night until now. Barbara rose from the bed, picked up the schnapps bottle, tipped it and drank a long pull.

She let the warmth slide down to her belly, then crossed the floor to the small sink built into the corner. She took a leather bag down from the shelf above it. The strap that held it shut ran through a brass buckle—she undid it, slid it out of its place and pulled the bag open. The light in the room glinted on the back of Johann's nickel-steel razor. She took it out, unfolded it, and looked at the shiny blade for a long time. She drank from the bottle again, put the bag on the shelf, folded the razor, and went to the living room with it in her hand. She laid the razor on the table in front of the sofa, then sat and stared at the heavy blackout curtains. A few minutes later, she stood and went to the cellar.

The bathing room was cold. Barbara lit the paper, wood, and charcoal in the water heater and waited for the fire to burn before leaving the room and going upstairs. She left a lit candle on the table beside the porcelain tub.

Goebbels had dropped his demand that Germans no longer sell or play Lili Marlen, and the record was now in plain sight on the phonograph. Barbara turned it on, lifted and set the needle in the first groove. The familiar music began.

Barbara had not been able to write to Johann about Lisa. Maria had written to him the day after her granddaughter had died, but Barbara's despondence was too deep to allow her to face Johann. She went to the desk in the corner of the living room and slid a piece of plain white paper off the small pile at the corner, lifted the pen out of the inkwell, wiped the excess on the edge. She wrote,

Meine Liebe Johann,

Barbara stopped. She felt Johann's caresses, his loving touch. She smiled. Then she wrote,

Ich liebe dich über alles, aber ich kann die Zukunft nicht mehr ansehen. Dass was ich tun muss, mindert meine Liebe nicht....

Barbara wrote of her love for him, but she couldn't bear to wait for the letter from the Bundeswehr announcing his death—the pain of Lisa's death was already more than she could stand. As she wrote, she sang softly with Lale Andersen, and when Lale's melancholy voice reached the last verse, Barbara heard it as though for the first time, and began to cry. "And, if I should die in battle, I will come out of the still, quiet other world, out of the earth covering my grave. As in my dreams, I will kiss your lovely mouth. In the late-night fog, I will meet you under the lantern, as I have always done, my Lili Marlen."

When the record ended, she lifted the needle and started it again.

The third time she played the record, she stopped singing before the final verse. She folded the letter and slid it into an envelope. She addressed it to Johann, stood up with it in her hand, and smiled as she laid the phonograph arm in its cradle and switched it off. She took the razor from the table, walked across the room and down the cellar stairs into the warm bathing room.

Barbara set the razor and the letter on the table next to the tub and turned on the taps. She slipped out of Johann's bathrobe and stepped into the tub, then slid down the sloped back until her feet were under the rushing water. She leaned ahead, increased the hot water, and let it flow until the mix was as hot as she could stand.

When the water covered her hips, Barbara turned both handles off. The water dripped ever slower as she lay back and looked at the arched white ceiling. The flickering candlelight danced across the rough plaster. The room was silent except for the slowing drip from the tap—it stopped within a minute, leaving a single drop holding tenuously onto the outlet. She took the razor from the table and opened it.

Barbara inexplicably thought of something she had read about American women shaving their legs and under their arms. She laid the razor on her leg, trying to imagine how that would look. Barbara had almost no hair there, but the razor collected a string of soft fine hairs when she stroked it upwards. She felt her skin...it was smooth... It burned where the razor had scraped it. She lathered some soap as she had watched Johann do and rubbed it on her leg, then tried the razor again... It was smoother, and her skin didn't burn. Would Johann prefer that she shaved her legs? Barbara looked at her triangle and wondered whether the American women shaved that too.

Barbara lay back on the slope, thought of Johann, of their lovemaking in the tub. She pushed the thought aside and sat up again, razor still in her hand. She touched the blade on her left wrist, nicking it. The slight pain didn't bother her as much as she had thought it would, and a few tiny drops of blood ran over the edge of her arm into the water, spreading out. Barbara watched it turn the water between the side of the tub and her body red and marvelled at how little blood it took. Leaning back, Barbara looked at the beautiful white ceiling, the candlelight playing games on the plaster. And she felt at peace.

Barbara lowered the blade to her wrist and prepared for the pain...

She felt Johann beside her and imagined his voice. "What about Thomas? What about me? We need you." She tried to push him away, but his presence stubbornly remained.

She pulled the razor away without cutting her soft flesh.

Barbara twirled her finger in the water, creating ripples, waiting for Johann to leave. She began to sing 'Lili Marlen'—softly at first, then louder. Barbara sang as loudly as she could, and when she reached the last verse, she slowed, waiting for the tears. But no tears came.

As she sang the final chorus, Barbara put the razor on the table beside the candle. She imagined Johann lying in the water while she stood over him, his tongue finding her. She unconsciously reached down with her finger, closed her eyes, matched his touch exactly.

Barbara stopped before her orgasm, touched herself lightly and slowly, remaining on the precipice as long as she could. When she felt herself going over, she stopped, breathed slowly and deeply, waiting for the tension to subside. She began again, letting her fingers follow the feeling that Johann was in control. She had not touched herself since Lisa died, and her nerves were electric as she stimulated them. She moaned Johann's name as she arched her back and succumbed. She slumped into the water, closed her eyes...and Johann was still there.

Barbara stayed in the water until it cooled, then dressed in Johann's robe and went upstairs to her room, taking the razor and letter with her. She took the schnapps from the bedside table and emptied the bottle down the sink drain. She thought of Lisa again, but Johann's presence calmed her.

Barbara looked out at the moonlit garden. She felt an overwhelming need to care for her little boy and her husband, and serenity displaced her pain. She relaxed into the soft bed, let her head sink into the pillow and fell asleep, peacefully, for the first time since Lisa's death.

The morning had dawned when Barbara put the razor back in its leather case, tore up the letter and flushed it down the toilet.

<hr>

Thomas bounded into the kitchen, and when he found his mother there, he hugged her and said, "Good morning, Mutti." He looked at the batter his mother was beating. "Pancakes for breakfast?"

She mussed his hair and spoke with a smile. "Yes, all you can eat! Now, wash your hands." She hugged Thomas, and he went to the kitchen sink. "Not there, in the bathroom!" She laughed, and Thomas, giggling, ignored her, ran cold water without soap over his hands and turned to smile at her. Excited, he wiped his hands on the dishtowel, another "no-no." She shook her head and hugged him, swung him around to his chair at the table and patted him gently on the bum. Thomas didn't object when she sneaked a peck on his cheek.

Thomas had his *Mutti* back, and this morning he would get pancakes and honey.

When Maria unlocked the front door, Thomas ran to greet her. Barbara heard him say, "Mutti is happy again, and she is making pancakes and honey for us!"

Barbara showed her face around the corner. "Did you bring milk? I can't find any."

Maria stemmed the flow of happy tears with the back of her hand. "Yes, I brought a litre of whole milk."

<hr>

When Thomas was out the door, Barbara sat down at the writing desk and wrote another letter to Johann. She wrote and rewrote the letter, taking most of the morning, and finally walked to the *Postamt* and mailed it before Thomas returned from school. She smiled all the way home from the post office, humming Lili Marlen as she looked at the daffodils and tulips growing in gardens along the street.

CHAPTER SEVENTEEN

APRIL 1943

Monsters

Krieg verzehrt, was Friede beschert.

(War devours what peace bestows.)

JOHANN SAT ON THE TAILGATE of one of the Lastwagen transporting Eighth Jäger Company westward toward Belorussia. Mired to its axles in mud, it waited for a *demag* half-track to pull it out. A young private handed Johann a letter from the bundle he carried, and Johann saw that it was from his mother. He sliced it open using his grandfather's knife.

> "Liebe Johann,
> I am so sorry that I have to write this letter, but I must. It breaks my heart to tell you that we have lost Lisa. She was at a birthday party at Angela's house when a British bomb struck it, killing Siegruna, a mother who was helping, and all of the twelve children at the party."

<hr>

Johann couldn't suppress a groan. His breath stopped, and, in an instant, he lost his will to live.

Wilhelm sat on one side of Johann, Ian on the other, enjoying a break from slogging through mud. Wilhelm watched Johann's weathered face turn white—watched tears fill Johann's sunken eyes. He waited while Johann's eyes went back to the page.

> "A British bomber dropped its bombs on the railway tracks, but one bomb missed the target and hit Siegruna's house. It is no consolation to me, but the bomber crashed and burned near Barntrup, killing the crew.

Barbara cannot write; she is in considerable distress and will need a lot of time. I go to the house every day to check on her and take care of Thomas, and I will take care of them as long as they need me. Theo and I force ourselves to keep going because we must, but our darling Lisa is all we can think about.

We have attended church every Sunday since we were children, but nothing has prepared us for this…God is somewhere else. There is so much misery everywhere these days, with no end in sight. God is severely testing our faith in Him.

I wish I had words to help you, but I have none. We must go on without Lisa; we must do our work and live for Thomas and Barbara, despite our pain.

Be careful, Johann—Barbara cannot stand any more grief—losing you would leave Thomas without a mother or a father."

◇◇◇◇◇◇◇◇◇◇◇◇◇◇◇◇◇◇◇◇◇◇◇◇◇◇◇◇◇◇

"Johann, what's wrong?" Wilhelm tried to see the writing on the page. Johann didn't try to speak; he doubted that he could. He passed the letter to Wilhelm.

The first paragraph was all that Wilhelm needed to read.

Johann slid off the tailgate onto the ground, took a long deep breath and tried to stifle a sob, but a shaky whimper leaked through his vocal cords. Wilhelm folded the paper, pushed it into the crack where the tailgate met the truck bed, then slid down beside Johann and took his right arm in his firm grip.

Johann shook him off, stumbled into the long muddy field that ran forever away from the road. He kept walking, slipping in the gritless soil until he could no longer see Wilhelm in the gloomy half-darkness.

In spite of the distance, Johann's men could still hear his cries of pain.

◇◇◇◇◇◇◇◇◇◇◇◇◇◇◇◇◇◇◇◇◇◇◇◇◇◇◇◇◇◇

Johann could barely see the ground beside his feet, and it had been dark for hours when he rejoined his men. He had no more time for tears or a broken heart—he had to lead his men. A unit of Russian artillery had begun shelling the encampment, and he knew that Eighth Jäger Company would lead any effort to locate the guns and silence them. Wilhelm already had the orders when Johann walked into the light surrounding his men's pitiful fire.

Wilhelm asked, "Are you all right?"

Johann answered, loud enough for his men to hear. "Don't worry about me. What I need right now is a fight!" Wilhelm observed Johann for a moment, then said, "I'll get the equipment we'll need." He took two men with him and left the group. Ten minutes later, they were back, carrying packs filled with explosives. Johann's Eighth Jäger Company set out in the direction of gun flashes on the horizon.

An hour later, lying in the mud, looking over the edge of a ditch bank at a line of six 88 mm guns, Johann counted a small infantry company guarding them. If he followed standard procedure, he would call in the coordinates and German artillery would do the job. Without discussion, he gave his orders.

"Ian's scouts and I will take out the sentries as quickly as we can, and when we're done, we'll signal the attack. Wilhelm's platoon will then take the guns before the crews know what's happening; the rest of us will take care of the infantry." Johann glanced at Ian and Wilhelm; Wilhelm nodded, but Ian turned away.

Johann tapped Ian on the shoulder, the signal to crawl over the bank toward the sentries they could see sitting in holes around the perimeter. Ian and his men spread out, slithering across open ground.

Johann led the attack, a mission he had always trusted to Wilhelm and Ian. He felt intensely alive—every sense heightened for the battle.

As they neared the relaxed sentries, Johann began running in a crouch, pulling ahead of Ian, straight toward a sleepy Russian soldier who sat leaning over his rifle. He cut his throat from behind, moved to another, killing both inattentive soldiers quickly and quietly while Ian's scouts killed eight men guarding the outer perimeter.

Johann signalled the remaining men of Eighth Jäger Company, and a line of dark figures appeared above the lip of the escarpment, running silently toward him. A Russian soldier spotted one of the dead guards, turned, raised his rifle and Johann, lying in the wet grass with the scouts, cut him down with his machine gun. Wilhelm's platoon then opened fire on the men guarding the guns, killing half of them in a few seconds. They were into their midst before the stunned soldiers reached their rifles. Screaming obscenities, Johann ran toward Russian infantry now directing fire at Wilhelm's men, leaving Ian and his men with no choice but to do the same. Shouting like a madman, Johann emptied a magazine, reloaded, and fired at anything that moved. He fired until almost a hundred Russian soldiers lay dead or dying.

The guns were silent—Johann's men moved around them like ghosts, removing breeches, rigging explosives that would destroy them. A wounded Russian soldier groaned. Johann emptied half a magazine into his chest.

Wilhelm joined Johann, thoughtfully lit a cigarette. "So, are we the Einsatzgruppe now?"

Johann looked at Wilhelm, then down at his Papa.

Wilhelm put his hand on Johann's shoulder.

"I can't imagine your pain, but I assume you still have a wife to go home to. You aren't going to make it, and neither are we if you don't go back to being a soldier. You very nearly screwed up—if the Russians on those guns had turned around when you were running to get to the sentries, some of your men, and maybe you would be dead! Next time, let our artillery take them out."

Johann knew Wilhelm was right, but he couldn't bring himself to say it. Wilhelm's eyes swept across the guns where the men worked. "Johann, you must listen to me. There is no time for this, and you cannot make time. We've been killing men for so long it seems to be normal, but it isn't." He pointed at the men working on the guns. "You have no time to feel sorry for yourself. Half of those men have lost as much as you have, and they must fight when you fight. We must follow you and no one else, so either kill yourself here where you will die alone and for nothing, or help us fight our way back home the way you know how!"

Johann's eyes cleared. His expression slowly changed, and he lifted Wilhelm's hand from his shoulder.

"You're right; I still have a son and a wife to live for." He stared directly into Wilhelm's eyes. "I will find a way to get us home before the Russians get there." He began walking—Eighth Jäger Company followed, gathered in a group around Johann. The guns blew up behind them.

Chapter Eighteen

April–May 1943

The Calm

When war isn't boring, it's terrifying.

Johann put his grief in a box, and with it, Barbara and Thomas. When he tried to see Barbara's face, only a vague likeness came to him. When he tried to write, the words that had always come to him so naturally seemed trite and insincere. He had given up and hadn't mentioned her name in weeks when he and Wilhelm were alone in a trench, and he said, out of the blue, "Why doesn't Barbara write to me?"

"Maybe she can't because of the pain. Perhaps she needs to hear from you."

Johann said, "I need her letter as much as she needs mine!" and immediately felt like a child in a tit-for-tat.

He looked around the trench he and Wilhelm had confiscated, picked up an empty cigarette package and tried to find something else to do. He had oiled his guns yesterday, and his knife was sharp enough to give a decent shave.

Vacated by its talented Russian architect and builder, the trench was luxurious compared to its German counterpart. It had two wide sleeping shelves, a stove, and a simple but effective sloped camouflage canvas cover. Johann could imagine spending a winter there in relative comfort.

Wilhelm interrupted Johann as he began sweeping the plank floor with the broom they had inherited with the trench. "Your wife lost her daughter, and now you are taking her husband from her at a time when she needs him the most. Perhaps she is sick or in shock, or both. She may need you to help her snap out of it."

Johann slapped his broom on the hard wall of the trench.

"That's enough!" He fought the urge to break down in front of his friend. "You don't know anything about my relationship with Barbara, and you don't know anything about me!"

"That's unfortunately true; I don't know anything about how you feel about anything except killing Russians. But I do know about Barbara, Thomas, and Lisa. I've been with you day and night for over two years. We've slept together as often as most married couples!" He laughed at the expression of disgust on Johann's face. "I hate to use the word love when it's between men, but I am closer to you than to my brother." Wilhelm added a note of regret, "And yet, I don't know you."

"You've got a brother?" Johann was happy to change the subject. "You've never told me about any siblings." He went back to sweeping.

"You've never asked," Wilhelm looked at the clean floor of the trench, "and I've never asked you about your family."

"I told you about Barbara and the children—you just said you knew about them."

"No, you didn't tell me; Stieff told me they existed, and he got that from your file!"

"Does Ian know about them?" Johann couldn't remember telling anyone. He had deliberately kept his personal life separate from his soldier life.

"He only knows that you lost your daughter. I haven't told him about Barbara or your son."

Johann felt uncomfortable but didn't know why.

"You must write to her!" Wilhelm poked at Johann with his finger, and Johann leaned on the broom.

"I have no paper. I've tried to write and wound up tearing up every piece of paper I had."

Wilhelm opened his pack and pulled out three folded sheets of regulation paper with the Wehrmacht logo on the top.

Johann put the broom in a corner and took the paper without thanking him. Wilhelm put his hand on Johann's shoulder and said, "I'm going to find some breakfast for us while you write that letter."

<hr>

The sun rose at the edge of the steppes in a blaze of red glory. Flat land stretched eastward to meet a layer of red cumulus clouds that covered the sky from the horizon to where Johann sat in a Russian trench on a wooden Russian ammunition box. It was the middle of the night in Detmold.

Wilhelm gave Johann a pencil and climbed out of the trench. When his steps receded, Johann wrote: *"Schöne Grüsse an dir und die Kinder"* and then stopped to think—he had used the plural of 'child.' He erased *"und die Kinder"* and stared at the rest of the heartless greeting. He decided to begin again.

As Johann carefully erased, his world slowed to a crawl; it took him thirty seconds to eliminate the greeting. The paper was thin, and even with careful light strokes, it would not stand a second erasing—he had one more chance to get it right.

He stood and pulled the canvas back, letting more of the pink morning light into the trench. The lantern Wilhelm had lit before dawn was still burning, so Johann turned off the supply of kerosene to the wick. He thought of Lisa and the Mendelssohn Violin Concerto as he watched the flame become dim, then die.

Johann put his pencil on the paper twice before writing, *"Liebling."* He stared at what he had written for a long time, then read the word of affection aloud. He closed his eyes, and memories of Barbara were suddenly there—the face he had not seen for two years was in front of him. She smiled—he could see that two bottom teeth overlapped slightly, something he couldn't remember noticing before. The slight offset of her nose—one side of her mouth wrinkled a tiny bit more than the other when she smiled—was also something he couldn't remember seeing. Her smile was sad, resigned to something.

He wrote quickly, afraid she would leave.

◇◇◇◇◇◇◇◇◇◇◇◇◇◇◇◇◇◇◇◇◇◇◇◇◇◇◇◇◇◇◇

"Ich liebe dich, Barbara. I have tried to write so many times I've lost count. I couldn't find the words I needed, so I ripped up the pages and threw them away. I know now that I couldn't admit that our Lisa was gone; I was afraid the pain would be too great.

Time has helped, and the men, especially Wilhelm, have been patient with me. To say I've been erratic would be an understatement, and sometimes, I have endangered men's lives with my poor judgment. Today, I can finally face the fact that Lisa is gone, but I find it almost impossible to bear the pain.

Your face is clear for the first time since we crossed the border into Russia, and I remember everything I love about you. I have let you down

205

when you needed me, and I ask your forgiveness. We have lost Lisa, as millions of families have lost their children, but we still have Thomas and one another. Without you, I would surely die, and just as surely, at least some of my men would die with me. I am leading a company of soldiers who count on me to get them through this war, and if I make a mistake, someone dies. My soul is sick, and I need you to heal it. And Thomas needs both of us.

One day, this war must and will end. At the rate we're killing one another, there will be no soldiers left to fight. Every day brings us closer to becoming a family again.

Johann stopped writing, picked up his eraser and poised it above the emotional outpouring. But a feeling of guilt made him relax his hand. He reread the words, *"Ich liebe dich Barbara..."*

He read everything he had written, defeated the urge to change it, and then filled the three pages Wilhelm had given him. He had to use the margin to write his emotional ending. *"Bis wir sehen uns wieder. Bis in die Ewigkeit. Deine, Johann."* He had taken the parting, 'Into eternity,' from their wedding vows.

Johann was sealing the envelope when Wilhelm called out, "It's me; don't shoot, I've got your breakfast!" He walked down the steps and gave Johann an oval-shaped tin container. It was still hot.

"I hope you've been writing a letter to Barbara; otherwise, I want that breakfast back."

Johann passed him the envelope with Barbara's name on it. "Take it to the Feldpost right now, or I may change my mind."

Wilhelm smiled and tested the letter for weight. "All three pages? Is it too hot for the censors?"

"Shut up and get out of here!" Johann swung a half-hearted hand at his friend, almost dumping his wurst, eggs, and hard army bread on the floor. Wilhelm made a show of jumping out of the hole and running with the letter.

◇◇◇◇◇◇◇◇◇◇◇◇◇◇◇◇◇◇◇◇◇◇◇◇◇◇◇◇◇◇◇◇◇◇◇◇◇

Johann and his men specialized in working quietly in the dark, rarely in daylight. They dealt in ambush and surprise, giving their victims little chance. Their reputation for efficiency spread through the Ninth Army, and the newly rebuilt Fourth panzer Army conscripted the Jäger

Company to help with their scouting needs. Replacements had arrived during the long winter, and Johann now had almost two hundred healthy men to command.

The food improved, the scouting became routine, and there was no interference from officers. Eighth Jäger Company's mission was simple—find targets for the tanks and artillery, locate potential threats to German armour, and do the job using their judgment. The mud dried, the roads and fields became firm, and the Russians waited for the Germans to make the next move.

Rumours of peace talks raced through the German ranks, and hope lifted its ugly head. Wilhelm and Johann didn't share such foolish thoughts as Wilhelm asked, "Why wouldn't the Russians attack us right now?" He enjoyed a withered apple that had survived the winter in a farmer's cold cellar.

Johann spoke while Wilhelm chewed. "Wrong question! The right question is, 'Why would the Russians attack us at all?' If they wait until we attack them, they will destroy at least some of our tanks and guns, and we don't have any to spare."

They had bought the withered fruit and a hundred eggs for the food cart from a Ukrainian farmer who seemed happy to get a captured Russian rifle and a box of ammunition.

Wilhelm leaned ahead where he could reach the little Esbit stove. "The Russians seemed weak when we retook Kharkiv and Bolgorod in March, and I don't believe they are in any better shape now." He checked the tea boiling in a tin pot.

"You always ruin the tea. You shouldn't boil it with the tea in the pot. Don't add the leaves until you take the water off the stove!"

"Only sissies drink tea that way. The full flavour comes out when it boils—otherwise, it stays in the leaves."

Sometimes, Johann thought that Wilhelm only boiled the tea to irritate him. No one could drink boiled tea without copious amounts of sugar and milk, and they had neither.

Wilhelm changed the subject. "I heard a rumour that General Manstein wants to attack the Kursk bulge immediately. The mud is almost dry, and if we wait, the Russians will dig in and move in fresh troops." He stood up, held the tin pot by its wire handle and tipped the hot pot with the blade of his hunting knife. Johann held out his tin cup and stopped Wilhelm when it was half full.

"If I drink more than that, it will eat a hole in my stomach." He put the cup on the floor beside him to cool. Wilhelm poured his cup almost to the brim and set the pot back on the Esbit tin stove. Johann shook his head when Wilhelm sipped the boiling-temperature tea.

Johann put his arms around his knees. "Yes, that's the rumour, but Hitler thinks he's a military genius, and even though Manstein wants to attack, he's going to wait for the new panther tanks and the new Ferdinand tank destroyers. The question is, what will the Russians do while they wait?"

Wilhelm took two gulps of his tea, then put it down. "I don't know about the Russians, but I could use a few more weeks without killing anybody... I could get used to peace."

Johann tested his tea and managed a couple of sips without burning his mouth. "It tastes like you used battery acid instead of water!" he accused Wilhelm, who smiled and took a gulp from his cup.

Johann looked at the steaming cup and wondered if it would hurt Wilhelm's feelings if he poured it on the ground. He searched for a place where it wouldn't kill something and said, "Remember how we got Hitler and the Berlin generals all excited when we took Kharkiv, and they wanted to chase the Russians to Moscow? Manheim was the one who talked them out of it; he wanted to wait. Now they're in the opposite positions. Maybe they should fight the Russians instead of each other."

Johann managed to drink a pull of the bitter brew, asked himself why he drank it and said aloud, "I wonder what the hell is going on." He exaggerated his gesture, purposely slopping his tea on the floor. "The Russians always seem to know what we're thinking! It's as though they are reading Hitler's mail!"

<hr>

While Hitler waited, Johann's company scouted the route the Fourth panzer Army would take on their campaign to reach Kursk. The spring sun shone as Johann and Ian, covered with a camouflage net, lay in grass and bushes on a slight ridge. They looked down on men and women, mostly civilians, laying anti-tank mines. They were two kilometres behind the Russian line, and Wilhelm was doing the same on the other end of the mine-laying project.

A hundred metres behind the minefield, groups of workers bailed dirt out of a ditch deep enough to trap German tanks. The workers appeared to be farmers with their wives and kids. The men used Horses to drag steel scoops filled with mud out of holes designed to trap German panzers, then dumped them on ridges where the women and children levelled them.

Ian talked while he looked through his binoculars. "Give them a few weeks, and that line will be a real problem." He swept the binoculars across the construction site. "There must be two hundred workers, and it's only six in the morning!" He put his binoculars down next to him. "Should we count them? I can't think of why we would do that, but German bureaucrats will appreciate a few more pieces of paper, especially if they have numbers on them."

"We've got nothing else to do until dark." Johann laid his notebook and pencil between them. "You count; I'll write."

Johann and Ian observed the work until dark, expecting it to stop for the short night. But when the sun dipped to the northwestern horizon, setting fire to the bottom of a solid layer of apple-blossom clouds, women drove poles in the ground and hung lanterns on them.

When Johann and Ian left, an hour before the morning twilight, the notebook had recorded two-and-a-half thousand mines laid in a thousand-metre by hundred-metre stretch of land the German tanks would need to cross to reach Kursk. At its peak, more than five hundred men and women had worked all the daylight hours and, when darkness came, had continued to dig by lantern light. Workers came and went, but at least half that number was always working. Johann and Ian watched until the workers had finished the minefield, and the ditch was deep enough to stop any tank Johann knew of. The farmers were still digging when he and Ian left their post and met with Wilhelm and a young Finn volunteer.

When they returned to headquarters, they immediately reported to the SS officer in charge of intelligence. Johann had never seen Obersturmführer Michael Hartmann use the Heil Hitler salute. He was the only SS officer Johann had ever seen who returned Johann's sloppy touch on the edge of his standard-issue hat with an equally half-hearted effort.

"What do you have for me, Leutnant?" He took Johann's cloth pouch of notebook pages and dropped them on a pile of similar pouches lying on the desk.

Johann pointed in a general way at the pouch. "I'm afraid it isn't good news."

Wilhelm passed his notes to Obersturmführer Hartmann; he dropped them on the same pile.

"Why don't you tell me what you saw? I'll get someone with more time than we have to read your notes and write a report."

Johann put his finger on a map spread out on the desk. "There is a minefield across our route to Kursk, about ten kilometres long and a hundred metres wide. We counted two thousand five hundred mines in a stretch less than a thousand metres long. Behind the minefield is a tank trap, a ditch that none of our tanks can cross without getting stuck."

Johann stopped, anticipating a question, but the Obersturmführer waited until Johann became uncomfortable and went on.

"Behind the tank traps, infantry and machine guns are dug into very well-built trenches, shooting over the ridge of dirt that came out of the ditch."

The SS officer smiled. "Primitive, as I anticipated. We will be through those defences before noon. What else?"

"There are two lines of defence, sir, and they have five hundred artillery pieces; they look like '88s, sighted on the killing field they've set up."

"We will destroy the artillery with our Stukas."

"If we don't attack soon, they will have a thousand cannons, then two thousand, and eventually...."

"You are insolent, Leutnant."

"Yes, sir, I am, and you are naïve if you think the Russians will stop building their defences." Johann could hear Ian and Wilhelm sucking air. "Sir, ten days ago, they had only one line of minefields across part of our route and almost no artillery. They've hidden hundreds of new T-34 tanks somewhere, but your aerial photographs don't show that."

"They show fewer than fifty tanks, and those are antiques—*Schrotthaufen—Fleischdosen!*"

Johann leaned over the desk, and the Obersturmführer stood up. Johann straightened his back and looked him in the eyes.

"Obersturmführer, you have been here for less than a month; you have no idea what the Russians can do."

"I know they are Untermenschen, and a thousand Russian soldiers are not worth ten Waffen SS!"

"Obersturmführer, you have just proven my point!"

"Then go and find the Russian tanks…" he leaned almost to Johann's face… "if there are any new tanks, and if you know where to look!"

Outside, Johann headed for the demag, walking as fast as he could.

"Scheisskopf!" said Wilhelm, and Ian added, "Arschloch!"

In the coming weeks, Johann and his scouts did as instructed—they found T-34s hidden in patches of woods, buildings, ditches, and in the open covered with camouflage. They found them under tarpaulins, buried in holes, covered with dirt. They photographed hundreds of T-34s, dozens of tank traps, and minefields with thousands of mines waiting for panzers, and Johann piled it all on Obersturmführer Hartmann's desk.

And yet, against the pleading of his generals, Hitler again postponed the battle, choosing early July as a potential jump-off date.

Chapter Nineteen

June 1943

Kursk

"All wars are civil wars, because all men are brothers."

Francois Fenelon

Two hundred panther tanks attached to the Fifty-First and Fifty-Second Battalions arrived directly from the factory in late June. Johann and his company helped unload them, guarded them during transport, and observed the initial trials.

Two of the panzers caught fire before they were off their rail car—another ground to a halt when the driver pulled a steering brake and the final drive snapped with a sound like a rifle shot. Two more didn't make it to the compound before their transmissions failed.

Mechanics traced the fire problem to a faulty gas-line design—the engineers had put it too close to the exhaust. When the exhaust became hot, the line vapour-locked, then ruptured. All two hundred panthers had to wait for the field mechanics to remedy the fuel line design problem by rerouting it. The crews solved the final drive gear problem by babying the tank through turns, and they solved the transmission problem by using less than full throttle and only four of the six gears.

A tank commander who had broken a final drive told Johann that every panther would carry a spare set of gears, and the tank's crew would learn how to change them.

Johann laughed—he thought the commander was joking, but when he scowled, Johann knew he wasn't. Johann asked, with a touch of mockery, "And do you expect the Russians will hold their fire while you change the gears?" Johann's attitude wasn't welcome, and he instantly regretted it. He felt sorry for the men who would fight in a tank that they had to drive gently. The crews saw no humour in repairing a stationary tank while Russian artillery used them for target practice.

The disgusted commander said, "Of course, we have discussed that.

We've considered all our options and have decided that if the gears break in battle, we will get out of that fucking pile of junk and run like hell!" Then he added, "The Russians won't steal them once they find out how useless they are!"

Johann and his men began their role in the battle for Kursk on the night of the fourth of July. They seized high ground held by a small platoon of Russian infantry and set up an observation post to observe and target Russian artillery and tanks. They took it in the dark, quickly and quietly, and without a loss. Johann's Jäger Company was ready when, a few hours later, at 02:00, the Russians thumbed their noses at the Germans by beginning an artillery barrage precisely three hours before the scheduled German attack.

Johann lay on the ground beside Ian, watching shells burst among the German tanks and infantry preparing for the attack.

"Scheisse, that's not a coincidence—they're listening to us!" He rolled on his side to face Ian. "Don't let your radioman say anything you don't want the Russians to hear...use runners if you can. Assume the Russians know when and how we will attack." He rolled back and put his binoculars up to his face. "Maybe we should lie a little."

While the Russian artillery fired, Johann sent a runner back to battle headquarters with a simple code. In the meantime, his men located and destroyed a few of the more vulnerable guns.

Battle headquarters verified the code, and it took only a half-hour for German artillery to silence the remainder, using Ian's mix of false and factual information. At 05:00, in the first grey promise of the morning light, German artillery began their scheduled barrage aimed at the fixed defences, driving the Russian tanks back from the minefield. With the first light, Russian planes flew overhead on their way to attack German airfields, but few returned as the Luftwaffe shot them down as fast as they showed up.

Dawn broke—a bloody sunrise heralded a bloody day as Johann and his men watched Goliaths, tiny mine-clearing robots, carry explosive charges into the minefield. Dozens of them self-destructed, taking at least one mine with them. Others, a more modern version, dropped a timed charge, then reversed out of harm's way. It took the robots an hour to clear a half-dozen paths through the minefield.

At 08:00, the first tanks drove forward while Russian cannons fired at them. Johann and his men radioed the coordinates to the men sighting the German guns and then watched them neutralize the Russian artillery. A few panzers lost a track to a mine the robots had missed, but almost all got across without incident. Bulldozers made short work of the ditches, quickly filling in the tank traps to create bridges that the panzers drove across to attack the third barrier. Machine gun emplacements and dug-in infantry were no match for panzers and StuGs. Dozens of T-34 tanks moved against the German tanks, and artillery, Stukas, and tank destroyers decimated them.

But the Russians kept coming—and coming. They crawled like insects across the open steppes—to be squashed by raw power. By nightfall, Johann and his men were ten kilometres into the Russian lines, searching for Russian artillery and tanks, and it looked like reaching Kursk was a realistic expectation. To Johann, the progress so far seemed too easy, and it looked suspiciously like the bulge at Barvenkovo. The Russian collapse looked suspiciously like a mousetrap.

◇◇◇◇◇◇◇◇◇◇◇◇◇◇◇◇◇◇◇◇◇◇◇◇◇◇◇◇◇◇◇◇◇◇◇◇

Johann's Jäger Company fought best in the dark, and the night of the tenth of July was as dark as night can be. A line of thunderstorms moved through the area, adding rain and noise to the darkness. Major Helmann, III panzer Corps, called Johann to his headquarters, a lean-to designed to keep the rain off his maps and nothing more.

"Johann, I have a problem I want you to solve." He smiled and raised his head from his map. "I need you to take a bridge for me."

"Jawohl, Herr Major. Where do I find the bridge?"

"It's not hard to find. It's over the Donets River, two kilometres that way." He pointed northwest. "Just follow the road. There are a hundred Russians and a couple of tanks guarding this side, and, as far as we know, only forty or fifty infantry on the other side. When you attack, Russian reinforcements will be about an hour from the other side of the bridge. We don't know how many tanks and men the Russians have in reserve, but if you take the bridge quickly, we will be there to help when they arrive."

Johann was skeptical. "All of this depends on your intelligence... Tell me how good you think it is."

"It's as good as any and as bad as the rest... In other words, we won't know anything for certain until it's too late!"

Johann hesitated a few seconds, then asked, "How soon do you need this bridge?"

"We need it at daylight tomorrow. The Russians are moving in behind us, closing the pincer our brilliant generals didn't predict, and I'm afraid that if our Stukas can't take them out, they will succeed, and in that case we will spend the rest of the war in a gulag."

It was a familiar story; the Russians had learned well. Progress toward Kursk had been easy until now—so easy someone with a modicum of intelligence and the whole picture should have recognized it as a trap.

Johann said, "I will get your bridge for you, sir. I need four inflatable boats and four panzerfausts. I've got everything else."

"Take whatever you need." He handed a folded piece of paper to Johann. "No one will question you."

Johann didn't read it; he slipped it into his pocket and saluted. "Sir, I will have the bridge for an hour before dawn. Can I count on you being there before those undetermined numbers of Russian reinforcements arrive?"

"We will be right behind you." The major looked straight into Johann's eyes, as steady as a rock. Johann broke away and went to get his boats.

◇◇◇◇◇◇◇◇◇◇◇◇◇◇◇◇◇◇◇◇◇◇◇◇◇◇◇◇◇◇◇◇◇◇◇

When he had his four sergeants together, Johann explained the problem, and Ian was the first to speak. "I'll take twelve men in the boats, and we'll take out the Russians on the other side. Everything depends on accurate intelligence—intelligence that we didn't gather. Am I right?"

Johann nodded. "Yes, you are right, and the major didn't give me any reason to believe it's accurate, but it's all we've got."

"That's what I thought." Ian shrugged.

Johann went on. "Wilhelm, you and I will take care of the soldiers and the tanks on this side. Do you have a problem with that?" Wilhelm exchanged glances with Ian and nodded. Johann said, "Enough talk—let's get to work." Both men left to get what they needed.

Two hours before dawn, Johann and Wilhelm joined Ian and his four twelve-man squads two kilometres upstream from the bridge. The rest of Jäger Company, a hundred and fifty men, waited in the small trees and bushes growing a thousand metres down the road from the bridge. The night was dark—the only light was an occasional flicker of distant lightning.

It took twenty minutes to inflate the boats and load the gear: four panzerfausts, two MG-42 machine guns, and enough ammunition, grenades and explosives to fight for hours.

Ian grinned and saluted as the boats floated away into the darkness. When they were gone, Johann turned to Wilhelm.

"Ian will take his time scouting and setting up his attack on the other side, and we need to know what we're facing—let's check on what the Russians have on this side." Wilhelm followed Johann straight back from the riverbank until they had five hundred metres between them and the water, then turned to intersect the roadway halfway between where their men hid in the trees and the bridgehead. Wilhelm scurried across the road and, sheltered by the trees on each side, he and Johann worked their way toward the bridge.

◇◇◇◇◇◇◇◇◇◇◇◇◇◇◇◇◇◇◇◇◇◇◇◇◇◇◇◇◇◇◇◇◇◇◇

Johann wasn't surprised when he heard voices and saw lights two hundred metres from the bridge. He stopped and waited before going forward. Wilhelm warbled a nightbird's song, and Johann made a sound that could have been a frog.

Johann dropped to the ground a hundred metres from the bridge and crawled toward the lights. The sound of voices came from two T-34s parked on the road with guns aimed in his direction. He had to assume either Major Helmann's scouts were blind or had never been within a kilometre of the bridge.

He could make out faces in a lantern's light fifty metres ahead of him, and he stopped and waited. A few minutes later, four men came out of a tent. One picked up a lantern and began walking toward Johann—the others followed. When they were twenty metres from Johann, two men in a hole surrounded by sandbags stood up. The lantern light reflected off a machine gun on the top row of bags. Two men replaced the machine gunner and his loader, and the others played out the same routine at another position thirty metres closer to the river.

Johann turned around, crawled away from the bridge until he knew he was safe, looked at his watch and waited.

At precisely the right time, the quiet whistle that sounded uncannily like a night bird came from the other side of the road. Johann joined Wilhelm there, and they said nothing until they were in the trees with their men.

Johann gave his assessment to the men.

"There are two T-34s at the end of the bridge with their cannons pointed this way. I saw two machine-gun placements on this side of the road, and I could see about ten men at the end of the bridge."

Wilhelm said, "A tank is a shitty place to sleep. The crew is in a tent not far from the tanks."

Johann went on. "Yes, you're right, the hatches of both T-34s are open—the men I saw were not the tank crews." He could only see Wilhelm's teeth in the dark, and only when he spoke. He changed the angle so he could talk to his sergeant's silhouette. "If you can, I would like to take the tanks without damaging them—no grenades. Those tanks might be useful."

"That should be possible," Wilhelm said after a slight pause. He looked around at the men who hung on every word. "There are two sleeping tents on this side of the road with room for about fifty men in each, and I found two machine guns. The total force on this side of the river is a short company—about a hundred men. I will need ten men to take those tanks before the crews reach them."

Lightning lit the sky, and three seconds later, thunder rolled. Johann said, "I want seven men to go with me to take out the machine guns on the north side of the road, and Sergeant Bayer will take seven men to take out the ones on the south side. The rest of you will wait a hundred metres behind us. We will try to keep it quiet as long as we can, but if you hear shooting, all bets are off, and we will take the bridge the hard way. If all goes well, Sergeant Bayer and I will return when we have neutralized the machine guns; Then Bayer will take twenty men and attack from the road, and the rest will go through the bushes with me to eliminate the men in the tents."

Johann could only see the outlines of a handful of his men; the rest were vague shadows, and he knew at least a hundred were invisible.

He tried to reach those he couldn't see by speaking louder than usual. "Ian's platoon is on the other side of the bridge, and they will attack at exactly oh-four hundred, hopefully after we take out the machine guns and before we move on the tanks and the men in the tents. Don't shoot across the bridge if you can help it—Ian might come from that direction."

The machine gunners and loaders died soundlessly, and Bayer was already there when Johann reached the trees where his company waited. At precisely five minutes before 04:00, they moved toward the bridge in a crouch. Two rows of men skirted bushes with Johann, a hundred-and-fifty-four skilled men, each carrying a Russian Ppsh 41, a 'Papa.' Twenty men followed Bayer down the edge of the road. When they were fifty metres from the river, and the Russians still hadn't discovered them, Wilhelm and his men sprinted ahead. When Johann's men reached the tents, two Russians sat outside at a wooden table with a lantern between them, talking and playing cards. Three men at the front of the line ran at the Russians, who didn't see them until too late and died in mid-sentence.

Wilhelm quietly killed the men sleeping in a tent near the tanks and, as expected, found empty T-34s. It was 04:00, and Johann took a few minutes to speculate on why the battle on the other side hadn't started. He decided to go ahead with the noisy part of the operation.

The company spread out to attack tents at the riverbank. Flashes of blue lightning froze the scene as over a hundred Russian submachine guns in German hands ripped the tents to shreds. Only a few men got out of the tents, but no farther.

Johann returned to the tanks. Lightning outlined Wilhelm's form on the top of one of the tanks before he disappeared into the turret. Thunder followed the lightning without a gap. The storm was close.

Johann stood beside one of the T-34s with his hand resting on its fender when Wilhelm poked his head out of the turret. Johann moved to where Wilhelm would see him and shouted over rolls of thunder, "Can you start that thing and turn the gun around?" Wilhelm waved his hand and disappeared. Johann suddenly realized his hand was on the tank's track, an excellent way to get killed in a lightning storm. He pulled it away and stepped toward the bridge, trying to see the other side. *Where the hell was Ian?*

A roar started in the woods, far away and faint, but grew and became a curtain of water, flattening trees as it came toward Johann. The wind and rain struck him so hard that he temporarily lost his balance and had to hang onto the T-34's fender.

Wilhelm raised himself out of the hatch, ignoring the water running down his face and back. "We're trying to figure it out. My dad has a tractor, but it doesn't look anything like this!" He disappeared, closing the hatch to keep the rain out. Two minutes passed; the engine rolled over but didn't start. A few seconds later, it cranked again, roaring to life with a hiss from the compressed-air starter. The hatch opened, and the top of Wilhelm's head appeared above the edge. He yelled down at his feet where one of his men was sitting in the gunner's seat: "Swing the turret slowly; I'll tell you when to stop."

The turret swung a hundred and eighty degrees, a jerk at a time, until Wilhelm yelled, "Stop... Back a little... Stop!" His head disappeared—lightning flashed, then a crack of thunder. Johann stood behind the tank. The gun pointed down the bridge's left lane, two to two-and-a-half metres above the deck. Wilhelm's head appeared, and again he yelled: "A degree to the right and lower... Stop! Lower... Stop!"

Lightning lit up the bridge.

Johann yelled at Wilhelm. "Get your head down; it's a fucking lightning rod!"

Wilhelm shouted above the rolling drumbeat of torrential rain, "We've got the gun loaded, and we're ready to fire as soon as... Hey, we just found what seems to be the trigger, but I don't think we need to test it."

"Get out of there, Wilhelm. Leave it running and set up the other tank. Teach someone to load and fire the other tank's gun—we might need them both." He had to shout over rain bouncing half a metre above the bridge deck.

Wilhelm climbed out of the hatch, slid down the front armour plate and jumped clear of the tank just as a hiss, a blinding flash, and blue fire danced across the tank's armour plate. Simultaneously, a loud snap, sharper than the sound of an '88' firing, numbed Johann's hearing. Wilhelm smiled and touched his cap as he passed Johann on his way to the other T-34.

Fifteen minutes later, the tanks were ready to fire, with three men in each. One of Wilhelm's men was a Finn and had trained on tanks, but Finland lost their tanks a few days into the war against the Russians. His unit managed to steal one from the Russians, and since he could speak Russian, he could read all the labels on the switches and levers. They used the tank until they ran out of gas. The man figured out the driving system and the gun, instructed a second man on the 75 mm cannon, picked out two drivers and gave them basic instructions on how to move the tank. Wilhelm put the drivers in the seats, ready to pull away if necessary. The second gunner was a good pick—he was trained in the Finnish Army to fire the howitzers they lost in the first week. Two other men got a crash course on loading the gun.

Wilhelm had just proclaimed his tanks ready for battle when Ian and his men emerged out of the downpour, walking down the river toward Johann. Ian joined him between the tanks and the bridge.

"Tell me again... How many Russians did Helmann say would be on the other side of the river?" Ian was not in a good mood.

"A few, maybe fifty."

"And tanks—what about tanks?"

"No tanks...the tanks are an hour away. We don't know how many."

"Well, the Russians have a surprise for him! Two, maybe three hundred Russian soldiers are dug in and waiting on the other side of that fucking bridge! And they've got a dozen T-34s." He waited for Johann to say something, but Johann was thinking, so he continued the rant.

"We grounded our boats upstream and worked our way down to them. If you ask me, and you did, someone told the Russians that Helmann is coming. They're waiting for him in trenches, and they've picked a damned good spot for an ambush!" He waited for a moment of silence in the storm. None came. He yelled over the pounding rain and thunder, "You ruined their plans when you killed their friends on this side, and they won't take that very well. My guess is they're probably going to try to kill us. When did you say Helman would arrive?"

Johann stared at Ian and said, "Soon... he'll be here soon. And yes, that's what they'll try to do. We had better get ready to spoil that." He had a plan. He would need Helmann's artillery.

Johann decided to conduct the battle from the turret of one of the T-34s while Wilhelm commanded the other. Ian would lead Eighth Company fighting the Russian infantry.

Rain hammered the ground and beat the leaves off the trees. Constant lightning and the continuous roar of thunder created the same chaos as an artillery barrage. Johann could barely hear Ian when he yelled in his ear. "I'm going to set up all five of our MG-42 machine guns where they can hit whatever comes across that bridge! We'll use the sandbags scattered around here to build a wall on the bridge and we'll hide grenade launchers and panzerfausts behind them." Thunder covered the next few words, but Johann heard enough to know that Ian's men would take a heavy toll on any force that tried to cross the bridge."

Johann said, "Okay, set it up, but do it fast." He pointed at the T-34s. "Wilhelm and I will try to kill a tank or two on the bridge. Maybe we can block it until Helmann shows up."

Ian smiled sarcastically. "Do you expect Helmann to be on time? He might postpone the battle because of the weather. He doesn't know that he might lose his bridge if he's late!"

Johann pulled out his pocket watch. "He was supposed to be here thirty minutes ago."

The rain slowed, the lightning became intermittent, and clacking tracks and powerful diesel engines across the river filled gaps in the rolling thunder—now reduced to the sound of empty wooden barrels rolling over a rough floor above the men's heads.

Johann said, "We'd better get ready," climbed on Wilhelm's tank and gave him the bad news. "Ian reported that at least two hundred Russians are waiting for us on the other side, and they've got a dozen tanks. Ian didn't show himself, so they don't know that we know they're there. I think there's a good chance they will wait for the rain to stop or at least slow down before they get things figured out and attack. Helmann might even get here in time to help us!"

Wilhelm looked pessimistically along the tank's gun barrel at the blackness where the lightning had shown the bridge should be. When it flashed again, it found relief in the ground a kilometre to the east, and by its momentary light, Johann glimpsed the bridge covered with men carrying sandbags. The Russians would also have seen the preparations, and would understand what it meant.

Wilhelm said, "Let's hope Helmann gets here soon... a dozen T-34 tanks will do a helluva lot of damage if they get across the bridge!"

"Are our maps and radio in that tent?" Johann pointed at the nearest tent.

"Yes. I sent them there to keep dry."

Johann slid down the front of Wilhelm's tank, picked the first man he saw and asked him to bring the maps and the radioman back to him. "I will be in that tank." He pointed to the tank beside Wilhelm's.

When everyone was in the tank, Johann closed the hatch, then cranked the cover up enough to see under the edge. The raised cover leaked. The gunner sat in his seat—the loader, the radio, and the man to operate it filled the rest of the cramped turret. Johann pulled the map out of its waterproof pouch and spread it on the front of his legs. He picked the coordinates for the other side of the bridge, memorized them, folded the map and returned it to the pouch.

"Get Helmann on the radio." Thirty seconds later, the radioman handed the receiver to Johann.

"Helmann here!" The signal was full of static, probably lightning, but it was clear enough to understand the Major.

"I need artillery. Your intelligence isn't worth a thimbleful of hen shit. Half a battalion of soldiers and at least a dozen T-34 tanks are waiting for us to cross the bridge. We have this side secure, but they will catch on and come to get us. Can you give support fire, and when can we expect you?"

"I can give you four 88s whenever you want them...you have the frequency. Lightning has set fire to a couple of tents, and the wind is tearing everything apart. We will be late—at least another hour, more likely two. You are on your own until then. Can you hold? Over."

"*Sheisse!* Understood. We will do our best... Hell, we'll get it done somehow! Make sure the 88s are loaded and pointed in this direction. When I say 'fire,' I need the shell to land a few seconds later! Out."

Johann handed the receiver to the radioman and recited his memorized coordinates. The radioman wrote them down on a cigarette pack, then held it in front of Johann, who checked them and nodded.

"Wait exactly five minutes, then fire one for range. Do not let them fire more than one shot before I return!"

Johann pushed up the hatch and climbed out. The rain fell heavier than it had at its worst, accompanied by a wind that threatened to blow him off the tank. He slid to the ground and ran to Ian.

"I've got a round of 88 coming in to get the range. Pull the men off the bridge."

When the gun fired, the exploding shell lit up the other side of the river. The shot was fifty metres to the right and too close to the bridge.

Ian looked at his boss. "Seventy-five metres farther would be nice, and fifty metres to the left. Then fire for effect."

Johann nodded. Ian tried to look through his binoculars. "How many of those do we get?"

"We have four guns for at least fifteen minutes...maybe thirty rounds, maybe more."

"We'd better make them count." Ian wiped the lenses with his sleeve and looked through the binoculars—lightning flashed, closer now. "They're coming—you had better get in your tank..." Lightning flashed again. "Fifty metres longer would work better...those T-34s are almost to the bridge."

◇◇◇◇◇◇◇◇◇◇◇◇◇◇◇◇◇◇◇◇◇◇◇◇◇◇◇◇◇◇◇

Johann climbed on the tank and lay beside the open hatch. When the shadow of the first enemy tank appeared, driving toward his tank on the precise path its gun was sighted on, Johann put his face in the turret and yelled, "Fire!"

The tank rocked, and the shell hit the slow-moving Russian in the centre of the front armour plate, scooted up the slope and pried a hole under the turret. It exploded inside the turret, and the tank commander flew out of the hatch, followed by a flume of flame six metres long. The tank clattered to a stop.

Wilhelm's tank fired, and a tank driving onto the bridge in the other lane blew up, its turret flipping into the river. Fire from the burning tanks lit up the bridge, allowing Johann to see Ian and his men run to the sandbags to prepare for the inevitable.

Johann shouted at the wide-eyed radioman, who had retreated to a corner.

"Tell the artillery to adjust up fifty metres and fifty to the left." He gave him the new coordinates and said, "Fire two rounds." The man's hands shook as he spoke into the receiver.

Johann tried to keep his binoculars dry enough to be useful but had to give up. Without binoculars, he could see four tanks facing him, two approaching each side of the bridge. They fired, guessing at the position of the rogue tanks. Two shells landed on the shore, thirty metres from their target. A pair of German 88s two thousand metres behind the battle fired, destroying one tank and blowing the track off a second. The flash lit up two more tanks, climbing onto the bridge with infantry around and behind them.

Johann said to himself, "They can't see us." He shouted into the turret, "Tell the artillery to drop the elevation twenty metres and fire everything they've got!"

Thirty seconds later, the other side of the bridge lit up, and even through the rain, Johann could see bodies and pieces of tanks flying through the air. He saw one of the T-34s take a direct hit, opening it up like a can of meat—another disappeared in a wall of mud, then reappeared lying on its side.

He waved at Wilhelm to hold his fire, and the T-34s that had made it to the bridge drove straight at the destroyed tanks blocking the lanes, using them for cover. When they reached them, they tied cables to the smoking hulks. When the line attached to the wrecked tank tightened, it skidded to one side, leaving the other T-34 in the open. Johann fired—the shell hit the tank in front of the rear sprocket and blew the track off. Wilhelm's shot hit his target behind the turret, igniting the fuel tank.

Before Johann could reload, the crippled Russian tank swung its gun and fired. Wilhelm's tank took the full impact of the shell, and Wilhelm disappeared, sucked into the black wall of the night.

Johann shouted at his feet. "Fire—fire before he reloads!" Seconds passed—the loader swore—the gunner yelled, "Hurry!" and a streak of fire came out of the barrel of the Russian, straight at Johann. The shell struck the side of the turret opposite Johann and deflected off, exploding on the road a hundred metres behind the tank.

Johann rocked back as his cannon fired. The shell pierced the T-34's armour plate—gas and flame forced its way out of every crack on the tank.

Constant lightning lit up Russian infantry climbing over their comrades' tanks. Two T-34s drove fast along the riverbank, heading for the bridge. One of them met an 88 mm shell before reaching its objective, and Johann's loader yelled "ready" just before the gunner fired and hit the other tank squarely on the side plate. The T-34 stopped. Men poured out of the hatches.

Johann yelled into the turret, "Tell the artillery to stop firing!"

A new threat roared over the sound of machine guns, grenades, and panzerfausts—the howl of an angry dragon. A wall of wind crossed the bridge and tried to suck Johann out of the tank. He put his hands under the lip of the hatch and pulled himself down into the turret. The wind lifted the hatch cover, and then gravity clanged it shut. Johann was only vaguely aware of the gunner saying something over the roar outside.

"What in hell is going on?" The gunner swung the turret, looking through his sight. "Men are flying through the air...some are going over the side of the bridge!"

Johann's mind fought to return to the battle, but he wasn't sure what or who were they fighting.

And then, just as quickly as it came, the dragon moved on. Johann lifted the hatch and pushing his head through it. The night's blackness had yielded to grey.

Shadows slashed at one another on the bridge, ignoring the storm. Fire streaked out of machine guns; black figures, rifles extended, ran at the men behind the sandbags, climbing over their comrades' bodies with bayonets fixed. The rain pelted the men as they fought for their lives. It ran off their bodies, cleaning the blood of their wounds and the enemy's. Shadows ran around and over the wrecked tanks, pouring toward the sandbags like a river.

Johann screamed at the gunner, "Use your machine gun on the Russians...fire at them!" The gunner mowed down the men running toward the sandbags like cutting long grass with a scythe.

Johann yelled at the loader, "Pass me a Papa, and when I pass it back, hand me another one..." The man laid a machine gun in Johann's open hand.

Johann targeted the Russians attacking Ian's men, picking off the closest ones while the gunner sprayed those farther away. The flow of men slowed as the pile of bodies grew.

The gunner called out that he had no more ammunition, and Johann emptied his last magazine, but the battle was over. Ian and his men shot the few Russians who still tried to resist.

◇◇◇◇◇◇◇◇◇◇◇◇◇◇◇◇◇◇◇◇◇◇◇◇◇◇◇◇◇◇◇◇◇◇◇◇◇

Silence fell like a blanket—the greyness won the battle against the night, and the last storm clouds drifted overhead as Johann slid down the front armour of the T-34. His radio operator followed him; Ian left his men to join Johann.

"The sun's coming up...." Ian pointed at a sliver of red inching its way above the horizon. "It looks like another hot one." As the men watched, the sun crept up, shooting blood-red light on the bottom of the remaining clouds, reflecting on the surface of the calm river. The dragon had gone back to its lair.

A man cursed in Russian; a Papa fired; a body splashed in the river.

"Let's go find Wilhelm." Johann led the way to the other side of Wilhelm's tank. Wilhelm was there—his legs were gone—he was dead. Johann turned and looked at the smoking turret.

Ian said, "I'll get someone to clean it out and take care of Wilhelm." and turned toward the men checking Russians for life and dumping those who had none over the side of the bridge. They put the wounded in groups on the sides of the roadway.

The reverberation of German tanks approaching the bridge from behind him brought Johann to the side of the road, and he walked to meet them. When the column of panther tanks and infantry reached him, Johann waved them past. They rumbled onto the bridge and rigged cables to drag the steel T-34 coffins out of the way. Helmann's infantry helped Ian's men clear the deck ahead of them. A demag APC stopped beside Johann, and Major Helmann greeted him from the passenger side. He spoke while looking at the carnage on the bridge and the bodies floating in the river.

"Did you leave any for us?"

Johann looked at the sky, ablaze with a spectacular sunrise. "You're late." He slapped the side of the demag. "I lost half my men; one of them was my best soldier, and he was my friend."

Ian and a helper carried Wilhelm's body to Helman's demag and loaded it into the back seat.

Johann said, "His name is Sergeant Wilhelm Neumann, and he's from Stuttgart. I want you to personally see that he gets home to his father." Johann tipped his hat brim and walked away, water sloshing in his boots.

◇◇◇◇◇◇◇◇◇◇◇◇◇◇◇◇◇◇◇◇◇◇◇◇◇◇◇◇◇◇◇◇◇

Johann spent the morning sleeping and the late afternoon walking, scouting ahead of Kempf Detachment and Leibstandarte's northeast flank. It was evening, the darkness wasn't far away, and he led Wilhelm's platoon; Wilhelm's natural successor had died in the tank with him.

Ian and his platoon moved ahead on Johann's right flank, and Johann's thoughts went to Wilhelm. He walked alone, chasing away those who wanted to walk at his side. He watched the sun retreat in a fading blaze as the night began to cover its red glory.

"Why don't I feel anything?" Johann spoke to the new night. He felt that someone was listening, so he continued. "I suppose I loved Wilhelm as much as a man can love another man, so why don't I feel sad?" No one answered.

Twice, Johann stopped and signalled his men to get down—his sixth sense was working overtime. He sensed someone was watching them, but nothing happened; nothing interrupted the night sounds. He heard a night bird warble, a sound so familiar that he waited five minutes before the feeling disappeared. And then he stood up and waved his men forward.

CHAPTER TWENTY

12 JUNE 1943

Heads they win, tails we lose

A true soldier fights not because he hates what is in front of him, but because he loves what is behind him.

G.K. Chesterton

IN THE GRAY PRE-DAWN LIGHT of the twelfth of June, Johann's Eighth Jäger Company walked uphill toward Prokhorovka, looking for Russian T-34 tanks. Convinced this would be the place the Russians would choose to hit the Germans with everything they had, Johann split Eighth Jäger Company into four groups to look for the Russian armour and artillery, and within an hour, they found them. Johann mapped the information, fitting it together until he thought he understood the Russian plan. Most of the tanks they found had their engines running, positioned to attack down a long slope to where SS II panzergrenadier Battalion waited. At 06:30, Johann called Leibstandarte headquarters to explain the Russian tanks' position and how he expected them to attack.

At 06:50, the panzer IVs and panthers of II panzergrenadier Battalion began working their way up the hill to meet the Russians, and the Soviet infantry withdrew ahead of them. At 08:00, Russian guns at the top of the slope began firing; the Germans spread out and kept moving. At 08:30, the artillery barrage stopped, and Russian tanks started down the slopes. Johann's scouts fired purple flares, the agreed-upon signal that Russian tanks were moving.

Five hundred Russian tanks and tank destroyers attacked in two waves, three hundred metres apart. At first, infantry rode on the Russian tanks, but they left them when the T-34s had to pick up speed. Clumps of tanks charged into the spread-out and badly outnumbered German panzer ranks.

And then, the Luftwaffe appeared; Stukas and FW190s attacked the Russians from nowhere and everywhere, flying between the low clouds and the trees, giving Russian anti-aircraft guns no time to sight on them. The T-34s drove fast and erratically, creating challenging targets but travelling too fast to fire accurately. Despite that, the German fighters and guns managed to pick a few of them off, and when groups of T-34s stopped to shoot, the German artillery batteries and StuG III and IV mobile guns found them, with disastrous results for the Russians.

With little or no infantry support, Russian artillery became victims of Wehrmacht Jäger units. Their scouts passed the guns' coordinates to ground-attack fighters and artillery, whose overwhelming power then devastated them.

<hr>

When the battle ended, the Eighth Company soldiers worked their way back to headquarters. It was dark; isolated shots broke the night silence, and Johann's company followed gullies, grass-choked ditches, and groves of trees. Towing tractors and healthy panzers pulled damaged tanks to safety, weaving around still-smoking steel carcasses and broken and bent pieces of what had been machines designed to kill men. Men's corpses lay where cleanup crews had sorted them—Russians in piles, Germans in rows, waiting for Lastwagen to haul them away. Specialists checked for life before cleanup crews piled dead Russians on top of their comrades.

"How can they keep coming?" Ian stopped beside a heap of at least a hundred Russian soldiers. "Where do they come from?"

Johann felt his first pang of grief for Wilhelm as he looked at the heaps and rows of dead students and engineers—and musicians like him.

"They are defending their homes, and no matter how many we kill, they will keep coming until there are no more of them or no more of us."

Ian nodded toward four Russian tanks, one of which looked undamaged except for a perfectly round seventy-five-millimetre hole in its side under the turret. "I've been counting Russian tanks and tank destroyers—they lost eight to one of ours. I know they have more, but surely we'll overrun them tomorrow!"

Ian's voice hinted at desperation—he wanted to be right.

Johann couldn't keep sarcasm at bay. Suddenly exhausted, he looked at the piles of bodies and said, "I wouldn't count on it. We threw everything we had at them, and despite what our generals say, they stopped us. I'll bet you my grandfather's knife that tomorrow, even if we can kill as many Russians and destroy as much equipment as we did today, we won't be any closer to Kursk. If I must tell the truth, I have to say that I don't think we'll ever get there."

When Ian responded, he kept his voice low enough that the men around them wouldn't hear.

"We must take Kursk or retreat... so you're saying the Russians will win the war!"

"I am telling you what I see—nothing will change because nothing has changed since the Russians chased us out of Stalingrad."

Johann stopped walking; Ian pulled up beside him. Their men gave them space but stopped and looked at them, waiting for something but understanding nothing.

Johann said, "When we escaped from Stalingrad, I believed we could reach home; I was even confident I would see Barbara and my children again. But since then, I've changed my mind." He wound his arm around the horizon. "What do you think Hitler means by Lebensraum? We all know what the Einsatzgruppe is doing to Russian Jews and Bolsheviks to get that room.

"The Russians will never allow Germans to stay on their land. And the Ukrainians who welcomed us, believing we would liberate them from Stalin, are now our enemies because we massacred their friends and neighbours. The Russians will chase us back across Ukraine, and the Ukrainians will fight us for every metre of land. We taught them to hate Germans worse than they hate Russians, and that's no small feat! Stalin starved a few million Ukrainians to death in 1932 and '33, an incident the Ukrainians call the Holodomor, just a few years before we shot another million, give or take a few hundred thousand, so now they hate all of us!"

His voice rose; his men listened. "Lebensraum, in Hitler's mind, means that we will kill all the Russian and Ukrainian Jews and communist bureaucrats so Germans can take over their farms and factories. If the Russians were occupying our country, killing our friends and family, murdering our wounded men, stealing our land, how long and hard would we fight?"

Johann, aware that he was losing control, turned away from his men. He had gone too far, and he regretted it. He turned to Ian. "Scheisse, Ian, you know what I'm saying."

"Yes, you are saying you miss your daughter and Wilhelm...."

Johann took a deep breath, shook his head, and returned to his rant.

"If you take everything away from a man, then tell him you're going to kill him and his family, you are leaving him no choice except to fight to the death! Whether that man is English, French, German, Jewish, or Russian, you are forcing him to fight you until his last breath. The power you think you have over him is an illusion—you can't win, even if you kill him. There will be another one, and they will keep coming; they will build planes and panzers, and eventually, you will tire, and then they will kill you.

"If you want someone to yield to you, you must leave him with something precious to lose if he doesn't do it—better yet, promise to reward him if he joins you. Hitler has given the Russian and Ukrainian people no choice but to fight us to our death or theirs. They have everything to gain and nothing to lose by fighting to the last man, woman, and child—and they have three times as many of them as we do."

Ian softened his voice as he would when comforting a child. "Despite your theory, annihilating one side is and will never be an option. At some point, the government of one country or the other will stop the war before it destroys them. We may not win the battle, or for that matter, the war, but we will still survive as people."

Ian put his hand on Johann's shoulder. "In Stalingrad, when the situation was hopeless, you promised to get us home..." He looked around at the men who had stopped and were now listening to every word... "and we believed you. If you give up now, what becomes of us?"

◇◇◇◇◇◇◇◇◇◇◇◇◇◇◇◇◇◇◇◇◇◇◇◇◇◇◇◇◇◇◇◇◇◇◇◇

A week later, Kursk was no closer; Russian tanks and men kept coming, and finally, Hitler gave up the offensive and ignominiously retreated. The Russians claimed victory, and Hitler moved half the German forces to Italy to defend that failing front against the Americans. Johann had lost half of his company, killed or wounded—the highest attrition rate in the Kempf division. He was happy to withdraw.

Behind the lines, Johann and Ian sat opposite one another in the darkness outside their Russian-built bunker, unable to sleep in the hours they usually spent fighting or skulking around looking for Russians to kill.

Ian asked, "Do you still miss Wilhelm?" He sat on his pack with his back against a big spruce tree, closely watching Johann as he waited for his answer.

Johann tried to decide what the answer should be and concluded that the truth wouldn't do.

"I certainly miss his abilities, but I can't say I've thought of him—I've been concentrating on keeping the rest of my men alive, and unfortunately, I haven't succeeded."

Johann sat on a canvas chair, using his grandfather's knife to whittle a big stick down to a small one.

Ian asked, "Would you forget me so easily?"

"I didn't say I'd forgotten him… He was my friend." Johann stopped whittling. "I don't give a shit if you remember me, and you won't give a shit if I remember you either—when you're dead." He examined the stick and then began carving a notch. "So, are you the philosopher now? Are you going to replace Wilhelm's nagging with your own?"

"And now you're a cynic? You've changed your mind; you think we won't make it home."

"I would rather think of myself as a pragmatist. When you're dead, there is no more, and nothing matters. Home could mean anything."

"But no heaven, no hell…no meeting your loved ones?"

"If there's a heaven, there has to be a hell, and when God finds out what we've been up to, we will burn there!" Johann laughed. "You'd better hope I'm right about there being neither!"

Ian laughed politely. Johann waited for him to take his turn, but Ian sat in silence.

Finally, Johann said, "I had a nightmare last night—I have a lot of them now, but this one was different."

"I have them too, but they are normally hard to figure out. I wake up in the middle, and there is never an end to the story." Ian snapped a dry stick. "What kind of nightmare is different?"

"I saw little fingers sticking through slits in a wooden wall and an SS soldier pointing a machine gun at Barbara and Thomas. The fingers had crying, pleading voices, but I couldn't hear what they said. The scene was so clear I woke and couldn't get back to sleep because the picture had stuck in my mind."

Ian waited. The full moon used black trees to create dark shadows. It would be a lousy night to hunt Russians.

"Okay...did the SS soldier shoot them?"

"I don't know. Barbara yelled something. There were other voices, and women screamed, but I couldn't understand what they were saying."

Johann pulled a sharpening stone out of his pocket, spit on it, and made circles in the spit with his knife.

Ian said, "Dreams don't mean anything." He put a piece of spruce gum in his mouth, then made a face. He tried to delicately pick a little piece of bark out of the gum but dropped it in the spruce needles that covered the ground.

Johann tested the knife's edge with his finger. "You're probably right, but they still bother me—I guess it's all the throats I've cut."

Ian said, "It's not so much killing men who would kill us if we didn't kill them... It's killing the helpless ones that bothers me." Ian bent over, felt around his feet for the gum, found it, meticulously removed the dirt and needles and put it in his mouth. He chewed it in what seemed like a pattern, then spit it out. Johann made a quizzical face, and Ian said, "I'm cleaning my teeth like the Indians do it."

Moonlight glinted off the bright enamel on Ian's teeth.

Johann put his knife in its sheath and threw the stick into the darkness. "You know, I think we might make it home."

Ian grinned and said, "Yeah, I know that."

Chapter Twenty-one

18 July 1943

Weil Sie Juden sind

(Because they are Jews)

Don't break their hearts and expect them to love; don't crush their souls, then tell them to be happy!

It was the fourth year of a worsening war, but Maria felt a joy she hadn't felt in months. She sang a Brahms lied that she had often sung with Lisa as she pulled her cart toward Barbara's house. Time had dulled some of the pain of losing her—enough that Maria could wrap herself in the memories of Lisa that accompanied the little song of a flirtatious maid and a young shepherd. She smiled as she sang despite tears that found the path of least resistance on their way down the curves of her face to fall on the brick sidewalk.

On this eighteenth day of June, the weather was sunny and warm, a hardly-ever occurrence in Detmold's average June. Today, Herr Strang had supplied the usual extras despite the Gestapo cracking down on black market activities. Publicly, he had decided to lay low for a while, but privately, among friends, nothing changed.

Strang the butcher and his wife owned a small farm with a few meat animals and chickens. They looked after it themselves and sold the trackable farm's production through proper channels, but gave their surplus to whomever they wanted, and fortunately, Maria was high on that list. It was technically illegal to grow food and give it away outside the ration card channels, and the Gestapo rewarded tattletales well if their help resulted in the arrest of those who cheated. The Office of Commerce and the Economy employed the Gestapo to stop black market activity, and those they caught faced an uncertain and sometimes painful future. Consequently, there were few repeat offenders.

Thanks to Herr Strang, Maria and Theo had more than most

Germans. Every Tuesday, Maria's friend put enough food in her little cart to feed the family for days.

Every adult German received cards of ration stamps from the Wirtschaftsamt, the 'office of commerce'…yellow for fat such as butter and margarine, blue for meat, green for milk, red for bread, and brown for tobacco. In the fourth year of the war, the coupons provided sixteen hundred calories per adult per day, but only if one used every coupon. The merchant had to reconcile the coupons he received with the goods he sold by glueing the coupons to a cardboard sheet. He received his product allotment based on those sheets of stamps. When his customer paid for the product, the vendor used scissors to cut out the appropriate ration stamp.

As with all regulated shortages, a black market grew out of the law, and less well-off Germans sold as many calories as they could eliminate and still sustain life. Brown coupons fetched the most money, then blue. The rich ate well—the poor ate what the coupons they could afford to keep would buy, and to fill their stomachs, they ate unrationed potatoes—lots of potatoes—prepared in dozens of innovative ways.

Maria was fifty metres from Barbara's house and thinking about Lisa when she saw Barbara running toward her. Barbara grabbed Maria's arm and bent over, gasping for breath.

"Maria…people…dying…in rail cars…at the Bahnhof!" she cried out, almost screaming, "We…must help!"

Maria stood her cart up, let go of it and leaned over to support Barbara. She wasn't sure she had heard right. She asked, "Dying people? What people?"

Barbara, hands on her knees, sucked air into her lungs so hard her vocal cords vibrated in a moan. "Jews…hundreds…locked in cattle cars."

Thomas, running from the same direction as Barbara had come, grabbed Maria's hand and pointed in the general direction of the train station.

"Maria, they're locked in the train—we must save them!" Thomas's frantic, beet-red face, streaked with tears, looked up at his grandmother and then at the cart. "Please, Maria, we must get some food and water… They can have mine!" He leaned back to get leverage as he pulled on her hand; she braced herself to keep from falling.

Confused, Maria suggested the first thing that came into her head. "I've already bought bread... It's in the cart, and I have stamps to buy more." A picture of Yvonne flashed into her mind. She had been in Auschwitz, but her captivity had begun in a holding compound in France, where French Pétain soldiers had herded her and hundreds of others into livestock cars. Those cars could have passed through Detmold.

Yvonne had described arriving in Auschwitz, half-dead from starvation and dehydration—sick, and filthy. She had told stories of terrified children torn from their mother's arms and taken directly from the train to the gas chamber—and the operation took place under the order of a man who was the camp doctor! Yvonne had described their screams, and Maria had cried.

Thomas grabbed the cart from her, shouted, "Come on!" and ran toward the station. He pulled the cart so fast that Maria feared the wheels would come off. He looked back, eyes wild, yelling, "Come on! Run faster!"

Barbara stopped and shouted as he left them behind, "You take the food, Thomas. Maria and I will get more bread and some water." He didn't turn around or slow in the least. She softly added as she swallowed a sob, remembering that Yvonne had said many in the rail cars had died of thirst, "They will need water—they will need a lot of water."

Maria followed her into the house, and as fast as the water would flow, they filled a ten-litre milk jug and a large pot. Barbara filled a sack with everything edible that she could find, then put it in the cart she took to market every week. They arranged a place for the milk jug, and Maria carried the pot as they returned to the street. Word had spread, and other women ran toward the train station with their arms loaded.

The shortest route to the railcars was through bushes growing on a slope between the siding and the road. Children, unwilling to walk an extra hundred metres to cross a pedestrian bridge, had trampled a forbidden path across the tracks to their destinations.

Barbara and Maria held hands, their sense of balance better together than apart. Despite that, Maria slipped on the rough stones and fell, upsetting the pot, spilling the water and pulling Barbara to her knees.

Barbara stood and lifted her, then locked her free arm around Maria's until they reached smoother ground.

∞∞∞∞∞∞∞∞∞∞∞∞∞∞∞∞∞∞∞∞∞∞∞∞∞∞

Barbara located Thomas, bent over beside a rail car, tearing at the buckles on Maria's cart while hundreds of wiggling fingers competed for his attention. Children's cries echoed from behind the fingers.

Barbara put down the milk jug so she could help Thomas. Maria tried to pull the top off, yanking at one side, then the other. She said, "Scheisse" every time she pulled, frustrated at gaining less than a millimetre with each cycle.

The stench drifting through gaps between the boards was overwhelming; the openings were there to keep animals from suffocating on their way to the slaughterhouse, and the smell passing through them told everyone there were no bathroom facilities in the cars. Pitiful cries echoed over the area between the railcars and the trees—cries in French and bad German begged the dozens outside to help the wretches locked in the cars. Thomas reached into a cloth bag filled with two loaves of bread, pulled one out, tore off pieces and put them in the tiny hands reaching through the cracks.

The hands cut their skin on the rough boards; splinters stabbed them as the children tried to pull their fists back through the narrow cracks while clutching the bread, dropping most of it. Thomas picked it up and attempted to return it to the hand that had lost it. He wiped his tears, working hysterically; there were too many hands and fingers to feed them all.

Barbara found a stone the size of her fist and tapped the edges of the milk jug's cover while Maria lifted it. The cover yielded, and Maria dropped it on the ground. Cries for water came from everywhere. Barbara looked at the board wall and wiped her face, desperately trying to think of a way to get precious water through the small cracks without wasting it.

Maria said, "I've got an idea!" She tore the hem off her dress, soaked a strip in the water and put it in a tiny hand. It disappeared behind the boards, and when she had wet a second strip and given it to another hand, the dry first rag reappeared.

Barbara ripped at her dress, imitating Maria's genius—they now

238

had a repeatable system. Others watching them replicated and improved the procedure. Forming a line, one woman passed wet rags to waiting fingers; another retrieved them, and two soaked them again. When the water ran out, women carried it from the train station—a system developed without apparent leadership. The water flowed steadily to waiting fingers, the cries lessened, and the people in the cars soon learned that it went faster if they took turns.

Thomas settled in a rhythm, passing a rapidly dwindling stock of bread to the little hands, using his small fingers to push larger pieces through the cracks so hands could get them on the other side.

He took a second to get his mother's attention and asked, resuming his work when she looked at him, "Mutti, do you know who these people are? Why are they in those dirty cars? What did they do?"

"Sie haben nichts getan…nur…Sie sind Juden," she said softly, "They did nothing wrong…they are only Jews… They are French Jews."

Thomas tore the last loaf of bread apart, pushed a small piece through a crack, and put a chunk between two fingers. "But what did they do? Why are they here?"

Barbara shook her head and looked at her son. "Weil Sie Juden sind! They are only here because they are Jews!"

Thomas began to tear pieces from a tube of Mettwurst, desperation driving him to work quickly. He muttered to himself, "But why? I don't understand."

Barbara heard him but had no answer.

When dozens of people arrived, the guards faced the choice of ignoring them or shooting them, and the soldiers chose to turn their backs and step away. They avoided confrontation and stood in a group smoking, chatting and avoiding looking where they would see their mothers and sisters committing a crime. The women didn't ask them for help—standing aside was enough.

A constant flow of new arrivals brought food. Volunteers ran to local shops to buy more, collecting precious ration cards and money from those who had it—no one kept track. The rescue grew to a hundred people working to help the people in the railcars. Many more brought food and water. When the soldiers showed no interest in stopping them, two old men found rocks and beat at the locks and hinges, but rocks weren't enough. A soldier came to help them, but when he aimed his gun at the lock, his comrades pulled him away.

The yard was in a state of organized chaos when a young SS officer crossed the tracks from the station, flanked by two soldiers armed with machine pistols. Ignored by women engrossed in the rhythm and necessity of their work, he stepped up on a rail, balancing himself on the highest point he could find. He shouted, "Hau ab, dumme Kühe!" Leave here, you stupid cows! A few glanced at him and then worked faster, but most paid no attention to him at all. He took his Walthers P38 pistol out of its holster and fired two shots in the air. Most turned to look at him, then looked at one another to see what their neighbour would do. And then, without pause, they returned to feeding the hands and fingers. The old men continued their search for a way to open the doors.

The SS officer stepped between the rails, took a machine pistol from one of his men and fired a burst in the air. Again, most stopped and turned to face him, but they made it evident in their expressions that they thought of him as a nuisance and unworthy of respect.

He missed the mood entirely when he said, "That's better. Everyone must leave immediately, and there will be no trouble!" He gestured to the Wehrmacht soldiers assigned to guard the train, still gathered like a school of fish. "Do your job—remove these people!"

The soldiers reluctantly turned toward the women, and the women picked up stones and turned to face the SS officer. Barbara had one in each hand, and Maria, closer to him, picked up a stone and confronted the young man. Maria twisted her face in an expression Barbara had never thought she was capable of. And then Maria stepped doggedly toward the SS officer, now only a few paces from her, screaming, "No, you leave!" and pointing at him with the extended index finger of her left hand. She drew her right hand back, aiming the stone.

The officer ducked when he should have done something else, and the badly thrown stone caught him on the front of his SS hat, knocking it off his head. He pointed at Maria and stepped back as she picked up another missile and cocked her arm. He held his arm rigid, pointing at her as he shouted without looking away, "Shoot her!"

The two soldiers with him levelled their guns at Maria. She stared from one to the other with an expression that dared them to shoot. They hesitated—the officer shouted, "Shoot her!" The soldiers lowered their guns. The officer screamed, "Shoot her or I will shoot you!" and lifted his Luger.

Barbara stepped in front of Maria, and Maria pulled her aside. The women at the front of the train began to walk toward the SS officer, increasing their speed as they closed the distance. Those who were late starting, ran to catch up to the line of angry women forming on both sides of Maria and Barbara, between the young officer and the rail cars, creating a stampede. He pointed his pistol at one, then another. His soldiers fired into the air, and the women slowed. Those closest to the SS soldiers gathered around Barbara and Maria. From one female voice, then another, and then all the women in one voice began the chant, "No! You leave...No! You leave..."

A woman stepped through the others and approached the young man, determination deepening the wrinkles on her face. She swung her open hand at the officer, but this time, he ducked in the right direction, grabbing her hand so she couldn't attack him again. She screamed at him as she struggled to free her hand.

"You are no longer my son!" The woman squeezed the words between her teeth.

"But Mother, I must do my duty!" He shouted, almost letting her hand go, but wisely held on when she yanked at it.

"Your duty does not involve shooting women and children. These people are starving and dying of thirst—we will help them, or you will shoot your mother first! I swear this by the Virgin Mary and the blood of her son, Jesus Christ!"

The officer let her hand go, and the woman dropped it to her side.

"If you are my son, you will leave us alone to help these people." The edge was gone from her voice, and she spoke softly. Every person in the silent crowd stopped breathing, and the sound of her voice carried even to the rail cars.

The women who pressed themselves into a wall behind the SS officer's mother and in front of the SS soldiers left them only two choices: they could retreat to the street or shoot the women. The SS mother walked behind her son, not satisfied until he opened the door of his grey car, got in, and drove away.

◇◇◇◇◇◇◇◇◇◇◇◇◇◇◇◇◇◇◇◇◇◇◇◇◇◇◇◇◇◇◇◇◇◇◇◇

The women and their children fed the starving, thirsty people on the train until darkness came, and a crew coupled an engine to the front railcar. The Wehrmacht guards climbed up on the cars, and the train began to move away. Shouts of "Gott schütze euch!" God protect you, went up from the people still running beside the train, trying to pass the last crumbs to still-waiting hands as the train slowly gained speed. Finally, it outdistanced them and disappeared into the darkness.

Maria, Barbara, Thomas, and now Theo, who had joined them, silently walked back to the house on Mühlenstrasse. There would be very little food tonight, but no one mentioned it. And potato dumplings would be a big part of their diet for the immediate future.

Maria said, "I fear for those poor people. And the children—what will happen to them? Yvonne said…"

Theo shook his head. "What has our country become? How can we live with this? Is this what Johann is fighting for?"

Chapter Twenty-two

August–September

The Letter

Major Helmann, Johann's new boss, was standing at a map table when Johann entered the command tent. He was alone, studying enemy and friendly forces positions. Johann thought the arrows and dotted lines that zigzagged the map looked like tracks left in the snow by a squirrel trying to remember where he had hidden his stash of nuts. Helmann saluted without straightening up, and Johann returned it while walking toward him.

Helmann pointed at the map, circling an area east of the Dnieper River with his finger. "This is Berlin's plan for our withdrawal to the Dnieper River. You will accompany a squadron of tanks commanded by Leutnant Reifschneider, and you will like him because he thinks as you do on the battlefield. But you both must remember that these orders came straight to General Manstein from the Führer, then to me, and now to you, and you must carry them out exactly as written!"

Helmann had just made it clear that Johann would not like the orders. Johann studied the withdrawal plan, could find nothing wrong with it and decided it must be something else.

Johann said, "You don't like the orders, and nothing on this map is the problem." Johann straightened and looked at Helmann; the major was reluctant to tell him something. "So, tell me what you think is Hitler's and Manstein's mistake." He was insolent but didn't give a rat's ass anymore.

Helmann put his hands behind his back and locked them together as he bent over the map, then turned his head toward Johann.

"We can't win against the Russians on the Steppes—they're building over two thousand tanks a month and almost as many aircraft. Intelligence estimates that they have moved three thousand T-34s against us since Kursk, added to the two thousand they already had.

The only way we can fight them is to restrict the battle to strongpoints, where our superior equipment gives us the advantage.

"The fighting front stretches from the Sea of Azov across Ukraine and Belorussia, fourteen hundred kilometres. The Dnieper River is two-thirds of that front, restricting their tanks' crossing points to bridges and shallows where tanks can wade without drowning the engine. We will guard these points with what Hitler calls his Eastern Wall."

Johann nodded. "That sounds reasonable. So, we must withdraw without retreating."

"Precisely! And that would be a simple procedure if not for the second part of the order."

"And you already told me that the order comes directly from Hitler, that it isn't your idea…."

"Of course, it isn't my idea—I'm only a major; I'm not permitted to have ideas." Helmann almost smiled but caught himself in time.

"The Russian people are starving… Their army exists on boiled weeds and potato soup. Since Stalingrad, our army has left nothing behind that the Russians could use—Hitler calls it our 'scorched earth' policy. We've burned houses, barns and granaries, and we've destroyed their farm equipment."

Johann was beginning to recognize the plan. "I take it that this is the SD or the SS Einsatzgruppe's new job. They murdered all the Jews on the way to Stalingrad and Moscow, and now they will starve and murder as many Russians as they can as we retreat— Excuse me, sir—withdraw." Johann spread his hands. "That only makes sense in Hitler's imaginary world."

Helmann lost control as much as he ever let his emotions rule his sense of logic. "Hitler's world, imaginary or real, is our world! We must carry out orders, and you are insolent to ask questions." He unlocked his hands and used them to support his body over the table.

Johann leaned over the table beside him. "I can't say I'm surprised we're…withdrawing, considering the number of Russian soldiers and the equipment we've seen. They are going to have to attack soon…" He looked sideways at Helmann… "because they're running out of room to park their equipment." Johann looked at the map but caught a slight upturn of Helmann's lip in his peripheral vision.

Major Helmann ignored the joke attempt and put his finger on the map, all business. "This is the withdrawal route Reifschneider will take, and your job is to protect his panzers. If you can do it on the open Steppes, I want you to set up ambushes against the Russians' forward units."

"What is my role in the 'scorched earth' plan? Are you ordering me to scorch the earth, Herr Major?"

"No, I am ordering you specifically not to do that. We have a special Vernichtungsgruppe for that purpose. They will do their dastardly deeds separate from you but close. If the Russians attack them, and they will, you and your men must defend them."

Johann hesitated. "Are they in any way related to the Einsatzgruppe?"

"If they were, would you defend them?" Helmann waited for the answer, and Johann hoped the major would go on, but after ten seconds, it was clear that only the honest answer would do.

"If we catch them raping and murdering civilians, we will do everything in our power to defend those civilians."

"Let's hope you don't have to. Remember that these are not the Einsatzgruppe; they are the Wehrmacht. But if you see them doing any of the deeds you mentioned, you are hereby authorized to arrest the perpetrators and bring them to me. Try not to kill anyone wearing a German uniform—at least not in front of witnesses."

∞∞∞∞∞∞∞∞∞∞∞∞∞∞∞∞∞∞∞∞∞∞∞∞∞∞∞∞∞∞∞

Johann and twenty of his men were behind Russian lines when, an hour before dawn, Russian artillery began a noisy, colourful, but ineffective barrage. Johann gave the coordinates of the guns to Ian; he spoke into the handset, a radio-equipped demag relayed the message to the German artillery coordinator, and less than a minute later, shells rained down on the flashes of the Russian guns. They stopped firing, and another group of guns began firing a few miles south of the first. Johann guessed at the coordinates, and the German shells fell short. He adjusted them, and in minutes, those guns stopped firing. Katya rockets flew over his head, playing their fearsome music, always on the same undefinable note. Knowing that the launching trucks would move after each salvo, Johann didn't bother to send the coordinates.

The bombardment stopped when daylight came, and Johann retreated to where his Eighth Jäger Company lay in a wheat field, waiting for the inevitable Russian advance. Twenty-four panthers, half of them camouflaged in a small group of fruit trees and the rest hidden behind the myriad of buildings necessary for the once-thriving farm, waited for a group of ten T-34s and a company of infantry. The Russian probing force worked its way toward Johann's men, the tanks lined up one behind the other, sticking to the roads. The fields grew Russian wheat destined for Russian soldiers' stomachs.

Ian said, "They must have orders not to ruin the fields." He put down his binoculars—he didn't need them anymore.

Johann had one hundred sixty men spread over a field, hidden by tall grain. A second company of Jäger infantry waited in the stalks on the opposite side of the road.

The T-34s moved at a walking pace, less than ten metres apart. The Russian infantry filled the space around the tanks, their rifles and Papa machine guns casually slung over their shoulders. Johann said, "I guess they haven't seen any Germans lately," and Ian grunted.

The lead T-34s were opposite Eighth Jäger Company when the two at the column's rear took direct hits from Reifschneider's panthers. The front tank's turret flew in the air, and it took less than a minute for the panthers' armour-piercing 75 mm shells to disable every Russian tank. Half the infantry died where they stood; those still able to run took to the fields, and the Jäger companies killed most of them before they had run thirty metres. The few who tried to surrender died with their hands in the air. Ten destroyed Russian tanks blocked the road—useless, motionless hulks.

Covered Lastwagen drove up to the blocked road; German soldiers carrying flamethrowers jumped out of them and began setting fire to the dry wheat. The fire raced across the field, reaching the other side in minutes.

"Will they burn the houses and barns?" Ian asked the question casually, knowing the answer. Johann didn't need to give him one, so he didn't.

"What about the farmer and his family?" Ian looked back; flames ran through all the fields he could see, driven by the wind—men with flamethrowers headed for the buildings, setting fire to everything that would burn. The sound of rifles and Papas carried to Johann's men, then screams—more shots, then silence. Johann considered taking his men back to the house but couldn't think of a scenario that would help the farmer and his family. He cursed... "Verdammt Krieg"... and kicked a lump of dirt on the edge of the road.

Ian said, "I guess that answers my question." He didn't look at Johann, but Johann knew that Ian was talking to him when he said, "Maybe Hitler should ask Stalin what he intends to do to German families and their houses when his soldiers reach Germany."

◇◇◇◇◇◇◇◇◇◇◇◇◇◇◇◇◇◇◇◇◇◇◇◇◇◇◇◇◇◇◇◇

The scene repeated itself a half-dozen times before Johann's Eighth Jäger Company reached Kyiv on the tenth of September. The Russians learned quickly, and every ambush became more costly. When they crossed the Dnieper River, a hundred and fifty of Johann's company were still alive, but eleven were on stretchers in the back of a Lastwagen. Another dozen limped or had their arms in slings or bandages covering various wounds. All but two of Reifschneider's tanks were still in acceptable battle condition, and the two that weren't had broken something. Both panzers' final drives had been their undoing—the crews had abandoned and scuttled otherwise operable panthers. In lieu of a design modification, the visionary Wehrmacht had issued explosives designed to destroy their new panthers in case of capture.

◇◇◇◇◇◇◇◇◇◇◇◇◇◇◇◇◇◇◇◇◇◇◇◇◇◇◇◇◇◇◇◇

Kyiv, occupied by German forces since September 1941, was the principal rest area for German soldiers in the vicinity. Johann located the hotel the Wehrmacht used for the rest and rehabilitation of their officers; he needed a bath, clean clothes, and an hour to read his mail. Officers at Johann and Ian's level stayed in a second-rate hotel with a bathroom for five rooms, and they flipped to see who would get the bathtub first. The toilet was in a separate room, leaving the tub free for extended soaks if no one came in with a gun. Ian had won the coin toss, bathed in record time and headed to the bar, so Johann took his time. When he met Ian there an hour later, he felt like a new man, and Ian was well on his way to complete inebriation.

Johann said to the bartender, "Bring me a beer... A German beer, if you've got one." The bartender shook his head. Johann looked at the dark brew Ian had in his hand; Ian nodded, and Johann said, "Whatever he's drinking will do." The Ukrainian bartender pulled a lever, slowly filled a tall glass, then scraped the foam off the top. Johann dropped ten Groschen on the counter.

The bartender slid the coins across the bar into his small, soft hand. Johann noted as the man wiped the counter that his fingernails were clean and neatly cut. Ian's, on the other hand, were filthy.

When the bartender was out of earshot, Johann spoke without turning. "As much as we deserve a little rest after two years, I'm afraid we have orders to move out tomorrow; we're joining the Nineteenth panzers near a town called Rzhishchev. It's south of here, close to the river." He sucked the foam off his beer and took a deep swallow. "The Russians will be at the river soon, and I'm betting that our fucking Vernichtungsgruppe has put them in the mood to cross it."

Ian switched on his sarcastic voice, "And here I assumed that killing four or five hundred of the enemy would earn us more than a night's rest... Man, do I feel stupid!" The tone wasn't Ian's usual approach, leaving Johann to speculate about his meaning. He hadn't dealt with sarcasm since Wilhelm's death—years ago in battle time.

Johann swallowed another gulp, lowering the level of the beer considerably. "Don't forget the tanks we destroyed." He made a face at the bartender inching toward them; the bartender shrugged, turned his back and moved away. Johann decided the man had been listening with a purpose.

"Do they add or subtract the farmers...and what about wives and children?" Ian pushed his empty glass across the bar and fished a five-mark note from his leather wallet. "Don't we get extra credit for the women and children those SD and SS bastards kill?"

"We didn't kill any farmers or their wives and children," Johann said emphatically. The bartender was closer and not paying any notice to a customer trying to get his attention at the other end of the bar.

Ian blew the foam off his beer onto the bar, and the bartender wiped it up before Ian took another breath. Johann guessed that Ian didn't give a fuck about the bartender.

Ian said, "Yeah, we didn't pull the trigger, but we didn't try to stop the bastards who did... that should be worth something." He slapped his open hand on the bar. "And are you going to tell me those animals didn't rape the women before they shot them?" His face suddenly twisted, and he began to cry.

Johann decided to stop what was becoming embarrassing. "Ian, you are drunk; I'm taking you upstairs."

Johann had to leave his beer unfinished; he hadn't had one in a long time, but this wasn't what he had missed. He took Ian's arm, half lifting him from the barstool.

As they climbed the stairs, Ian leaned against his commander and twice forced Johann to stop while he cried and declared his intention to let the Russians kill him— "To atone."

When Johann opened the door to the room, he saw that someone had delivered their mail, a single letter, and left it on the bed. Ian collapsed and rolled on top of it. Johann reached under him and pulled the letter out. It was from Barbara.

◇◇◇◇◇◇◇◇◇◇◇◇◇◇◇◇◇◇◇◇◇◇◇◇◇◇◇◇◇◇◇◇◇◇◇

Johann slid down the wall under the only lamp in the room. Sitting on the floor, he sliced the end with his grandfather's knife and fished two sheets of paper out of the envelope with his fingers. He unfolded them, apprehensive but, at the same time, hopeful.

She began with the usual *"I miss you"* and *"Thomas is fine, and so are Maria and Theo,"* but something wasn't right. Barbara's love and positive outlook, always between the lines in her letters, died at the end of the greeting.

Without a smidgen of joy, she wrote about Maria's daily visits, Theo's successes in the theatre, and two new boarders at family friend Waltraut's house. Waltraut's grandnephew—a young man of fifteen and a violinist like Johann, had brought his girlfriend with him from Dortmund, where they had both lost their parents in a bombing raid that had destroyed the city.

Johann could hear her desperation, but more, he sensed sadness in her words that he had never felt before. He put his hands and the letter in his lap and called up his memory of Barbara: her hair, beautiful eyes and soft skin. The details were there, but he couldn't put everything together; he was losing her again. Johann tried to remember Lisa, but her face wasn't clear. Tears filled his eyes—he had lost her too.

Ian stopped snoring, cursed, rolled over and muttered, "I pissed in the fucking bed." He landed on his knees on the floor, said, "Verdammt Scheisse!" and staggered to his feet. He went out into the hallway, heading, Johann presumed, for the bathroom. Johann began the last page.

"Maria and I helped some people on a train that stopped at the station in Detmold. They were on their way to Poland, and they were starving and thirsty. The whole town came to the station to feed them and give them water. They were French people, people like the Bielefeld Opera House manager. They will stay in Poland, where the Party has jobs for them. Some were old, but most were young women with their children. I feel so sad for these refugees, as I do for all the victims of the terrible British bombing raids."

Barbara's code wasn't difficult to interpret—She had seen French Jews transported like animals to Polish work camps. Johann remembered the dream, the fingers sticking through cracks between the boards, the train wheels, and Barbara screaming at an SS officer who had a gun aimed at her. It made sense now, and he had no trouble figuring out what Barbara had sneaked past the censors—His mind tried to avoid thinking about what was likely to be their final fate.

Barbara closed with an unusual,

"I pray for those people., I pray for Germany, and I pray that you return home as the man I loved and will love until I die."

Ian returned, grabbed the only pillow from the bed, then lay on the floor in the fetal position. In seconds, he was snoring.

Johann wept as he reread the letter, blurring Barbara's beautiful handwriting. He wiped tears out of his eyes, went to the bathroom, and then tried to sleep on the floor.

Chapter Twenty-three

October 1943

Like Ants under the door

If ten times the enemy's strength, surround them

If five times, attack them

If double, divide them

If equal, engage them

If fewer, evade them

If weaker, avoid them

Sun Tzu

During the lull in fighting, twenty-eight Finnish soldiers joined Johann's First platoon, bringing Eighth Company's depleted numbers to one hundred forty-eight healthy men. Johann wouldn't have traded the Finns for a hundred recruits fresh out of training, especially, he surmised, after December froze the ground. All twenty-eight Finns came from Lapland, and winter in Lapland is long and hard for anyone but a Finn. Lapland soldiers, tactical wonders in the snow and cold, had almost defeated the mighty Russian army during the first winter of their Finland invasion.

Unfortunately, the German soldiers fighting alongside the Laplanders were unaccustomed to the harsh arctic winter, and by the time they had adjusted to the temperatures, spring had come. The Russians used their overwhelming numbers and a short summer to force a stalemate in Lapland, keeping the Murmansk supply route open for the Western Allies to ship war material to Russia. Following the defeats at Stalingrad and Kursk, Finland saw the writing on the wall and began peace negotiations with Russia. The German and Finnish soldiers shared their hatred for the Russians, and disillusioned Finnish soldiers joined the German army, forming "Viking" units. Germany used some of these forces to bolster their specialist units fighting in Belorussia and Ukraine.

<hr>

Eighth Jäger Company was an essential part of the defence of a loop in the Dnieper River called the Bukrin Bend. The Russians chose the bend as the point where they would test the German defences, a decision they would regret. Russian infantry tried to swim across the river or paddle across on makeshift rafts, but they swam and paddled into a hail of bullets. In a terrible blunder, planes carrying paratroopers dropped their loads of men in the wrong places, and those Russian paratroopers that the Luftwaffe didn't shoot down jumped into the arms of German soldiers. The Russians lost over half of the men who crossed the Dnieper and accomplished nothing. The magnitude of the slaughter appalled even the toughest of Johann's men.

The Ukrainian underground, reinforced by the Russians who escaped capture, was initially far more effective than the Russian Army. They harassed the Germans from their forest hideouts, and the Eighth Jäger Company found them only when they walked into an ambush. The Underground Ukrainian Army was a ghost that eluded them.

When Major Helmann called the company back to temporary headquarters north of Dubari, Johann had a hundred and thirty-three men who could fight, but eight had minor wounds, and ten were green replacements.

Major Helmann said, "You are now part of the Twenty-Fourth panzer Corp." An adjutant handed Johann his orders. "I tried to keep you, but they have a special job for Eighth Jäger Company."

When he returned to their tent, Johann handed Ian the single sheet of paper. "We go north, back to Rzhishchev. The new boss's name is General Walther Nehring."

Ian read the paper twice, then passed it back to Johann.

"It looks like they want us to do something that's too fucking dangerous for anyone else."

The XXIV panzer Corp, part of the Fourth panzer Army, was tasked with keeping the Russians in the Bukrin Bend, and when General Nehring called Johann to his tent to give him his orders, the Corp controlled the west side of the Dnieper River from Bukrin north to Kyiv.

When he stepped into Nehring's tent, the first thing Johann saw was a beautiful chessboard set up on a small table between two chairs. He stared at it, forgetting to salute.

Nehring asked, "Do you play, Leutnant Finke?"

Johann picked up the flawless white king, carved from pure white onyx. Likewise perfect, the sculptor had made the board from black and green onyx, polished and fitted together, interspersed with narrow rivulets of wandering white lines.

Nehring looked lovingly at the chessboard and said, "I picked that up in a small market in a village a couple of hundred kilometres northeast of Milano. An old man told me it took him ten years to carve those figures and make the board. He wouldn't put a price on them, and I was ashamed to offer him a hundred thousand lire, but it was all I had." Nehring waved at the board. "As you can see, he was desperate to feed his family. I have his name, and someday when this shit is over, I will pay him what it is worth."

Johann adjusted his opinion of the general to the plus side and said, "Yes, I play, but I haven't had much chance lately."

"I wish we could take time to play right now, but this is a new job for me, and I have too much to do."

Johann remembered that he hadn't saluted and moved his arm up, but General Nehring caught it.

"No, Johann, don't worry about that. Winning this brutal game means working together as equals, and winning means going home to our families. And besides, if you do that at the wrong time, a sniper might get the idea that I'm an officer."

"Okay, sir, what do you want me to do?" Johann looked for an envelope or a packet of papers. The desk was clean.

"I want your company to scout the Dnieper from Rzhishchev to Kyiv. Be thorough—the Russians will cross the river soon, but everyone on my level believes we can restrict them to two or three crossing places and decimate them there."

Nehring observed Johann's reaction with an interest that told Johann he had better think before he spoke. He decided to say what he knew to be true.

"Sir, only someone sitting behind a desk could believe such

Vogelscheiss! I've been fighting Russians for two years, and they are a cunning and resourceful adversary. They will cross the Dnieper when they're ready and at places of their choosing. Based on two years of fighting those bastards, my best guess is they will cross where and when we don't expect them."

Nehring seemed relieved with Johann's honesty and nodded as he said, "Yes, I agree with your assessment of the Russians, and that is why I insisted on having the Eighth Jäger Company under my command. I need you to find out where and how they will do it.

"You will report directly to me—not a word to anyone else—what you say is off the record. Scout the river, take no chances, and above all, do not engage the enemy! If you find something, make sure the Russians don't know you know what they're up to."

General Nehring held up his hand when Johann started to speak. He lowered his voice and said, "I need you and your men to be invisible. I do not trust the information I receive, and the Russians seem to know what we will do before I do. Be careful using the radio. Don't trust anyone but me with anything more important than the time of day!"

"Yes, sir." Johann saluted smartly, a twinge of hope in his heart, and General Nehring grimaced.

◇◇◇◇◇◇◇◇◇◇◇◇◇◇◇◇◇◇◇◇◇◇◇◇◇◇◇◇◇◇◇◇◇◇

Johann's company began their scouting mission at Rzhishchev and headed upriver. They moved slowly, searching the shores where narrow or shallow sections with low banks made a crossing possible. They searched the banks for two days, picking out minor irregularities on the Russian side too often for it to be a coincidence.

Late in the afternoon of the second day, Johann and Ian lay on top of a bluff, looking down at the forest on the Russian side of the river. At that spot, the Dnieper River's western bank was considerably higher than the eastern, and the river was narrow and deep. Using binoculars, Johann could see irregular patches of missing trees, and the opposite shoreline looked unnatural. Something, likely men's boots, had disturbed the mud close to the water.

Johann tapped Ian's shoulder. "Let's move back into the woods and wait until it's dark."

An hour later, at the beginning of a night that promised to be partly cloudy with some light from stars and a sliver moon, Johann and Ian lay down on their Zeltbahn groundsheets, spread on the soft, dry moss between the trees. They made themselves comfortable—it would be a long night.

A half-hour later, when the darkness was as complete as it would get, Johann was snoozing when Ian shook him and asked, "Fireflies?"

Johann got up on his elbows, and Ian pointed at the river. Tiny spots of light burned above the water, disappeared, then reappeared.

Johann looked through his binoculars. "Cigarettes..." He put his binoculars down. "In the middle of the river? Without boats under them?" He paused, not sure, trying to find an explanation. He raised his binoculars again—the tiny lights were closer, close enough that Johann could see men's shadows. The men appeared to walk on water.

The two men nearest Johann carried a square timber between them. They stopped, turned it sideways, and laid it down. It floated; a man stepped on it while two men drove spikes in both ends. In a parade of men carrying timbers, the next two laid their load in the water, tight against the one the first men had just nailed. The nailers drove their spikes, and another beam splashed in place.

"It looks like they're building a submerged bridge." Johann passed the binoculars to Ian and waited for his interpretation.

Ian said, "Yes, and I will bet my Lederhosen that it will carry a T-34."

Johann rolled on his side so he could see Ian's face. "This can't be the only bridge like this... I bet my Lederhosen that there are more than a few of these between here and Kyiv."

Ian didn't lower the glasses. "You are Prussian... You're not allowed to wear Lederhosen."

"I will buy a pair and give them to you if I'm wrong. If you're wrong, you can keep yours. Barbara would laugh at me if I brought Lederhosen home."

Ian interrupted him as he cleaned the lenses on his binoculars with spit and cigarette paper. "That's the first time in months that I've heard you say your wife's name or mention anything about home." He raised the binoculars to his eyes with his elbows on the ground, searching the opposite bank.

Johann knew Ian was right. He began thinking of Barbara and was trying to form her picture when Ian said, "That's a boat at the edge of the river." Johann had his mouth open to speak when Ian continued.

"Yes, there are also cigarettes, but there's the shadow of a boat or a big raft." Ian rolled sideways to look at Johann. "I think it's a ferry... They covered it with trees and branches, and now men are pushing it across the river with poles. It looks like a rehearsal, maybe a test to see if they can handle it."

The raft swung downstream and disappeared. Johann searched the bank where the raft had come from. A hole in the clouds let a stream of moonlight shine on the opposite bank, and Johann picked out another raft, with men removing branches and tops of trees from it. Six men with poles climbed on it, and within minutes, the raft floated into the river and disappeared in the wake of the first one.

Ian whistled softly. "They've built a raft factory over there...."

Johann and Ian watched most of the night, counting cigarettes and shadows while the rest of Eighth Jäger Company slept in their make-shift Zeltbahn tents a kilometre into the woods behind them.

When pre-dawn daylight arrived, the forms of men on the other side of the river became distinct, and a few minutes later, they disappeared like ghosts.

"There are hundreds and likely thousands of Russian soldiers on the other side of the river." Ian lay on the soft needles covering the forest floor, binoculars resting on his hands and against his eyes. "I see camouflaged tanks… Yes, they are tanks for sure... and big guns… eighty-eights, covered with branches." He steadied the binoculars on a single spot. "I can see bald trees and thick branches growing where there are no trees. T-34s? Guns? Naked trees? There's something serious going on!"

Johann said, "Let's go," and put his binoculars in their case. They crawled back from the river until they could no longer see it. Ian struggled to his feet and limped around in a circle, dragging his foot.

"My damned foot is asleep."

While Johann waited for Ian's foot to wake up, he said, "By the way, Ian, you were right; I had given up the idea of reaching my family again, but Nehring has given me hope."

"What the hell are you talking about? You're the one who says hope delays the inevitable." Ian shook his leg and jumped up and down to test it. "My foot's okay now…let's go."

Johann didn't move. "Nehring is smart; he doesn't want to die for the Führer. He wants to go home as much as we do."

"That sounds okay to me." Ian began walking, limping slightly. Johann thought he heard skepticism in his voice, and Ian added, "It also sounds like a classic case of naïve optimism."

<hr>

Two days later, Jäger Company returned to headquarters, and Johann reported finding eight bridges and some thirty ferries south of Kyiv. They had also found several half-hearted attempts. Johann noted them on the map as false bridges, deceptions, and red herrings. After close examination by the engineer in Ian, he ruled out the possibility of taking anything heavier than a wheelbarrow across those bogus structures.

General Nehring listened to Johann's report, and before the day was over, the Fourth panzer Army sent out scouts all along the river from Kyiv north beyond Lyutezh. They found eighteen more submerged bridges and fifty-seven ferries. On the last day of October, the Fourth panzer Army was prepared for battle.

Nearly too late for Abendessen, Ian and Johann followed the men still under their command past a line of tin trays that were now almost empty of meat and potatoes. A thin, short man with a big spoon looked at Johann, the second last man in the line, ahead of Ian. He asked, "One or two?"

"One." The wet mash splattered on Johann's clean uniform. He said, "Sheisse," and stepped ahead to a pan still holding a few pieces of dry meat of uncertain ancestry, a bad sign. He delicately tried to remove the splattered potato from his uniform and wound up spreading it.

The big man in charge of the meat had a voice like a foghorn. He looked at Johann, then Ian, then back at Johann. "I can give each of you two pieces." He speared two of the four pieces in the tray using a well-rehearsed staccato motion, then pushed them off the sharp fork onto Johann's plate with his big middle finger. While the man performed that feat, Ian grabbed the last two buns from a basket.

Johann made a face. "Isn't this supposed to be better than field rations?"

Ian didn't laugh. "I'm not sure about that, but I am sure it's better than the food the Russians are eating...we sure as hell didn't leave them much!"

Johann asked, "If you had to fight a bear, would you rather fight a happy, well-fed bear or a starving one?"

"Do I have a choice?" Ian nodded toward two empty places, but before they could sit, a soldier at the end of the middle table picked up his plate and moved. The men waved Johann and Ian to their places. Jäger Company had three long tables, and their Leutnant traditionally sat at the head of the middle table. They hung on Johann's words; the good, the bad, and the terrible—he always told them the truth.

Ian tried the dull table knife on a piece of meat, then pulled his fighting knife out of its sheath.

"Speaking of Russian bears, how many do we think are on the other side of the river?" The blade was sharp, but he still had to lean on it to make two pieces of one.

Johann went straight to his grandfather's hunting knife.

"There are thousands, tens of thousands this side of Kyiv, hundreds of thousands east of there, and hundreds of thousands on the river north of Kyiv. Altogether, I would guess there are close to a million."

"How many do you figure we have?" Knowing the answer, Ian asked Johann while balancing a piece of meat on the tip of his knife. Johann put a piece of meat in his mouth and chewed, putting all the strength in the work that his jaw could muster. He decided it resembled pork more than beef, but it could have once been a goat—he worried about breaking one of his rotting teeth. He chewed, waited for the piece of meat to shrink and soften enough that he had a chance of swallowing it, gave up and pushed it into his cheek to marinate in his saliva.

"The Fourth panzer Army has about two hundred thousand men, two thousand artillery pieces, and two hundred tanks. Facing us, the Russians have about four times that and lots more where they came from!" He swallowed the piece of meat whole, forcing it through his esophagus, but he could feel that it didn't make it to his stomach. He cut a smaller chunk and began the rubbery chewing process again, swallowing the smaller lump after a minute of no gain. The piece found its way to the first one and stopped.

"Do you think we can hold them back?" Ian had finally swallowed his first piece, took a big bite of mushy potatoes mixed with onion and began work on the second.

Johann put a spoonful of potato and onion in his mouth, copying Ian. When he swallowed, the potato pushed the meat ahead of it. He pointed with his fork at something that wasn't in front of him—and his men silently waited.

"I think of Russians as hungry ants coming under the door. They're ants that like human flesh, especially Germans, and they're coming straight at me! I brush a few off, stomp on a few more, and stand beside the crack under the door, crushing ants as fast as they come in." He pushed his plate aside and lit a cigarette while his men waited. He sucked in the smoke, then blew it out and showed the cigarette to the room.

"I light a cigarette, and while I do that, a bunch of ants get past my foot. I jump to where they are trying to escape and stomp them." He slapped the table, and a few men near him jumped, startled by the suddenness.

"A couple of ants get on my boot, and I swat them, squeeze a couple more between my fingers, and return to stomping ants at the door."

Grinning men lined both sides of the tables. The Finn scout, Väinü, said, "Stuff something in the crack to stop the ants while you kill the ones that got by you."

Johann flopped the fork with the handle between his fingers in the Finn's direction. "A great idea, and that's precisely what I will do! So, I stuff my jacket under the door and kill the stragglers. And then, I sit down. It's been a lot of work, and I take a little snooze to get my strength back." He looked at his men's expectant faces while he worked on what would happen next.

"I wake up an hour later, covered with ants; the fuckers ate my jacket while I was sleeping! The damned things are biting me, and there's a line of them coming under the door, a fucking parade, two or three ants high and four ants wide! I take off my clothes to brush off the ants, and I jam the clothes under the door. I itch all over, and it takes me a long time to kill all the ants in the room, but eventually, I get it done. I am dead tired and bleeding from bites, so I sit down again. But I don't sleep this time—I watch the clothes I jammed under the door.

"In about half an hour, the clothes move, and I run over to stuff the crack full, tighter than it was. I sit down and wait, and it takes another half hour before the ants chew through the clothes. But there isn't enough fabric to fill the crack."

"Okay, so the ants kill you?" Väinü spoke with a heavy accent; he wasn't grinning, but Ian was.

Johann jammed the last piece of meat in his mouth, stuffed it in his cheek to soak, and answered the Finn's question.

"No, I'm not done yet... I run out through the back door into the cold, as naked as I was born. The bastards follow me, but outside I'm a lot faster. I don't dare stop to rest for more than a minute or two—they're slower than I am, but they are relentless. I stop and kill some of them with a piece of wood I carve for the purpose, then run for a while, believing I will eventually whittle them down.

"But nests of local ants join their numbers, making up more than I've killed!" He paused to force the lump of meat down his throat, and the table was quiet. He gagged, then succeeded in pushing the blockage into his stomach.

"They chase me, sometimes stopping to let fresh ants join them to replenish their losses. Their numbers grow. When they are ready, they advance again." He stamped his feet on the board floor, making a marching sound.

"One day, they reach my home, hundreds of kilometres from here."

"Do they eat you in your home?" This time, it was Ian, and the grin was gone.

"When I arrive, they are already there, waiting for me. The fucking ants have gone around me and eaten my wife and my kid!"

"What about you?" The Finn was hoarse.

"They leave me alone...I surrender. They make a deal with me. When they become hungry, I must find food for them. And then I must build houses for them, care for their young and fight their enemies."

Chapter Twenty-four

1 November 1943

Schachspiel

(Chess game)

Early morning—a crappy day.

General Nehring said, "Leutnant, you don't know how close you are to a firing squad!"

Johann, aware that he was standing opposite the commander of the Fourth panzer Army, a half-dozen rungs above him on the rank ladder, understood that the General wasn't asking for comment, so he stiffened his back and waited.

"Half the men in the camp have heard and repeated that little ant story you told yesterday. Everyone, including the Gestapo, is talking about it."

Johann was flabbergasted. He had told the ant story to lift his men's spirits, and perhaps it had become something more, but he hadn't committed treason! Or had he?

"Did one of those men complain?"

The General smiled. "Our Gestapo friends questioned every one of your men, and, despite their usually effective methods, every man denied that you had mentioned ants in any context except to 'stomp' a couple that tried to cross the table. They said you had told them a bedtime story, but none of them could remember what it was about."

"Thank you, sir. That's the truth."

General Nehring put his hands behind his back and began to walk back and forth in front of Johann, using all the spare room in the small tent.

"I can't do anything about the Gestapo nonsense… they have their agenda. But I had planned to send you and your men to patrol the Russian lines anyway, and it might be a good idea to get you out of sight for a few days."

He leaned over the map and slid his finger along the Dnieper River.

"I want you to cross the river where you feel you can do it safely—I need more information. I guarantee the Gestapo will not follow you there, and this will have blown over by the time you return."

"Herr General, it is never safe to cross behind the Russian lines, but I know what you need, and we will get it." He smiled and added, "The men would be happy if you told those bastards where they can find us... and you can tell them that if they want to join us, we will look after them."

"Of course you will." The general smiled but with no joy. "I heard a detailed recounting of your ant story from a Gestapo rat who was listening. I was very interested in his version of your assessment of the coming battle and, for that matter, the fight to save the Vaterland. I want to discuss that with you."

He paused and, when Johann looked straight ahead without opening his mouth, said, "Unter Vier Augen. Sie haben meine Guarantie." Under four eyes and a guarantee that the conversation would be private; Johann wasn't ready to believe that yet.

◇◇

Johann looked at the chessboard, and Nehring said, "After we eat." He made a noise that carried outside, and two soldiers came in with trays of boiled eggs, almost-fresh buns, two kinds of jam, and a pile of Wurst. They put the food, eating and drinking paraphernalia, a pitcher of apple juice, and a pot of coffee that wasn't real on the table and disappeared.

"Breakfast, Leutnant?" Nehring swept his hand toward a chair on Johann's side of the table and motioned for him to sit. Johann waited until the general was seated, then poured coffee and juice before sitting down. He began to think this man might be who he seemed to be.

"Eat, Johann... you haven't had breakfast, have you?"

Johann had already eaten a stick of ration but hadn't seen a German breakfast for two years, so he didn't intend to spoil Nehring's surprise. He tore a bun apart and peeled one of the three eggs on the tray.

Nehring leaned ahead so that his face was over the table, with a table knife in one hand and half a bun in the other. "I want to know what you think of the Russian soldier, and I want you to compare him to the German soldiers you know so well."

"Herr General. Stalin thinks of the Russian soldier as a commodity, of which he has an inexhaustible supply. He teaches them how to carry a gun but not how to fight. Russia gives their soldiers a uniform and a handful of ammunition and then sends them to certain death. And the question is this: why would he do such a thing? Do our generals believe Stalin is an idiot?"

Johann drank half a glass of juice, and Nehring spread butter on his bun. Johann put the glass down and continued while remembering his lengthy discussions with Wilhelm. He found himself thinking more of his friend every day and could finally admit he missed him for more than his fighting skills.

"Every dead Russian soldier costs Hitler a gallon of petrol, an artillery shell or two, and a dozen, maybe a hundred, bullets. Mission accomplished for Stalin." Johann drank a swallow of what was supposed to be coffee.

"On the other hand, our generals think the German soldier is unique. The country cannot mass-produce them, and the supply is strictly limited. A German soldier is well-trained, cherished and protected—his superiors recognize his value."

Nehring slathered butter on the other half of the bun and said, "Yes, I understand; it's the ant analogy for the Russians. And I understand your comparison of Russian and German soldiers." He bit a piece from the bun and drank a swallow of coffee. "Now, tell me about your family. I read in your file that you have a wife and boy and that you lost your daughter in a bombing raid."

General Nehring's expression softened in a way that discouraged Johann from talking shop, and they ate their food while reminiscing about their families.

◇◇◇◇◇◇◇◇◇◇◇◇◇◇◇◇◇◇◇◇◇◇◇◇◇◇◇◇◇◇◇

When they had finished with the food, General Nehring stood and walked around the table to Johann, who had stood up. Nehring put his hand on Johann's shoulder.

"Relax, Leutnant; I will order a beer for you, and we will sit at this table." Nehring surprised Johann when he indicated his leutnant should take the chair on the white side of the chessboard. There was room for a glass of beer beside it. "You did say that you play chess, Leutnant?"

Johann sat down, and two beers appeared. He reasoned that there was a high likelihood they were German beers. A sip confirmed it.

Johann always carried a miniature chess set in his pack and constantly searched for a worthy opponent. The Finn often beat him, but he always apologized. Lately, either Johann's chess was improving, or the Finn was sucking up to his boss.

"Yes, sir, but I may not be a worthy opponent."

Johann began with the ubiquitous king's Gambit. Nehring returned traditionally, and Johann moved his 'f' pawn up to tempt his opponent. At this point, the usual decision was to accept or decline the pawn and, therefore, the opening. General Nehring chose to take the pawn.

Johann moved his knight, preferring this more unconventional and aggressive answer because it allowed white to castle unimpeded.

"I see you play as aggressively as you fight." General Nehring made the exchange of pieces, and Johann castled. "What do you think the Russians will do?"

Johann lifted his eyes from the board and leaned back in his chair. It creaked, threatening to collapse, so he found a better balance point. "The Russian tanks and infantry will cross the river at the sunken bridges above and below Kyiv, and we will stop them by drawing forces from the city. And that's when the Russians will take Kyiv." Johann picked up his queen, examined her, and then put her back. "We don't have enough panzers and men to stop them."

Johann looked at General Nehring. "But first, they will try to deceive us by attacking where they have been openly building fake bridges and rafts. Those men will die so that we will hesitate when the real attack begins. Their immediate objective is to encircle Army Group Centre and then destroy Army Group South when they stand and fight. I am betting those are Hitler's orders, but please tell me I am wrong!"

Nehring moved his queen for the first time; it was the last piece preventing him from castling on the long side. Johann crossed his bishop to threaten the king if black castled. The general made a sour face and said, *"Maskirovka."*

"Excuse me? *Maskirovka?"*

The general moved a pawn ahead, blocking the bishop's slant attack, then put his chin in his hand and studied the board; Johann freed his knight by moving it to the side. They were well into the middle game, past either player's ability to remember a pre-set attack or defence.

Nehring explained, "Maskirovka means deception and is considered a virtue in Russian politics, business, and, of course, the Russian military. Germans traditionally value directness and honesty, especially in those endeavours. But I would say that Hitler's politics have changed that—lies and deception are now standard in German politics—he and his followers laugh at anyone who believes his lies. He signed a non-aggression pact with Russia and then attacked them with everything he had. That's one of the many reasons the Russians hate us so much."

Nehring touched his king, then pulled his hand back.

He said, "Hitler signed that treaty with the Russians knowing that he would attack them when the time was right. I don't think he ever intended to attack the British, except by bombing English cities to try and get Churchill to agree to divide Europe between them. When Churchill made his speech about 'fighting on the land,' on the sea," and so on, Hitler turned to Russia, as was his original intent. And don't forget all those countries between Germany and Russia. They would be collateral profit."

Johann looked up from the board and asked, "Why not invade England? I would think that would be easier than what he's doing now."

Nehring considered the board as he answered. "Because the Royal Navy would have sunk whatever ships we took into the English Channel. They rule the seas, and we have nothing but submarines, which are no good for an invasion and would be dead meat in the channel."

"That makes sense."

Nehring reached for a rook, discarded the idea and said, "The Russians were an easy target because they believed the treaty's terms and didn't prepare for war. Until Hitler crossed Russia's western border in June 1941, Germany had always been honourable. But now, the world will always remember Barbarossa!"

Johann nodded, and General Nehring castled. Johann moved the knight, sitting inconspicuously to one side, and his boss gave him a look that didn't bode well for Johann's future.

Nehring tipped his king. "You may not know the term Maskirovka, but you certainly know how to apply it!" Johann had caught his king and queen in a fork move, and the queen must die.

General Nehring said, "I would like to play again sometime when you have time." General Nehring began putting the pieces in their places on the board. "But this morning, I would like to talk about ants."

◇◇◇◇◇◇◇◇◇◇◇◇◇◇◇◇◇◇◇◇◇◇◇◇◇◇◇◇◇◇◇◇◇◇◇◇◇◇

Johann had learned a lot about General Nehring in the past hour and realized that he had anticipated the reverse of what he had found. Most important, General Nehring was honest. He was not egotistical, but he was confident. He was intelligent, and Johann expected to lose the next game. The fork move was too apparent for a chess player of Nehring's calibre to have missed it.

Johann accepted a cigar, although he wasn't fond of them. His father had smoked them in the evening with brandy but never with beer, and Johann had inherited his father's individuality. General Nehring offered a light from a standard-issue steel lighter.

"They call your company Die Musiker, and they say it's because you direct your men as though they were musical instruments in an orchestra. They say the music they play for the Russians is Chopin's second sonata, better known as the 'Death March.'" Nehring passed the lighter to Johann and leaned forward so he could light his cigar. Nehring sucked in enough air through the cigar to burn the end square, then blew the smoke toward the tent roof. "But there's something else, isn't there?"

Johann said, "Nothing to do with ants, but yes, there is something else." He sucked in and blew the smoke up to join the cloud his general had created. "I played the fiddle in the Bielefeld Opera orchestra and was promoted to concertmaster the day I received my orders."

Johann's voice had no tone of bitterness, but General Nehring's smile said he knew the truth of how Johann felt.

Nehring nodded, leaned back, and his chair cracked. He smiled and leaned forward slightly; it creaked, but the sound wasn't ominous.

266

"I have been a soldier since before the Great War. I was wounded twice before the armistice, and in this war, I was injured in Africa. Fighting is my career, and fighting with tanks against tanks is my specialty." He sucked on the cigar and blew the smoke to the side.

"For the past twenty-one years, I have had a wife, Annamarie, whom I love very much. We have three children, two boys and a girl, and my family is more important to me than being a soldier, or for that matter, my survival." He put his cigar on the edge of a brass ashtray, leaned forward, and spoke softly. "Hitler has endangered my family and my career. I fight first to return to them, and then for my country. I do not fight for Adolph Hitler." He leaned back. "I promised Annamarie I would get back to her before the Russians arrived." He leaned back. "Now, tell me why you fight."

"I lost my daughter to a British bomb, but my wife and son are still alive, as far as I know. As you do, I fight to stay alive and return to them." He paused, and Nehring waited expectantly.

"Sometimes, I don't believe I will ever see them again."

"I understand that, and we will discuss that later. Now, tell me about the ants." General Nehring picked up his cigar, flicked the ash into the ashtray, leaned back and crossed his legs.

Johann lost interest in his cigar, aware that he sat opposite a general, one who had possibly thrown a chess game to earn his confidence.

"What do you want to know about the ants? They are just ants, nothing more."

"Leutnant, I have shown you enough about who I am that you should know you are safe to talk to me." Nehring put both feet on the floor and looked expectantly at Johann, but Johann waited, and General Nehring continued.

"Your unambiguous attempt at hiding your belief in Germany's defeat by using an allegory about ants would never save you from a firing squad! What has saved you is your outstanding record and your intelligence—and, of course, the absolute loyalty of your officers and men. They would die for you while other soldiers are deserting their posts." He sat back in his chair and crossed his legs. "My interest is in the attitude of yourself and your men. I want to know why you are fighting if you see no other option but defeat.

Why risk your life when you and your men could probably broker a better deal with the Russians?"

Johann didn't dare answer.

"I want you to call me Walther and forget my rank. I worked hard to gain your trust, and I need to know what makes you fight for the Reich and not the Russians. And there is always the third option… not fighting for anyone."

Johann decided to start with the truth. "You threw the chess game; you are a better player than the one who moved his queen into an obvious trap."

"I thought I was very convincing." Nehring shrugged and briefly laughed. "I guess I'm not as good at Maskirovka as I had hoped." He held the cigar over the ashtray, rolled it between his fingers with a snap, and the ashes fell in a steady, clean stream. Johann was impressed.

"General…" Johann had no intention of calling him Walther… "I was telling my men the truth. I don't have to worry about letting those men know what I think—they have hope because they have trust. They will follow me to hell if I tell them we must go there before we go home. They trust me to get them to Germany ahead of those Gottverdammte ants."

Nehring picked up Johann's thread. "And the truth is what I want you to tell me. Please call me Walther and tell me about the ants—tell me how you would get to Germany before they do."

Johann waited, decided what the truth was, and spoke carefully.

"Herr General, the truth in the story is what you want to make of it. I see more of the battlefield than any general, and I know that the Russian tactics are based on overwhelming numbers, not on the efficient use of assets. The Wehrmacht is vastly outnumbered by forces that are significantly less skilled.

"The Russians attack in waves, committing everything they have, and if the attack falters, they bring up more men and equipment. They keep committing their forces until the enemy tires and walks backwards or stands his ground and dies. They take some of the land their enemy occupies, and then they wait while they build up their reserves."

"And how do we attack? How do you think we should attack?"

Johann leaned toward General Nehring, leaving his cigar burning on the ashtray, a long ash cylinder cantilevered two centimetres from the burn. "We attack in moving lines. When the forward line reaches its objective, the second line passes the first and drives for the next objective. We distribute the risk, and we always have a strong, fast withdrawal as an option, one that will cost the enemy more than they can afford if they push too hard."

Nehring pulled hard on his cigar, then set it on the edge of the ashtray.

"And in the story of your retreat from the ants, you kill as many as you can, run away, construct a killing field, then kill again. Your success and survival depend on your speed in both directions."

"Yes, I ambush the ants when they least expect it, but…" Johann observed General Nehring closely. "I have a serious problem with the colonies of ants that help them along the route."

"Ah! The partisans?" Johann nodded, but Nehring wasn't satisfied. "The Jews?" Johann nodded again. "The Free Polish Army!"

Johann smiled and said, "I didn't know there was a Free Polish Army, but yes, the people will organize liberation armies against us, all with 'free' or 'freedom' somewhere in their name. I have some knowledge of the Einsatzgruppen, and they've made many formidable enemies who now have more than a passing interest in our demise." Johann believed the Nazi's past would eventually destroy his country. "They have, in our name, created millions of Russian, Ukrainian and Polish fanatics who will fight us to the last breath!" He pointed at the roof of the tent. "And God is on their side."

General Nehring's hand shook when he picked up his cigar, knocking the long ash into the tray. He tried to hide the shaking by making it look like he did it to remove the ash. He pulled on the cigar, blew the smoke upward, and returned it to the ashtray. "Is there a solution to the problem as you see it?"

Johann looked straight into General Nehring's eyes. "We," he pointed to Nehring and then to himself, "can try to look better than the Russian alternative. That would be a good place to start."

Nehring picked up the cigar, took a short puff, held it in his lap, and pointed upward so the ash wouldn't fall.

Johann continued with something that had bothered him since

he crossed into Russia. "We must stop our 'scorched earth' policy and send the Vernichtungsgruppe far away from here! Hell would be an excellent place for them—they wouldn't need to carry those heavy flamethrowers." Johann decided he was already over his head and waited for the verdict.

General Nehring puffed on his cigar and blew the smoke upward.

"The Russian army will use what food we leave. Why should we leave it to strengthen their men?"

"Because it will then be the Russians who steal the farmer's food and rape his wife. And then, if we are smart, they will be the ones who fight the partisans and the Free Polish Army while we concentrate on getting home."

General Nehring nodded. "You think we should leave the peasants alone and mind our own business."

"No, we should protect them, especially those who want to return to Germany with us! We should defend those who choose Germany over Russia until they are safely behind our borders. They will clog the roads, and they will drive the Russians crazy, like the Belgians, Dutch and French refugees drove our invading army crazy." Johann made eye contact. "We should protect them and share our food so they will want to stay close to us."

Nehring rubbed his chin and carefully pinched the burn off his cigar as Johann had done.

Nehring said, "They will slow us down." He didn't sound as though he believed that.

He put the cigar in his shirt pocket. "Tell me why they wouldn't get in the way."

"They will get in everyone's way, but they will slow the Russians more because they will fight the Russians who attack them to get at us, and they will buy enough time for the British and Americans, who will be coming through France, to save our wives and children, and perhaps Berlin."

The general shook his head. "I will forget you said that." Johann knew he had gone a bridge too far, and anything more on the subject would work against him. He decided to change it.

"Then, consider that Hitler is right, and we will have his wonder weapon if we can buy enough time. That should pass the treason test."

"Now, that I will remember." General Nehring rose from his chair, and Johann stood up with him.

"When will the Russians cross the Dnieper, Johann?" He extended his hand, and Johann shook it.

"I'm surprised they haven't attacked already." He saluted smartly, and the general winced. "Herr General, I expect the Russians no later than Wednesday, and they will attack all along the river, but strongest above Kyiv, where the banks are lower and where there is a forest to hide them until they are on the bridges or the ferries. I would also worry about the area around Lyutezh."

"It's been an interesting morning, Leutnant."

CHAPTER TWENTY-FIVE

OCTOBER 1943

Ashes and Daffodils

Sometimes silence is the loudest sound a woman can make

WHEN BARBARA WALKED DOWN THE STONE STEPS, Thomas was already on his way to school and out of sight. The October dawn was beginning to colour the twilight sky, and she was on a mission she had contemplated for weeks.

It had been six months since Lisa's death, and overwhelming grief still sometimes woke Barbara in the night. She no longer needed Thomas to come to her room, but sadness wasn't far behind in the rare moments when she was happy. She burst into tears when something reminded her of Lisa, and reminders were everywhere. Even working at the train station, Barbara saw glimpses of Lisa in the crowds of people who got on and off the trains. Sometimes, she had to force herself not to call out to someone who looked like her. Lisa's hat, wool coat, gloves, and how she walked were everywhere. Every little girl with blond curls became Lisa.

Barbara wanted an end to her grief and thought she might find it in the hole that had been Siegruna's house. She had avoided visiting the site, believing that she couldn't bear it, but today, Barbara convinced herself to face that fear—this would be the day she would defeat it. Barbara walked fast, reaching the corner of Wiesenstrasse quickly. She hesitated before turning the corner—and stopped when she could see the wreckage of what had been three houses. Barbara stared at the desolation—she had forgotten that the bomb had destroyed the homes on both sides of Siegruna's.

Walking slowly, Barbara looked down at the concrete sidewalk blocks. They reminded her of Lisa and Angela's hopping games— the chalk marks had faded but were still visible. She reached the hole that had been Siegruna's house and stood looking into it with her woollen coat bundled against the raw October wind. Barbara tried to hold the tears back but finally collapsed to her knees and began to cry.

The sun rose quickly, creeping up through the bright yellow leaves on a beech tree behind a house farther down the street. Barbara stood up, still sobbing but pushing away the tears as beams of light shining through the tree created a beautiful glow in the hole. Barbara chose a route to a spot where a ray reflected off something bright. She worked through the debris until she found a broken mirror reflecting the beam onto a small pile of ashes and dust. As the sun rose, the light moved on, but Barbara's attention stayed on the ashes.

"Lisa?" Barbara's tears began again. She tried to reason that Lisa couldn't be there, but logic was now the enemy and couldn't be trusted. She knelt and touched the ashes.

Maria's voice came from the sidewalk.

"Barbara? What are you doing?"

Barbara looked up but didn't stand—she waved but couldn't answer.

Maria descended the slope, picking her way through the rubble until she reached Barbara and squatted beside her.

"A beam of light shone on this little pile of ashes, and I want to take it home with me." Barbara pointed at the pile. "I can't tell you why because I don't know."

Maria waited quietly, looking at the ashes. She finally said, "I was coming to your house to spend the morning and Mittagessen with you when I saw you turn the corner. I hope you don't mind that I followed you."

"I don't mind." Barbara touched the ashes. "Do you think I should take those ashes home? Does that seem silly to you?"

"No, that's not silly at all." Maria touched Barbara's hand. "If you want this pile of ashes, we can't leave it here."

Maria unwound the silk scarf from her neck and spread it on the ground beside the ash.

Barbara stared at the little pile, then at the scarf. "This seems stupid to me. Why do I want them? I don't know what they were before…"

"It's not stupid, Barbara—why are the ashes in such a neat pile, like they knew you would come? Stop asking questions and help me."

Maria put her hands together to make a scoop, picked up a handful of ashes and dumped them gently on the scarf. She used her fingers to push the remaining fine ash into a pile and carefully moved it onto the scarf.

When Maria had gathered all the ashes, she said, "Why don't you wrap it up?"

Barbara nodded, then carefully folded the scarf so it covered the little pile. She brought the corners together at the top, tied a knot, and passed the bundle to Maria. Maria put her hand out in a stop signal. "I think you should carry them home."

"This is really silly, Maria." Barbara looked at the scarf. "Why do I feel I must take this pile of dirt home?"

"You have lost a child, and you will say and do what some people may say are stupid things for a while. You should do the small stupid things so you won't do the big ones. Right now, if your heart tells you to do something, that's reason enough to do it."

Barbara and Maria returned to Mühlenstrasse 45 with the bundle in Barbara's hands. Although Barbara tried to hide it, Maria caught her caressing the scarf and holding it as though it were something precious. Maria looked at it occasionally, and finally asked, "Do you have a plan for them?"

Barbara answered in a small voice. "If you and Theo will let me, I would like to bury them in your garden. She loved the daffodils."

"Of course, and Theo and I will help you."

Barbara took the scarf into her bedroom and closed the door.

◇◇◇◇◇◇◇◇◇◇◇◇◇◇◇◇◇◇◇◇◇◇◇◇◇◇◇◇◇◇◇◇◇◇

Maria dragged her little cart into the kitchen, removed the items she had brought, and put her cart in the front entrance.

Dinner wouldn't be for another four hours, but Maria wanted something to do, so she began preparing the sauerbraten Barbara had soaked in its spicy marinade. She poured the marinade into a bottle, turned on the gas and lit the stove. She put olive oil in an oval cast-iron roasting pot, waited until it was hot, and then put the sauerbraten in the oil. It sizzled and spit, and Maria turned down the heat. She browned all the sides and then added two cups of the marinade she had saved. She lowered the heat until the liquid barely bubbled.

Maria went to the living room to read the newspaper, but her mind strayed to Barbara, the daughter Johann had given her, and she was worried. She got up twice, intending to go to her, but stopped herself and instead went to the kitchen to check on the roast. At noon, Maria added vegetables, carrots and potatoes, and Thomas burst through the front door an hour later.

She picked up the coat he had thrown on the floor and handed it to him. "You dropped your coat. And I want you to be quiet; your mother is sleeping in her room."

Thomas knew what that meant and hung his coat in the hall Schrank. He closed the closet door and asked Maria, "Is Mutti sick?"

"No, she is in her room because she is tired and wants privacy. She will come out when she wants to see us."

Thomas tried to squeeze past Maria. "I want to see what you brought today."

"Not until you promise me you will leave your mother alone."

"Does that mean I can't play chess in my room? I can hear noises from Mutti's room, so she must be able to hear me in my room."

"What noises have you heard in Mutti's room?" Maria moved to the kitchen, smiling, and Thomas followed.

"Wow! Honey and plums from your tree!"

"And sugar and fresh milk." Maria pointed to a litre bottle and a small brown bag.

"Are you going to make *Pflaumenkuchen* with the sugar?"

"Yes, I will make a plum torte. Do you want to help me?"

"Wow, can I?" He headed for the knife drawer and pulled out a paring knife. "I'll cut up the plums while you make the bottom part."

"I guess that will be alright. That knife wouldn't cut you if you tried."

"I'll go down to the basement and sharpen it with Vati's stone!" Thomas started for the basement stairs at the front entrance, and Maria caught him with her long arm around his waist.

"No, not now. Theo will sharpen the knives when he has time. Maybe he will let you help him."

"Great! When will he be here? That knife won't even cut a plum."

Maria looked at the cuckoo clock on the kitchen wall. "He will be here in fifteen minutes, but I need to have the Kuchen in the oven before then." She steered Thomas back to the table.

Thomas talked a steady stream while cutting the plums into wedges as fast as Maria arranged them on the dough. Theo came in so quietly that Maria and Thomas didn't hear him until he bent over to hug his grandson.

He said, "I see Pflaumenkuchen," and Thomas stopped talking long enough to hug his grandfather.

Thomas let Theo go and resumed talking. "Maria has some sugar— and honey too! Can we sharpen Mutti's knives when I finish? This one is so dull it won't cut…" he looked around the kitchen… "goose fat." He congratulated himself with a smile.

"Okay, if Maria and Barbara are willing to wait a few minutes before we eat." Theo looked around the corner into the living room. "Where's Barbara?"

Maria slid the Kuchen into the oven and closed the door. "That's a long story. We may have to eat without her."

"Why don't you tell me what's going on?"

Thomas collected knives from various locations and headed for the cellar. "Mutti is tired, and Maria said she wants us to leave her alone."

"Tired? Is she sick?" Theo followed Thomas, turning his head to look inquisitively at Maria. Maria shook her head, and Theo disappeared down the cellar stairs.

◇◇◇◇◇◇◇◇◇◇◇◇◇◇◇◇◇◇◇◇◇◇◇◇◇◇◇◇◇◇◇◇

It took twenty minutes to sharpen the knives, and when Theo and Thomas returned to the kitchen, Barbara was helping Maria. She pointed at the sauerbraten sitting on the counter.

"Try out one of your sharp knives on that roast. It's tender and will fall apart if the knife isn't sharp."

Thomas reassured his Oma. "These knives are really, really sharp! Theo taught me how, so I can sharpen them from now on." Thomas dumped half a dozen knives on the counter, and Maria put them in the sink.

"You can't use them until I clean them," She ran water into the sink, "And you will need Theo's help for a while yet." She looked at Theo while she washed the knives, adding, "You can remind Theo to sharpen them before they get so dull."

Barbara sat sideways on a chair with her left arm draped over the back. "Everything takes practice—sharpening knives more than most things. Johann tried to teach me, but there is something about it that I can't seem to get."

Theo sliced a thin piece of meat and put it in Barbara's mouth. "Try that and tell me what you think."

"Why? I marinated the meat, Maria cooked it, and you are slicing it. What does slicing have to do with taste?" Barbara laughed. "But it is more delicious than usual; maybe it is the knife." She winked at Theo.

"I sharpened that knife!" Thomas looked at his mother, and Barbara put her arm around his shoulders. "So, that's why it tastes better!"

Maria took the browned potatoes and carrots from the iron roaster and put them in bowls. Barbara put them on the table and filled the water glasses while Maria made the gravy.

<hr>

The family joined hands, Theo said grace, and everyone chattered about food while they filled their plates. Thomas complained that he couldn't drink that much milk, and when Maria pulled the Kuchen out of the oven, every eye followed her every move. She put it on the top of the stove to cool and sat down.

"Guten Appetit" worked its way around the table.

Halfway through her meal, Barbara immediately got everyone's attention when she put down her fork.

"I walked to Siegruna's house this morning…it's the first time I've gone there since Lisa died. I want to live without crying so much—and I thought I might find peace there."

Everyone put their utensils down and waited. Thomas looked at Maria; she nodded, and he put his spoon on his plate.

"While I stood on the sidewalk, the sun rose through the neighbour's trees, and the rays that made their way through the leaves shone into the hole. A piece of a mirror reflected the sun into something on the bottom and lit up a patch of ash and dust."

Maria and Theo fought their tears, and Thomas quietly watched his mother, listening intently.

"I climbed down to the little pile, and although it seems strange, I felt Lisa's presence there."

She looked at Maria. "Didn't you feel her there?"

"I feel Lisa with me so often it's become normal for me. She was with me today when I went to look for you; I knew where you would be."

Thomas said, "I talk to Lisa all the time," as though it were the most normal thing in the world. "She doesn't answer me, but I know she hears me."

Barbara smiled at Thomas and touched his arm. "I know you do, Thomas, and you have since the day she died. I've never felt her with me like you feel her until today. Maybe we lose those abilities when we get older." She hesitated for a moment, and no one spoke.

"Maria gave me her scarf to carry the ashes, and I brought them home. I've been with them all morning and decided that these ashes are Lisa—maybe not all of them, but enough for me to feel her in them."

Maria spoke for Barbara's ears only. "You must do what your heart tells you, not what you think is reasonable. Logic and reason became irrelevant six months ago."

Barbara looked around the table. "I want to move on with my life. I've got a son and a husband who need my help, and Lisa would want me to put everything into that."

She stopped, put her head down, and Maria asked, "What do you want us to do, Barbara?"

She lifted her head. "I don't want you to do this unless you feel it in your heart as I feel it in mine."

Theo lost his fight with his tears. "Tell us what to do, and we will do it. Whatever you feel right now, we feel it too. My heart feels what your heart feels, and we will do this together."

"Do you remember how Lisa loved daffodils? Every spring, she watched them come up in the garden at Gartenstrasse 18, and when they bloomed, she sat down in the flower bed beside them."

Barbara looked around the table. "I want to put the ashes in the daffodil bed. We could plant some fresh bulbs, and next spring, Lisa would be with them."

Everyone laughed when Thomas shouted, "Mutti, Lisa would love that!" so he cut the volume when he continued. "I will dig the old ones out and loosen the dirt, and we can mix the ashes in." Thomas, excited, left his chair and hugged his mother.

Theo found fifty daffodil bulbs at a greenhouse in Holzhausen, and two days later, the family said goodbye to Lisa.

Until spring, when the daffodils bloomed.

Chapter Twenty-six

The Russians are coming, again.

"Women and cats will do as they please, and men and dogs should relax and get used to the idea."

Robert A. Heinlein

JOHANN AND HIS MEN SPENT THE NEXT FEW DAYS on the Dnieper River exploring the banks above and below Kyiv, crossing the river at night to count tanks and guns, and reporting Russian activity. On the third of November, when the Russians began their withering barrage along the Dnieper above and below Kyiv, the Fourth panzer Army had prepared their withdrawal plans and tactical traps.

As anticipated, the Russians attacked the Bukrin Bend, where Johann and his men had beaten them back a month earlier, and, as Johann had predicted, was a preliminary to the main assault, a test of the German defences. The XXIV panzer Corps followed the plan, trapping the Russians in a soft, fifteen-hundred-metre-deep loop. They used machine guns, artillery, and Stukas to slaughter thousands of Russian soldiers and finally pushed the survivors back across the river at the cost of one wounded soldier.

General Nehring speared a fried Schnitzel and flopped it onto his plate. He had left the smaller one for Johann, and Johann took it before it disappeared. A bowl of bean salad and a larger bowl full of fried potato slices made a meal to satisfy Johann's Gods. Christmas Eve, 1943, was turning out to be the best Johann could remember since leaving Detmold.

"How many men did you lose, Johann?"

"One, sir. He shot himself in the foot, and the lucky bastard gets to go home. You ordered me to scout and find targets for the artillery and Luftwaffe and specifically not to engage the enemy unless I had an overwhelming advantage."

"I don't remember the last bit—the bit after 'unless.'"

"Well, we had nothing to do once the artillery had done their work, so we set up a trap in the loop and called in the Luftwaffe. When they finished, we helped chase the Russians back across the river."

It didn't occur to Johann that he had disobeyed Nehring.

The general showed a hint of a smile. "While you were at the bend, Kyiv fell, but we expected that, didn't we? When the Russians crossed the river, they pushed Army Group Center northward—now a hundred kilometres of Russians are between them and us."

While he chewed, Johann said, "But look at the cost! Surely, the Russians can't take casualties at this rate for much longer." He cut his second piece of schnitzel, popped it in his mouth and followed it with a forkful of bean salad.

Nehring swallowed before he said, "Yes, I hear you, and Russian losses are certainly appalling if we were talking about a regular army in a normal war. Our intelligence estimates Russian losses of one hundred eighteen thousand since they began their offensive and 'only' sixteen thousand for us. According to them, the Russians lost about four hundred tanks, mostly to our artillery and the Luftwaffe, while we lost two dozen, and most of those had mechanical issues."

Johann's tone showed his disdain for reports of battlefield successes. "So, if intelligence is telling the truth about Russian losses, why would the Russians keep going? Why won't they stop at the Polish border and leave the German army in Poland?"

General Nehring put his fork and knife on his plate.

"Because, even with those losses, Stalin gained a hundred and fifty kilometres toward Germany, and Berlin is the prize the Red Army is after. In fact, despite his losses, Stalin can claim a victory because of the ground he gained—Polish and Russian ground. Stalin doesn't care about losses as long as his army gets closer to Germany and Hitler.

"Hitler is apoplectic—I would even say, under four eyes, that he is scared. Stalin plans to crush Germany, kill Hitler and his gang, and keep whatever ground he crosses to accomplish that!

"But the cost...." Johann put his fork down. "Hundreds of thousands of men and hundreds of tanks for a few kilometres of land? Hitler won't be in Berlin when and if the Russians get there. When was the last time a politician paid for his crimes?"

In a tone more befitting a father, Nehring said, "Remember your ants? You killed thousands, ran away and rested, but they multiplied and followed you. When they attacked again, you killed thousands more, but they repeated their strategy until they were in your home." He gave Johann time to respond, but Johann waited, knowing Nehring was right and having no answer.

Nehring said, "You were right, Johann—the Russians won't stop until they are in our homes, and Poland is only a bridge—one that Stalin intends to keep."

"But these are men, and my story was just a story. How can Stalin let thousands of men die fighting for Poland—a country that doesn't even speak Russian and has done nothing to hurt him?"

"As you know, you shouldn't take our intelligence reports of Russian casualties too seriously. As for Poland, Stalin only wants all the land attached to the land he has at any given moment. He will send thousands more men to the front than we killed or captured and two thousand tanks to replace the actual two hundred that we destroyed. And Stalin will do it before the end of January!"

The general split his last piece of schnitzel into two large, barely edible parts. "I can't even guarantee we will replace the panzers we lost, and we won't get sixteen thousand replacements for our lost soldiers. All the men who would make good soldiers are already in the Wehrmacht or the SS."

Canned pudding topped off a perfect Christmas dinner.

<hr>

General Nehring made a rookie mistake in the Queen's Gambit opening. Ten moves later, he tipped his king and sat back, puffing on his cigar like a train, directing smoke rings to his right. Johann took a long pull on his cigar and aimed the smoke at the rings twirling beside the chessboard. As the smoke rings collided, Johann waited for Nehring to tell him what was on his mind. He didn't have to wait long.

"There is something you should know." Nehring tapped his cigar on the edge of the ashtray and leaned forward with his elbows on the table. "England and America met with Stalin in Tehran a month ago, where

Stalin demanded a 'Land for Blood' reward for continuing to fight Germany. Otherwise, he threatened to stop at Russia's borders and let the Allies sort out Western Europe."

Johann suddenly understood. "So that's why the Russians want to 'save' Poland and Czechoslovakia—Russia will take those countries as booty!"

In Johann's mind, any hope for stopping the Russian advance at the Polish border evaporated. The fight would go on for months, perhaps years.

Nehring added, "Stalin's hordes will chase us to Germany, but will the Allies let the Red Army cross the German border? I suppose that would depend on where the Allies are when the Russians get there."

Johann twirled the ash from his cigar. "The Russians won't stop at our border unless the British and Americans are standing there. Stalin will tear Germany apart to get his hands on Hitler!"

"The Russians got more than Poland and Czechoslovakia in the 'land for blood' agreement—they got a dozen countries between him and Germany: Ukraine, Belorussia, Romania, Yugoslavia, Bulgaria, Hungary, Poland, Czechoslovakia…virtually all of them. The Allies did refuse one item on Stalin's agenda. He wanted to execute fifty thousand German officers that he has in his prisons. Roosevelt said no. The report claims Stalin laughed at him."

"So, how does this affect what we do?" Johann figured that one more pull would take the cigar halfway, and then he would pinch it off and save it for later.

The adjutant opened the tent flap and saluted. "Scouts report that the Russians are preparing to attack. General Hoth is on the phone."

Johann stood, pinched his cigar and put it in his pocket. "It's time to go to work. Thanks for dinner." He saluted, ducked through the tent flap and headed for the Kubelwagen reserved for his drive back to the camp. "Christmas! For God's sake, couldn't they wait a few days?" He trotted to the car and sat in the front passenger seat.

◇◇◇◇◇◇◇◇◇◇◇◇◇◇◇◇◇◇◇◇◇◇◇◇◇◇◇◇◇◇◇

It was cold and dark when Johann arrived at the Jäger Company camp, frozen from the drive in the open Kubelwagen. His men sat around fires—burning tires donated by the maintenance crew.

"Put the fires out; the war's still out there, and we've got to go to work." Johann motioned toward the flames and the circle of soldiers around it, including Ian.

Ian stood. "Yeah, we know; we're the ones who reported the Russians getting ready to attack." He pointed at the end of a chain tied to a burning tire. "We're moving the tires to that field—it will make a fine target for Russian artillery." On cue, two men picked up the end of the chain and began walking, leaving a trail of faltering flames on the snow. Half a dozen other fires got the same treatment.

Ian waved at the Finn. "Väinü came up with this one; apparently, it worked well in Finland. We passed it on to the regular troops, and if the Russians take the bait, their first half-hour with the big guns won't be entirely useful."

◇◇◇◇◇◇◇◇◇◇◇◇◇◇◇◇◇◇◇◇◇◇◇◇◇◇

When the Russians attacked, Johann had fewer than a hundred men broken into two platoons—one commanded by Ian, and the other was his responsibility. The Finn, Väinü, assisted Johann, fitting in as Wilhelm's replacement. Jäger Company was not a defensive force, and when the bombardment began, their standing orders were to find the guns and tanks and target them for German artillery and planes.

Johann and Ian led their platoons toward the Russians, using what sparse cover they could find on the flat land. Houses and barns, occasional thickets of small, bare trees, and occasional ditches or tall grass around frozen ponds supplied some cover. But between hiding places, the landscape was open. It had snowed several times since the beginning of December, and the wind had whipped and pounded the dry powder into drifts, like waves on a turbulent, frozen ocean, hard enough to support a man's weight.

The Finnish soldiers had brought camouflage and deception skills Johann had not thought possible. They knew how to make themselves invisible in or on snow and happily taught their German comrades how to create and wear white camouflage. Johann's soldiers now carried their rifles and Papa machine guns in white bags, wore white hoods with flaps that covered their weathered, bearded faces, and extended pant legs to cover their boots. When they folded their three-man white canvas tents, each man put his share of the tent in a white pack, to be used as a groundsheet when it wasn't a third of a tent. When they travelled through falling and blowing snow, they were visible only to two or three men beside them. Thirty feet of separation was enough to become lost in a three-dimensional sea of white. Without gravity to help, up and down would have been impossible to establish.

The cold north wind whipped grains of snow into the air, blowing it in wisps and eddies higher than a man's head. Johann's men moved silently, using hand signals passed down the line. Walking in 'V' formations, each man followed the one beside and in front of him, and the only sounds were boots crunching hard frozen snow and a howling wind that blew any other sound away. Snow swirled around the marks their boots made, and the tracks disappeared in minutes.

Jäger Company was ten kilometres southeast of Zhytomyr when the predicted barrage began, and they found themselves less than a thousand metres from the Russian guns. Big guns, eighty and hundred-fifty-millimetre howitzers, fired high heavy shells into the frozen air, launched on streaks of fire easily visible a kilometre away. And the white tails of Katya rockets screamed overhead.

◇◇◇◇◇◇◇◇◇◇◇◇◇◇◇◇◇◇◇◇◇◇◇◇◇◇◇◇◇◇◇◇◇◇

The snow and wind lessened for a few minutes, and Johann saw a farmhouse typical of Ukrainian family farms isolated on the flat Steppes. He decided the house was unique enough to make a good meeting place in the featureless landscape and signalled a halt to discuss the next phase of their mission.

He crouched on one knee, and when his sergeants had gathered around him, he said, "Ian, I want you and your men to work your way to the Russian guns and send the coordinates to our artillery. Then I want you to go north and see what you can find; I will take Väinü and go south." Ian nodded, and Johann pointed at the house. "We will meet south of that farmhouse in three hours. If one of us is not there, the other will wait half an hour, then report to headquarters."

He looked around the circle. "Do not engage the enemy—run away if you must. Don't shoot unless someone shoots at you!"

Ian grinned, nodded, slung his bagged Papa over his back and ran in a crouch to the north, vanishing with his men into a wall of snow. Johann checked his compass, picked a course well clear of the rocket launchers, and jogged away to the south. Väinü ran on his right, and Private Werner Schäffer, one of several new German recruits forced on him after Kyiv, ran on his left.

The boy, Schäffer, was incompetent but didn't know it, and Johann kept him close so he wouldn't shoot someone he shouldn't. Until now, he had answered every attempt Johann made to clarify an order with, "Yes, I know that," and Johann feared the private would be dead in a week—perhaps before the day was over if he said it one more time. Despite that, Johann still held a glimmer of hope that bullets whizzing past his head might broaden the boy's perspective and break his oversized sense of self-importance. Johann's experience with arrogance had shown it was not conducive to learning or change and, in battle, survival. Arrogant soldiers usually became forgotten dead heroes.

While the platoon moved south at a jog, Johann sent Väinü and his Finnish squad to look for tanks. They pushed ahead of the platoon and vanished. Private Schäffer waited less than a minute before he asked the obvious question. "How will he find us again?"

"I don't know; I sure as hell couldn't!"

"But he shouldn't run off like that if he can't find us again."

"I didn't say he couldn't find us; he will find us when he wants to. Meanwhile, we will find tanks in this direction."

"I don't think there are any tanks. I haven't seen any." The boy was obviously in good physical shape. He spoke clearly and breathed quietly, even though the jog wasn't easy.

Johann's voice wasn't as clear, and he had to breathe twice to finish a short sentence. "That's why we…must find them… They will attack us today."

"Why are you sure they will use tanks today? Maybe they will fire artillery at us and use tanks later—when the snow stops."

"Experience." Johann wanted to trip him but controlled his urge. Maybe if he shot him by mistake… Yes, his men would pretend it was an accident, or the Russians might…

<hr>

Half an hour later, Väinü appeared out of the swirling snow.

"There are a hundred T-34s and at least fifty eighty-eight and one-oh-five tank destroyers about five hundred metres dead ahead. Their crews are in them, their engines are running, and they are pointed where you would expect."

Johann purposely ignored Schäffer's open mouth. "Let's get an accurate count and some coordinates. Lead us as close as you dare, and we'll work our way around them."

The frozen ground under the Steppes was unbroken by anything but an occasional drainage ditch—and hard snow and ice filled the furrows and holes in the fields, making travelling easy. It was a perfect location for a tank battle; the only advantage the Germans had would be what reconnaissance would give them. The Russian tanks were up to the jump-off line, ready to hit the XXIV panzer Corps on two fronts. If Johann's company could find them before they attacked, the Fourth panzer Army artillery could save their tanks.

The scouts walked over the same ground they had walked over several times in the past week—ground where they had seen no tanks until today. Now, Väinü had found more than a hundred tanks in a tight formation, engines running, facing the heart of the XXIV panzer Corps line. There had to be dozens, maybe hundreds more, hiding in the snowstorm.

Johann put his hand on Private Schäffer's shoulder. "Do you know where we are?"

"Uh...no, sir...not exactly." Private Schäffer hadn't expected the question.

"I need you to run back to our demag and send the coordinates of those tanks."

"But I don't know the coordinates, and I'm not sure I can find the demag." Private Schäffer was uncomfortable.

"Then how can you tell our artillery where to target their guns? Isn't that why you are here?"

"Uh...I can't, sir." His voice faltered.

Johann said, "Then I guess I will have to shoot you!" He turned away, finished with Schäffer for the moment.

Väinü briefed one of his men in Finnish and sent him to the demag.

Snow fell from low clouds, so an airstrike against the Russian tank formation was out of the question, but the German artillery might do some damage, if they received the coordinates soon enough.

Johann's men kept up their pace for another five kilometres and found another two hundred tanks and fifty tank destroyers that hadn't been there three days ago.

Johann stopped, and the Finn stopped beside him. "We can expect another hundred T-34s this side of Berdychev, but we don't have time to find them; we have to meet Ian and get what information we've got to Nehring." Väinü nodded.

Private Schäffer interrupted. "Shouldn't we count those tanks to be sure? I could take some men with me and meet Ian later."

Johann said quietly, "Which way would you go from here?"

Werner pointed toward Moscow.

"I think you had better stay close to me. If you lose sight of us, sit down and pray that we will find you. Do you speak Russian? Can you say, "I surrender… Please don't shoot me?""

"No...but..."

Väinü saved Werner's life with a withering look that closed the boy's mouth.

Johann's platoon reached the farmhouse a few minutes after Ian and found him crouching in a depression surrounded by tall frozen grass and snowdrifts. Two months ago, it had been a pond—now, it was a slab of ice.

Ian reported three hundred T-34s and at least a hundred heavy tank destroyers between them and Zhytomyr. He had also seen thousands of infantry soldiers ready to move up with the tanks. He had taken the only radio with him and had already sent the coordinates to Nehring's headquarters. Johann gave Ian's radioman the coordinates of the tanks they had found, and the man tried to send them, but the batteries died before the message was complete.

While trying to warm the batteries with their hands, Johann and Ian heard male laughter, then shots from the farmhouse, muffled to a dull thump by the falling snow. Johann, Ian, Väinü, and every man in both platoons dropped to the snow—except for Werner. He went as far as his knees, then stretched his neck to see over the grass. A blow from Väinü's rifle butt felled him. He yelped, but the Finn covered his mouth before a full sound could get out.

Johann and Ian crawled to the edge of the grass and parted it with the barrel of their Papas. Väinü crawled up beside Johann, and they watched two women running toward them, with six laughing Russian soldiers trying to catch them. The Russians fired their rifles in the air and yelled what Johann presumed was "Stop!" The women ran faster.

Väinü whispered, "They are saying, 'Stop! We won't hurt you!'" Väinü pushed the barrel of his Russian sniper rifle through the grass and lowered his eye to the sight. Johann put his mitten on the barrel, shook his head and said, "Not yet!"

The men gained on the women, who ran straight for the frozen pond. The Russian soldiers were twenty metres behind them when the women burst through the grass and cattails and threw themselves down in the snow behind cover in a desperate attempt to hide. They were a dozen feet from Johann and his men but didn't see them. Their laughing pursuers stumbled as they ran, clearly drunk on fermented potatoes. They followed the women's tracks and broke through the grass where they lay in the snow. The last sound the Russians made on earth was a triumphant laugh—a dozen of Johann's men burst out of the snow, knives ready, targets picked, and in seconds, all six Russians either lay still or were taking their final breaths in the bloody snow. No one had fired a shot, and Johann relaxed. Sound carried a long way on flat land, and the Red Army was close. These men were doing the same job as Johann's.

Private Schäffer threw up.

<hr>

The older woman stood, and Väinü pulled her down, speaking softly in Russian. She lay very still—shock glazed her wide-open eyes. Tentatively at first, then in a torrent, she uttered a blur of Russian words. Väinü waited with his hands coiled around his knees, fingers locked together, nodding occasionally.

She finally stopped babbling, and he turned to Johann. "She said there are no more soldiers." He paused, thinking about something, then said, "They could be a patrol, or perhaps scouts, like us, but what would they scout behind their own lines? I think we will find Russian soldiers between us and our demag! We should get out of here as soon as we can."

"What else did she say? That was a lot of words for one sentence."

"She said her husband is dead, killed by the Germans a year ago, on their way to Moscow. She is Ukrainian, and the Russians hate Ukrainians." He paused… "I'm not sure… Do Germans hate Ukrainians?"

Johann ignored the question, rolled over, parted the grass, and looked toward the house. It was snowing too hard now to see it. "Tell her she should be safe to return to her house. These men aren't going to tell on her." Johann looked at her. She was terrified and hadn't understood a word.

Väinü relayed the message, and she talked for a full minute.

"She says she has no food, no fuel for the fire, and they can't go back. The Russians took everything, and they will kill her and rape her daughter if they return to the house." Väinü's expression answered the question Johann was going to ask. "She wants to come with us. We saved her life, so she thinks we can't be as bad as the Russian soldiers!"

"Germans killed her husband, and she still wants to go with us?"

Väinü nodded. "She knows who we are. She says that Germans can't possibly be as bad as the Russians."

"She said that?"

Väinü spread his hands and smiled. "I modified it a little…so you wouldn't be offended."

"Yeah, you can smile—you're a Finn! Everyone likes Finns!"

The young girl, dressed only in a woollen dress and low shoes like her mother, watched the two men as the conversation progressed and then suddenly threw herself on Johann's boots, buried her face between them, and lifted her tearful face up to look in his eyes. She sobbed as she spoke, and even though the words were foreign, Johann didn't need a translator.

Scheisse. He lifted her to a sitting position beside him and brushed her hair away from her face while thinking of Lisa. He turned to Väinü. "Give them warm clothes and camouflage." He turned to Private Schäffer. "You will look after them. If they get away or you lose them, I will shoot you!" The private's face moved. "If you speak, I will shoot you now and let someone else look after them!" Unhappy, Schäffer stood up and pointed at them, ignoring Johann's threat. "They may be Jews. You cannot order a soldier of the Reich to protect Jews!"

Johann kicked Private Schäffer's feet sideways, and the boy fell backwards, landing on the hard pond ice with a thud and an expiration of breath. He gasped, trying unsuccessfully to fill his empty lungs. Johann looked down at him and hissed, "They can't be Jews… Nazi murderers like you killed all the Jews when they went through here in forty-one!" He drew his boot back but stopped short of kicking the boy.

"These are civilians, and that's all you need to know! Their religion has nothing to do with you—do you understand?"

"Y-y-yes, but…" he gasped; Johann drew back his foot, and Werner wisely quit trying to speak.

"If you ask them if they're Jews or if anything happens to these people, I will let the Russians kill you. If you are lucky, they may offer you a job in a salt mine! On the plus side, you will learn Russian." Johann shook his head in exasperation. "I don't think there is any hope for you."

Väinü smiled at the young Nazi, then spoke to the women. The older one rambled on, pointed here and there, then stopped, pulled her knees tight with her shaking hands and laid her head on them. Väinü turned back to the boy.

"Private Schäffer, I have excellent news! You are safe. They are Orthodox Christians. And Johann is right—she confirmed that your fellow Nazis killed the Jews that lived in the villages near here in the summer of forty-one on their way to Moscow. She says they buried many of them in a ditch not far from here." He squeezed Schäffer's leg. "You are safe, my son. These women are not dangerous, and you will benefit if they convert you to Christianity."

Private Schäffer furrowed his brow and started to open his mouth, but Väinü shook his head. "No, Private Schäffer, you are not a Christian!"

Väinü returned to the women, leaving no doubt that the conversation with the boy was over.

Sixty men gathered spare white capes and hoods to clothe ten women. Dry boots appeared, and the women found two pairs that fit well enough, if a little loose. Extra socks fixed the looseness.

Johann and Ian took two of the fastest runners and ran ahead of Väinü and the women. Russian artillery and rockets began their second barrage as the Eighth Jäger Company headed for the demag and XXIV panzer headquarters. Standard Russian protocol would mean the attack would follow in a few hours.

◇◇◇◇◇◇◇◇◇◇◇◇◇◇◇◇◇◇◇◇◇◇◇◇◇◇◇◇◇◇◇◇

Five minutes after arriving at the battle command tent, Johann reached General Nehring's intelligence headquarters on the Corps telephone. Because it was wired directly, the line had no unwanted listeners. Johann described the Russian attack positions to the intelligence officer, and when he finished, General Nehring took the handset on the other end.

"You've seen what they've got and where they are—where would you try to stop them?" Nehring's question surprised Johann, and he waited while his leutnant's mind adjusted. General Nehring had asked him what he would do if he were a general. He decided to answer honestly.

"They will attack the line between Zhytomyr and Berdychev. The engines in the northern and southern tank units are running, but the tanks between them are quiet. They will try to force the ends but retreat or hold in the centre. The tanks will form a pincer behind us, and when they've closed it, the infantry will bring reinforcements to the centre, and their artillery will bomb the hell out of us. The Soviet Air Force and artillery will destroy our armour; this is a twist on the tactic they have used since forty-two when we taught them how to do it."

The phone was silent for so long that Johann wondered if the general had hung up. He eventually spoke.

"I believe you are right." Nehring hesitated, then asked, "Is there something else you want to tell me?"

Check, thought Johann, the general knows me too well. He said, "We've played too much chess," and decided to tell him. "Remember our conversation about the Russians raping women and stealing food if our men didn't?"

"Yes, and we no longer carry out that policy. The penalty for soldier rape is death."

"Yes, sir, and I must congratulate you; the plan is working."

"What is it, Leutnant? What do you want from me?"

"While on patrol, we rescued a Ukrainian woman and her daughter from some nasty but now dead Russians, and we couldn't leave them to freeze or to be killed by the dead soldiers' friends."

"Don't tell me what I think you are going to tell me."

"No, sir, but I'm afraid I did what you think I did."

"They are in the camp?"

"They just arrived... They are standing beside me, sir." He paused, but Nehring didn't jump in, so he continued his pitch. "They are very nice and intelligent women, sir. Surely you could find something for them to do in your headquarters... make coffee, sweep the floor..."

Nehring sighed. "Yes, you're right; they can't stay on the front, and they can't go home. Bring them to my headquarters, and we will discuss the situation."

Johann hung up and said, "Checkmate, General!"

Chapter Twenty-seven

Winter-spring 1944

A Triumphant Retreat

Wenn das Haupt krank ist, trauern alle Glieder.

(When the head is sick, every part of the body suffers.)

Johann took Private Schäffer with him when he drove the Ukrainian women to Nehring's headquarters. He had two motives: first, the usual protocol would require a second man for security, and second, Johann wanted to leave the private with Nehring. It would be appropriate to give him a job looking after women he couldn't understand and who couldn't understand him.

Johann drove the cold Kubelwagen to Nehring's headquarters, open to the minus-fifteen-degree elements. The mother, who had revealed her name as Katherine, sat in the front seat with him behind the windshield's shelter. Her daughter, Natasha, crouched behind the front seat beside Private Schäffer.

It took half an hour to reach General Nehring's headquarters, and enough cold air blew through their coarse woollen coats to cause grave danger of dying from exposure if the journey had been longer. They entered the general's heated tent, stamping their feet to get their blood flowing. Johann moved everything he could still feel.

General Nehring greeted the Ukrainian woman with a broad smile; one would think he was glad to see them. He said, "I assume you are Katherine." and extended his hand. She took it warily.

Johann guided a shy Natasha forward. "And this is her daughter, Natasha." General Nehring shook her ice-cold hand warmly. Natasha kept her eyes respectfully down, turning the corners of her mouth barely upward, not quite smiling, but Johann gave her an 'Eins' for effort.

Nehring said, "You will stay here until we can make other arrangements." He looked at them, but the comment was for Johann's benefit.

Katherine couldn't understand a word he had said, and the expression on her face said she was worried. She asked Johann what he assumed was a question.

"Adjutant!" General Nehring shouted, and a young man stepped through the flap. "Bring Schröder."

The general answered the question before Johann could ask. "Sergeant Sergei Schröder is my Russian expert. He's from Bavaria but speaks perfect Russian, which he learned from his Ukrainian mother. He spent six weeks every summer on his grandparents' farm in Ukraine. And, incidentally, he's also a fine chess player."

Schröder entered and Nehring indicated Katherine.

"Ask her what she said to Leutnant Finke."

The cold may have frozen Katherine's lips, but not her tongue. She babbled until the sergeant cut her off.

"She's afraid of you." Sergei nodded to General Nehring and waited.

"Tell her what a nice person I am."

The sergeant rolled his eyes and talked for what seemed a long time. While he spoke, Katherine's face broke into a smile, and she laughed when he finished.

The sergeant smiled. "Sir, she's no longer afraid of you."

"It's probably better that I don't know the details." General Nehring turned to Johann.

"Is this the young man you told me about...the one who will get everyone killed?" Private Schäffer looked at Johann and then returned his attention to the general. He opened his mouth but closed it again when Sergeant Schröder elbowed him.

Nehring said, "Leutnant Finke says it will save lives if you stay here. You will look after these ladies and run confidential errands for me. Can you drive a car?"

"Yes, Herr General!" the private stiffened and audibly exhaled, likely relieved that General Nehring wouldn't shoot him in the immediate future. He clicked his heels and stuck out his arm in a Nazi salute.

"Very impressive..." General Nehring pulled the boy's arm down, "but if you do that again around here, you will sleep outside—in the snow—without a blanket." He put his hand on Private Schäffer's shoulder and looked into the confused boy's eyes. "If you reveal anything I tell you, or if any documents you carry fall into any hands other than the ones I assign, I will either kill you outright or give you to the Russians."

Johann smiled.

General Nehring turned to the adjutant. "Sergeant Schröder, take the ladies to their tent; it should be warm by now." Then, as an afterthought, "Take Private Schäffer with you. Explain his duties to him and show him where he will sleep."

"Yes, sir. The tent is warm, and I found a few things they will need. I will see that they are comfortable." The sergeant faced Private Schäffer, "You must come with me."

General Nehring sighed and spoke to Johann. "Leutnant, I need some fresh air."

They exited the tent into a blast of cold air. Johann watched the sergeant guide his charges to a nearby tent, smoke rising from its tin chimney, and wished he could go somewhere warm. He noted that General Nehring hadn't worn the standard-issue heavy woollen coat; the walk would be short.

"Johann, Hitler has ordered us to hold to the last man."

Johann nodded. "There is nothing new in that."

"But simultaneously, he diverted our every available source of reinforcements to France, where the Allies will eventually attack."

"Yes, sir. Every man here knows about Directive Five One."

"The tiny hope he left us is independence to stop the Russians in any way we see fit."

Johann nodded thoughtfully. "So, we need to retreat in an organized way that will make it appear we are holding and winning."

"Exactly!" General Nehring slapped his hands together and rubbed them to create friction. He used a very efficient hand-washing motion.

"I want you to keep track of the Russians and report directly to me. Do not use wireless except in emergencies. You will send runners to meet Private Schäffer and only Private Schäffer. You may request that he meet you at coordinates—I will assign a demag half-track to him." He turned 180 degrees and headed back to his tent, walking a little faster. Johann stayed beside him.

"Sir, Schäffer couldn't find the ocean if he were standing on the beach, let alone find a point on a map, and I wouldn't trust him with a tracked vehicle like the two-fifty. A Kubelwagen is his limit."

"I will send Schröder and three of my best men with him. Sergeant Schröder can find whatever you can find. He is our Cochise." He smiled at the reference to Ian. "Send your Cochise to meet our Cochise, and Private Schäffer will drive the wagon." He chuckled at his little joke.

He stopped to think, and Johann asked, "Is there something else I should know?" He had learned a lot while playing chess with Nehring, and the general had more to say.

"Yes, I'm afraid so." They approached the tents and would be heard if they went farther, so General Nehring stopped. "Hitler replaced General Hoth, commander of the Fourth panzer Army, with General Raus, a Hitler fanatic. Unfortunately, he subscribes to the 'fighting to the last man' theory. Equally unfortunate, he is my commander, and I fear he will find a way around Manstein's standing orders. Manstein believes, as I do that, we must fight our way back to Germany, slowing the Russians to give time for peace negotiations to succeed. Failing that, it would be better if the Western Allies met the Russians on this side of Germany."

"So, you want me to know that even though the Russians might encircle Raus's Fourth panzer Army, you will move the Twenty-Fourth Corps' panzers back?"

"Let's see how this works out, but yes, I will move the Twenty-Fourth panzers before the Russians destroy them, and Raus may change his mind when he realizes he will be the last man standing. You will know what to do if you read my orders carefully and use your chess skills."

The drive back to XXIV panzer Corps' field headquarters was cold, but Johann didn't notice it until he tried to straighten his fingers to let go of the wheel. He had talked to himself for the entire half-hour drive.

<hr>

Although it was now March, the ground was frozen and covered with snow as Johann and Ian stood in the back of their demag half-track, watching Russian tanks driving along Raus's Fourth panzer Army's southern flank. The Russian T-34s herded the remnants of Raus's forces toward a pocket north of Johann's Jäger Company, where it was evident to Johann that they would destroy them if Raus didn't do something.

Johann lowered his binoculars and passed them to Ian, frustrated that Raus didn't see the trap. "Why in hell doesn't Raus swing and attack the Russians? Manstein ordered him to do that two days ago!"

Ian watched the Russian tanks through his binoculars, as frustrated as Johann. "Hitler told him to hold, and Raus thinks Hitler is a military genius." He lowered the binoculars. "Don't you think it's time to talk to Nehring?"

"I sent him a report two days ago, and no reinforcements are available. The Third panzer Corps is fighting for its life, and the Russians have encircled the First panzer Army a hundred and fifty kilometres south of us. General Nehring wants us to meet with Schröder, probably to tell us to withdraw and leave Raus to his fate."

Ian said, "The Russians have moved twenty-five kilometres in the last two hours. Someone must wake up, or Raus will lose the Fourth panzer Army and General Nehring's Twenty-Fourth panzer Corps along with it!"

Johann looked southwest toward the meeting place ten kilometres away. Schröder would be there in half an hour. "When we meet with Nehring's messengers, I will tell them to tell Nehring that the Twenty-Fourth panzers have to withdraw."

"Nehring knows that."

Johann tightened his hands on the binoculars. "You're right; Nehring promised me the Corps would pull back to save themselves... But they must do it today—tomorrow, the Russians will be behind them."

When Johann and Ian arrived at the meeting place, Nehring was in the demag, Sergeant Schröder was driving, and Private Schäffer was at the machine gun. Johann climbed out of his demag and slid into the back seat of Nehring's. The general handed him an envelope.

"These are the orders for the Twenty-Fourth panzer Corps, signed by General Manstein and me. You should know that Manstein just returned from a meeting with Hitler, and the Führer refused his request to allow the Fourth panzer Army to withdraw. Despite that, Manstein told Raus he is ordering the Twenty-Fourth panzer Corps to pull back, and Raus can either swing his line with them or spend the rest of the war in a Russian Gulag!"

"Yes, sir. What do you want the Eighth Jäger Company to do?"

"As we discussed—ambush, thrust and parry, and keep me informed. You know how to do that job better than I do. Make the Russians afraid of you."

"Yes, sir." Johann slid off the seat, stepped down from the half-track, and was turning to his own demag when the sound of shots and bullets zipping around him flipped a switch in his brain. He turned back, jumped up on the demag, grabbed Nehring's arm and dragged him to the ground as bullets struck the half-track, some of them hitting Werner Schäffer, who cried out as he swung the demag's gun.

Men in white camouflage appeared out of nowhere, but Ian's machine gun cut them down before they got close. Väinü picked off targets farther away.

Four men almost reached the demag, but Schröder cut them down with his Papa. Johann got two more as they ran for safety. Väinü shot the last man in the back.

As suddenly as the battle had begun, the only sound was the moan of a wounded man. Väinü fired a single shot, and the silence was complete.

Johann helped General Nehring to his feet. The general wasn't frightened; he spoke evenly and naturally. "It looks as though they were after me… How the devil would the Russians know that I would be here?"

Johann helped him brush the snow from his clothes. "I sent a message to headquarters earlier, using code, to confirm the meeting. Someone who knew our frequency may have been listening—maybe someone in your office… But without today's code, why would they go straight for you? You are wearing the same uniform as the rest of us, yet you were the target. How did they know that you would personally deliver those orders?"

"Every order has a piece of paper, and the Gestapo is everywhere. Manstein and I are mavericks right now, and perhaps…"

"…someone told the Russians? That seems unlikely because it takes too much time." Johann asked, "Did you send that information anywhere else?"

Nehring looked shocked. "Yes…Manstein and I have exchanged

coded messages..." He paused, thinking... "The code? Is it possible they have our codes?"

Johann said, "Perhaps you shouldn't use that coding machine for a while. At least, not for anything that has to do with me."

"No, it's not possible...I can't believe the Russians have our codes. But that would explain the timely artillery bombardment at Kursk...."

Johann nodded. "You should use couriers for anything you don't want the Russians to know. Do you still want us to 'hit and run'?"

"Of course! Nothing has changed for anyone but poor Private Schäffer." Ian was laying the dead private in the rear seat of Nehring's demag. He jumped to the ground, and General Nehring got into the front seat.

Johann watched the demag until it rounded a corner and disappeared. He turned to Ian and Väinü. "We're on our own." They looked at one another, and Ian said, "That's the best news I've heard today."

◇◇◇◇◇◇◇◇◇◇◇◇◇◇◇◇◇◇◇◇◇◇◇◇◇◇◇◇◇◇◇◇

The XXIV panzer Corps fought its way out of the trap and south to the Bug River, and to no one's surprise, Raus decided to move his Fourth panzer Army with them.

The ground thawed a day later, too soon for the XXIV panzers to drive a wedge south to free the First panzer Army. The First panzers, two hundred kilometres south of the Fourth panzer Army, had obeyed Hitler's orders until it was almost too late—the Russian Army had surrounded them, leaving the First panzers with three choices: surrender, fight to the last man, or take the bitter medicine and fight their way out! They chose to follow Manstein's instructions to take the pills, formed a wedge, and broke out of the Russian encirclement, but at a terrible cost. Nehring told Johann that the First panzer Army had lost almost all its armour and nearly half its infantry. Nehring dismissed claims coming out of Goebbels' Ministry of Lies of victory and much lower numbers. The truth was that the battle had been a tragedy of epic proportions.

The Russians had won two hundred thousand square kilometres of land when the spring rain and mud stopped the T-34s and panthers from killing one another. Stalin declared victory and stopped his advance.

The Russian 'victory' had cost a million men, thousands of guns and tanks, and seven hundred aircraft.

Furious that his army hadn't stood its ground, Hitler fired Von Manstein and replaced him with General Model. For reasons known only to Hitler, he changed the name of Army Group South to Army Group North Ukraine.

Johann and his men prepared for the mud season.

Chapter Twenty-eight

Spring 1944

"Music has charms to soothe the savage breast."

William Congreve, from "The Mourning Bride"

Ian's foot went out of sight in a hole hidden in a puddle of water, and he cursed for the twentieth time in an hour. *"Gotverdammter Beschissener Schlamm!"* And he continued to swear at the mud as he worked on getting his foot out of the hole with the boot still attached. He finally gave up, pulled his bare foot out of the boot and sock, and tried to stand on one leg. Failing at that, he plunged his bare foot into the cold mud. Väinü chuckled, used the butt of his Papa to dig Ian's boot out of the hole, then washed both in a puddle.

Johann laughed as he balanced himself on a narrow ridge of mud pushed up by a passing panther. "I wouldn't curse the mud too loudly; I'll take mud over fighting the Russians! And don't forget that every day the mud holds them here means another day they won't be in Germany."

A screech broke the early morning quiet, immediately joined by a familiar dissonant chorus.

"Katyas!" Johann yelled superfluously and dropped into the muck on the road's edge. Väinü, Ian, and the fifty men with them threw themselves into the mud and water, cursing, trying to stay out of the water-filled tank tracks.

The rockets landed short of the dozen panzers the Jäger Company guarded, and the Wehrmacht artillery fired in the general direction of the katya launchers. A second volley screamed over the Jäger Company's heads and past the panzers.

The tanks had nowhere to go but down the road. The fields were too soft for forty-ton panthers, and a bridge five hundred metres ahead, barely wide enough for single-file trucks and tanks, squeezed traffic through a narrow hole. The Russians wanted the bridge saved for their own purposes, so any vehicles near it basked in its protection. katyas had a 'general direction' targeting system, and the Russians ensured the kill zone was well short of the bridge.

German artillery fired continuously and accurately, adjusting quickly to the Jäger scouts' instructions. The third volley of katyas was a fraction of the second volley and was short of the target, and the panthers made it to the bridge and crossed it before the Russians could load and fire the rockets again.

Slipping in wet mud, not caring now whether they fell or if the water topped their boots, Johann and his men followed the panzers, joining them on the other side of the river.

A half-track stopped at the end of the bridge, and five of Johann's men unloaded boxes of explosives while the rest of Eighth Company and the panthers formed a perimeter close to the bridge. The Russians didn't launch any more katyas.

A rifle shot split the air, and one of the men carrying explosives to the bridge dropped to his knees, let go of the box and fell backward. Väinü cursed in Finnish and dropped to the ground beside Ian and Johann. The dead man was one of the Finnish volunteers and Väinü's friend.

Ian, lying in the mud next to Johann, tapped the binoculars, and Johann passed them to him. Ian picked a section of the horizon, searched it carefully, then moved to another sector, searching for a movement or something that didn't belong.

Väinü clawed a notch into the ridge of mud in front of him, then steadied his rifle on his hand.

Another bullet broke the sound barrier with a crack, and a man fell off the bridge where he was wiring an explosive charge.

Ian said, without emotion, "I've got him—under a bush—light is reflecting from his sight." Ian remained stationary, and Väinü followed the line of his binoculars as Ian said, "Another flash…."

Johann knew how this would end; he hoped it would end before a third shot.

Ian said, "There's a small branch just a little from the right edge of the bush…he's under it. I can see the barrel, and he's going to…"

The sniper fired again, and another man collapsed on the bridge.

Väinü swore, breathed and fired. Two seconds passed, and he said, "Got him…"

Ian continued to stare through his binoculars. He said, "He's trying to get up. Shoot him again!"

Väinü fired again. "Now he won't get up."

Johann rolled sideways and tried to stand, but Ian pulled him down. "There's another man beside him, and he's got the rifle—he's a fool…" Väinü fired, and Ian declared, "That one won't get up. You hit him in the head."

Johann waited until Ian and Väinü finished searching for snipers before he got to his feet, soaked through to his skin with muddy water.

It took an uninterrupted half hour to set the explosives, and when the engineer twisted the handle on the detonator, both ends of the bridge fell into the river.

Johann and his miserable, wet, cold men, all of them covered in mud, rode the panzers and half-tracks to their temporary camp downstream from the bridge. The men stripped, washed the mud off their bodies with cold water from the river, dressed in their alternate winter uniforms, and went to the riverbank to wash the clothes they had been wearing. They spread them on makeshift racks set up around a roaring fire built from wood scrounged by the resourceful arsonists who were responsible for starting the fire.

◇◇◇◇◇◇◇◇◇◇◇◇◇◇◇◇◇◇◇◇◇◇◇◇◇◇◇◇◇◇◇◇◇◇◇

Dressed in dry winter uniforms, the men found the May evening comfortably warm, boding well for the summer that was hard on its heels. The first generation of biting, flying insects was still working through the pupal cycle, not yet ready to feast on human blood. A hundred war-weary soldiers sat on a dry grassy slope, watching the fire downwind from them. Steam rose from the drying clothes spread around the upwind side of the fire.

Like most of the men, Johann had spread his Zeltbahn groundsheet under him. Thanks to an hour of diligent work, he was clean, and the fire revived a sense of peace in him. He let his mind wander to Barbara's letter telling of Lisa's symbolic burial in Maria's garden. In the month since that letter, early April would have brought the daffodils out of their winter sleep, and by now, the flower bed would be a mat of yellow blossoms. Lisa's memory was, for the moment, trapped between grief and joy.

"Is that smile for Barbara or for me?" Ian sat cross-legged next to Johann, eating a can of wurst he had taken from twenty tins warming at the edge of the fire. The sausage tins, cracked open so they wouldn't explode, were placed there courtesy of the Wehrmacht kitchen. And there was soldier's bread, toasted and softened on a tilted wire rack that faced the fire.

Johann breathed a slight scent of woodsmoke, thinking of Barbara and home. Reading his mind, Ian pointed at the flames with his fork and said, "There are a hundred men here who find the love of home in that fire!"

Leaning back on his elbows, his legs stretched toward the flames, Johann said, "The daffodils are blooming in Detmold. Somehow, it doesn't seem so far away tonight, and I was thinking of Barbara."

A baritone voice began singing "Erika," a song of a sweetheart left behind, and the talking stopped. The man's beautiful voice resonated from the forest at the top of the slope and a wall of trees on the other side of the fire. A second voice, as clear and strong as the first, joined in the second verse, and within a few minutes, a hundred-voice men's choir sang the marching song of departure from their girlfriend, wife, or perhaps their sister or mother. They sang of leaving the women they loved to join in the fight for their country.

Men came and went, carrying beer in both hands. They cried, laughed, drank too much, dreamed of sweethearts and mothers, "Fussball" games, and fishing.

An accordion appeared in the hands of a musically talented Black Forest tree-feller, and an equally gifted Bavarian tenor sang songs of "Mädel in den Bergen," complete with spectacular yodelling choruses. Men clapped to the rhythm, laughing partly at his musical acrobatics but mostly because they had pushed the noise and chaos of war farther back in their minds than it had been for a long time.

Finally, they got to the bar songs, accompanied by roars of laughter. Men strayed to the hill from other units until there was barely room on the slope to sit down. They sang themselves hoarse and eventually became quiet, speaking in low tones while watching the hypnotic flames.

Katherine approached the fire with a violin in her hands, and when she stroked the bow to tune it, a hush crept up the slope until anyone who spoke was immediately silenced. Sitting beside Johann with his hands locked in front of his knees, Ian looked sideways to see his boss's reaction.

Johann, his emotions running wild, looked at the ground, found a small stone and tossed it into the darkness.

Satisfied with the tuning, Katherine stroked her bow across the strings. The pure sound vibrated against the trees, reflecting to the listeners and mesmerizing them with its sweetness. Johann knew the song; it was a universal song of home, "Songs My Mother Taught Me," from Antonin Dvorak's "Gypsy Songs." A young Czech soldier stood up and spoke to her in Russian, and she began again. His beautiful baritone voice, singing in his native language, carried through the peaceful night, and the melancholy sound softened the toughest heart.

When the young soldier finished the song, his comrades sat quietly. Katherine lowered her bow and looked at the expectant faces, her violin in one hand and her bow in the other. She looked at Johann, and, satisfied with something, she lifted the violin, stroked it, and a haunting, homesick Russian melody filled the air. The slow sweetness continued for a minute, then gradually gained speed and energy until a pulsing dancing rhythm resounded through the forest. The men stood up, reluctantly at first, individually stamping their feet, then dancing enthusiastically in pairs. A few gathered in groups mimicking the Cossack arm-lock crouch. They fell, laughed at their pitiful efforts, then got up and tried again. Katherine danced while she played her violin, and the men hooted and shouted, some using Russian words.

Sitting above most of the men, Johann clapped in time with the rhythm, but when Ian stood and offered his hand, Johann shook his head. Ian insisted and took Johann's hand by force, but the mood died. Johann locked his hands together in front of his knees; Ian gave up and joined his men, jumping like a bunch of kids around a maypole.

The men began to tire and dropped out at an ever-increasing rate until Katherine skillfully resolved the seventh chord and lowered her violin. The men clapped, and shouts of "bravo" echoed back from the trees.

The soldiers returned to their beer. Some quietly talked while others watched the fire with the faraway look they reserved for wives and sweethearts. A low murmur grew, occasionally punctuated by the laughter of a young soldier pretending to be drunk. Katherine spoke to Natasha, and her daughter walked up the slope to Johann. He didn't notice that he was her destination until she reached out her hand to him. He looked up at her, and she smiled, holding out her hand as though she would never pull it back.

"Please come with me. My mother wants you to play your violin." It was apparent she had worked hard at her German. He stood up, and Natasha waited, looking directly into his eyes, shamelessly using her innocence to charm him.

Tears formed in his eyes. Lisa's memory flooded his senses—her sweet voice, the way she curled a smile—Lisa returned in a rush that overwhelmed him, and he swallowed so he wouldn't sob.

Natasha waited patiently. He said, "I can't play anymore. Please, not tonight." He breathed in loudly and deeply, fought to keep from blubbering, and, for an instant, resented Natasha for bringing Lisa back. He turned away from her and began walking toward the moon rising behind the trees.

She looked at her mother, who waved her hand, then chased Johann while the men on the slope, sensing something was happening to the man they loved, waited. She circled, cut him off, and stepped sideways to block his way when he tried walking around her.

Natasha wrapped her arms around him and pleaded, "You must play the violin for me."

Johann pushed her back, held her shoulders in his hands and looked into her eyes. It was a mistake; he had never said no to Lisa. "I will play for you, but only if you play for me." He suddenly recognized the exact conversation with his daughter when she had gone through a self-doubting period.

Natasha smiled broadly and nodded vigorously.

"Yes, I will play for you, but you must help me." He smiled, beaten; she had left him no way out without hurting her, and he could never do that. She took his hand and led him on a circuitous route through the silent men to the bottom of the hill. Katherine gave the violin to Natasha.

A soldier took two dry sticks from a pile and threw them on the fire. The flames crackled, spewed sparks, and the soft wind took them away, dancing through the branches of the trees. Silhouetted against the blaze, Natasha raised her bow and stroked the strings expertly. A hundred men held their breath.

Johann recognized the voluptuous music, a romance written by Dvorak. Written for orchestra, it worked beautifully as a solo, and Natasha played it with the innocence of her age. Filled with emotion and giving, of caring without thought of reward, it brought tears to men's eyes. Johann silently cried to himself, one by one untying the knots that imprisoned his soul.

Katherine moved to his side and took his hand. He looked down at her, grateful for her presence. She leaned against his arm and tipped her head to touch his shoulder.

Men cried openly with Johann, their hearts at home. Natasha played reprise after reprise until the sadness evaporated. And then, demonstrating an incredible sense of timing, she modulated into a cheerful folk melody they all recognized but didn't know the words. When she stopped, the men clapped and cheered, and she handed the violin to Johann. He took the instrument carefully, touching the soundboard with a reverence he reserved for music and Barbara.

"Please, play for me." Natasha smiled, and Johann touched her hair as he had touched Lisa's. A pang of guilt tweaked his soul.

The song Johann played, familiar to every man on the hill, was the march they sang when they left home as a soldier and then in the bars and caserns as they fought their way across Europe. "Muss Ich Denn?" was a song about leaving loved ones and someday returning to them. Using his bow, Johann stressed the rhythm as the men sang, trying to strengthen the violin's sound so they could find the pitches. Alas, they drifted off-key, and each took his own tempo. Just before everything went to hell, the accordion appeared. Johann played as loudly as he dared without breaking the strings on the bow, matching the men's tempo and the sound of the accordion. A few near the fire picked out the key, and it moved from the men at the front back and across the hill, and the majority drifted back, dragging the others and saving the day.

A dozen raucous songs followed, and finally, vocal cords raw and emotions spent, the men sat down when Johann indicated they should. They were quiet as he tuned the violin for the song they all knew and loved more than anything in their repertoire. Every night, at five minutes before ten, German Armed Forces Radio, 'Soldatensender Belgrad,' read letters from home and played Lale Andersen's 'Lili Marlen' before they signed off. A sorrowful song of a soldier's longing for the love he left behind, Lili Marlen was the most popular song in Germany and England.

Johann played the tune once before the men came in and quietly sang every verse until the dead soldier rose from his grave to meet Lili Marlen under the lamppost. When the song ended, Johann lowered the violin and looked from one man to the other. They smiled back at him, and a few saluted.

Katherine stepped in front of him, and he passed the violin to her. She gave it to her daughter, then stood on her tiptoes and kissed Johann on the lips. The men cheered until Johann put his arms around her and kissed her. They laughed and clapped, and when they realized the party was over, they gradually picked up their groundsheets and wandered away.

Johann asked Katherine, "Where did you learn to play the fiddle?" more to gain time for his churning emotions to cool than to get information. She was reluctant to leave his side, and Johann fought the urge to kiss her for real.

"Before the war, I make music professor at academy in Kyiv." Katherine struggled but still spoke confidently.

He stroked her cheek. "Thank you, Katherine. You gave me back my family. It's been so long; I had almost lost them."

"I ty dal nam nashi." She touched his cheek, smiled, and took Natasha's hand. As she turned to follow her mother, Natasha said, "And you gave us ours."

The men returned to their tents, some softly singing bits of "Lili Marlen" or "Erika," others quietly talking while watching a full moon rise over the steppes. There wasn't a killer's heart in the crowd. If the Russians had appeared, they would have hugged them.

Chapter Twenty-nine

June–August 1944

Go ahead, back up

Laufen ist eine Schande, aber gesund.

(Running away is shameful, but healthy.)

General Nehring pushed his queen's pawn forward two squares and said, "The Allies landed at Normandy this morning." Johann pushed his black pawn to d5, Nehring moved c2 to c4, and Johann moved e7 to e6, declining the gambit to begin the opening of their now almost daily chess game.

"Do you think they will succeed?"

Nehring moved his knight. Nc3. "What do you call success?"

"Getting beyond the beaches." Johann moved his knight to f7. "If they get past the beaches, so they have a place to put things, the Allies will send everything they own across the Channel."

"The British and Canadians are already off the beaches, and there is a traffic jam of ships going both ways across the channel. The air is full of Allied planes, and Göring's Luftwaffe is notable in its absence." Walther moved his bishop to g5.

Johann sat up straight, pulled a cigar out of the box, gave it to Nehring and selected one for himself. "What about the Wehrmacht? They would have orders to 'Hold to the last man,' wouldn't they?" He lit a match on his sleeve and held the flame at the end of Nehring's cigar. Nehring sucked the fire into the tip until it glowed, and Johann quickly shifted to his own. He barely got it glowing before the flame touched his finger. Walther grinned at him when he dropped the match and stamped it out with his foot.

Nehring blew perfect smoke rings. "'Hold to the last man' only applies if the enemy would kill you anyway. The worst American or British prisoner-of-war camp is probably better than this tent, and there is a rumour that the Western Allies don't shoot prisoners. What would you do if they were over the next hill when the Russians attacked us?"

Johann was silent for ten seconds, and Nehring smiled. "It's only a matter of scale, isn't it? The British and Canadians are in the French coastal towns, and the Americans will be off the beach tomorrow. The Wehrmacht has American paratroopers behind their lines, and the Allies control the skies. Minutes after we fire a big gun or move a tank, an aircraft drops a bomb on it, shoots a rocket at it, or both.

The Résistance has effectively disabled the railway system, making reinforcements and panzers difficult to move. They've blown up bridges, destroyed hundreds of locomotives, and torn up thousands of metres of tracks. Our forces can only move safely at night, and our panzers must use roads." He blew smoke at the open door as he examined the board, then went on talking when he realized it was Johann's move.

"But that's a moot point because Hitler won't commit our panzer forces or our reserves—he believes the main attack is yet to come, north of what he calls a diversion. But the truth might be that Hitler is afraid that whatever he commits, the Allies would destroy from the air. However, if he doesn't commit them, it's only a matter of time before bombers find and destroy them where they are."

Johann sucked on his cigar until he felt dizzy, then blew the smoke to the roof of the tent, a mixture of sadness and excitement invading his conflicted mind. He reasoned that his family would likely survive if the Allies crossed Germany before the Russians. He wanted to save his family more than he wanted to save Germany for the bastards now in Berlin.

But if the Russians get there first... Johann tried but couldn't construct a scenario where the Wehrmacht saved Germany from both.

He said, "We are in deep trouble—it looks like we're the meat in the sandwich, squeezed between the Russians and the Western Allies."

"Yes, and every general in the Wehrmacht expected this. The English and Americans have more men and equipment still on the British Islands than we've built and destroyed since the war began, and, contrary to a popular misconception, it's now the best technology in the world.

The Western Allies can afford to send a hundred Lancaster bombers, each with nine tons of bombs, to kill a dozen tanks. They don't care what it costs in equipment and fuel; they will destroy us without sacrificing a man if they can do it. If a panzer fires a single shot at their soldiers, someone will dial up a fighter on the radio. It will swoop down, fire a rack of rockets and a thousand rounds from its cannons, and the panzer is dead!"

Johann began looking for a move as he said, "That's all probably true, but if they try to fight a war without casualties, they will move ahead slowly. Meanwhile, the Russians will sacrifice men and equipment for speed."

General Nehring sucked in and then blew smoke at the roof. "Yes, your assessment is probably correct. Unfortunately, we who are stuck on the eastern front must deal with the Russians, not the Americans and British." He indicated Johann should move a piece. "And yes, I would say we are in trouble."

Johann moved his bishop to e7. "Perhaps the Allies will pause to ask Hitler for peace."

Nehring moved his second knight, Kf3, to consolidate his forces. "Churchill doesn't want peace; he wants revenge, and the Allies will throw everything they've got at us until their lust for German blood is satisfied. After Stalingrad, Churchill made it clear that only unconditional surrender would do. But if Hitler surrenders, he will be committing suicide and taking his staff and most of the SS and Gestapo officers with him. He won't do that, even if they would let him."

Nehring lost interest in the game and leaned back in his chair.

◇◇◇◇◇◇◇◇◇◇◇◇◇◇◇◇◇◇◇◇◇◇◇◇◇◇◇◇◇◇◇◇◇◇◇◇◇◇◇

"It's a race for the brass ring—control of Germany when this is over—and hangman's justice for the criminals who run the "Third Reich." It's safe to say the Russians will keep everything east of Austria and Italy under their control, except perhaps Greece and Turkey. They want Poland, Hungary, Czechoslovakia, Latvia, Lithuania, Romania, and every square metre of Germany they can take before the Americans and British get there. The Russians, not the Allies, will be the biggest winners in this war. They will meet the Americans and British as far west as possible and keep all the land they cross. The unknown will be

Berlin, but my money is on Stalin!" He stood up, brushed his head on the wet roof canvas and pushed it up with his hand, dumping rainwater down the roof to the rain-soaked ground. He swung back to Johann. "They are two wolves fighting over a rabbit…and neither wants to hear from the rabbit."

Johann pinched the glow off his cigar, dropped the ash in the ashtray, and put the cigar in his shirt pocket. The chess game was over. "Then we must do our best to make the meeting point as far east as possible."

"Johann, maybe we can save Berlin for the Americans, but I doubt the Allies will sacrifice anything to get it. In the end, they will go home, and if Europe doesn't restore sanity on its own, it will slide down to hell on a Russian sled!"

Johann hopped his chair back from the table and stood up. "The most difficult part of every mission is getting my men safely out. The enemy now knows where we are, and they know our strength. I can't imagine retreating with an entire army!" He picked up his hat.

Nehring nodded. "An unplanned withdrawal quickly becomes a rout. But a planned withdrawal, if carried out as a strategy before it becomes an emergency, can do more damage to the enemy than standing and fighting. As long as I am here, we will withdraw as a strategy. We will never retreat because the enemy forced us to. Despite our orders to stand and fight, we cannot do it. Many Russians will die if we stand our ground, but, like your endless ants, many more would replace them, and we would be lost, leaving the Russians a leisurely drive to Berlin. We must choose whether and when to stand and fight or to run like hell, and we must never sacrifice the option of a tactical withdrawal."

Nehring put his hand on Johann's shoulder. "You must use your head; you are my eyes and ears, and your job is to tell me what the Russians are doing—I can't be beside you to tell you what to do. We are in the middle game now, and we lost our queen. All we can do is wait for mistakes, and when we see them, we must pounce with our claws out! Even the Russians have a limit to how much they can lose."

Johann left the general's quarters in pouring rain, headed for the tents, where his men played Skat and Doppelkopf. Fighting men get bored quickly, and intelligent officers keep their tightly-strung minds and bodies busy. Johann decided that when the card games wound down, he would discuss the future of their war. He would run them for an hour when that discussion ended.

◇◇◇◇◇◇◇◇◇◇◇◇◇◇◇◇◇◇◇◇◇◇◇◇◇◇◇◇

A few days later, Johann and General Nehring were in the middle of another chess game when Nehring lit his cigar and announced, "Hitler fired General Raus because he didn't sacrifice the Fourth panzer Army. I've been told the Führer considered shooting Raus for treason, and the result is that I am the new commander of the Fourth panzer Army."

Johann, stunned at the news, said, "You've never mentioned that Hitler might promote you...."

Nehring shrugged. "If he was considering it, he didn't tell me. He also fired General Model—General Josef Harpe is now in charge of Army Group North Ukraine."

"Scheisse!" Johann moved his queen. "Check." He looked at Nehring. "What about the twenty-fourth? Who will command it?"

"I will keep the XXIV panzers under my direct control. We will continue using your Apache tactics." Nehring tipped his king.

◇◇◇◇◇◇◇◇◇◇◇◇◇◇◇◇◇◇◇◇◇◇◇◇◇◇◇◇

The Russians attacked on 23 June. Before the battle began, Hitler's latest strategic move was to give his forces a list of "Feste Plätze," points that Hitler ordered them to "hold to the last man" using practices from the Middle Ages.

Nehring ignored the orders and fought a "hit and run" war, saving the Fourth panzer Army by fighting an organized withdrawal until they were north of the Vistula River and a hundred kilometres east of Warsaw. Meanwhile, the Russians encircled the Army Group Center and, using Maskirovka deceptions and Hitler's stupidity, wiped them out, killing or capturing four hundred thousand German soldiers. The Russians then had a clear path to Warsaw but stopped on the southeast bank of the Vistula River just short of the city. They set up bridgeheads on the river as far east as the Polish border with Czechoslovakia before beginning a period of rest and regeneration, preparing for its mortal enemy's final and absolute destruction.

Early in August, on a rare hot evening, Johann and Nehring stood smoking outside the command tent. Inside was stifling, too hot to play chess, and outside wasn't much better. There was barely enough air movement to stir the leaves in the nearby trees!

Johann noted there were no cigars on the small table. He looked at Nehring, got a slight head-wag, shrugged his shoulders and pulled on his cigarette.

Nehring wiped his sweaty brow. "No more cigars in this war, but you will have all the cigarettes you want." He picked a piece of tobacco out of his mouth and announced, "They tried to kill Hitler." He inhaled again, creating a six-millimetre ash cylinder.

"Who?" Johann had heard the rumour, but no one wanted or dared to talk about it.

Nehring waited for a soldier to pass before he spoke.

"You've heard of the Schwarze Kapelle?"

Johann nodded. It was the worst-kept secret in the Wehrmacht, but the Gestapo, in their inimitable way, discouraged any rumours of an organization devoted to killing Hitler and launching a coup.

General Nehring sucked on his cigarette, scrutinizing Johann. He chose his words meticulously.

"They say that the 'Schwarze Kapelle,' the organization the Gestapo claims never existed, exists no more." General Nehring paused and gave Johann an opening, but considering the situation and his rank, Johann had no idea what to say. The general pointed toward a path winding down a slope along the edge of a field.

Nehring pulled on his cigarette as he began walking, blew the smoke downwind away from Johann, spit a piece of shredded tobacco into his hand and said, "On the twentieth of July, Hitler was supposed to have died in an explosion, but he claims that divine intervention saved him so he could eliminate the scourge of the Schwarze Kapelle, which until now he has never admitted exists. He arrested thousands of officers and civilians and, so far, has executed hundreds. Hitler is trying the remainder as quickly as he can. Admiral Canaris and General Rommel are ostensibly two of the plotters."

Johann looked into Nehring's eyes but found no opinion, no pity, and no anger.

"Scheisse!" Johann emphasized the universal expression of a German's frustration."

"Do you mean, 'Scheisse they failed, Scheisse they were caught, or Scheisse, they deserve to die?'"

Johann didn't hesitate. "If Hitler had died, the Allies would have negotiated with the Schwarze Kapelle, wouldn't they?" He fought against the depression that seized him. "So, Scheisse, they failed, and Scheisse, they were caught!" He added as an afterthought. "You can shoot me right now if you think that's treason."

Nehring looked around before he continued, a good sign he wasn't going to shoot his leutnant. "There was a revolt planned if the attempt had succeeded… It was called 'Unternehmen Valkyrie.' When Goebbels officially announced Hitler's death, he deceived those in charge and triggered the operation.

"When, a few hours later, Hitler announced that God had saved him, Wehrmacht soldiers killed other Wehrmacht soldiers, ambushed because their officers believed it was safe to come out in the open!"

Johann saw pain in his general's eyes, evaporating any doubt he may have had about him.

General Nehring bowed his head, hiding his eyes. "We must now fight without hope of peace before the total and final destruction of Germany."

Johann stopped and stubbed his cigarette on his pant leg. "I cannot fight without hope. I will fight my way back to the family I still have, and I won't allow the Russians to get there before I do!"

Nehring looked up. "That is not what you've said before."

"I feel differently now. Having Katherine and Natasha around has helped me—perhaps I'm beginning to feel human again."

◇◇◇◇◇◇◇◇◇◇◇◇◇◇◇◇◇◇◇◇◇◇◇◇◇◇◇◇◇◇◇◇◇◇◇

Nehring nodded. "If we try to stop the Russians, we will die where we stand. As the American cavalry feared Cochise, we must make the Russians fear us enough to hesitate. I want you to help the Twenty-Fourth hit hard like a hammer, move away, and set up an opportunity to hit them again. The Twenty-Fourth must not fight unless they have an absolute positional advantage and an escape plan. We must be the bad guys, and we must play dirty.

"But I don't expect to have replacements for tanks or men, and it's difficult to predict how long we will have fuel and ammunition." Nehring put his right hand in his pocket.

Johann nodded and said, "I understand, sir. When do you expect the Russians to move again?"

"They stopped at the Vistula River to let the SS take care of the Free Polish Army in Warsaw, and the Germans are obliging by murdering all the Polish patriots for them. But the Poles are a stubborn, willful race, and the SS has problems they hadn't anticipated. The city is a pile of rubble, and still, the Poles fight from behind the piles. They cannot possibly win, but to surrender to the SS is to die.

They are unintentionally buying time for Hitler by making the Russians wait. The Russians want Germany to wipe out the Polish democratic movement—represented by The Free Polish Army—so they can install their communist ideology in Warsaw without opposition. They won't move until Hitler finishes with the destruction of Warsaw, and then it will be with Berlin and Adolph Hitler as the objective."

Johann tried to be positive. "They must build up their forces before they do that. We have hurt them badly in the past few months, and as they get closer to Germany the area we have to defend will become smaller. The price for every metre will go up!"

Nehring turned around, gestured at the tent, and picked up the pace. The sun was hot, especially where there was no shade.

"They won't attack today, and we will have mud in a few months. We have time for a few chess games—perhaps we should set up the board outside."

When they reached the tent, Johann talked as he opened the flap. "Will Hitler move you again?"

Nehring was behind him and said in his ear, "I have my replacement now. General Fritz-Hubert Gräser."

Johann yelped, *"Our* General Gräser? *He* is taking over the Fourth panzer Army?" He stuck his head outside and looked around to see if anyone had noticed his outburst. He lowered his voice. "But what about you? What will you do? Who will lead the Twenty-Fourth?" He hesitated, shaking his head. "Gräser will destroy the Fourth Army and our panzer Corps with it."

Nehring smiled as he gathered the chess pieces. "I am not as pessimistic as you are, but I know more than you do. To tell the truth, I requested the move. I am returning to the Twenty-Fourth panzer Corps, and so are you. Hitler doesn't like my 'hit and run' tactics and wants to limit them. For my purposes, I am too visible when I'm in charge of an Army, and Hitler wants me out of sight, so we both win."

Johann carried a handful of pieces and the board. He set the load on the small table, sat down, and they began the game.

Nehring moved his pawn to c4, and Johann immediately moved his to c5.

"Is this the new General Nehring? The English opening?"

Walther smiled. "It's time to learn how to play it." He moved his knight to f3, and Johann moved his to f6.

Nehring said, "You are going to hit my flank? Is this the new tactic of the Twenty-Fourth panzers?"

Johann smiled and took his finger off the knight. "No more head-on attacks. I will always come from where you least expect me. You must learn to predict my moves, but even if you do, it will be too late

Chapter Thirty

December 1944

Lead me not into temptation... Amen

GENERAL NEHRING SOMEHOW GOT PERMISSION from General Gräser to move his XXIV panzers back from the Russian bridgehead at Sandomierz. But Gräser left XLVIII panzer Corps close to the Russian line, within range of their artillery and rockets.

Hitler insisted that the German forces along the Vistula River set up two defence lines: the Grosskampflinie, closest to the enemy, and the Hauptkampflinie, the line from which there would be no retreat. General Gräser placed the XLVIII panzers at the Grosskampflinie and instructed Nehring to defend the Hauptkampflinie, 2,000 metres behind them but still within range of Russian artillery and katya rockets. Hitler's orders were to "hold to the last man" no closer to Germany than the second line.

A horrified General Nehring watched Gräser place the Fourth panzer Army infantry at Hitler's designated 'defend to the last man' points, thinly spread over two long defensive lines, leaving significant gaps.

General Nehring, recognizing the futility of committing his panzers and artillery to a tactic guaranteed to fail, cheated on the Hauptkampflinie Hitler ordered him to defend. Over Gräser's objections, he backed it up ten kilometres, beyond the range of the thousands of Russian guns and rockets set up along the river. The Fourth panzer Army, outnumbered and outgunned five to one, waited for the Russian onslaught that would take them to Germany's border, Berlin, and Hitler's bunker.

◇◇◇◇◇◇◇◇◇◇◇◇◇◇◇◇◇◇◇◇◇◇◇◇◇◇◇◇◇◇◇◇

While waiting, Walther Nehring and Johann returned to their chess, and it was during one of their games that General Nehring lost his usual calm.

"I lost a friend, and I don't know why." Nehring had finished setting up the chessboard, and Johann passed him a beer.

Johann sipped the foam off his beer. "I've lost a few friends lately, but I know why and believe me when I say it doesn't help!"

"This is different." Nehring put his beer beside the board. "She was a doctor in Warsaw and had no part in the war except to help those who suffered from it. She was German, married to a Polish businessman."

"I thought the SS took care of the Free Polish Army in October. Warsaw has been peaceful since then, hasn't it?"

"Yes, but at that time they shot her husband for sheltering Jews in his factory. They took her to Auschwitz, and a week ago, the guards shot her—they said she tried to escape!" Nehring shook his head and looked away for a moment. "Do you know about these camps…?"

Johann paused, then nodded. "I've heard they force the inmates to work for German companies." he paused again, deciding whether to tell Nehring the latest from the army rumour mill. "There are rumours of executions if they can't or won't work."

Nehring made a sound of disgust. "You shouldn't repeat that kind of nonsense. There are things that even Hitler wouldn't do!"

Johann said, "Sir, we are near Krakow and not far from those camps. We will soon know what is going on there. Perhaps your friend is still alive."

"Yes, Elsa was not the kind of person who would try to escape from anything... I suppose it wouldn't hurt to hope."

◇◇◇◇◇◇◇◇◇◇◇◇◇◇◇◇◇◇◇◇◇◇◇◇◇◇◇◇◇◇◇◇◇◇◇◇◇

The weather at Christmas was not yet cooperating with the Russian plan. In November, mud had stopped any thoughts the Russians had of moving forward, forcing them to wait for weather that would turn the soft fields into hard-as-iron playgrounds for their T-34s. Both sides made the most of the respite by celebrating the birth of the Prince of Peace.

The temporary headquarters Nehring had chosen for the XXIV panzer Corps was a heated, comfortable compound formerly the property of the Polish Army. It included a large barn-like structure for games, concerts, or whatever purpose pleased the German army. On Christmas Eve, Nehring used it to feed his men Christmas dinner, and following the ham and peeled potatoes, Katherine and Johann treated them to a sing-along.

Christmas carols and songs of home, accompanied by Katherine's sweet violin and Johann's piano virtuosity, were capped with "Stille Nacht," leaving every man with a lump in his throat and tears in his eyes.

Johann said, "We can't leave them sad," and smiled at Katherine as the men clapped and stamped their feet for more. Five minutes brought no respite, and finally, Johann spread his hands for quiet and asked, "Would anyone like to sing our panzerlied?"

The men stamped and clapped louder, shouting, "Jawohl! Das panzerlied!"

Anticipating the request, Johann had taught Katherine a violin part for the song and worked out a creative arrangement for the piano. They had rehearsed with a panzer gunner known to Johann as Corporal 'Sturm.' He had a fine voice, and Johann announced that 'Sturm' would sing the first verse.

The rousing march, at first sung only by Waffen SS panzer crews but now by any soldier in a panzer unit, brought every one of over a thousand men to their feet. Corporal Sturm stood at attention as Johann and Katherine finished playing the end of the first verse as an introduction, then began in a clear, resonant voice. *"Ob sturm's oder schneit, ob die Sonne uns lacht…"*

The corporal finished the first verse, Johann lifted an arm in a gesture for the men in the room to join in, and they sang loud enough to drown out the violin. Johann had to punish the piano so that it carried over them, keeping them on the pitches. Corporal Sturm's resonant voice steered those close to him in the right direction, and the rest of the men followed.

The final verse, of death in battle and their last resting place in their panzers, brought reality close, and the men began to pull back the tempo, but Johann and Corporal Sturm drove them on.

"Und lässt uns im stich einst das treulose Glück,

"Und kehren wir nicht mehr zur Heimat zurück…"

At first, the men sang loudly and enthusiastically of their luck running out, never to return home to their families and their country, but then, bit by bit, their enthusiasm waned. Johann understood; he was one of them. The battle-weary soldiers dared not think of dying before they could reach their families—they must stop the Russians—and they must stop them this side of the German border.

But every man in the hall knew that thousands of Russian T-34s were only hours from where the war-weary men stood, and their crews were also singing of victory. Germany was within a day's travel for those T-34s—a single tank of fuel would get them to the border.

Johann's audience had left a sad trail of lost battles and dead comrades behind them since Stalingrad; two years of 'one step ahead, then two back' meant that confidence was a rare commodity in the hall. Excited Russians, only a few kilometres from where German soldiers sang their anthem of sacrifice and death, were dancing, singing joyful songs, and looking forward to the destruction of the Third Reich.

Johann sang with his audience, "… *Trifft uns die Todeskugel; ruft uns das Schicksal an…Ja Schicksal an,*
    dann wird unser panzer ein ehernes Grab…"

The words described a warrior's death and the panzer as their noble grave. But as romantic as the song made it, the men knew that an honourable death was meaningless if it didn't stop the mighty Russian horde—and a coffin was a waste of a panther.

There was a moment of silence when the song ended. The corporal on the stage waited, then smartly raised his arm in a Nazi salute.

He shouted, "Sieg Heil!" and half the men in the room straightened their arms and shouted, "Sieg Heil!" He stood motionless, then lowered his arm to attention before performing a perfect Wehrmacht salute. Without a word, every man returned it.

Johann stood beside Katherine and bowed to the silent crowd. She cradled her violin and turned to leave the stage but paused to look into his eyes with an expression Johann recognized. When Barbara looked at him like that, he knew what she wanted, and to turn her down was to suffer her wrath for days.

The room's silence quickly became awkward, and Johann decided it was time for the coup de grâce. He looked from man to man until they became restless, then raised his arms and said, "I have another surprise for you." The men waited, anticipating another song, though not many were in the mood. Johann grinned. "We have connected the speakers to '*Soldatensender Belgrad,*' and it's time for 'Letters from Home.'"

The men cheered. They spent as many evenings as possible in front of miserably inadequate radio sets, catching bits and pieces of the German Forces radio station. They sat quietly, waiting for the connection to become clear, and cheered when it fed through speakers into the room.

The program began precisely on time. Some letters, obviously creations of Goebbels' Department of Propaganda and the People's Education, drew jeers and catcalls. Still, most were genuine and elicited silent tears and lowered heads—until the inevitable inserted words at the end.

Letters from sweethearts, parents, brothers, and sisters somehow always mentioned the great German cause, the Führer leading the country to inevitable victory, and the honour his soldiers felt when they fought for him. Every night, every letter mentioned the soldier and his family's devotion to Hitler, limiting the number of different phrases the creative propaganda spinners could conjure up. Many men in the room knew the propaganda words by heart, and when they appeared, the killjoys in the crowd mockingly repeated them with the commentator. Occasionally, someone would chant the words as a parody. Every night, a brave, creative Klassenklown thought of a new way to get a laugh.

"Aren't they mocking Hitler?" Natasha sat between Johann and her mother while the men softly sang "Lili Marlen" as Soldatensender Belgrad closed the program with the song for the multi-hundredth time.

"No, they are mocking the people who make up these words, believing these soldiers are too stupid to notice. The soldiers can laugh at it, or whistle their disgust—laughing is less likely to get them punished." Johann looked at Katherine to see if she understood, and Natasha immediately translated the conversation.

Johann watched the men's mood change as they sang with Lale Andersen. He explained to Natasha, "Most of them don't care about Hitler anymore—they don't even care about Germany—they only want to see their families. The Gestapo have their spies here, but even they have had enough. What would have meant a firing squad a year ago is now ignored."

Katherine nodded as Natasha translated Johann's soliloquy. She spoke a short phrase in Russian, and then Natasha turned to Johann.

"It's a saying in Russian. Mother said, 'But for tonight, let's eat and drink, for tomorrow we may die.'"

Johann stood, thinking, 'I was afraid it was something like that.' He looked at Katherine. "I'm going to bed now because I must rise in a few hours. The Russians are getting restless; it's going to snow, and General Nehring needs to know what they are up to."

Natasha translated, and Katherine got to her feet, but Natasha remained seated.

"I hope you sleep very well," Katherine said clearly but with a heavy accent and an expression that put the lie to her hope.

Johann took her outstretched hand and bowed to her. He quoted from something he had read, "Madame, if you truly wish it so, I surely will." When he released her hand, she laughed, a musical, sexy laugh, and his heart gained speed like a truck losing its brakes on a steep hill. He had flirted with Katherine, and he wanted to kick himself—the hole he dug frightened him.

◇◇◇◇◇◇◇◇◇◇◇◇◇◇◇◇◇◇◇◇◇◇◇◇◇◇◇◇◇◇◇

Ian wasn't in the room when Johann opened the door on its squeaky hinges and switched on the light beside his narrow bed. He hadn't needed a key until now, and when he checked the door and then the room, there was none and no way to lock the door without one. Johann shrugged, picked up his leather shaving kit and a towel from his chair, then headed for the bathing room, expecting to see Ian in the hallway or the bathroom. But when he reached the bathing rooms, they were empty.

Johann peed in the gutter, then went into one of three bathing rooms. He locked the door, turned on the taps, adjusted the temperature until it was about right, then undressed. As he eased himself into the hot bath, someone entered the toilet room, and he recognized the sound and rhythm of Ian's nightly ritual.

"I thought I saw you leave the party before I did." Johann's voice echoed against the stone and brick walls.

Ian didn't sound surprised to hear his roommate in the bathing room. He said, "I'm sleeping in the Finn's room tonight. It's going to be an early morning, and you snore."

326

Johann said, "Hah! You would never hear me snore over the racket you make! You sound like a train on a hard hill. I'm so used to it that I can't sleep without it."

Ian chuckled. "So that's why you haven't mentioned it before?" He was silent for a few seconds, then added, "She's in love with you, and you know it."

Johann breathed deeply, immersed himself a little lower in the water, washing while trying to think of anything but Katherine.

"I have a wife and son, and I love them too much to betray them." He turned on the taps and splashed clean water on his hair. He slid down in the tub—the water reached up his back and over his rising problem.

Ian's voice bounced off the walls. "This is not betrayal. You are fighting a war, and by definition, someone is trying to kill you. You may not be alive tomorrow... especially if you turn down Katherine."

Johann heard Ian turn on the tap to brush his teeth; he waited until the noise stopped.

"I would not be happy if I found out Barbara had slept with someone while I was fighting to get back to her."

"And if you didn't find out? Would it bother you then?" He paused, Johann didn't speak, and he went on. "You've been away for three years, and Barbara is intelligent; she won't ask you that question."

"That's a stupid argument." Johann pulled the plug and stood up. He rinsed himself with cold water straight from the tap. It didn't help.

Johann heard Ian put his kit together and walk toward the door. There was a finality in his voice when he said, "I will see you in the dining room at four."

"You might as well go back to our room, and we will go to breakfast together."

"I don't want to be there if you tell her you won't sleep with her, and I don't want to be there if you sleep with her." The door creaked when Ian opened it. "I will see you in the dining room."

Johann wrapped himself in his towel and shaved. He took his time, praying the room would be empty. He shaved with the dull razor; he hadn't brought the strap. Nothing was going right, and he saw no possibility of that changing.

The door to his room was closed, and the light from a lamp shone under it. Johann had deliberately left it open a crack with the light off and now deliberately waited before opening it. He tried to think of words, but the right ones didn't exist, and she wouldn't understand them if they did. Johann tried to breathe normally while pushing the handle down and opening the door as casually as possible under the circumstances. But he tripped over the raised sill and stubbed his bare toe, ruining the effect. He said, "Verdammt..." and swallowed the second word before it exited his lips.

"So long in water. You must be very clean." Katherine's honey contralto came from the bed—she had arranged the lamp so that the light shone on her in a very sexy way. And she was naked. "That is very good for me." Johann tried to decide to run away but wound up rooted to the spot.

Katherine was not at all like Barbara. She was half a head shorter, her hair was dark, and her eyes were soft brown. Her triangular face, Slavic forehead, and strong cheekbones radiated strength. Her dark eyes glowed, and her smile bewitched; in that detail, she was just like Barbara. He tried to imagine how strong this woman could be, and decided that, as with Barbara, there was no limit.

Johann's towel didn't hide his desire. He let his free arm fall casually over the lump and turned toward Ian's bed, his other arm loaded with clothes. He dumped them on Ian's chair.

"This your bed?" Her struggle to communicate made her sexier.

Johann turned away and sat on Ian's bed. He opened his mouth to tell a bald-faced lie but couldn't do it. "I care for you very much, Katherine, but I can't do what you want. I have waited almost four years, and I must wait until I get home to Barbara." He looked at Katherine. He would have preferred to face a well-armed Russian.

She made a supreme effort not to cry—he had to keep talking—if she cried, he was lost!

"I can't hold Barbara in my arms without telling her that I love only her; I can't lie to her; I can't hide the truth. She would know, but she wouldn't say anything, and that would make it worse. If I told her, she would forgive me and never mention it again, but I would know, and it might ruin what I have fought for. I have killed many men, and many friends have died so that I can be with Barbara. And I am so close!" He knew she probably hadn't understood a word, and Katherine confirmed it.

"I not understand what you say!" Katherine's beautiful eyes shone with the tears forming in them. "I must understand." She stood up, which was not what Johann would have preferred.

<hr />

Early that morning, after breakfast, General Nehring and Johann had played chess. Both men knew that they had to find a solution to the problem of Katherine and Natasha, and Johann had decided to tell him that the women were his superiors' problem, namely General Nehring's. Once the battle began, it wouldn't break until the Russians were across the Oder, and perhaps not until Russian T-34s drove under Berlin's Brandenburg Tor.

Nehring's English opening was a disaster, so he lit a cigar and offered one to Johann. When both cigars glowed, Nehring began the discussion Johann expected.

"The Russians will attack soon, and speed is the XXIV panzer Corps' only advantage. Katherine knows that she and Natasha can't stay with me because I will have no time for them, and I hope we can find another solution."

Nehring blew smoke at the small open crack at the bottom of the window, and it miraculously flowed outside to pollute the rest of the world. He waited, and Johann took the opportunity to clear up any foolish ideas the general might have.

"I can't take them with me—I will only come back to report if ordered to. What would I do with two women in a 'hit and run' action? That is not an option!" Nehring stared at him.

Johann went on. "I can't have non-combatant women with me while I make decisions that will sacrifice men's lives. But they aren't stray cats, either! We can't just put them out..."

General Nehring put up his hand. "Stop! Stop! I never assumed you could take them with you—I wouldn't let you if you wanted to!" He looked at Johann curiously. "Be very careful, Johann; if you become soft, you may start feeling sorry for the Russians."

Johann realized that he had made a mistake. He relaxed, embarrassed. He asked, "So, what do you think we should do? The Russians will rape and kill both of them if they are still here."

Somehow, the conversation was ruining Johann's cigar. He pinched it out, then thought he saw 'mission accomplished' in his boss's smile.

Nehring said, "The trains are still running, and I've decided to send them to Dresden, where the Auslanderamt processes refugees and distributes them around Germany. They will be safe there… Goebbels has declared it a non-combatant city."

Johann hated to think of Natasha in a refugee camp, but it was preferable to facing the Russians. He had an alternative but said nothing.

Nehring said, "I would send them to my home, but it is close to Berlin, and my wife will take the children to Switzerland." He waited for the obvious reply from Johann.

Johann finally relented; he had hoped to avoid this. "I knew it might come to this, and I wrote to Barbara and my parents."

Nehring grinned. He knew Johann too well for there to be secrets between them.

"I told them about Katherine and Natasha, and they wrote that, if the need arose, they could stay in Detmold. So far, the war has mainly passed Detmold, and Barbara offered Lisa's empty room to them. There is also the possibility of the upstairs apartment at Gartenstrasse 18. The only problem is how to get them there."

Nehring was visibly relieved. "I know this is not ideal for you, but it is impossible for me. However, I can get them to Detmold if they have a place to stay when they get there. They will still have to go to Dresden for processing, and I will give them a letter to speed that up and give them enough money for the trip. I have a few Swiss francs and enough Reichmarks to get them to Detmold and perhaps even a little to help with expenses they and Barbara might have when they get there."

Johann couldn't hide his surprise as Nehring went on. He thought about offering what little money he had but forced himself to hold his tongue.

"I have the letter ready, and I thought it wise to give them a German husband and father. I have said that the Russians murdered him, and you rescued them from certain death. I also changed their last name to Schneider. Like most refugees, they have no formal papers but will have this letter stating they are under my protection."

Johann tried to hide his amazement that Nehring would sign a letter that was a blatant lie—many had died for lesser crimes. He spread his hands and said, "Alright, I will tell Katherine and Natasha, unless you want to do it."

"Wait until you come back from your mission. In a few days, we will know better what we're facing." General Nehring shook Johann's hand with a wide grin on his face. "I guess a little humanity won't hurt us too much…if we keep it in perspective."

<hr>

Johann stared at Katherine for a long second, and she stared back. He forced himself to look at the floor.

"I get Natasha now." Katherine's feet pattered toward the door, then stopped. Johann peeked as she reversed course and pulled the heavy woollen coat she had laid on Johann's chair over her nakedness. She opened the door, and Natasha immediately stepped into the room. Katherine started chattering, and despite being around Katherine and Natasha for almost a year, Johann couldn't pick out a single word. He grabbed his shirt from Ian's chair and put it on, almost losing the towel in the process. He caught Natasha's quick glance and smile as she nodded at her mother, who finally stopped chattering.

"My mother is in love with you and wants you to sex with her." Natasha looked at Johann as though pimping for her mother were the most natural thing in the world.

"I can't. I couldn't face Barbara if I did." He wanted to add, "Why am I telling you this?"

Johann turned his attention to finding a way to get into his pants without dropping the towel. He thought briefly of asking the women to turn around but then gave up on the pants.

"Why did she suddenly fall in love with me?" He turned to Katherine. "You've been living with Walther; why not him?"

Natasha looked at the wall for a few seconds, the wheels in her mind spinning. Johann knew he was about to hear a Ukrainian lie, but

Katherine cut Natasha off before she spoke. The tone of her voice left no question that her daughter was getting instructions.

"She say that she love you since you save our lifes. She want to sleep with you long ago, but no chance."

Johann deliberately ignored her mother, easier now that she wore a woollen coat. He said, "Natasha, I want you to tell me the truth. What's going on?"

Natasha blurted out the truth before Katherine could interrupt.

"She try to sex with general, but he say no. She work in kitchen and know they put powder in food so men won't want to sex."

Johann mumbled to himself, "I think that either she's hearing false rumours, or it doesn't work on me." and Natasha giggled.

"Mother wants to stay with you and General Nehring until you kill all the Russians, but general tell he must send us away before the Russians come again! He say you might not can kill them all!"

Natasha was visibly upset, ruining the "sexing" mood. Johann decided to come clean.

"Yes, we discussed that this morning, and we were going to tell you about our plans when I got back from scouting, but perhaps this is the time."

He discarded the notion that he might be disobeying an order.

"Nowhere on this side of the German border will be safe for you and your mother. When the Russians attack, we will slow them down, but we can't defeat them—they will surely drive us back into Germany. General Nehring and I discussed this only a few hours ago, and I have already written to Barbara. We must send you on the train to Dresden, where you will get papers allowing you to stay in Germany. You will go to Detmold, where Barbara and my parents live, and they will care for you. General Nehring will give you a letter giving you a German name and enough money to get you to Detmold."

The relief on Natasha's face was pitiful, and Johann emphatically added, "Please remember that Walther has lied for you in the letter, and the Gestapo will shoot him if they find out!"

Natasha looked at her mother and translated what Johann had said. Katherine's reaction was a mixture of relief and worry. Natasha translated her response to Johann, although her mother hadn't said a word.

"General Nehring is good man. It make my mother sad that he take so much chance for us. We never tell!"

Johann decided to clear up another doubt they may have had. "When you get to Detmold, you and your mother will live with Barbara."

Natasha looked like she was going to ask a question, so Johann added, "Both of you can sleep in my daughter's bedroom. It is a big room. Barbara will have it ready when you get there."

Natasha nodded slowly, puzzled, and turned to her mother.

Katherine pulled her oversized coat tighter as Natasha translated, becoming happier with each sentence. While looking at Johann, she responded with a three-word sentence; it sounded like she was glad to be out of the situation she had feared.

"She said she is sorry that she cannot sex with you, and she is sure you are very good sexer, but if she going to live with wife, sex with you is not now possible."

Katherine issued a short command to her daughter, and Natasha opened the door.

"She also say she very happy you are such fine friend. She thank you for teaching her daughter the violin and helping her with her German so we can go to Germany." Katherine was through the door before Natasha finished talking.

Johann told a beaming Natasha, "Tell your mother our time together has made the war bearable for me. I thank both of you for that."

Natasha seemed comfortable standing still, looking at Johann. Katherine took her daughter's hand and yanked her through the door.

Chapter Thirty-one

December 1944

Snow for Christmas

"The woods are lovely, dark and deep,

But I have promises to keep,

And miles to go before I sleep,

And miles to go before I sleep."

Stopping by Woods on a Snowy Evening

Robert Frost

CHRISTMAS DAY DIDN'T DAWN; the light filtering through the falling snow simply turned the blackness to gray. A capricious wind blew snow across the road, whipping it from the ground, mixing it with the whirling blizzard, and creating a pulsing cone of whiteness around Johann's demag. When the cone suddenly contracted to a white void a metre from his face, Johann's driver lost his sense of space and direction, and the half-track left the road.

Ian's demag followed the leader into the ditch, but fortunately, the ditches were frozen and not deep, and the effective steering system dragged the front wheels sideways across the wind-packed snow and back up the ditch bank.

The engine on Johann's demag groaned, the driver found second gear, and the tracks pulled the machine back onto the narrow, featureless road. Johann's driver left the transmission in the more powerful but slower gear, and Ian's driver followed his lead.

A demag 250 half-track could carry a crew of two with room for four skinny and friendly passengers behind them. Väinü, the gunner and observer on Johann's machine, had chosen the driver from his Viking contingent. Johann sat behind his Finnish sergeant in the passenger compartment with two of his Stalingrad veterans. He crouched behind Väinü, who appeared to be impervious to the driving snow or the biting cold wind, though Johann suspected that despite appearances, the Finn hated the wind and whipping, stinging snow as much as he did.

Ian followed in the second demag with three of his best fighting men and a radio operator who would report what they found. Still, Johann had no intention of using the radio except in an emergency. Convinced the Russians listened at every level, Johann suspected they knew the German battle plans before General Nehring did. Since before Stalingrad, the Russians' tactical moves were too accurate and convenient to be only coincidence. Scout and 'hit and run' units who used radio communications regularly did not fare nearly as well as Johann's, often running into suspiciously coincidental ambushes.

◇◇◇◇◇◇◇◇◇◇◇◇◇◇◇◇◇◇◇◇◇◇◇◇◇◇◇◇◇◇◇◇◇◇◇◇◇◇◇

Johann called a halt a thousand metres from the Russian lines and parked the half-tracks in a small opening in the woods. Two kilometres north, the vulnerable XLVIII panzer Corps waited for the Russian attack, and it was Johann's job to assess the timing and intensity of that attack. Nehring would share what he knew with the XLVIII panzers so they could withdraw if necessary, and if General Gräser would allow it.

Johann, prepared for an argument, met Ian in the snow between the vehicles. The men moved a few paces away from them, led by Väinü, who wanted no part of the fireworks.

Ian put one hand on his hip, swung the other through the swirling snow and asked in a distinctly sarcastic tone, "So, how are you planning to count tanks and guns in this weather? Intuition? Magic?"

Johann stayed calm. "Don't worry. The snowstorm will eventually slow down so we can see, and until then, it will cover us so we can get behind the Russians." He put his compass on his left palm, levelled it and pointed east with his gloved right hand. "The river is in that direction, and we will have the cover of the forest all the way there. After that, it will stop snowing enough to count tanks and guns."

Ian looked at the forest, the three or four trees he could see in the blizzard, and Johann followed his eyes, waiting for the inevitable sarcasm.

"How stupid of me; of course, this is a perfect day to look for Russian guns and tanks. So, do I understand that you have a deal with God?

336

Right now, I wouldn't see a tank before I ran into it, and you want me to believe that you are going to find them before the Russians find us?"

Johann shrugged. "Believe what you want, but it will stop snowing; we will find Russian guns and panzers, and we will count them!" Johann began walking. Väinü and his men followed. Ian brought up the rear, annoyed, muttering words that, fortunately, Johann couldn't hear over the howling wind.

The storm worsened as Johann led his men farther into the woods, where walking was less impossible. They reached the river without seeing anything but trees that bore a remarkable resemblance to one another—and snow, a lot of snow. The wind sighed in the branches as he stopped and leaned against a spruce tree. A clump of snow dislodged by the wind landed in front of him with a soft thump.

Ian caught up, plodding through drifts to the top of his boots, sometimes to his knees. He smiled sarcastically and said, "Okay, when are you planning to turn off the storm?"

Johann looked up; he couldn't see the tops of the trees. He grinned at Ian. "It will stop in a few minutes… I want it to fill in our tracks first." Johann unslung his pack and unbuckled the straps. "When we finish eating, the storm will let up enough to see guns and tanks."

Ian looked up toward where the sky should be. "Okay, God, did you hear that?" He checked his watch. "You've got fifteen minutes, max twenty. We're lost, and we need to count guns and tanks, so if you don't mind, it's time to stop your storm. Amen."

Väinü pulled out a knife and opened a can of sausage while speaking to Ian. "I'm not lost, so you're not!" He held out the opened tin; Ian cut off a slice, and Väinü said, "You know it will stop soon, and Johann will win, don't you?" He kicked the pack to Ian. "I have bread in there." Ian pulled the bread out. There was no butter, but slices of the canned sausage had enough grease to supplement it. The men sat with their backs against trees, and the snow slowed as they ate. Johann smiled at Ian when he got up but decided not to rub it in.

He asked, "Are you ready to go?" and Ian stood up, growling as he pulled his white hood over his head and fastened the drawstring. The flap on the front of the hood flopped down to cover his forehead. He peeked under it and smiled at Johann without a hint of sarcasm. He followed in Johann's footsteps for a few minutes, then trotted around him to join Väinü breaking the trail.

Despite the storm's reprieve, when he turned his head, Johann could barely pick out the last man in the group, and he was only ten metres behind him. Väinü assumed the point from Ian, leading the men along the top of the Vistula riverbank, then along the edge of a thicket that extended northward.

◇◇◇◇◇◇◇◇◇◇◇◇◇◇◇◇◇◇◇◇◇◇◇◇◇◇◇◇◇◇◇◇

A cannon barrel appeared out of the whiteness, where sky and ground blended into a featureless void, pointing skyward. Two more, and then a row of cannons grew out of the snow like branchless, leaning trees. As Johann and his men waded through the snow, the endless lines of modern artillery stunned them. Silently, they walked around a sand-bag guard station, working north along the river through a forest of cannon barrels, passing hectare after hectare of potentially devastating force.

It began to snow heavily, and Ian, walking beside Johann, raised his eyebrows as his boss looked at him through snow that became thicker by the second. Johann said, "I don't want to hear it. We found the guns—now we need the protection." Johann whacked Ian on the back and laughed. Ian grunted and forced a sarcastic "Ha! Ha!"

The men moved closer together so no one would get lost, and the guns disappeared behind a white wall as the whipping, swirling snow encircling them closed in. Väinü slowed, raising his voice above the wind's rising lament. "Should we stop? I can't see a thing."

Johann pointed away from the river. "Let's find the edge of the guns. Go west, and we will likely find the tanks there too. The snow will eventually slow again."

Väinü consulted his compass, kept it in his hand and checked it often. He weaved his way between gun emplacements, turning away when, in one instance, he got close enough to see men working. Johann noted they hadn't seen any sandbags or structures near the guns, and the barrels pointed in random directions and elevations. The installation was a work in progress.

They walked a thousand metres past lines of guns, small calibres grouped between heavy ones with no discernible pattern. There were

338

ever-increasing walls of sandbags and piles of cannon shells around ever-increasing numbers of guns. Most of the time, snow obscured the cannons until they were within a few metres of them. Still, sometimes the impulsive wind blew the snow upward and away, revealing cannons impossibly close to one another in disorganized groups.

Väinü stopped, and Johann stepped up beside him while Ian took a roll call of the men.

Peering through a break in the swirling blizzard, Väinü said, "We are a kilometre from the river, and we haven't seen a soldier—don't you think that's strange?"

Johann said, "They're either in their barracks or their holes. It's Christmas Day, we're in the middle of a blizzard, and vodka is how they eat potatoes in the Russian army." He swept his arm around an arc to the east, where they knew the wall of snow masked thousands of guns. "The good news is, half of the guns we've seen aren't ready for an attack. The Russians are still bringing them in and setting them up, and this snowstorm will surely slow them down."

"Should we still try to find the tanks?"

Johann thought about the blizzard, tried to guess whether it would die or intensify, then tried to estimate their chances of finding the half-track before dark. The barely visible white ghosts of his men gathered around him, whispering their opinions to one another.

"Let's figure out the course to the demags and see what we can find between here and there." He looked at Ian and tried not to laugh when he added, "The snow will stop soon; we don't want the Russians to catch us in the open!"

Väinü looked at his compass, stuck his arm out, and Johann bobbed his head. He looked at Ian, who nodded his consensus.

They walked southwest with the cutting wind at their back. The stinging snow no longer forced Johann to pull the flaps of his white hood in front of his face, and he constantly turned his head to look around. Ten minutes later, he whistled, and Väinü stopped.

He pointed to the right. "Katyas?"

Väinü grunted, looked at them for a few seconds, then started walking again.

Katyushas, or "Stalin's Organs," were the most feared weapon in the Soviet arsenal; rockets fired from trucks that couldn't be located and eliminated because they moved as the situation developed.

The wind increased, and the snow thickened as they worked their way through lines of trucks loaded with rocket launchers and fitted with chains on their wheels. Most of the trucks were American, a hodgepodge of brands and configurations, but the rocket launchers were all Katyushas.

Johann tapped Väinü on the shoulder, and he stopped.

"Let's head north and see how many rows there are. And then we have to work our way back to the demags, or we will never find them in the dark. We must find the edge of the woods while we can still see the trees."

There were eight long rows of parked Katya trucks—and then the T-34s began. The tanks, guarded by infantry in dark uniforms, became visible to Johann and his men long before the Russians could have seen the camouflaged Jäger patrol. Weaving between groups of tanks, the nearly invisible men easily avoided the inattentive soldiers who stood around in groups or crouched behind the tanks for protection from the wind. Johann estimated they had seen several hundred tanks in an hour, and there was no reason to assume they had seen more than a fraction of the number parked there.

"Are we headed for the demags?" he asked Väinü, who checked his compass.

"More or less." The Finn stuck out his arm. "We will find the edge of the woods if we go in that direction. From there, even you could find them."

The snow came well over their army boots, but white pant legs pulled down over them and tied tightly with heavy string prevented it from getting in. The wind that blew snow into the ditches and holes obliterated tracks seconds after a foot lifted out of them.

They worked their way around and along a second line of tanks for another kilometre, and Johann lost count, not that it mattered. When they reached the trees, Johann estimated that the Russians had parked over a thousand tanks between them and the river. He decided he could safely assume twice that number of artillery and hundreds, possibly more than a thousand rocket launchers, occupied the same general area. It was enough destructive power that precise numbers became irrelevant. The Russians outnumbered the Fourth panzer Army by a significant enough factor to sacrifice half their men and equipment and still destroy the largest and most effective German army facing them.

When the trees appeared, Johann was fighting a deepening depression, and when Väinü turned right to follow them, Johann was trying to create a survival scenario for Germany. As they waded through the drifts, Johann became more exhausted and discouraged. Survival for his country was impossible, and survival for him and his men was unlikely. He felt no pleasure when the demags' shapes appeared out of the darkening gloom. Strangely, his most profound regret was that he couldn't see how Katherine and Natasha could escape the Russians. He believed his family would survive without him; distance, time, and geography had put them in a separate world. He tried to think of them in danger, but Katherine and Natasha's more immediate problems kept bringing him back.

◇◇◇

The drive back to the base with the demags was eventful; they slid on and off the roads, but nothing was life-threatening. Every ten minutes, Väinü stepped away from the steel vehicle so that his compass would work and verified that they were going in the right direction. Once in a while, a road sign or landmark confirmed it, but the roads were impossible to differentiate from the surrounding fields unless they had power poles along them. Even with the poles, visibility was so limited that only one was visible at a time, and the only way to find the next one was to follow the wires.

It was midnight when they arrived at the compound, and although Johann was so tired he staggered, he went into General Nehring's sparse quarters and found him sitting beside the window, playing chess.

"Don't you know that if you play chess against yourself, you will become neurotic and paranoid?" Johann dropped his pack on the floor and sat opposite his general.

"I can't become what I already am, and I can't lose to myself." Nehring didn't smile. The expression on Johann's face removed all humour from the room.

Johann was about to tell him that he couldn't win against himself either when General Nehring interrupted him.

"I want more than the report version; I want to know what you know, but I also want to know what you think."

"Walther, my friend, I don't know what I know, but I am certain we won't survive unless we can run faster than the Russians."

Nehring smiled at the first-name greeting and familiar pronouns. "That many? How many guns, and where are they?"

"They're on this side of the river. The guns can't reach us, but the Forty-Eighth panzers are doomed if they stay where they are. There are at least a thousand artillery pieces, more likely double that and about a thousand Katya trucks aimed at the Forty-Eighth. They must withdraw before the first barrage; waiting until the Russians begin firing might be too late.

When?

Two weeks, probably sooner. Meanwhile, they should keep their engines running!"

Johann noted the anguish on Nehring's face, hesitated, then mercilessly continued.

"There are at least a thousand T-34 tanks and hundreds of one-oh-five tank destroyers, all less than three thousand metres from the Forty-Eighth's northern flank. A half-hour after the barrage begins, the forty-eighth will have nowhere to go. They will be doomed."

Johann looked at the chessboard. "Black's move?" Walther nodded.

Johann forked a bishop and a pawn with the black knight.

Walther moved the bishop. Johann moved the knight again, rejecting the pawn, and said, "Check." He leaned back. "You are tired, aren't you?"

Nehring moved his king, Johann took the white queen, then studied his general.

"We've got to get Katherine and Natasha out of here."

Nehring grunted his agreement. "I rewrote the letter for Katherine and Natasha Schneider into two letters in case they get separated." He nodded toward a chart table that served as a desk. "But I'm afraid the train ticket must go through channels. Jesus Christ can't get on that train without a permit from the Wehrmacht God!"

"How long will that take?"

"That depends on too many things to get it right. My guess is a week." He leaned ahead, closer to Johann's face. "I requested it yesterday. How long do you think we've got?"

"I still think we have a couple of weeks; I suggest you plan on half that, but don't count on more. If they were in a hurry, they would have been working today; some guns point the wrong way, and most rocket trucks are empty. We didn't see a tank with its engine running; they parked them in rows, covered them with white tarps and tree branches, and I doubt they've started them in a while."

Nehring's shoulders relaxed. "We should be able to get Katherine and Natasha on a train out of here before the attack. Berlin is moving units from Poland and Germany to the east, and trains are returning to Germany empty, except for a few medical emergencies." He paused, then shifted gears.

"I don't know what could be more important in Hungary than the battle against the Russians here..." Nehring tipped his king..., "but they don't tell me everything." He looked up from the board. "It's been a week since reconnaissance aircraft could fly over the Russians, but their estimate confirms yours. The Russians outnumber us in every way by five to one." He coughed. "Hitler thinks that's a fairy tale... so, I guess we have nothing to worry about."

Johann put on his pack and shuffled to the door. He staggered as he whacked it on the door frame, stumbled down three steps into thirty centimetres of snow and headed for his barracks. He tried to think of how he would trap the Russians when they came for the Twenty-Fourth's panzers, and his mind began to churn out possibilities.

Chapter Thirty-two

12 January 1944

A hit and run war

Some of those we assume brave simply don't have the courage to run away.

Stormy weather continued to be a problem for a week—alternating days of snow, rain, mud and frost. And then, on January 4, the cold, sunny deep freeze began. Everything with moving parts had to be 'winterized.' Mechanics added kerosene to the oil in every engine, thinning it so they would turn over and start, no matter the temperature. Lastwagen drivers left stubborn diesel engines idling all night to keep them warm. Tank crews cleaned the tracks on their panzers and kept them free of dirt.

It only took a day of minus-twenty weather to dry up all the mud and water and then another day to free everything up so that it moved as it did in summer. Train wheels, tank tracks, and brakes worked as well as ever. The dry frost and snow lubricated panzer tracks so they ran over the ground smoother than in summer. The Russia campaign had taught the men how to adjust to cold weather. Everything started, engine power noticeably increased, and men kept warm by working hard. The war functioned as well in winter as it did in the summer.

Nehring ordered his tanks to spread out through the forest, camouflaged so they were invisible to prying eyes and overhead camera lenses. Artillery crews hid their guns from snooping aircraft by lowering the barrels and covering them with appropriate camouflage.

The Gulash Cannonen, the Wehrmacht field kitchen, pulled behind horses or half-tracks, cooked hot food for freezing soldiers, and delivered it to them. A hundred thousand soldiers waited comfortably for a starving army with five times their numbers to attack them.

<hr>

It was cold, clear, dark, and ominously quiet at twenty-two hundred hours on 12 January 1945, two hours before midnight. General

Nehring and Johann stood on the steps outside the barracks, waiting for Natasha and Katherine. Their breath froze the instant it left their mouth, creating small clouds of ice fog in front of their faces. Walther had finally received a permit for the women to travel to Dresden on the train, and they had reluctantly agreed to go. Ian drove Johann's demag up to the building, and Johann got in the front while Walther got in the rear seat. Minutes later, Natasha and Katherine climbed in the rear with General Nehring. The demag had no top, but the Finn driver had brought a tarpaulin, and the heaters running at full blast kept everyone from freezing.

During the one-hour trip from the base to the train station, Johann checked twice to see that Katherine and Natasha had the Detmold information in case of separation. Nehring repeated the instructions on the processing they should expect at Dresden's officialdom, confirming that they had the contact name in the Auslanderamt and checking their money twice. He added a hundred Reichmarks to the money they carried, just in case.

<hr>

It was almost midnight when they arrived at the station, and the train was due to leave in an hour. General Nehring inquired about the status, and the traffic coordinator said he must hold it because of problems somewhere up the line. Johann and Walther waited with the women for two hours, checking periodically with officials, but no matter how much weight he put behind the questions, Nehring could not get any more information. Finally, the general decided that he and Johann must return to the base. He put the women in the hands of a young German officer he could trust, and he and Johann said their goodbyes.

He spoke to Katherine, trying to reassure himself while comforting her. "It's probably the partisans again; the rabbits kick the wounded wolf." Johann wasn't sure, but the Russian attack couldn't be far behind if the Polish underground had attacked the rail lines. General Nehring was nervous, and Johann guessed that his general's thoughts were leaning in the same direction as his own.

Nehring put his arms around Katherine, then Natasha. "We can no longer protect you—I'm afraid we have a war to fight. I would say

I will pray for you, but at this point, God isn't listening to German generals."

Johann kissed Natasha on the cheek. "We will see one another when this is over."

He hugged them both; Katherine cried, and Natasha smiled through tears. They vowed to meet at Gartenstrasse 18, and Johann and General Nehring left them in the station.

They were halfway back to the base when the Russian artillery bombardment began, and Nehring sent a message for his officers to meet him at the operations tent. The shelling stopped an hour later, and Pale gray light—a harbinger of impending dawn—combined with wisps of ice fog to lend an eeriness to the shadows of buildings and streets.

<hr>

The sun peeked above the horizon as the train pulled out of the Ostrowiec railway station, a critical six hours late with the sun's rays already tinting the sky. Katherine and Natasha sat in a compartment with three officers, two of them wounded. The third was on his way to the western front to fight the Americans, and General Nehring had tasked him with looking after the women. Although he was curious why a general would ask such a favour, the officer promised to protect them.

Katherine spoke only a few words of German, and only when she couldn't avoid it. On the other hand, Natasha chattered with little encouragement, telling the officers of their lives in Ukraine and her imaginary German father. Her story was worthy of a novel, and it mesmerized the young soldiers who hadn't spoken to a pretty girl or any girl who didn't hate them in a very long time.

Artillery fire from the northeast interrupted Natasha's ramble, and the officers, noticeably nervous, told Katherine and Natasha the Russians had begun the attack but that the German panzers would push them back.

Katherine and Natasha didn't tell them that General Nehring had told them the Russians would push the German Army back to Germany, and the end, one way or another, could not be far into the future.

IL-2 was the short designation for the primary Russian ground attack aircraft nicknamed Fliegender panzer, the flying tank, by German ground forces and the Zementbomber by members of the Luftwaffe.

Egor means 'farmer,' and the surname Smirnov means 'meek.' Egor Smirnov, the pilot of an IL-2 flying southwest along the railway tracks, was neither meek nor a farmer. The Germans had killed his entire family, including his sister, mother and grandmother in Kharkiv, and they had done it intentionally, personally, and without mercy. His soul burned with a desire to kill Germans, and it burned hotter than his will to live.

Feliks, erroneously named by his parents, sat in a canvas sling behind Egor, his hands on the grips of an American fifty-calibre machine gun. Feliks—his name meant happy—was anything but happy. He had flunked out of flight school, and the Russian Air Force had punished him with the most dangerous job they had—rear gunner in an Ilyushkin IL-2. Armour protecting the pilot started at the aircraft's nose and extended under his seat but stopped before the gunner. To the Russian Air Force and Egor, rear gunners were expendable, not worth the weight of the armour needed to protect them. But, on the bright side for the Russian Air Force, the high death rate among gunners kept the flight-school failure rate down.

Egor was on his third gunner and hadn't bothered to remember Feliks's last name.

The day started early for Egor and Feliks; they were in the air before full daylight, hoping to reach their objective before the German fighters went hunting. As they climbed out to the south, the sun's edge splashed a small patch of fire on their starboard wingtip until Egor turned west.

The IL-2 flew to the Vistula River and followed the railway tracks west, away from the river, looking for targets. Egor was about to turn north when the smoky haze from a westbound train's coal-fired boiler caught his attention. He closed rapidly on the train, and the smoke led to ten railway cars behind a six-wheeled locomotive. Egor flicked the protective covers off his cannon switches and the bomb release and said into the intercom, "After I drop the bombs, I will climb and turn left so you can fire at the train... Do your best not to shoot our tail off!"

Egor had set the fire in his forward cannons to converge at two hundred metres, too close for most pilots, but he liked to attack ground targets low and slow. He cut the throttle by half, added two notches of flap to push the nose down, and pressed the firing button when his sight was on the last car. The cannons seemed to slow the plane, and Egor added throttle as he touched the rudders to keep the hits in the centre of the targets.

Small explosions and pieces of railway cars flew into the air ahead of his fighter, and Egor held the button down until he passed over the engine. Cannon-shell explosions destroyed the engine's cabin and the men in it, and just before he passed over it at twenty metres, Egor dropped his 200-kilogram cluster of bombs on the locomotive. He opened the throttle, tipped the control stick to the left rear corner and instinctively pushed the left rudder far enough to synchronize the turn. He centred the stick when the American-built artificial horizon indicated thirty degrees of bank.

Egor held the turn until he was flying parallel to the left side of the burning cars. The heavy machine gun in Feliks's hands shook the aircraft as he raked the train with steel bullets, and the American Browning's fifty-calibre barrel smoked when the train passed out of his field of fire.

Feliks said, "I've got enough bullets for another five seconds; let's go back!"

"No, we might need that if a German fighter finds us. We must return to the airfield for ammunition." Egor looked at the American gyrocompass and steered to the easterly bearing that would take them to the field they had left. The train's engine boiler exploded behind them, and Egor said to the intercom, "I don't think that train will make it to Germany." He chuckled. "If we're lucky, it was full of German soldiers!"

The train's rear car was a mail and freight car; the next two were flatcars designed to carry panzers, and the fourth and fifth cars, marked with a bullet-riddled red cross on the roof, were stretcher cars carrying seriously wounded soldiers home from the front. The five railcars at the front of the train were for passengers, the walking wounded, and soldiers moving from one theatre to another.

The officer in charge of the women heard the fighter's engine and propeller, then cannon fire. Natasha screamed as the young man pushed Katherine and Natasha on the floor and lay on top of them. He could have saved himself had he been the first on the floor.

The cannons' converging fire blew the compartment apart, killing all three German soldiers, but the young officer had been successful in saving Katherine and Natasha.

The fighter roared overhead, bombs destroyed the locomotive, and Katherine pushed the soldier's body aside as the sound of the plane retreated. The chatter of a machine gun began as Katherine struggled to get to her feet—the exploding boiler shook the train, still rolling down the track. Someone pulled on the brakes, and steel wheels screeched against steel rails. The coasting train slowed, then stopped with a jolt. Screams and shouted orders to get away from the train prodded Katherine to move—she could smell fire; it was time to run, and she pulled Natasha to her feet.

Katherine pointed at the hole where the window had been. "Jump! Now!" Natasha hesitated; Katherine pushed her into the opening, and Natasha pushed herself away from the window ledge with her feet. Katherine followed her, landing in the weeds, snow and gravel beside the burning train. She pointed away from the railway tracks. "Go that way…hurry!" Uniformed men running along the tracks toward the screams from the hospital cars paid no attention to the uninjured women.

Katherine stopped, looked back at the chaos and swore in her native tongue. She said to her daughter, "We need our clothes!" She turned toward the train, and Natasha followed. Katherine yelled at her daughter as she reached the front of the car they had jumped out of a minute before, "Help me… Lift me onto the step!" Without a platform and standing on the slope of the gravel roadbed, the bottom step was at her waist, too high to get onto.

Natasha put her arms around her mother's thighs and lifted her so that her knees were on the hard corrugated steel step—Katherine grimaced and swore, grabbed the hand bars and hoisted herself to her feet.

"Wait here." She disappeared but returned a few seconds later with their bloody suitcase in one hand and two equally bloody army greatcoats draped over the other. She threw them on the ground and jumped.

Pulling on the coats, they ran through a line of bushes into a snowy pasture. There was a road two hundred metres away on the other side of the field, but they first had to wade through the piles of snow that wind had drifted and jammed into deep drifts against the bushes.

Katherine said, "We will walk to Germany!" and pointed at scattered groups of people on the road. "We will walk with them." She waded through the snow, dragging the suitcase and cleaning the soldier's blood from it. She used snow to clean her coat and Natasha's. And then, shivering despite the heavy coat, she held back her tears and broke the trail for her daughter.

The sun was cold, but German Army winter uniforms made it bearable. Ploughing through knee-deep snow, they were sweating when they reached the road and joined the people walking toward the German border. The refugees moved aside when Natasha and Katherine caught up to them, and Natasha said, "Walther said these uniforms are SS—they're afraid of us."

General Nehring had removed the markings, but every Pole knew what that uniform meant. Katherine told Natasha not to tell anyone where they had gotten them.

Chapter Thirty-three

January 1944

The beginning of the End

But if there must be an end, let it be loud. Let it be bloody. Better to burn than to wither away in the dark.

Mike Mignola

Although twenty-five kilometres from the guns, the men in the demag could hear the first Russian guns above the noise of the demag's engine and tracks. It was 04:30, and Johann and General Nehring were halfway to the base. The general nodded when Johann turned around. They exchanged glances—the guns confirmed what Johann had predicted eighteen days ago. Today, the Russians would start the final stage of their campaign to take Berlin and eliminate Adolph Hitler.

The initial bombardment was over when they arrived at the base and entered the war room, where a dozen officers stood around a table staring at the map of the area where German forces would fight the coming battle. The officers saluted and stepped back, and General Nehring immediately asked for a briefing on the Russian attack and the damage assessment from the bombardment.

A young officer said, "The Russians shelled our decoy base on the Grosskampflinie—we assume the bombardment wiped it out—but since we had evacuated it, there were no casualties. We have lost communication with the Forty-Eighth panzers and Sixty-Eighth Infantry. The Ninth Army was also hit hard and is bracing for an all-out assault. The Russian guns couldn't reach the Twenty-Fourth panzers' tanks and men, so there are no casualties to report."

Nehring put his finger on the map. "We are here, on the southeast side of Kielce." General Nehring slid his finger to where the officers knew they should have been according to Hitler's orders. "This is our decoy base, and, as predicted, the guns targetted it as soon as the bombardment began. The Russian artillery obliterated it, but they will soon realize they accomplished nothing and figure out our 'Maskirova' and our actual location." Nehring traced a line to Kielce with his finger. "And when they commit their armour, we won't be able to stop them before they reach Kielce."

Nehring tapped his finger on their present position, then looked to his men. "We must buy time for the Ninth Army, or the Russians will be in Berlin by the end of next week, and we can't do that by 'holding to the last man!' But we can delay the Russian advance by making them afraid to turn a corner or climb a hill. Our *modus operandi* will be to 'hit hard and run like hell!' When we're not fighting, we will be hiding."

General Nehring circled an oval between their location and the Forty-Eighth panzers at the Hauptkampflinie. "We will delay the Russians for a few days by hitting them opportunistically in this area. We will ambush them when they are most vulnerable and when they least expect it!" He straightened up and smiled. "We've kept the forests clear of Russian eyes for the past couple of weeks, and we will sweep them again before we set our first trap."

Nehring looked at Johann. "You have Leutnant Klaus's Waffen SS panzers; he's our best commander and has two squadrons of four pan-thers in the woods not far from where you want him—please try not to waste them."

Johann said, "Yes, Klaus and I have met, and we have made prep-arations. He knows where and when we will ambush the Russians." He slid his finger along a field in the northeastern part of the oval. "As soon as this barrage stops, they will send T-34s and tank destroyers through this narrow field between these two patches of forests. The Russians always probe our defences before they begin the real attack. They send a small force as sacrificial lambs to find out where we are and what we have. If they stay with that pattern, they will go through that funnel. My scouts are coordinating the ambush as we are talking about it."

Nehring's expression said he was satisfied, and he told Johann, "The artillery is ready and waiting for your call when you need them." He looked at his artillery officers, and they nodded. Nehring's silence when he turned back to Johann meant that Johann didn't need to hear the rest of the briefing.

◇◇◇◇◇◇◇◇◇◇◇◇◇◇◇◇◇◇◇◇◇◇◇◇◇◇◇◇◇◇◇◇◇

Johann saluted, a little more like a regulation effort than usual, and headed for the demag. Väinü's Finnish driver had it running, and Johann joined Väinü in the back seat.

"Is Ian ready?"

Väinü said, "He's got the men hidden in the woods." He pulled a white tarpaulin windbreak up on a makeshift frame. "I just came from our panzers, and there are no living Russian scouts within five or six kilometres—and there won't be until after we finish our job."

The demag jumped forward, headed for the edge of the woods. It turned east when it reached the trees, and the only thing on it that wasn't white was the gray smoke coming from the exhaust.

It took thirty-five minutes to reach the pre-arranged meeting point with Ian—a shallow valley at the bottom of two opposing slopes, five hundred metres wide, with tall trees at the top of the slopes on both sides.

Ian was already there, waiting for Johann, and after they shook hands, he said, "First, the bad news: the Forty-Eighth panzers are no more, and Russian tanks and infantry will soon destroy the Sixty-Eighth infantry if they don't get out of there! Our panzers can't protect them—we will lose them if they try. Hundreds of T-34s and tank destroyers are coming right at them. They will hit the infantry as soon as the barrage is over!"

◇◇◇◇◇◇◇◇◇◇◇◇◇◇◇◇◇◇◇◇◇◇◇◇◇◇◇◇◇◇◇◇◇

Following an hour of constant racket, the second barrage waned, and rose-coloured light crept into the eastern sky. Both Ian and Johann knew the Sixty-Eighth infantry wouldn't withdraw against Hitler's orders, and the Russian armour and infantry would roll over them in a matter of hours.

Johann kicked the snow, angry at the immense cost of such gross incompetence. "Hitler, the fucking military genius, has lost half of the Fourth panzer Army, and the sun isn't up yet!"

Ian shrugged his shoulders and switched back to the report.

"There are twenty T-34s and a couple of one-oh-five destroyers on their way to see what we've got, but they aren't sure where we are. Our scouts will stay ahead of them and advise if their route changes, but they are headed for this field right now. Our men are in those woods." Ian pointed toward a black wall of trees.

"You've been using the radio?" Johann's voice had a tinge of criticism in it.

"We need to know where those tanks are, and we only use today's code."

"Use it as little as possible..." Ian opened his mouth to protest Johann's implied assumption, but Johann ignored him and went on. "We will ambush them and get the hell out of here before their planes find us."

Leutnant Klaus, a stickler for detail, looked at his watch as Johann approached panzer 227. He knew Klaus well and climbed on his panther with a friendly grin. Klaus didn't salute, but when Johann sat beside the cupola, he reached for Johann's hand and shook it.

"Grüss' dich, Johann. Wie spät ist es?" Using sarcasm was safer than directly criticizing a superior for being late.

Klaus was a small, dark-skinned man, handsome to a woman and envied by other men.

"Grüss' dich. It's time to get into position to kill Russian tanks." Johann took his hand back. "The Twenty-Fourth panzers is all we've got to hold Kielce, and we want the Russians to think we are stronger than we are."

Klaus said, "We won't hold them for long."

Johann smiled. "We won't hold them at all. We'll kill as many Russians as we can, and then we'll run like hell!"

Men came out of the shadows as Klaus's panthers moved along the edge of the trees. Klaus had covered his panzers with tree limbs, white tarps, and snow. Half of Johann's company climbed on the panzers while the remainder walked through the trees where the snow was not as deep.

Johann stopped Klaus's tank at the western side of the field, and Ian led the Eighth Jäger Company to the trees on the southern edge. They left tracks in the snow, but it would be too late for the Russians when they discovered them. Johann climbed up on the tank's rump, sat beside Klaus's cupola, and pointed across the valley below them.

"Twenty T-34s and two one-oh-five destroyers will come from the southeast." Johann pointed at a narrow stand of trees on each side of the killing field. "My men will be in the trees on both sides and will take care of the infantry…Ian says there are about two hundred of them. They will leave their rides as soon as the artillery fires, so concentrate on the tanks and leave the infantry to us."

Johann pointed at a large dark rectangular shape a hundred metres on their left, then swept his arm to another dark building across a narrow field road to their right.

"The light on the snow makes even camouflaged tanks visible, and I recommend that you take two panzers to each of those barns. Park them against the north side of the barn so the shadow hides the tank's silhouette. The bright light from the sun will be on your right, and they won't see your tanks until they're in serious trouble. When the artillery fires, you can move all you want." He pointed at trees beyond the field, the first point the Russians would pass. "Hide the rest of your tanks in those trees, well spread out. Tell them to wait until the Russians pass, then shoot them in the ass!"

Klaus shook his head. "I know the Russians, and they wouldn't attack without scouts. They will have set up observation posts overnight and are probably watching us right now."

It was Johann's turn to shake his head. "I assure you there are no observation posts or forward Russian scouting parties to report your tanks."

Johann glanced past Klaus at a young man sitting in the loader's seat, no more than a boy.

"Is the Waffen SS stealing children now? He looks like he would have trouble lifting a dinner fork, let alone a cannon shell."

"Don't worry about him—he can load and shoot as well as any man I've ever had."

"How old?"

"Seventeen…almost…and you're right, he is too young to play soldier."

"So are we all, but he is a child." Johann muttered, *"Kindersoldat,"* and slid down from his perch.

The Russian tanks showed up in the full daylight, crawling through deep snow, gathered together in two bunches as though trying to keep one another warm. Wading on foot through the deep snow was difficult, and infantry clung to the twenty tanks and both tank destroyers.

"I wonder if they draw straws," said Johann, talking to himself as he watched men struggle in the snow-packed tracks left by the tanks, "or do they go by rank?" Johann watched them creep toward him through his Zeiss binoculars, thinking that a worse example of military tactics would be hard to find. They advanced toward the enemy without reconnaissance and in a formation that invited disaster—actually, more a clump than an organized formation.

The Russian tanks worked their way past the camouflaged panthers Klaus had backed into holes in the forest, moving at the speed of men wading snow to their knees. Johann waited until the Russians were past the mid-point between the two groups of German tanks before he spoke quietly into the radio, where six eighty-eight gun crews, the coordinates already calculated and set, waited for the order to fire. Two-and-a-half seconds later, a single eighty-eight-millimetre shell, fired to test the range, exploded a hundred metres in front of the Russian tanks.

It took a full second for the sound of the gun firing to reach Johann and the Russians—a short time if one is eating an apple, but confusing to Russian tank commanders who didn't expect it. Thinking that the shell could have been one of theirs, they stopped, guessing they were driving into a Russian barrage. Unfortunately, they had guessed wrong and now presented a stationary target for eight panthers and two MG-42 crews. The panthers' gunners had their fingers on their triggers and fired before gravity stopped the upward arc of dirt and snow blown into the air from the German shell. Six T-34s took hits that ended their day, and a seventh lost a track.

Johann spoke into the handset. "Range plus one hundred fifty and fire everything!" Seconds later, the field exploded—the tank destroyers died, and eighty-eight-millimetre shells rained down on the T-34s before they could make up their minds which way to go, raising clouds of snow and mud. A flurry of machine-gun bullets met Russian infantry running for the trees and tank crews who bailed out. They lay down, trying to hide in the snow, but there was no safe place. The panthers, eighty-eights, and machine guns finished their work in five minutes, leaving the field littered with bodies and the snow red with Russian blood.

Johann met Ian and Väinü on the south side of the killing field, where Jäger company had scattered through the forest. panther 227 stopped beside Johann, and he climbed up the front armour plate to talk to Klaus.

Johann said, "We have a man seriously wounded. Ian will take him to Kielce in the demag and report to Nehring. So, if you want to send a message… You haven't used your radio, have you?"

"Of course not, and I will brief Ian before he leaves. But perhaps it would be better if we send the wounded straight to the medical station with one of the panthers."

Johann shook his head. "The medical station you're thinking about is no more, and the same applies to our tent headquarters. Nehring moved everyone to Kielce a few days ago. I have orders to take care of you and your panzers, so at the moment, we must get out of range of Russian artillery and hide from the Russian Air Force. If we're lucky, we'll get a chance to ambush the next probe, but we need to disappear right now. Keep close to the trees, just in case those Russians had time to call home."

Klaus instinctively checked the sky for aircraft. "Are the Forty-Eighth panzers fighting a defensive action while we regroup?"

"The Forty-Eighth panzers, and likely the Sixty-Eighth infantry, are useless to us. The Russians have destroyed almost all their tanks and at least half of their infantry. What's left has surrendered or is retreating. The Twenty-Fourth panzers is the only panzer defence standing between the Russians and Berlin in this sector and we have orders to set hold at Kielce, or the Russians will flank the Fourth and Ninth armies and have a clear path to Berlin."

Klaus said, "Too bad that little skirmish is not how our war is going."

"Yes, Twenty T-34s is a drop of water in the ocean!"

Chapter Thirty-four

If we don't get there first

Hell is empty, and all the devils are here.
William Shakespeare

THE TWENTY-FOURTH PANZER CORPS was the only force on the Fourth panzer Army's southwestern flank that could slow the Russians, and Hitler ordered them to hold Kielce "at all costs." General Nehring showed Johann the order.

In the late morning of the twelfth of January, Johann sat in Nehring's command vehicle, his metal mapboard between him and his boss. Nehring put the order in his pocket, and Johann slid his stiff, frozen finger across the map. He said, "They will try to hit us here, on our southern flank."

The constant rumble of cannons firing in the background disturbed both men. Although the shells landed far from Nehring's forces, the sound of battle ominously crept westward as the morning progressed.

Johann had left panther 227 and Klaus's well-camouflaged squadron in a small forest close to the route the Russians would have to take to reach Kielce. Ian, Väinü, and ten men were busy tracking and eliminating Russian forward scouts in the area, a 'cat and mouse' game in the snow, and the rest of Jäger Company waited for orders with Klaus and his panthers. Time was pressing; the Russians were moving forward.

Nehring confirmed what Johann knew. "We have reports that our Forty-Eighth panzers and Sixty-Eighth infantry have surrendered. General Gräser is still trying to hold at the Grosskampflinie with what's left of our Fourth panzer Army, but he has personally withdrawn well behind our lines. Hitler's lines mean nothing now."

"Sir, what about our southern flank?" Johann had not yet scouted the area between Kielce and the Czech border, and he didn't like flying blind. He hated asking the question, but General Nehring seemed willing to discuss strategy with him. "How is the Seventeenth Army doing?" He was afraid of the answer.

"For now, the Russians aren't taking them seriously. I suspect they plan to move on Kielce first, then swing southeast to cut off the Seventeenth." Nehring's frustration showed. "The Seventeenth should withdraw immediately so that our collapsing line is at right angles to the Czech border, hardening our defences on the shortest possible line. If they hold as the Russians drive us west, the line will swing and lengthen, spreading out our forces, and it won't take long for the Seventeenth to become isolated and irrelevant."

Johann said, "Hitler has done this before, and the Russians are planning on him doing it again."

Frustrated, General Nehring put his finger on the map as he said, "We're going to lose another army."

"Let me guess: Hitler told the Seventeenth to 'hold to the last man.'"

With his eyes, Johann estimated the distance from where he was to the Seventeenth and guessed that the Russians would cover it in a week. "The Russians will run over them at a time of their choosing, and a few days after that, they will finish off the Fourth Army!"

Johann put on his gloves, then his mittens. He could feel desperation taking over and wanted to hit something as he said, "Either he doesn't understand the geography, or he assumes that if he orders an army to hold, that will automatically stop the Russians. If...no...when the Seventeenth Army folds, the Russians will have cut off any escape toward Czechoslovakia, giving them the southern flank of the Fourth panzer Army on a platter."

Desperation was rapidly becoming depression as Johann said, "Klaus's squadron might be able to keep the Russians clear of our southern flank for a day or two while you withdraw the rest of the Twenty-Fourth west, but if the Seventeenth is gone, you must move fast, before the Russians close the pincer on the Fourth Army!" What Johann left unsaid was that Nehring could be sacrificing Klaus's squadron.

Nehring said, showing Johann's same sense of lost hope, "Yes, if the Russians pass the Fourth panzer Army on one of our flanks and pinch in front, we're done, leaving them an easy drive to the German border.

You and Klaus must protect our southern flank by setting up ambushes that will slow the Russians. I will keep our artillery ready to help you for as long as I can. All we can do is our best."

Johann was relieved. "So, you won't sacrifice Klaus's panthers or hold in Kielce to your last man, no matter what?"

"No, not in Kielce or anywhere else. If Gräser doesn't allow an orderly withdrawal, the Fourth Army and their panzers will become immaterial; he must ignore Hitler and save our army so they can protect the Ninth Army's southern flank. If he doesn't, we will withdraw with as many men and panzers as we can save."

Johann shook hands awkwardly in the confined space, then reached for the door lever.

"If I call this afternoon, will I get my artillery?" He stepped onto the packed snow around the command vehicle and waited to close the door. "I marked the approximate spot on your map, and I will give the gunners the exact coordinates and time when I know where the Russians are."

Nehring looked at Johann, visibly concerned. "I'm afraid you and your tanks are on your own. We can give you what you need this afternoon, but I can't promise anything tomorrow!" He looked at Johann with the same desperation that his leutnant felt as he pleaded, "Please don't lose those panthers."

<hr>

Johann spread his map out on his demag's warm hood with Ian on one side and Klaus on the other. The barrage that had begun at ten was likely the last before the Russians moved forward en masse. They would send spikes of Jäger-type infantry and small armoured units ahead to test German defences, and the main attack would come behind them—the modus operandi for Russian assaults, and Johann planned an ambush to eliminate one of the forward spikes.

The Russians' plan would include taking Kielce, and the armoured probe would give them vital information. If the probe failed, the main attack would hesitate, buying time for General Nehring's panzers.

Johann said, "If I were the Russians, I would try to flank the Twenty-Fourth to the south and get behind the Seventeenth before it withdraws. To do that, they need to probe our defences, and logically, they will send a bunch of T-34s and infantry up the gut between this forest and that creek." He put his finger on the small forest in the aerial photograph. "I need two panthers here..." He moved his finger to a ravine five hundred metres opposite the trees. "I also need two panthers in the ravine... here. And I want you to cover them with tarps and snow as soon as possible. The Russians will arrive soon, and I don't want any tracks leading to your panzers!"

Klaus interrupted Johann just as he was about to tell him not to cross the field from the woods. With his finger on the photograph, Klaus traced as he spoke.

"I will take the panthers northwest, staying close to the trees. We will cross the field using this plowed road and follow field roads back to our position, leaving no tracks that will be noticeable at first glance from the air." He looked at Johann. "It's not perfect, but does that work for you?"

"Okay, so I'm a nag." Johann smiled. Ian and Väinü usually let him finish before correcting him.

Väinü arrived with his half of the scouts and immediately reported to Johann.

"There are no Russian tanks within five kilometres, and the forward scouts they sent are not going to report anything. The only eyes they have now are their planes."

"How do you know you got all the scouts?" Klaus smiled at Väinü as he asked the question. Väinü gave him a sour look—his voice adopting the tone of a mother telling her child the obvious.

"Tracks in the snow lead to everything that passes through it. We also took out the only half-track they had. I guarantee they didn't get to their radio!" He looked at Klaus with an expression that dared him to question his abilities again.

"The Russians are coming; they're a couple of hours away, but they are moving without scouting reports. You will have the surprise you want."

Klaus nodded, and Johann said to Väinü. "We have an hour, and I would like to check out our escape route. Ian will call us when he has more information on the T-34s." He pointed at the demag. "We'll take that. Find a couple of men."

Väinü touched his hat and left to round them up.

Even in deep snow, the demag could cruise at twenty kilometres per hour, and, in fifteen minutes, they were southwest of the ambush and headed north. Staying close to the trees, driving over frozen ponds and shallow brooks, they left only a shallow depression to indicate where they had been. The snow ahead of them was unblemished, and when they drove up to a road heading west at a right angle, Johann instructed the driver to swing the demag onto it.

Ian had camouflaged the half-track with tree branches and white tarps, and when an Il-2 flew to the west of them, the driver stopped—camouflage loses its advantage when motion catches the eye of an observer. The fighter, probably out of ammunition and headed for home, didn't change course.

While the stopped demag's engine idled, excess gasoline poured into the carburetor through a stuck needle valve, choking the engine to a stop. In the first few seconds of quiet, sounds of shots fired in the calm, cold air carried to the men's ears, punctuated with what could only be a woman's screams. The Maybach engine's starter ground through one revolution before Johann said, "Stop! Don't try to start it! Listen..." Johann grabbed his binoculars and swept the horizon where he thought the shots had originated. Another scream confirmed the direction. All he could see, low on the horizon and at least five hundred metres west of them, was a farmhouse and a large barn.

He told the driver, "We will leave the demag, and when you get it started, I want you to hide it in that line of trees." He looked at his driver to be sure he was paying attention and pointed to a line of mature evergreen trees half a kilometre down the road. He had his feet on the ground when he said, "If we aren't back in thirty minutes, or if it looks like things are going bad, go back to Klaus and tell Ian to organize the ambush. We will find you later."

Väinü didn't offer an opinion like Ian would, but Johann felt his unease.

Johann pulled up his white hood and decided to clear the air while they walked. "What are you thinking, Väinü?"

"I wonder what this has to do with scouting an escape route for our tanks. But, of course, it's none of my business."

Johann began to jog toward the farmhouse, and Väinü followed with two men.

"You're right about it being none of your business, but I need to know if that's a Russian scouting party." Johann was surprised when the logical explanation came to him so quickly. In any case, the women's screams left him no choice.

The Finn caught up to jog beside Johann. "Whoever it is, what they are doing isn't good."

Johann could see two dark figures running from the barn, headed for the house. One was a child, and the other was a woman. A man at the barn raised his rifle, and a puff of smoke and fire exited the barrel. The bullet struck the woman before the sound reached Johann. The man lowered the gun, levered another shell into the barrel, then raised it, aiming at the boy who had stopped and begun to shriek.

Väinü shouted, "Get down!" and Johann looked back as he dropped to the ground. The Finn, on one knee, fired with his sniper rifle resting on his other knee. The bullet passed within inches of Johann's head.

The man beside the barn fell in a heap, and the boy stopped screaming. He ran to the woman, and a second man stepped out of the barn, then fell back through the doorway shortly after another bullet zipped past Johann.

Four men appeared at the barn door, looked at their dead comrades and exited cautiously, holding their Russian machine guns ready to fire. Väinü let them get into the yard, away from protection, watched them search for the source of the shots, then cut them down with four bullets in eight seconds.

The child, ignoring everything else, knelt beside the woman, and even from two hundred metres away, his howls were heartbreakingly distinct.

Johann stayed on the ground, fighting the urge to go to the boy, and a minute later, a man ran from the barn in a low crouch. Väinü fired, missed and cursed, and the man snatched the boy. He ran toward the house using the child as a shield, but the child screamed, "Mutti, Mutti," and wiggled free. The man hesitated—and Väinü's bullet hit him in the neck, spraying a cloud of blood.

Johann waited a few minutes, then said, "That could be the last one. We might be able to save the woman."

He crouched, pulled the white flaps of his hood over his face, and ran toward the child as fast as he could without giving in to the urge to run flat out.

Väinü said, "Let's hope so," as he caught up to him with his men on his heels.

The men ran straight at the barn, expecting any resistance to come from there, but two men exited the house with Papa's firing blindly into the whiteness. Simultaneously, four others rounded the turn from the rear of the house. Johann and his men dropped to their bellies and cut them down with their machine guns.

Johann got up and ran to the child, now wailing over the fallen woman.

The dead soldiers wore a lousy attempt at camouflage, and Johann was still five metres from the one who died trying to use the boy as a shield when he recognized the man's boots. He checked the woman; her eyes were closed, and the hole in her back wasn't bleeding, so he assumed her heart had stopped. He went to the dead man, pulled the coat sleeve back and exposed a Totenkopf, the skull emblem of the Waffen SS, embroidered on his sleeve. The man groaned, opened his eyes, asked, *"Wer sind Sie?"* and Väinü answered by putting a bullet in his chest.

"Mene helvettiin!" Väinü spat out the words that paved the SS officer's road to the afterlife, then looked at his commanding officer. Johann knew that Väinü was not asking his forgiveness for sending a murderer to hell as much as he was daring him to say something about it. While Väinü stared at his commander, several more short bursts marked the end of other SS soldiers.

Seconds later, Väinü's corporal walked across the yard to report to him. Johann's eyes went to the boy, who was now trying to get his mother to stand up.

The corporal spoke as a matter of fact. "There is a woman in the house who is still alive." Väinü nodded, and the corporal stared at the exposed Nazi uniform.

Väinü asked, "Can she walk?"

"No, sir, and if you don't get to her quickly, she won't be telling you what happened here." The corporal looked around the yard, his eyes stopping on each body to count it.

Johann couldn't take his eyes off the little boy trying to pull his dying mother to her feet and said to Väinü, "Why don't you go to the woman in the house...I will take care of the boy."

Johann knelt beside the boy. The woman moved, and Johann carefully turned her on her side. She was still alive, and he held her head while she fought for breath. Young and beautiful, like Barbara, she gasped in Polish-flavoured German, "Please take care of Reuben. He's a good boy and won't give you any trouble." Her breath escaped; she shook, gasped once more and died.

The boy was about nine, the same age as Thomas had been when Johann left home. Johann stroked the boy's hair and looked into his eyes. "Is she your mother?"

"Ja. Warum steht sie nicht auf?" He looked at his mother, bent over and tried to lift her head. *"Steh' auf, Mutti."* He sobbed, trying to pull her limp body up. Johann took the boy's hands away, gently rolled his mother onto her back and closed her eyes.

The boy lay down on the packed snow beside his mother and cried with his face in her hair. Johann waited silently for as long as he could. Time was the enemy now.

"What's your name?" Johann asked the question softly, and the sound that escaped his vocal cords was uncontrollable.

"Ich bin keine Jude...Ich bin keine Jude...Ich bin keine Jude!" The little boy stood up and screamed in Johann's face, wiping his tears with his sleeve.

The boy tried to retreat, but Johann grabbed his arms.

"It doesn't matter to me whether you are a Jew. Please believe me... I won't hurt you."

The boy gave up and buried his head in Johann's chest. Johann put his arms around him and waited while he cried.

"The woman inside died too." Väinü's voice broke through to Johann. "She told us what happened, and it isn't something you will want the boy to hear."

Johann picked the exhausted boy up in his arms. "He needs to lie down for a few minutes." He passed the boy to Väinü's corporal, and the man carried him to the house.

Väinü avoided looking at Johann as he watched the man walk to the house. "They raped and murdered two women in the house, and they killed three women and two old men in the barn. The people in the barn were Jews, and the people in the house were hiding them from your German patriots." His eyes wandered to the barn and then settled on the dead woman at Johann's feet. "I suppose she is one of the Jews since she came from the barn."

"Yes, and the boy is her son." He looked at the dead soldier. "I'm afraid we killed twelve Waffen SS soldiers."

Väinü shrugged and looked at Johann. "They aren't so tough, and they can't shoot worth shit!"

Johann choked on a comment that stuck in his throat and said, "We have to set up our ambush. Tell your corporal to take the boy to the road, find some refugees to care for him, then follow our tracks back...." His eyes wandered over the bloody scene, then to a house three hundred metres away. Two figures stood in front of it. "The locals heard the shooting and will clean things up here. The corporal could try giving the boy to those two, but I doubt they will take him when they find out what happened to their neighbours. The road is probably a better option."

Väinü looked at the bodies, paused, and then saluted Johann by touching his hat. He modified the orders slightly. "Understood, sir. I will send two men to take the boy to the road while you and I go to the demag."

Väinü went to the house, and the boy returned holding the corporal's hand.

Johann knelt in front of the boy. "This man will take you to the road and leave you with people who will help you get to Germany." The boy looked at Johann, waiting for something else.

"I have a son just like you. His name is Thomas, and he wouldn't mind if you used his name. My last name is Finke, and you can use that name too."

He knelt and looked into the boy's eyes. "Now, what is your name?"

"Ich bin keine Jude!"

"You are safe now and must use my son's name. I'm Johann Finke, and my son is Thomas Finke; now, what is your name?"

"Thomas...Finke." He said it hesitantly, then added, *"Ich bin keine Jude."*

"You don't need to say that you aren't a Jew. Thomas Finke is not a Jew's name. Repeat it for me."

"Thomas Finke...*Ich bin Thomas Finke, und Ich bin nicht eine Jude."* The boy nodded as he spoke, then put his arms around Johann's neck. Johann pulled the boy's head to his shoulder, then let him go.

He stroked the boy's black hair and put his hat on his head. *"Höffentlich sehen wir uns wieder."* Before Johann could stop him, the boy ran to his mother. He followed the boy, now lying across his mother's body, his arms around her, crying. Johann knelt beside him and stroked his back. "Your mother is dead, and I'm sorry, but you must go now. There is no time. Bad men are coming, and you must leave." The boy stood up, threw his arms around Johann and cried. "I want to go with you!"

"No, you can't go with me. I must fight, and you must go to Germany, where you will be safe. Look for a friend who will help you. Find a woman, like your mother, one with a child."

Väinü looked at the woman's body, kicked at the snow and spoke softly, but the boy heard. "You know damned well that you will never see him again...."

Johann gave Väinü a look that stopped him in mid-sentence. He took the boy's hand and led him to the corporal.

"This man will take you to the road. You must walk with the people who are going to Germany. Ask for food and water, and always sleep with women and children."

The boy looked back at Johann, and as the corporal led him away, Johann waved and forced a smile.

Väinü said, "That boy will never see Germany," and shook his head.

Chapter Thirty-five

14 January 1945

Sometimes you win…

In War, winning and losing are sometimes born as identical twins.

JOHANN, VÄINÜ, AND ANOTHER FINN whose name Johann could neither remember nor pronounce walked back to the demag. Johann felt a rage in his soul he had never believed could exist there.

Väinü said to Johann, "Someone will put this all together." He motioned to his man with his hand, indicating he should slow down and get out of earshot. The man couldn't understand German well enough to make sense of the conversation Väinü wanted to have with his boss, but Väinü wanted Johann to speak freely. He said, "They will follow our tracks to the demag—the Russians don't have demags that leave tracks like ours do—and it won't take a genius to figure out that the Twenty-Fourth's Jäger Company was the only German force in this area. From there, a few questions and answers will lead to us, and then there will be a firing squad."

Johann didn't answer immediately. The sun's reflection on the brilliant white snow hurt his eyes, forcing him to close his lids to narrow slits. The air was bitterly cold, and as he stepped, the snow under his feet crunched and squeaked in protest. When he had thought everything through, he said, "The people who live here heard those shots, and they knew what their friends on that farm were doing. They fear reprisal more than any sympathy for Germans and will bury those men or drag them far from here. The hate these people have for our SS is limitless, and anyone who kills those bastards is a hero—German or Russian is irrelevant."

When Väinü didn't comment, Johann continued. "The war has taken away the time and circumstances we need to make rational decisions, and the result is what those men did. The world has lost its collective mind. Without the war and guns in their hands, those monsters would never kill anything bigger than a mouse! The bastards would be home with their wives and kids, drinking beer with their friends."

"Don't you mean they would be at home beating their wives and children? Those men are criminals if they have the opportunity—the proof is on that farm." Väinü didn't try to hide his hatred.

Johann stopped walking.

"Think about why they were there. Those soldiers knew the Russians were coming, and they knew the Russians would kill them when they caught them, so the bastards ran away from their unit; maybe they were all that was left. The skull on their sleeves is the mark of beasts to the Russians—beasts that deserve to die!"

"So why didn't they keep running?"

"Run where? The Waffen SS soldier is a professional trained to win or die. Those men knew they had nowhere to hide, and they've probably done things that rule out anything but hell when they die. Those were men with nothing to lose, with every glimmer of what we consider morality squeezed out of them by this war!"

Johann began walking again.

Väinü said, "You know that Klaus and his men are Waffen SS; are they the beasts you are talking about?"

"Some of them are, but not all of them. No soldier can have sympathy for their victim, and when their friends die, they must erase them from their minds. Fighting and murder is everyday life for a soldier on the Eastern Front—Russian or German—whether or not it is a crime depends on your point of view."

Väinü shrugged. "That sounds familiar, but repeating it doesn't make it true."

◇◇◇◇◇◇◇◇◇◇◇◇◇◇◇◇◇◇◇◇◇◇◇◇◇◇◇◇◇◇◇◇◇◇◇◇◇

The demag was running when they reached it, and the drive back to Klaus and the panthers took twenty minutes. The unmarked snow reflected the low sun off countless ice crystals, except for a patch of blood and hair where a rabbit had given its life so a mother fox could feed its unborn young. Johann found it hard to reconcile the world he lived in—the little boy Reuben who had lost his Jewish mother and insisted he wasn't a Jew—Katherine and Natasha on their way to Dresden, where the future was as uncertain as it was in Poland where, after killing a dozen of his comrades-in-arms, he was on his way to murder as many Russians as he could.

Johann had his driver park the demag in the woods with instructions to make it invisible. Its machine gun had a forty-five-degree field of fire through an opening in the trees, and the Finn driver and Väinü became the gun's crew.

Ian met Johann ten metres from the demag.

"They're still almost an hour away—sixteen T-34s, a tank destroyer and at least five hundred infantry."

Johann checked with Klaus when he joined them. "How is your ammunition?"

Klaus jerked his head toward his tanks. "We have full bins and belts...our fuel is good for another six hours, and when this is over, we know where to find more."

Johann shaded his eyes with his hand and squinted, looking at the gully, searching for Klaus's panzers. He said, "I don't see your tanks in the gully."

"I assure you, they are there."

Johann turned to Ian. "Are you certain there are no Russian scouts ahead of their tanks?"

Ian nodded and said, "I am positive."

Johann turned to Väinü. "The MG-42s are set up on this side, spread along the line of trees?"

"Yes, sir, and the men are hidden. Just make sure the eighty-eights don't hit the trees."

Johann turned to the demag and stepped on the running board. "I put the approximate coordinates on a map I left with General Nehring, and you can check the exact ones with me right now." He pulled himself into the demag behind the gunner, picked up his metal map box, lifted the top and took out a folded contour map of the area. He pointed to the exact spot where the ambush would take place and noted the coordinates from the margins. "Those are close to the exact coordinates I gave Nehring. If you agree, I will call now and have our artillery set up the guns for a range shot." Ian, Väinü and Klaus nodded and grunted their approval.

Johann called the leutnant in charge of the guns and was assured they had four eighty-eights they could give him as long as he needed them. They would fire one ranging shot and then, on his command, rain shells as fast as they could load until he stopped them or they ran out of ammunition.

Johann and his men spent the next thirty minutes reassuring themselves that ammunition belts would not jam, that they had access to more ammunition, and that their 'papas' were ready to fight. Every man knew what he had to do; some had been doing it for so long that killing people had become nothing more than a job. They had no fear of dying themselves; they acknowledged that the end might come in the next hour. But they had seen death, and it wasn't worse than the life of a soldier on the Eastern Front.

◇◇◇◇◇◇◇◇◇◇◇◇◇◇◇◇◇◇◇◇◇◇◇◇◇◇◇◇◇◇◇◇◇◇

The men ate their midday ration in the woods and fed pieces of Feldbrot to little grey-capped chickadees. When the food was gone, the friendly little birds continued to flit here and there, looking for more, finding missed crumbs in the snow. Johann took a piece of the standard field ration out of his pocket and crushed it on his hand. A chickadee immediately landed on his thumb, picked up one of the crumbs and flew away, replaced immediately by another brave little bird. Within a minute, four little chickadees rotated their flights from a nearby tree to and from his hand, sharing in what seemed an organized way.

Väinü pointed at a chickadee sitting on Johann's hand. "I'm curious. Which is more important to you…those little birds or the life of a Russian soldier?"

"That's an easy question. The Russian soldier can't kill my family if he's dead. The chickadee loves me for a few breadcrumbs and would never harm me." He smiled at Väinü. "So, of course, the life of the Russian soldier is more important to me."

The chickadees picked the last crumbs from Johann's palm and waited patiently on their branch. Johann made a show of dusting off his hands, and the little birds disappeared.

◇◇◇◇◇◇◇◇◇◇◇◇◇◇◇◇◇◇◇◇◇◇◇◇◇◇◇◇◇◇◇◇◇◇

The tanks approached as before, bunched up and covered with infantry. The snow was deep, and their progress was slow—it took a lot of effort for soldiers to keep up with tanks while wading snow to their knees.

374

Forward probing units seldom used troop carriers; the infantry rode on the tracked vehicles, as many as could hold on without falling off. The T-34s drove in three groups, each slightly over three metres from the surrounding tanks. The unfortunate soldiers who hadn't found room on a tank walked in the mangled tracks left behind them in the snow.

When the first group of tanks passed Johann, one of the walking soldiers looked straight at him without seeing. Johann waited for the soldier to pass, then spoke quietly into the radio mouthpiece.

"Fire one for range."

The artillery on both sides had been quiet for two hours, and the explosion of the shell behind the lead tanks, followed by the crack of the cannon and the scream of the shattered air, startled Johann, even though he knew it would happen in that sequence. The shell, travelling at three times the sound's speed, arrived half a second before the sound of the gun.

"Fire! Fire! Fire!" Johann spoke into the telephone, and three eighty-eight mm cannon rounds landed amidst the tanks and soldiers now climbing off their rides. The Russian tanks stopped—one of the T-34s and a dozen men around it took a direct hit.

In seconds, Klaus's tanks killed three T-34s and a tank destroyer. The Jäger company machine guns, the driver of Johann's demag firing the forward machine gun, and Väinü on the rear gun cut down the Russian infantry as they ran around, firing wildly, trying to find an enemy. The trees were the only natural cover, and the Russians hopelessly ran for them.

A few of the T-34s, now scurrying around like lost ants, located and fired at the panthers, and Johann heard a loud clang as a dud shell bounced off the front armour of 227. Klaus's gun fired point-blank into the front armour of the T-34 that had fired it, and its turret's sixty mm of armour offered insufficient protection at that range against the high-velocity armour-piercing ammunition Klaus's panther used. The shell exploded inside the tank, blowing the turret and its gun off the body. The crippled T-34 coasted to a stop, flame and smoke exiting the hole where the turret should be.

The eighty-eights' withering bombardment took out one Russian tank after another, despite their attempts to find the source of their dilemma or a place to hide. Every direction led to panther tanks firing point-blank at them, invisible in the short time they had to find them. At times, flying dirt and snow obscured the Russian tanks from Johann's view altogether. A single T-34 broke out of the melee and churned directly toward Klaus's 227, firing its machine gun while lining up its cannon. Klaus's gunner fired first, and at a hundred metres, the shell easily penetrated the front armour. The turret stayed fastened to the body, but the shell exploding inside the tank made that irrelevant. The tank looked undamaged except for the clean hole in the front armour, but it stopped moving, and no one opened a hatch.

The eighty-eights kept up their barrage for another five minutes before the T-34s stopped trying to move, and a hundred Russian soldiers put up their hands in the faint hope that the Germans would let them live. No one fired at those with their hands up, encouraging more to do the same.

Johann's radio crackled as Klaus's tanks left their cover to surround the remaining T-34s.

"What do you want me to do with the guys with their hands up?" It was Ian. Johann paused. He knew the question's meaning and had an answer ready, but the Russian air force arrived first.

◇◇◇◇◇◇◇◇◇◇◇◇◇◇◇◇◇◇◇◇◇◇◇◇◇◇◇◇◇◇◇◇◇◇◇

Egor Smirnov and his gunner Feliks received the distress call while flying west to attack German armour in Kielce. Egor had three IL-2 Shturmovik fighter/bombers with him, and together, they represented considerable firepower. The Luftwaffe was not out in force, and his tank-killers had an additional escort of five fighters high above them. The clear, cold air and snow on the ground meant no low-level thermals would disturb their aim.

The call directed him to turn southwest, and he informed the flight of his intentions. The formation turned with him, and, in a shallow dive at over two hundred and fifty knots on his American airspeed indicator, Egor found the target in minutes. He slowed the plane, added a notch of flap to lower the nose, and the aircraft behind him slid into attack formation, staggered so they wouldn't shoot one of their own when they fired their cannons and machine guns.

Egor hesitated for a second when he saw what he recognized as Russian soldiers standing among T-34s with their hands up. He turned slightly, putting a German panther in his sight, and pushed the firing button. The stream of shells followed a straight line to the panther, and he smiled as he saw the stream pass directly over the turret, ripping the commander apart before he could close the hatch. Egor touched the rudder; the tracers tore through a line of German soldiers standing beside the surrendering Russians with their guns trained on them. He held the button down until the tracers snaked a path through the men with their hands up. He released his bombs, and they fell onto the surrendering T-34s, but Egor was past them and didn't see that he had destroyed two Russian tanks, killing their crews. He turned ten degrees so that his rear gunner could have a clear shot at the men and tanks in the field, and Felix fired his machine gun without distinguishing friend from foe. Egor saw men in the woods and tightened the turn to point the nose of his aircraft at them.

The aircraft behind Egor followed his example, strafing and bombing the helpless tanks with no regard to whether they were Russian or German, then followed him over the forest, raining cannon and machine-gun fire into the trees until their guns were empty.

◇◇◇◇◇◇◇◇◇◇◇◇◇◇◇◇◇◇◇◇◇◇◇◇◇◇◇◇◇◇◇◇◇◇◇

Twenty of Johann's men were crossing the field when the Ilyushkins appeared. Some of them made it to cover behind crippled T-34s and huddled there with the Russian soldiers. The planes hit two of the panthers guarding the Russian tanks, and when the attackers turned and lined up for a pass at the woods, Johann screamed on the radio, "Ian! They're going to strafe the trees!" Ian didn't acknowledge, and the Ilyushin tank killers raced over Johann with a roar, leaving the demag 250 and panther 227 undamaged. Out of ammunition and bombs, they vanished over the horizon, and the sound of their engines faded.

Johann found Ian and Väinü, already struggling through snow to their knees, checking on the wounded, mobilizing the uninjured to carry those who couldn't walk.

It took an hour to clear the field of Russian and German soldiers, leaving almost a hundred enemy soldiers to thank God for another chance at life. The flying tank destroyers would return; the Russian Army and Air Force now knew where to find them.

Johann radioed Nehring's headquarters with the bad news and, using the day's code told the controller where he would be in an hour. The man assured him that transport and medical personnel would meet Johann's Jäger company there.

Only five of Klaus's eight panthers were still mobile, and four men from the three destroyed panzers could still fight. They confiscated the only mobile T-34 and then, using explosives, scuttled the three damaged panthers.

Johann counted his dead. He had begun the battle with a hundred and twenty men, and thirty-five could still fight, including Ian and Väinü. Only one Finn other than the three with Johann had survived—they had been the first into the field and the first to die when the "flying tanks" had caught them in the open.

When they left the battlefield, thirty-two wounded men covered all the horizontal space on Klaus's tanks and Johann's demag.

The panthers unloaded their bloody cargo an hour later, then left to join the XXIV panzer Corps' main force. Johann headed southwest with his demag and thirty men to scout the Twenty-Four panzer Corps' southeastern flank.

Ian walked ahead of Väinü in the parallel track to Johann's, keeping his feet in the narrow channel broken by the demag. He had something on his mind.

"Tell me, sir…are we letting the Russians go so they can fight us later? Aren't we taking prisoners?"

Johann didn't want to talk about that particular subject. He knew how Ian and Väinü felt. "Our orders are to take no prisoners."

"And you think that order means we should let them go?" Väinü said it incredulously.

"Shooting prisoners is illegal and immoral. Tell me what I should do that doesn't involve killing men who surrender to us."

Ian and Väinü walked in silence for a long time. Finally, Ian said, "I suppose it will matter more to those men's families than it will to us."

Väinü grunted, then said, almost cheerfully, "Those men will be on the front line before the sun goes down, but sixteen of their T-34s won't." He paused for a few seconds, then said reflectively, "We should have taken the names of those Russians. They could defend us at the trial."

Chapter Thirty-six

17 January 1945

Truth has consequences

The worst dilemmas force one to decide which bad is worse.

Johann searched for Russians east and south of Kielce, and on January 16, he found them. Looking down from a low hill, he could see their fires and, by the light of a bright frozen moon, T-34 tanks, rows of them covered with camouflage and invisible from the air. There was nothing but flat, frozen fields between them and Kielce, and the clear, cold weather was perfect for tank operations.

He prodded Ian to put his binoculars away. "Let's get back to the demag. We have to give the bad news to General Nehring."

Johann and Ian had ventured out on foot to check Nehring's southern flank while the rest of the company either fanned out to search for hidden enemy armour east of there or stayed with the demag. It was 18:30 and an hour after dark when they reached the half-track—a three-quarter moon shone between clouds moving in from the northeast. Johann used the radio to send the bad news in the day's code.

"Found battalion of infantry, anti-tank guns, 200 T-34 tanks, 20 tank destroyers 20 kilometres southeast of you." He told the operator to send the coordinates twice.

It took ten minutes to code and send the description to the intelligence officer and receive confirmation. Fifteen minutes later, General Nehring called in the open on a pre-arranged frequency. Johann hoped the Russians weren't listening.

"There are not supposed to be Russian forces there! Our Seventeenth Army should be south of those coordinates, and we have no reports of Russians getting past them. Are you saying those Russians flanked us and got behind the Seventeenth's lines? Over."

"Yes, General, the Seventeenth is southeast of these Russians and will be cut off if they don't move. They must attack this force from the south, or the Russians will cut off your southeastern flank. They could be in Kielce tomorrow night!"

He took his thumb off the button, then pushed it and said, "You have two choices. If you withdraw the Twenty-Fourth tonight or tomorrow morning, the Russians will attack the Seventeenth from the northwest and leave you alone. Otherwise, the Twenty-Fourth must attack this force from the north while the Seventeenth attacks from the south." The radio was silent for a few seconds; Johann added, "I don't like the look of these guys—everything from their camouflage to their perfectly organized lines says they are ready to fight. Even if we stop them, the cost will be high. Changing to alternate frequency. Over."

Johann flipped the switch to 'receive,' changed the frequency, the radio crackled, and Nehring said, "We need the option to withdraw west toward Wroklaw, so I need to know what is southwest of those Russians. There is also a battalion-strength force northeast of us, and if we don't get out of here, the Russians will clamp us in a pincer between two—possibly three battalions. We must go west to protect the Ninth Army's southern flank, and if the Seventeenth can withdraw now, we can cover their western flank, but we can't stay here, and I don't want any more surprises!"

Johann waited. Nehring clicked his mike and added, "In southeastern Poland, the Twenty-Fourth panzers and the Seventeenth Army are all that lay between the Russians, the Oder River, and Germany... out!"

A few minutes later, Johann, Ian, and Väinü bent over a map spread on the demag's hood. "We need to know what's on Nehring's southern flank." Johann put his finger on the map. "Let's see what's between here and south of Wroklaw."

Johann sent Eighth Jäger Company to Kielce while he, Väinü, and Ian took the demag, a driver and two men and cut across to the southeast, reaching Katowice in the dark before the dawn of the 17th. They found no Russians, only refugees on the roads heading northwest.

A patch of woods was their refuge for the daylight hours, and they parked the camouflaged demag under the trees. They slept on groundsheets with blankets and every piece of clothing they could find pulled over them, but the cold and worry kept Johann awake. At 17:30, all daylight had faded, and they drove northwest under clear skies.

An hour later, Johann's demag and four men approached SS soldiers walking on the road, prodding what appeared to be sick and starving people with shouts, curses and blows from clubs and switches. It was impossible to pass the wall of humanity, and Johann stopped the demag.

Fifty metres before them, a man staggered, fell, tried to rise, then gave up. He rolled on his side to look up at an SS officer who had pulled his Luger out of its holster. The officer fired, missed the man's head, then adjusted his aim to the old man's withered chest.

A burst of machine-gun fire splattered the snow and gravel at the officer's feet. He jumped aside, staring at Ian, who sat behind the demag's MG-38.

"Sind Sie vollkommen verrükt?" The officer bellowed the question of Ian's sanity. He was angry but not frightened.

Ian said evenly, "The answer is yes—I am as crazy as everyone else around here, and I am going to shoot you if you don't drop that pistol." Ian tapped the side of the trigger guard and began to count, "One… two…"

The officer carefully put his Luger on the ground and then, without taking his eyes off Ian, ran to an officer standing on the road behind him. The second officer tentatively raised his hands as the first one approached. Johann ordered the driver to park the demag beside the man on the ground, sheltering him from both officers, and the man looked up with a pitiful glimmer of hope on his face.

The second officer opened his mouth, but Ian spoke first. "Tell me what's going on here!" Ian tapped the trigger guard while he waited. Ian was usurping Johann's authority, but he was doing so well that Johann decided to wait and see what happened. Neither he nor Ian had insignia on their uniforms, and Ian could have been a general.

A full moon rising in the middle of the road behind the mass of humanity silhouetted a ragtag caravan of scarcely-clad miserable souls. Johann estimated he could see a kilometre on the straight, moonlit road, and the end of the caravan was beyond that. He decided to let Ian finish what he had started. The old man and the arrogant

SS officer were enough to convince Johann that this was a battle he would gladly fight.

"We are moving these prisoners to safety," the second officer stated. "The Russians will be in Auschwitz in a few days, and they will kill them." He looked hopefully at Johann. "We need your demag to escort us."

Two SS officers on a motorcycle and sidecar came out of the darkness; the senior officer sitting in the sidecar spoke as he unfolded his legs and clumsily exited the tiny pod.

"What's going on here? By Himmler's order, we are escorting these prisoners to safety—you must not interfere!" His back foot hooked the edge of the coaming, and he caught himself with his right hand before his head hit the ground.

Johann stood and pointed to the old man, now trying to drag himself across the shallow ditch, not happy to be the centre of attention.

"My name is Leutnant Finke; we are the Eighth Jäger Company of the Wehrmacht Twenty-Fourth panzer Battalion. How many prisoners do you have, and are they all in the same condition as this man?" The senior officer, now standing beside the sidecar, unbuttoned his holster.

"Not a good idea," Ian barked as he fired a two-second stream of bullets over the man's head, close enough to take the fuzz off his SS hat.

A half-dozen soldiers ran out of the darkness and stood on both sides of the officer. They carried rifles. Ian smiled, moved the machine gun to point at them, and they shrank back, leaving the officer on his own.

"How many prisoners did you say you had?" Johann asked again.

"That is not your concern. I will not answer to a Wehrmacht leutnant. I am a major in the SS, and I am confiscating your vehicle."

Johann had to breathe deeply before he could speak. Ian was tightening his finger on the trigger when Johann said, "Relax, Ian… don't shoot him until I tell you."

Johann, concentrating on the major, asked curiously, "Do you always shoot them if they fall?"

The SS major spread his hands helplessly. "They are only Jews, and we have no food or water for them. Most of them are too weak to work effectively—if they can't walk, they can't work. We can't carry them, and we can't leave them behind. What do you suggest we do?"

Väinü leaned behind Johann and whispered in his ear, "Don't do anything stupid, Johann."

Johann turned his upper body so he could look into Väinü's face. He spoke loud enough for the SS officers to hear him clearly.

"And what would you consider stupid in this case? Look at those people! These are the Jews that we've heard about, the ones we've been murdering! Where are the children? Look! For God's sake, look at these people! I need to be able to sleep at night, and I need to do something that you call stupid!" More SS soldiers approached out of the darkness, and Johann decided to take control. He turned to Ian, believing these would be the last moments of his life.

"Shoot them all if they don't immediately do what I tell them!"

Johann and the two men in the rear seat racked their Papas, Väinü racked his, and Johann looked at the Major when he spoke to the SS soldiers, who had four Russian machine guns and Ian's MG-38 pointed at them.

"Immediately pile your rifles and pistols in front of the demag." No one moved—Ian fired close to the clean black boots of the officer; a ricochet nicked the left boot's sole. The soldiers hurried to the front of the demag, except the officer. Ian raised his aim to the man's chest and smiled. The SS officer spat on the ground and marched defiantly toward the growing pile of weapons. He jerked his shiny Luger from its holster and laid it gently on the ground.

Johann said, "Run over them!" The driver drove ahead, then reversed.

While the demag moved back and forth, grinding the weapons into pieces, Johann watched people leaving the column. At the edge of his vision, Johann watched as other people came out of the darkness to meet them.

Väinü asked the furious officer, "How long is the column?" and Johann leaned to the side as much as he could so that Väinü's Papa could fire unimpeded.

"More than a kilometre," the officer answered quickly, "and we have two such columns guarded by over two hundred SS officers. You cannot win!"

The officer moved forward a few steps, confident he knew what he was facing. "These are Jews, Untermenschen, not worthy of life unless they can earn what they eat. You can't help them, and we are taking them to food and water, to a safe place." He opened his arms. "Do you understand? When the war is over, we will all be friends!"

Johann looked at Väinü and pointed past the officer. "Väinü, I want you to go down the line and see what's happening here. Take two men and shoot anyone who tries to stop you. If we hear shots, we'll shoot these assholes." He looked at the officer. "If Väinü or anyone else fires a shot, I promise I will let Ian shoot you first!" Ian grinned hopefully.

The officer spread his hands in a gesture of futility. "Then I must go with him."

"Go then." Johann shooed him away with his hand. "And in that case, Väinü is authorized to shoot you for whatever reason he sees fit, and when we hear the shots, we will shoot your men."

It took fifteen minutes for Väinü and the officer to return, with no shots fired. Väinü climbed up on the demag and reported to Johann.

"The major is right…the column is at least a kilometre long, but not all the guards are bashful, and there aren't two hundred. When I threatened to cut one of the bastards' throat, he immediately volunteered that these Jews are from a camp called Auschwitz. The Russians are close—their soldiers are in Krakow. Yesterday, the guards shot as many prisoners as they could with the ammunition available, then organized this march. The sick were left to die. They have only a little ammunition for the march; he said that they may have to stop shooting the stragglers to save bullets."

Johann tried to rationalize what he was seeing. "I guess that's a good thing."

Väinü grunted, "I suppose that depends on whether you'd rather have a bullet in your head or your skull crushed with the butt of a gun."

"*Scheisse!*" Johann hurt his hand when he slammed his fist on the side of the demag. "We can't shoot this bunch of vermin, and we can't take time to rescue these poor people. We've got a job to do that might save an army." Ian pointed at the SS officer. "Him, I would like to shoot, but the Russians are enemy enough for now." Johann indicated that the driver should reverse, and the Finn complied, but a little more aggressively than he intended.

Johann said, "Stop!" before the demag had gone more than a few metres. The old man had reached the ditch and attempted to stand but fell. He raised his hand in a pathetic plea for help, and Johann had to help him.

"Get him into the demag." Ian jumped down, picked up the man, little more than a pile of bones, and passed him over the side of the demag to Väinü. The man groaned, but when Johann looked into his face, he was smiling.

Ian opened a bread can, and Väinü covered the man with a spare woollen coat and a tarpaulin. Ian gave him water, but the man didn't drink. His eyes brightened as he said, "My wife?" The man spoke so quietly that Johann had to put his head down to hear him. "My wife, Rachel. Please, you must find her!"

Johann spoke sharply to Ian. "Go find his wife; her name is Rachel."

Ian mumbled something under his breath about a kilometre of people that Johann figured would be better not to hear, and Väinü climbed down with him. The officer was screaming orders at his men when Ian and Väinü approached him.

Ian shouted at the officer, "I want this man's wife. Her name is Rachel, and you are going to find her!" He levelled his Papa at the man's chest, but the officer didn't flinch.

"Meinetwegen, wenn Sie sie finden kann…Ich kann's nicht." He turned and walked away, muttering obscenities.

Ian walked back to the demag. "He isn't happy…says he doesn't care what we do, but she doesn't have a name now, only a number on her arm. He won't try to find her even if he thinks we will shoot him." Johann sensed that Ian's patience was wearing thin. "The men and women are scattered everywhere…a kilometre of them…she could be anywhere."

Johann stood up in the demag and shouted as loudly as he could, "Rachel, I'm looking for Rachel!" Three women put up their hands.

"Is one of these your Rachel?" Johann held the man up so he could see the women. He pointed to the one nearest to them.

"That's Rachel. She was walking near me."

The SS officer followed Ian to the woman. Ian took her by the hand and led her to the demag, a broad smile on her face.

"David, mein Liebling." She put a bony arm on the demag to steady herself and looked into her husband's eyes. Johann could hardly hear her voice over the idling engine as she said, "I thought that animal shot you!"

Ian passed her to Väinü, and she immediately touched David's face. He kissed her hand and said, *"Ich liebe dich, Rachel!"*

<hr>

The two soldiers that had come with them had to jog behind, and they drove slowly and in silence for five hundred metres in a field parallel to the road full of Jews and turned west on the first field road they crossed. Three men appeared out of the darkness; two carried panzerfausts—anti-tank weapons and bad news for a demag.

The driver braked, seizing the tracks and stopping the vehicle in the length of itself. The old man and woman slid off the seat onto the floor. Johann caught Ian before he could swing the machine gun. "If they wanted to kill us, we would be dead."

A fourth man whose beard didn't hide his youth stepped onto the road in front of the panzerfausts. He appeared unarmed and beckoned to Johann. Johann climbed out of the half-track and walked up to him.

"We want the man and woman." The man spoke perfect Polish-flavoured German.

Johann didn't look back. He knew that Ian and Väinü were getting them out of the demag.

"You're Free Polish Army?"

The young man nodded. "You are still alive because we saw what you tried to do. We are saving Jews who sneak away from the column, and we got a lot of them while you were keeping the guards occupied. We don't have the equipment or men to eliminate the guards, but you and that demag would make a big difference until the Russians get here."

Johann didn't react. He wanted to be far away when the Russians arrived. "Have many of them escaped?"

"Many, yes, surprisingly, hundreds. The guards are terrified of the Russians, and there aren't enough of them to fight even a small company of regular infantry." He made a face of disgust. "These men are not fighters; they are rats, vermin, and we will kill them when the time is right. If you would help us, we could succeed now."

The old man could stand but couldn't walk. A man appeared, pulling a two-wheeled cart, and the man in charge helped load the old Jew. The cart disappeared in the darkness, and the old woman left when a second one appeared. Johann paused before he went back to the demag. "They seem old—but they are young, aren't they?"

"They are in their forties, no older." He seemed anxious to talk, so Johann listened.

"Until a month ago, we had a man on the inside who gathered evidence, including the names of prisoners. He got information out—documents—witness statements, and a few photographs. He helped a few prisoners escape, and we got them to Germany. But his sacrifice was for nothing. Neither the German people nor the Allies believed them, and no one came to rescue them."

Johann wanted to say he didn't know, but the lie stuck in his throat. He said, "I suspected something, but not this...." He pointed back at the convoy of dying people.

The partisan's eyes softened. "Our man was a lawyer in the Warsaw Ghetto who tried to use the law against the Nazis. They put him in Auschwitz and killed his children—they gassed all children too young to work. Six months ago, the SS caught him trying to get someone out of the camp. They killed him."

A wave of depression crushed Johann. It was so strong he had difficulty walking to the demag. The partisan called out, "Leutnant, are you sure you won't help us?"

Johann stopped and turned around. "We must fight the Russians. As far as I can see, they are no better than the SS, and they want to destroy Germany. If we join you, we will soon have no fuel or ammunition. We will die without protecting our families."

CHAPTER THIRTY-SEVEN

13 FEBRUARY 1945

Dresden

Matthew, Chapter 13, Jesus says:

"41 The Son of man shall send forth his angels, and they shall gather out of his kingdom all things that offend, and them which do iniquity; 42 And shall cast them into a furnace of fire: there shall be wailing and gnashing of teeth."

KATHERINE AND NATASHA REACHED THE MAIN ROADS heading west on their second day of walking. Small groups of refugees became a more or less continuous river of humanity who believed that safety and an escape from their misery could be found at the head of the line. People chatted, found soft hearts that could help them, or, in Natasha's case, found suffering that needed what she could offer.

Some had carts loaded with clothes and even furniture, usually pulled by their own hands but, in rare cases, by a horse. Poland's starving population had eaten most animals that couldn't directly earn their keep, and horses fell into that category.

People covered the roads, and German Army vehicles, on their way to a battle or running from one, forced them into the ditches and fields. Soldiers cursed the river of humanity, threatening to shoot anyone who didn't get out of their way, and those who couldn't speak German gave any man carrying a weapon a wide berth.

Most of the refugees were German-speaking to some degree, making it difficult to differentiate between ethnic Germans trying to return to their homeland and Poles who were running away from the rumours of Russian cruelty. The *Russische Schwarm* had a well-earned reputation for their brutal treatment of Polish and ethnic German women, and hundreds of thousands of people left their homes and everything they owned rather than face the *'Russische Bestien.'*

With roads overwhelmed by thousands of desperate people came criminals who used whatever means necessary to separate the refugees from what little they had left. Katherine and Natasha hid their money in their underwear, and both women carried knives that Johann had given them—slim knives, easily hidden—knives that could slide past a man's ribs to reach his heart with only the strength of a frightened girl behind it.

When a man offered a withered apple for sex, Natasha and Katherine pushed him into the ditch. Later, when Natasha stopped to pee on the roadside, an evil-smelling creature grabbed her and tried to entice her to give him sex for a tiny bag of potatoes. She pushed the man away so hard he fell backwards. She shrieked, "Why are you so mean?" and drew back her foot to kick him, but Katherine, who had been discreetly watching her daughter, pulled her away before she struck.

The next day, Katherine stopped in front of a man who blocked her way. He leered at her and rubbed his crotch. She pushed him aside. He grabbed her arm, and she deftly pulled out her knife, holding it a millimetre from his throat. The man backed up and moved on to find what he wanted from a more vulnerable target.

There was no law on the road. Polish and German police had all they could handle in the chaos ahead of the Russian wave. Bodies of starved and murdered people lay frozen in the ditches and fields, ignored by any type of authority and by the river of misery attempting to survive another day.

<hr>

Katherine spent a lot of time thinking about their situation and concluded they would not survive without help. She decided to try to explain the circumstances to Natasha.

"We look as though we have money—we have excellent boots, very comfortable clothes, and I think it's obvious that we aren't starving. Even if we sleep in shifts, we are helpless women in the predators' eyes, and eventually, they will kill us for what we have. It's time to do something about this."

"We could give away our coats."

Katherine smiled at her daughter's naiveté but didn't want to destroy her noble attitude, so she waited, hoping logic would filter into Natasha's teenage mind.

Finally, Natasha said, "We would freeze without them, wouldn't we?"

Katherine nodded.

"We could find someone with a ragged coat and trade them for ours!" Natasha was excited to have such a great idea, but Katherine threw cold water on it.

"It's not only the coat. It's the food we eat and the flesh on our bones. We have warm, dry boots, warm clothing, and money. We would need to give up all those things, but we would still be women, which is perhaps the most dangerous problem. Are you sure you want to give everything away?"

Natasha drew the line. "No, not my boots."

"Then, giving away our coats will do no good."

Katherine searched for the solution to their dilemma among the faces they passed. She pushed her daughter to walk faster than the human river, working their way ahead in the stream, pushing people aside when she could find no easier way. Katherine zigged and zagged, forcing Natasha to stay close enough that the holes her mother made wouldn't have time to close behind her.

Late in the day, Katherine spotted what she was looking for—a family with a cart—and bonuses. A healthy-looking horse pulled the cart, and the man wore a Great War wehrmacht uniform. The German Mauser 98 rifle from the same war sealed the deal. When Katherine reached them, she slowed alongside the woman. Natasha walked behind her mother.

Katherine asked the woman, "Do you speak Ukrainian?" and the woman ignored her.

Natasha asked, "Do you speak German?" and the woman turned her head.

"Your accent is Russian. I hate Russians."

"We are Ukrainian, not Russian," Natasha clarified in almost perfect Prussian German.

"Same thing...." The woman's tone softened slightly.

"The Russians killed my father and tried to rape my mother and me. German soldiers rescued us, and we have worked in their camp for the past year. That's where I learned German."

Katherine pulled out the letter General Nehring had given her and handed it to the young woman, who stopped walking so she could read it carefully.

"This is from General Nehring! Is this how you will cross the border?"

Natasha was bright enough to know the value of what Nehring had written in the letter. "Yes, and anyone who crosses with us will have the same protection!"

Katherine smiled—the woman's excitement was a good sign.

Natasha added the sugar. "We are going to Dresden, and we have the name of someone there who knows we are coming and will give us a travel permit for all of Germany." This last bit would discourage the woman from stealing the letter.

The woman caught up to her husband, who occasionally looked over his shoulder to check on his wife. She took his hand and stopped him, showing him the letter. A boy leading the horse looked back, but the man waved him on.

The excited woman pushed the letter up to her husband's face. "You must read it; it's a letter of protection signed by General Nehring himself! It belongs to these women, and perhaps they will help us when we reach the border!" She pulled on her husband's hand, and he turned to face Katherine and Natasha. "Georg, they are going to Dresden, and they know someone there who will give them a travel permit!"

He looked them over. "You picked us out…such generosity must have a price. What do you want from us?"

His tone was suspicious, not friendly. "We have no money and only enough food for our family—not enough to share. We have only what you see on the cart and the clothes we wear."

In her mind, Katherine had already worked out the deal she wanted—if she could find the right people. She decided on an "all or nothing" approach. If they didn't immediately agree, she would not waste time negotiating; she would find someone else.

Katherine spoke to Natasha, and Natasha translated. "We want to walk with you for our mutual protection. We are women alone, and you have a gun." Natasha pointed to the rifle cradled in the crook of the man's arm. "We can help you when we reach the border—we will use our letter to witness for you—when we cross the border, you will cross with us."

The man looked at the cart, now well ahead of them and widening the gap. He made his decision quickly.

"If my wife agrees, you can walk with us, and I will protect you. I have bullets." He patted the rifle's butt and turned to go but turned back and pointed his finger at Katherine. "But you must promise to help us cross the border and also to get travel papers in Dresden. It does no good to be in Germany without papers!"

Katherine, not confident she had understood, looked at Natasha and got a nod. She said emphatically, in heavily accented German, "I promise."

◇◇◇◇◇◇◇◇◇◇◇◇◇◇◇◇◇◇◇◇◇◇◇◇◇◇

Katherine assumed the man's claim of poverty was the usual denial of convenience, stated to discourage those who had nothing from begging or stealing. He said it loud and often... But he had a cart and a horse.

When darkness arrived, the woman—she had introduced herself as Sabrina—cut up a single potato into tiny pieces for her family. Georg, at least ten years older than Sabrina and the man with the gun, refused to accept his portion and offered it to his daughter, who spent most of her time on the cart, her short, four-year-old legs unable to keep up with the pace set by the horse.

Katherine and Natasha sat together on a small tarpaulin on one side of the road ditch, facing the family, their backs against the cart's wooden-spoked wheel. The horse munched on a handful of hay from a trove pressed under the seat. To quench its thirst, it ate a pile of snow gathered by the boy.

Natasha confirmed the offer her mother said she wanted to make, then opened her army pack and unfolded the cloth that bound their food. Katherine nodded, and Natasha said, "We have cheese and bread. My mother says you are welcome to share it."

Georg shook his head. "I cannot accept your food, but I will allow you to give a piece of cheese to the children."

Georg's tone left no room for discussion, and Katherine spoke softly to her daughter in Ukrainian. Natasha nodded and translated for Sabrina, "We have enough for everyone and enough money to feed your family and your horse until we reach Dresden." Natasha's happiness when she repeated her mother's offer was nothing short of euphoric.

Sabrina took her husband's hand. "It does no good for our children to survive if we don't." She leaned over and kissed his hand. He reluctantly spoke to Natasha, glancing at Katherine as he did.

"I accept your offer, but only if you accept my promise to repay you."

"Agreed." Katherine had understood enough. She added, "When you can."

The family spent the cold night under a cloudless sky; the children cried, and their mother tried to keep them warm. Natasha gave the children her coat and slept in her mother's arms.

They spent the second night in a more or less warm Polish barn, paid for by Katherine after protracted negotiations using the universal 'point and grunt' language. Georg and Sabrina piled loose hay around their children as they lay on coarse woollen blankets Katherine had purchased from the farmer. The children slept as only children can when they feel warm and safe. Georg slept fitfully, rifle loaded, a bullet in the barrel and the safety off. Katherine made a note not to wake him suddenly.

◇◇◇◇◇◇◇◇◇◇◇◇◇◇◇◇◇◇◇◇◇◇◇◇◇◇◇◇◇◇◇◇◇

Everyone on the road had the same objective, and many had children with them. Food prices rose with the demand, and peddlers with food, clothing and boots preyed on the refugees' desperation. People traded family jewels, valuable art, and what few saleable possessions they had for something to eat or a warm coat. When their belongings ran out or were too worthless to sell, they traded sex or stole.

General Nehring and Johann had given Katherine more than enough Swiss Francs and Reichmarks to reach Detmold, but most people on the road had no money or food. Natasha had a soft heart, and without knowing precisely how long the money had to last, Katherine had to bridle Natasha's naive generosity, leading to mother/daughter confrontations that embarrassed their companions.

On February 6, tired, hungry, but elated, Katherine, Natasha and their adopted family reached the Lusatian River at Görlitz and crossed into Germany. Twenty-five days of walking had not damaged Katherine and Natasha's German Army boots, and their woollen coats over three layers of clothing had kept them warm.

Georg and Sabrina's family had improved their situation over the days with trades of obviously frivolous items when survival was at stake. The cart was almost empty when they reached the border, but everyone was warm, and no one was hungry.

The border was chaotic. German officials, trained to administer regulations in an orderly and timely fashion, were overwhelmed. When they asked the refugees before them for papers, seldom did the document technically satisfy the law. The bureaucrat scanned whatever the refugee had for a few seconds, and if it contained most of the right words, he stamped it, passed it back and waved the refugee on. They turned away very few people who could speak even a little German.

Katherine and Natasha claimed Georg's family as theirs, and General Nehring's letter carried the day. The process took less than five minutes—and then, they were in Germany. When they were thirty metres from the bridge, Georg threw his cap in the air and whooped. Sabrina hugged Katherine and Natasha and thanked them over and over. König, the horse, well-fed with hay and grain that Katherine had purchased, neighed, shook his head, dropped a string of turds, and everyone laughed. The children caught the jubilant mood, suddenly relieved of the tension they had been under for a month.

The hundred kilometres from the border to Dresden were the quickest they had made. The road was not as busy because many refugees had other objectives that didn't include Nazi officialdom, and they dispersed over half a dozen alternative routes to other towns and cities.

They slept in a Dresden park on February 12 and were in the Auslanderamt early the following day. They waited an hour before the official named on the paper General Nehring had given Katherine could see them, and they descended on him en masse. He looked at the letter, put it in a file and stamped papers for Katherine and Natasha.

Katherine and Natasha insisted that the documents include Sabrina and Georg's family. The overworked and frustrated bureaucrat shrugged, said, *"Meinetwegen,"* and filled a form with relevant family details. He stamped two more *Reiseausweisen*, the travel papers that allowed the holder to travel anywhere in Germany, and handed them to Georg.

◇◇◇◇◇◇◇◇◇◇◇◇◇◇◇◇◇◇◇◇◇◇◇◇◇◇◇◇

Katherine and Natasha reluctantly bade goodbye to their extended family. The family's final destination was Kassel, and Sabrina assured Katherine she needn't worry. "We have relatives who live on a Bauernhof near Kassel, and we must walk there because of the horse and cart. We will spend the night in the park near the river and leave in the morning." Georg shook Katherine's hand. "There are no words to express my gratitude to you for saving my family."

Natasha translated, and before her daughter finished, Katherine pulled Georg to her and kissed his cheek. With tears in her eyes, Sabrina wrapped her arms around Natasha, then kissed Katherine, who pressed a hundred Reichmarks into her hand, a fortune in that time and circumstance.

"I saved this for you. We have enough, and we are safe now." Katherine smiled and touched her friend's face. "I wish you and your family safety and health." Her German was awkward, but it said enough. The children hugged Katherine and Natasha, and they parted. Katherine and Natasha went to the train station, and Georg and Sabrina went to the park on the bank of the Elbe River, where there would be water for their faithful König.

◇◇◇◇◇◇◇◇◇◇◇◇◇◇◇◇◇◇◇◇◇◇◇◇◇◇◇◇◇◇◇◇◇◇◇◇

The news at the Bahnhof wasn't good; no traffic except the military could board a train leaving Dresden. The clerk recommended they walk toward Meissen, checking the local train stops along the way. With a guilty smile, she said the military 'probably' was not monitoring those small stations, and they could 'possibly' catch a local train headed west.

In the worst case, the twenty-six-kilometre journey to Meissen would take eight hours on foot, and Katherine laughed at the clerk when it was apparent she thought it a significant undertaking.

"We still have more than four hours of daylight." Katherine adjusted her load as she led Natasha out of the Bahnhof. "If we leave now, we reach Meissen tonight, and the most important thing for us is to keep moving toward Detmold."

Natasha followed her outside, where Katherine consulted the sun, a train schedule, and a map she had purchased in the station, then pointed her arm northwest, parallel to the tracks. "There is Detmold. We will walk in that direction."

The southwest side of the Elbe River was flat and downhill to Meissen, making walking easy. The road followed the railway tracks through a small village where Katherine found a store willing to sell her food without a ration card. When Natasha explained their dilemma, the friendly woman recommended that Katherine try to catch the local train at their little station. With a wink, she assured Katherine that there were no guards.

When they arrived at the station, only one other person was there. No one was at the ticket window, but the train stopped, the doors opened, and they boarded. The train stopped twice before a conductor boarded and checked for a ticket just before reaching the Meissen Bahnhof. When Natasha offered a lengthy explanation for their missing tickets, the female conductor looked at their SS soldier's clothing, said, "Welcome to the Third Reich," and moved on.

Meissen's stores were still open when they stepped off the train and booked a room in the Ross Hotel across from the Bahnhof. The next order of business was clothes, and Katherine solved that problem in an hour. They left their quasi-SS uniforms with the curious store clerk and walked out as women again. On their way back to the hotel, they checked at the Bahnhof, and the ticket clerk sold them a *Fahrkarte* to Leipzig, assuring them they could get on a train the next day and purchase a ticket to Detmold in Leipzig.

◇◇◇◇◇◇◇◇◇◇◇◇◇◇◇◇◇◇◇◇◇◇◇◇◇◇◇◇◇◇◇◇◇◇◇◇

Katherine and Natasha bathed in warm water for the first time in over a month. And, for the first time in years, Katherine looked forward to eating a meal served by another woman from a menu intended to tease her palate, not merely sustain her.

The *Gaststätte* had no other clients on this cold February night, and Katherine had chosen the most expensive room—on the third floor facing southeast—toward Dresden and Poland, where she knew the Russians were crushing the German army. She imagined she could hear the sound of their guns and rejoiced in the feeling that she and her daughter were far away from them and the war. She worried about Walther Nehring and Johann.

Abendessen, even in a restaurant, was subject to the rigours of rationing. Still, an innovative chef had somehow gotten around the rules with rabbit stew, potato *Knödel,* dried garden greens, and a honey-sweetened bread pudding. Mother and daughter emptied a bottle of *Spätauslese* white wine, paid the bill and went to their room, a little tipsy and a lot happy. Katherine turned out the lights and pulled back the blackout curtain so they could sit in wicker chairs and watch the moon rise in a sky full of clouds scudding away to the east. The moon dodged between them, finding increasingly larger spaces.

"We made it, Natasha. We are finally safe, and we have a place where we will be welcome. Tomorrow, if God wills it, we will meet Johann's family and sleep in their house!"

Natasha squeezed her mother's hand. "I feel as though I am the richest person in the world, but I'm frightened for Johann and General Nehring."

Katherine sat silently for a minute before she spoke. "I fear we may have seen them for the last time. Walther told me that the Russians would try to encircle the Germans, and Hitler would never allow them to retreat. This is why they sent us away, and they may already be dead or in a Russian prison."

Natasha tried to control her tears, but in a few minutes, she gave up.

She asked, "Mother, will the Russians come here?"

"Walther said the Americans are already in Germany, coming from the west. He promised that the Americans and British will be in Detmold long before the Russians can get there." She looked at Natasha. "We are safe now; the Americans and British are civilized— they are not like the Russians!"

"But the Germans… they killed the Jews in our village!" Natasha stared at the moon. "They are no better than the Russians, so how can we trust them?"

Katherine and Natasha watched the moon and the running clouds through the tall windows. Katherine said, "We are not Jews," and nodded off, dreaming of Johann in his towel.

The air raid siren screaming in the cold and still night air woke Katherine from her dream. Minutes later, the sound of faraway engines and propellers thrashing the air twenty thousand feet above them carried to her. Natasha woke as the sound grew to a rumble.

She asked, frightened, "What is it? What's that noise?"

The rumble strengthened and appeared to come from all directions, and Katherine went to the window to search for the dark shapes. They were there, crossing the moon, already passing Meissen.

"They must be British bombers... They're probably going to bomb the German army in Poland."

"I'm frightened, Mother—what if they bomb us? Shouldn't we hide?"

"No, the man at the desk said they have no shelters in this small town, but we would be welcome in the cellar." Natasha nodded, then hung her head. Katherine said, "I am not worried; this little town is not a target for the British. There are only women and children here."

Natasha shivered. Her mother asked, "Are you cold?" and offered a blanket, but Natasha shook her head.

The sky over Dresden suddenly lit up like daylight: a single plane crossed the moon, lower than the others. Three minutes later, a bomb exploded, and a red glow appeared over what could only be the centre of Dresden.

Katherine cried and shouted, "My God, no...that can't be! What are they doing? The city is full of people! There are women and children with nowhere to go! No, no, no! Georg and Sabrina, their children..."

Second by second, the rumble of a thousand engines increased. The horrible sound came from everywhere as rows of bombers passed overhead, drowning out her sobs. The building shook, and the river of black shapes blocked out the moon.

Hundreds of creeping shadows stretched away from the hotel, moving ever closer to Dresden. When the river of aircraft reached the bright light over the city, red and orange welts rose from the horizon; distant explosions mingled with the roar of engines and the beat of thousands of propellers. In minutes, the eastern edge of the world was a pulsing red and orange line—flames flared upward, then fell back into a fiery lake.

Minutes, what seemed like hours later, the rumbling of bombers faded, and the constant roar of bombs echoing through the cold night from Dresden began to die. Still, the lake on the horizon grew, and a red cloud rose out of the city's centre; a horrifying glow reflected in the window, although Dresden was twenty kilometres away.

The smoke, a black wall rising from the fire, found the moon and blotted it out.

Katherine cried with her head buried in her hands until something dark in her soul brought her back to the fires. She imagined it spreading toward the river—surely, Georg and Sabrina could jump in the river with their children, and König—would he get in the icy water?

An hour passed, then two. Katherine and Natasha lay on the bed, exhausted and confused. First, Natasha fell asleep, and then Katherine, exhausted, went to sleep on top of the *Federbett*. But Katherine awoke what seemed like minutes later. She lay still, staring at the ceiling, holding her breath as she listened; perhaps she was dreaming—it couldn't be real!

A steady low reverberation that had begun as a distant, innocuous pulse gradually increased, coming toward her from the west. Natasha woke, sat up and screamed, "The bombers are coming again!"

Katherine tried to understand. "It can't be bombers! Dresden is burning; they already destroyed the city! The British are good people—they wouldn't do this!"

The rumble grew until it shook the building as bomber after bomber, rows of them, layers of rows, passed the hotel in the sporadic moonlight. The clock beside the bed said one-twenty in the morning when explosions from Dresden shook the hotel.

"Why?" Natasha stood in the centre of the room. "Why, when the city is already burning? What kind of monsters would do that?"

"Monsters don't do these things—only men hate enough to murder their own kind without reason."

"But mother, you told me love is stronger than hate." She looked at her mother, tears streaming down her face.

Katherine pulled a handkerchief out of her sleeve and wiped her daughter's tears. "My dear, years ago, I thought that was true, but I know now that sometimes love is not enough. Hate lasts for generations; it is passed from father to son, from mother to daughter. It is insatiable, and the only weapons we have to fight with are love and hope." She wiped her face with her sleeve and stared at the inferno. "And that is not enough."

Chapter Thirty-eight

Operation Solstice

JOHANN AND THE THIRTY-TWO MEN IN HIS UNIT who were still fit to fight arrived in Stargard on February 14, assigned to the newly formed Eleventh panzer Army and renamed First Company. Their assignment in the coming battle was to find targets for the panzers of panzergrenadier Nord.

The fifteenth of February dawned grey—a cold rain mixed with big wet snowflakes soaked everything, and when news of a bombing attack on Dresden reached Johann and his men, it put the finishing touches on their dreary mood.

Ian put his hand on Johann's arm. "Don't worry, they won't be in Dresden yet. The Russians hit their train a month ago, and it's over six hundred kilometres."

As he climbed into the demag to drive to their "jumping off" point, Johann asked the quiet morning, "Why would the British bomb an open city? They are supposed to be civilized, and It's a city of art and music, of men like Telemann and Bach, not animals like Hitler, Himmler, Göring, and Goebbels!"

Ian sat beside Johann. Väinü sat in front with the Finn driver, and the remaining men from Johann's Jäger Company found seats in two Lastwagen.

Ian said, "Do art, music, and civilization matter anymore?" He talked without looking at Johann. "Only Goebbels calls Dresden an open city, and I doubt the British would consider any German city 'open' just because Goebbels says it is! And why would you think the English are civilized? Churchill said he would annihilate Germany, didn't he? He is just trying to be meaner than Hitler, and it looks like he just might be!"

Until now, Johann's source for the truth, a truth that had never resembled anything Goebbels said, had been General Nehring. But lately, Nehring had no time for chess or chatter, and Johann rarely saw headquarters. Johann's intelligence source was now Ian, who was always current on the latest war talk and ready to update his superior officer.

"They're saying the fires in Dresden killed two hundred thousand people, and Goebbels says Germany will try Churchill for war crimes when we win the war."

Ian didn't miss the mixture of shock and doubt that crossed Johann's face and added a qualifier to the gruesome news. "But, of course, Goebbels is a pathological liar, as is Hitler. For that matter, every Nazi in Berlin falls into that category. Maybe the British just bombed the industrial part of Dresden—that would make sense—aren't they supposed to be the civilized country in this war?"

Johann didn't feel like laughing, but although sarcastic, Ian's laugh broke the ice, and Johann smiled. He tried to reconcile the bombing timeline with Katherine's arrival in Dresden but admitted that he could be wrong by a week. He told himself that she and Natasha could already be in Detmold but then had to concede that they could just as well be in Dresden.

Ian leaned back against the demag's steel side. "Why should the Russians be the only ones murdering Germans? The animal is down— why not let all the dogs have a piece?" He checked his Papa, then looked at Johann. "I just want to go home…I don't want to play soldier anymore."

Väinü laid his Papa on his lap, brushed wet snow from his coat, and the driver started the demag. Drizzle gradually replaced the snow, and as they drove, the rain stopped; wisps of ground fog began to accumulate in the hollows.

Väinü said, "What a miserable day to kill or get killed—we should only have to fight on sunny days!"

The temperature had risen during the night, from a damp, bone-chilling minus ten to above freezing, creating a strange atmospheric condition that put Johann's head above a layer of mist that hugged the ground. The fog bathed the demag in a low, wispy cloud whose top was at Johann's shoulders. Johann had a strange feeling as the demag parted the mist like a boat—forming twirling eddies behind it.

For the past two weeks, frustration had grown in the ranks of Johann's men as they did nothing but move from place to place for no stated or apparent reason. Rumour piled on rumour as Johann lost access to Nehring, the truth, and chess.

Goebbels's official line was that German forces were decimating the Russians while fighting a planned withdrawal. According to the Propaganda Ministerium, the German Reichswehr had the Russians right where they wanted them and would destroy them "soon." The timeline for the Russian's demise had shifted until "Our army will finish off the Russians if they try to cross the German border." The German army wanted to fight the Russians in Poland, where German citizens and their property would not become targets, and, according to Hitler and Goebbels, "Everything is going according to the Führer's excellent plan." Johann and officers like him ground their teeth and fought what they knew was an unwinnable war.

The initial objective of Hitler's new plan was Arnswalde. They would rescue the encircled garrison there and then open the road to Küstrin on the East bank of the Oder River. Küstrin was the last town in Poland the Russians had to seize before taking their spear across the river into Germany. It was the Eleventh SS panzer Army's job to either stop the Russians from reaching Küstrin or, failing that, to establish a defensive line that would keep the Russians in Poland. The Wehrmacht's last desperate hope was to make land in Germany so expensive the Russians would not want to pay the price. There was also the unmentionable possibility that, given enough time, someone would kill Hitler and beg the Allies for peace.

Johann and his men had spent the recent nights scouting ahead of the attack on Arnswalde, accumulating an impressive list of targets for the new 'king tiger' battle tanks and elefant mobile guns. The overconfident Russian Sixty-First Army and the equally arrogant Belarussians had positioned their anti-tank guns, artillery, and tanks in the open, and Johann's scouts had marked them as primary targets. He unfolded the map and studied the Russian positions, picking the anticipated order of their destruction.

Väinü purposely deflected Johann's attention by touching his arm and pointing to the new king tiger panzers. "What do you think of the king tiger?" Two of the monster tanks led the column with four panther escorts. "I was told they weigh seventy tonnes, have almost two hundred millimetres of front armour plate, and a gun that can kill a T-34 at four thousand metres if they can hit it."

When he had seen his first king tiger, Johann had visually estimated the area of the tiger's tread on the ground to be little more than the panther's, almost doubling the weight on every square centimetre. He looked at a rivulet of water running down the ditch and voiced his worry.

"With almost twice the ground pressure of a panther or a T-34, I wonder how they will do in the mud. If this warm weather holds, they may be unable to travel in fields or on unpaved roads."

Ian looked at him. "We can't change the weather, and for today at least, they don't have to leave the road."

"I have another problem. The tiger uses the same engine as the panther to pull almost twice the weight—I'm guessing that speed and maneuverability won't be their strong points."

Ian slouched in his seat. "Yes, but that six-metre seventy-calibre barrel with eighty-eight-millimetre high-velocity ammunition will send the Russians to hell when the king tigers are still outside their range! Of course, that depends on us finding the Russians before their T-34s or 150mm tank destroyers get close enough to fire."

The monster king tigers drove on the roads while the lighter panthers moved out onto the fields. The infantry moved with the panzers for their mutual protection. Johann's demag moved ahead of the lead formation, the point of a spear aimed at the Russian Sixty-First Army's heart. Four identical groups widened the gap behind them, an impressive force that the Russians weren't expecting.

Johann said, "That kind of optimism depends on whether we have enough ammunition and gas to destroy the Russian tanks." He leaned ahead to the driver and pointed his arm. "Let's go along that line of trees and locate some targets for those tigers. The Russians are waiting for a fight five kilometres down the road, and we won't disappoint them."

◇◇◇◇◇◇◇◇◇◇◇◇◇◇◇◇◇◇◇◇◇◇◇◇◇◇◇◇◇◇◇◇◇

The king tigers at the head of the line headed for the east side of

Stargard, where intelligence said the edge of the Belarussian and Sixty-First Russian Armies' northern flank was waiting for them. The plan called for the heavy tigers and equally massive *Elefant* tank destroyers to stay on the main road, stopping for nothing except to shoot.

Using information supplied by Jäger scouting specialists, the remaining ten tigers would widen the slot left behind the panzergrenadier Nord point tanks. With the ground thawing, battle command ordered all twelve tigers to stay on the asphalt to the objective but gave the panthers freedom to roam.

The entire operation had three days' supply of fuel and two hundred rounds of ammunition for each tank in supply vehicles following at a safe distance. The force had to be in Arnswalde before those critical supplies ran out.

◇◇◇◇◇◇◇◇◇◇◇◇◇◇◇◇◇◇◇◇◇◇◇◇◇◇◇◇◇

General Guderian put General Wenck in charge of the Eleventh Army and the entire operation, and Wenck nixed the typical pre-attack artillery barrage in favour of surprise. Consequently, the overconfident Russians were not ready, and it was child's play for Johann's men to target the unconcealed guns and tanks. Using Johann's coordinates, the artillery made short work of stationary Russian anti-tank guns and field artillery. The tigers and panthers took care of the Russian armour from a range that left them defenceless.

Although camouflaged, Johann decided that his demag was conspicuous and thus vulnerable and used it exclusively as a communications base from which his scouts fanned out.

Ian reported over his two-way *Feldfunk-Sprecher*, using the 'secret code of the day.' He informed Johann that a dozen T-34s and a 105 destroyer were in the fields ahead, preparing to intercept the German attack. Half an hour later, Johann and Väinü had joined him, lying on a small tarp with a camouflage net over their backs, watching the T-34s shepherd the heavy tank destroyer across a field. Ian instructed his radioman to send the coordinates to the demag, and in less than a minute, German artillery shells created bedlam in the ranks of the T-34s. The king tigers and elefant destroyers added their cannons to the attack on the confused Russian armour, and seconds later, eight of the T-34s and the tank destroyer were scattered pieces of junk.

"Du Liebe Himmel!" Johann looked at the burning wreckage through his binoculars. The eighty-eight mm armour-piercing shells from the tigers had destroyed every tank they had hit. The equally potent elefant had taken out a T-34 and the tank destroyer. Four T-34s had used their impressive speed to escape.

Johann said, not entirely under his breath, "What can stop those tigers?"

Väinü ruined Johann's day. "Airplanes. Sturmoviks can stop them. And the IL-2 panzer destroyer can kill any tank…that's why we travel at night, and that's why we attack when it's snowing. Today is good for us; however, the flying weather might be better tomorrow, or the day after tomorrow, or…." Väinü stopped when he sensed that Johann had gotten the point.

The only hiding places for Russian armour were behind buildings or under sparse trees along the narrow roads. Johann's scouts looked in the obvious places, found them, and then reported their location to the advancing tigers, tank destroyers and panthers. The king tigers and elefant destroyers picked them off from two kilometres, one by one. At almost no cost to the German juggernaut, wrecked Russian tanks and dead infantry littered the roads and fields behind them. The column arrived in Arnswalde ten hours after firing the first shot, leaving thirty-five kilometres of death and destruction behind them. Before darkness on the first day, they had shocked the Belarusians and given Hitler the first real reason to celebrate in more than a year.

<hr>

The weather continued mild, warming to ten degrees above freezing, and Wenck rolled out his plan to beat the Russians to Küstrin, stopping them before they could get a foothold on the most vulnerable place on the German border. He needed to move immediately, or the thaw could spell disaster for the heavy tigers.

Before the attack reached Arnwalde, Wenck sent Johann's Company to scout the road to Küstrin, and they found acceptable but rapidly deteriorating conditions for the heavy panzers. They found no Russians, and there was still enough frost under the gravelled field roads to carry the tigers. The firm fields would support a panther or a half-track.

When the company returned, Johann immediately went to headquarters to report what they had found, but when he returned to the room they had confiscated in a local hotel, he flung his gun in the corner and threw himself on the bed.

Väinü said, "I suppose we can assume that didn't go well?"

"Scheisse, und verdammt Scheisse! That little bastard has done it again! Hitler called Wenck back to Berlin for a newsreel stunt. Our first victory since Stalingrad, and Goebbels has decided to make Wenck a hero!"

"And I suppose that means we can't go to Küstrin until Wenck returns." Ian pulled on his cigarette and blew a neat smoke ring.

Johann pulled out a new pack and tore it open.

"Yes, and two days of this weather will be bad enough, but the Russians aren't stupid—they know what we're going to do next, and they have a couple of armies they can put in front of us if we give them enough time to do it!

"Well, I guess your initial reaction was right then." Väinü, stretched out on a cot stolen from a tent, closed his eyes. "But a simple *Scheisse* would have made your point—things can get much worse, so you should save some words for that. The way I look at it, this gives me a couple of days to get some sleep."

"Good luck with that!" Johann stood up and began to organize the pack and machine gun he had thrown on the floor. "Unless the weather clears so recon planes can fly, Wenck wants us to keep track of the Russians until he gets back." He grinned at Väinü. "That's what the extra curses were for."

◇◇

On the second day following Wenck's departure, Johann's company returned to the news that the general had taken over the driving from his exhausted chauffeur on the return trip and had fallen asleep at the wheel. He was in a Berlin hospital and wouldn't be returning. Hitler postponed all military operations until he named a replacement.

When Johann gave Väinü and Ian the news, it was their turn to curse. Johann filed his report that Russian forces were setting up artillery and moving tanks toward Küstrin. In the report, he estimated it would take the Russians another two days to block the Eleventh Army's route and set a pincer trap for them.

As the day passed, the critical layer of frozen ground so essential to the tigers and panthers became thinner and weaker, turning to mud that became deeper and more slippery by the hour. Johann and his men restlessly watched the snow melt, exposing the dreaded slime. Meanwhile, they knew the Russians were filling the route to Küstrin with guns and armour, and what began as a sure success became a foreseeable disaster.

Late on day two, Ian walked into a field with a heavy steel bar—and drove it through the frost with one blow. He pulled it out of the ground and looked at Johann. "It's too late unless it freezes tonight; the king tigers and elefanten can't leave the roads, and it would be risky for a panther. There isn't much asphalt or gravel that can carry seventy tonnes between here and Küstrin, and the Russians are setting up and sighting their big guns on the only roads we can use."

The night was the warmest of the winter thaw, and before dawn, two days after Wenck's accident, the tigers began moving on the road to Küstrin under the orders of Wenck's replacement, General Hans Krebs. The twelve king tigers split up as they had before, with two in the lead flanked by panthers. When the asphalt road ended, the tigers travelled on narrow, built-up gravel roads separating the fields, and the panthers flanked them using fields and service roads, staying slightly ahead to sniff out a Russian ambush.

Johann and his Jäger scouts moved forward during the night, marking targets and searching for ambushes. The tigers advanced slowly in second or third gear, stopping to fire at targets the scouts had marked. Progress was slow but steady, and Johann began to believe they might reach Küstrin. He had a driver, Ian, two riflemen, and a radioman in his crowded demag. Using the half-track's ability to traverse soft ground, they worked the south side of the attack's spear.

They avoided roads, followed tree lines and depressions, and Klaus and his squadron of panthers stayed a kilometre behind them. When Johann's demag was five hundred metres south of the narrow road 227's squadron used, they spotted two T-34s hiding in trees growing at the edge of the road. Johann's driver parked the camouflaged demag behind a wooden fence, and Johann got on the radio.

"First Jäger Company to two-two-seven. Two T-34s hiding in the trees a thousand metres ahead on your right." Johann spoke softly, as if the enemy would hear. He could see both the T-34s and the panthers from his vantage point.

Immediately, 227 pulled behind a barn close to the road, and Johann watched a figure he assumed to be Klaus climb down and walk to the corner of the building. The panther behind 227 moved to the other side of the road and parked between the bare trees in an orchard, leaving himself a clear shot down the road.

When Klaus returned to 227, he quickly moved his panther into the road beside the barn, facing the T-34s. The cannon fired as soon as the treads stopped, and the nearest T-34 blew up in a giant fireball.

The other Russian tank fired, but the shell exploded harmlessly on the road between the panthers. The second panther fired, hitting the second T-34 low on one side, blowing the track apart. The crippled tank tried to run, but the dragging tread spun it sideways. It stopped broadside to 227's next shot, which struck the fuel tank behind the crew.

The driver of the slow-moving lead tiger heard Johann's radio report and the first shot from 227. When the T-34 blew up, he ignored his real job and tried to see what was happening by looking out the corner of his narrow slit. His hands followed his eyes, slightly turning the steering wheel and seventy tons of steel to the left. Realizing his mistake, the driver corrected, but it was too late. The tank slid sideways on the greasy mud, and he yelled a hopeless "Scheisse!" into the intercom as he felt the left track drop off the gravel road, dragging the rest of the tank with it.

The layer of gravel on the road was thin and narrow; agriculture transport trucks and farm machinery only used it in the summer. Widened areas allowed vehicles to meet, but on average, the gravelled surface was scarcely wide enough for trucks. When the left track broke the frost on the shoulder and buried itself in the soft ditch, the commander swore and ordered the driver to reverse, sealing the tiger's fate.

◇◇◇◇◇◇◇◇◇◇◇◇◇◇◇◇◇◇◇◇◇◇◇◇◇◇◇◇◇◇◇

Hearing the chatter on his radio, Johann told his driver to head toward the troubled king tiger, and the demag was almost to the burning T-34s before Johann could see the stranded tiger lying at a thirty-degree angle with its tread in the ditch.

411

The tiger's commander sat on the edge of the hatch, engaged in a conversation with the commander of a panther who had come to his rescue. After much arm-waving and pointing, the panther backed up to the tiger. Two soldiers unwound the tow cable on its rump, fastened it to the front tow hook on the tiger, then stepped back.

The panther tightened the cable, and the commander signalled both tanks to go. The panther spun its treads; the tiger moved ahead, tried to climb the ditch bank, and had success in its grasp when it slid sideways down the slope, deeper into the mud. The panther swung on the end of the taut line, belching black smoke and spinning its treads. The tiger commander ducked below the rim of his hatch to avoid a stream of mud and stones thrown back by the panther's tracks, and when he realized it was slewing toward the ditch, he was too late signalling a stop. The panther slid into the ditch in front of the tiger, burying its left side in the mud and effectively blocking the monster from going ahead.

Johann watched the drama with his binoculars, his worry meter registering in the red as he realized the tiger could not return to the road in time to preserve the attack's momentum.

He spoke to Ian, who stood beside him without comment. "Russian scouts are looking at the same scene we are, and their tanks will seize this opportunity." He pointed ahead, parallel to the road 227 was travelling on. "We had better find out what's coming at us!"

◇◇◇◇◇◇◇◇◇◇◇◇◇◇◇◇◇◇◇◇◇◇◇◇◇◇◇◇◇◇◇◇◇◇◇◇◇

Three kilometres from the tigers, the demag met Väinü and two Finnish helper scouts he had confiscated from the regular infantry. He gave Johann the news with an "I knew this would happen!" attitude.

"Thirteen T-34s and two one-oh-fives are headed for the tigers, and they are moving fast!" Väinü stood on the running board. "The main Russian body is behind them but moving cautiously. It looks like they sent one of their suicide groups out to see if we could kill them."

"Get in. We have to know where the main body is and where the artillery and infantry are waiting."

The demag was moving, and Johann was on the radio before Väinü sat in his seat. One of the extra Finns had to sit on the other's knee.

"Jäger one to panzer two-two-seven. Thirteen T-34s and two destroyers are approaching from the east! Range, three thousand metres and closing! Over." Johann sent the message on the open battle channel so every tank and infantry commander would hear it.

A kilometre farther down the road, Johann told the driver to hide the demag behind a barn while everyone got out for a group talk. The sound of big guns behind them told Johann that the probing T-34s were catching hell.

"The main body is on the other side of those trees." Väinü pointed across the fields at a patch of dark forest.

"Okay, let's take a look." Johann began jogging alongside Väinü, parallel to the road. He wasn't yet out of breath when they rounded the end of the line of spruce trees and found a frozen lake before them. The wind had blown it clear of snow, and the warm weather had covered it with puddles of water. Twenty artillery pieces lined the shore behind the line of trees. A line of T-34 tanks on the road running along the lake's edge drove west to meet the Germans. Trucks loaded with infantry and men walking in groups around the tanks moved toward the German king tigers.

When they had finished counting the tanks and guns, Johann and Väinü trotted back to the demag.

Johann picked up the handset and said, "Two-two-seven, Finke. Over."

Klaus confirmed he was listening, and Johann went on. "Twenty pieces of heavy artillery straight ahead on the edge of Lake Jezioro, and at least a hundred tanks and a battalion of infantry headed in your direction. There are probably more guns hidden in the forest. Over."

The Russian artillery fired before Klaus answered—shells screamed toward the German line and the stuck tiger, and the Russian infantry and T-34s picked up their pace. Klaus's panther rounded a turn in the road and appeared in front of Johann, his partner close behind and to one side. The Russian artillery spotted and targeted the panthers, but 227 reversed seconds before the guns fired, and the shells fell short, leaving craters in the road. The panthers disappeared in the direction they had come, so the artillery again focused on the king tigers' situation.

Russian infantry and tanks covered the fields, heading for the point of the German spear. Johann shouted at his demag driver, "Take us south around these trees, and keep changing directions!"

Johann's half-track circled back, rejoining 227. When he reached Klaus's panther, the king tigers, caught out in the open, were smoking hulks, and the German infantry was in full retreat. One of the panthers was on its side, but the others were intact and moving, a difficult target for artillery and dangerous to the advancing T-34s. Battle Headquarters ordered the panthers back to the main body, and they swung to the west toward Stargard.

◇◇◇◇◇◇◇◇◇◇◇◇◇◇◇◇◇◇◇◇◇◇◇◇◇◇◇◇◇◇◇

As the demag drove parallel to the road occupied by 227 and a squadron of panthers, Johann said, "If we had attacked two days ago, none of this would have happened! We could have beaten the Russians to Küstrin!" He leaned ahead so he could speak in Väinü's ear. "What do you think, Väinü?"

"I think we have one chance to live our lives, and we should not waste it speculating on fairy tales that we think might have turned out better. It's time to figure out what to do next, not why we failed."

Ian laughed at Johann. "He just said that history is irreversible, and you should accept that the past does not determine our fate unless we let it." Johann couldn't help thinking about Wilhelm. He had parried and thrust with his literal sword like a verbose Zorro.

"But every historian says that if we don't learn from history, we are doomed to repeat it..." Johann said it as though no comment were necessary or wanted, but Ian couldn't help himself.

"You should put that little tidbit in a memo to Hitler. You might mention a Frenchman named Napoleon Bonaparte who also thought he could defeat those *Untermenschen*."

Chapter Thirty-nine

The Fish

The biggest fish story is generally about the one the fisherman almost caught, not the one he took home.

JOHANN CAREFULLY SLIT OPEN THE ENVELOPE, pinched two thin sheets of paper between his fingers, and pulled the most valuable thing in his life out of its sheath. Barbara's words fed his soul with the sweetness of home and love, connecting him to an almost-forgotten reality. His deep depression lasted from one letter to another, to be quenched for a few hours by the words he read. But it was enough to keep him fighting—not for Germany or the Third Reich, certainly not for Hitler, but for the possibility that he might see Barbara and Thomas again.

Each day, each battle, every man he killed made "home" a smaller word until it had become something he could no longer see clearly. Although he tried, it had been a long time since he could imagine himself lying beside Barbara, touching her, hearing the music of her laughter. A cup of coffee with her in the morning, playing the violin in an orchestra, walking down a peaceful street—Johann could no longer call up the feeling of home out of his imagination. He felt himself slipping into a new dark place where he feared Barbara could no longer find him.

He stared at the first word in every letter he got from Barbara. It meant Barbara was there, speaking to him. He knew she loved him, and he felt her presence.

Liebling

The war has come to Detmold, and it could have been the disaster it has been everywhere else, but our tiny city is safe because we now have the British Army, where we had the Nazis. The English arrested everyone in Gestapo headquarters, and English soldiers took over the building. I still have a job, but I work for the British Army as their liaison with the people of Detmold, and we can thank Thomas for that."

Johann began to cry. He was alone in the darkness except for a single candle, sitting on a stone wall. No one was there to hear his sobs of relief. He tried to think of a scenario where Thomas would get his mother a job with the English but couldn't come up with anything.

◇◇◇◇◇◇◇◇◇◇◇◇◇◇◇◇◇◇◇◇◇◇◇◇◇◇◇◇◇◇◇◇◇◇◇◇

Barbara took Mittagspause seriously, as did everyone in Detmold. Everything in the city stopped at 13:00 and didn't begin again until 15:00, and the typical resident began the mid-day pause with Mittagessen, then followed it with a nap. Maria, Theo, and Corrine, a girl who lived with them, left after the meal. Barbara went to bed for her usual rest, leaving orders for Thomas to do his homework.

The weather was mild for February, meaning the ice was gone from the ponds, and as soon as his mother closed her bedroom door, Thomas sneaked out of the house with his fishing rod and secretly met Gunther outside. The sun shone, the crocus's heads poked out of the flower bed, and Lisa's daffodils would soon be blooming. It was a perfect day to catch a fish. Thomas and Gunther headed for the Palais Teich, a pond full of big fish, which was only a ten-minute walk from the house. Thomas led the way.

Maria and Barbara had made the mistake of saying that the new rationing allowance meant the family would soon have nothing to eat, and Thomas had decided to do something about it; Gunther, as usual, was in it for the adventure.

"We'll use a piece of this red cloth to catch a fish." Thomas gave a piece of a discarded shirt to Gunther. "Carp like bright colours."

"How do you know that?" Gunther sounded skeptical.

"Theo and I caught a big one last summer, and we used a hook with a piece of red and yellow metal on it."

Gunther pointed across a large field, a shortcut to the palace pond, and said, "Let's take the shortcut."

Thomas grabbed his shirt and held on, stopping him. "Mutti said I should stay out of that field. It belongs to Herr Strang, a nice man who gives us meat and vegetables."

Gunther kicked a stone off the street. "We won't hurt anything if we stay on the grass…it's too soon to plant anything."

"We would leave tracks, and Mutti would know…Mutti knows

416

everything!" Thomas closed the discussion and started walking down the street; he had the fishing rod, so Gunther followed.

Halfway along the edge of the field, Thomas and Gunther noticed Wehrmacht soldiers moving behind buildings. Others had rifles and machine guns pointed out of windows at an unseen enemy on the other side of the field.

A soldier ran out of a brick-and-beam shed and approached the boys.

"You must get out of here! Sofort! Go home and lock your door!" He tried to turn Gunther around, but the boy was having none of that; he was going in the other direction; he was going to catch a fish!

"My house is that way!" He pointed toward the Palace, where a pond full of fish awaited him.

"And your house?" the soldier asked Thomas, and Thomas reluctantly pointed in the same direction.

"Go then, and go fast!" The soldier pushed the boys toward their destination.

Gunther was more than willing to hurry, but Thomas held back. He stopped fifty metres from the soldier and looked back at him. The soldier waved them on, shouting impatiently, "Geh! Schnell!"

Thomas didn't move, but Gunther took a few steps, then turned back. Thomas said, "I think we should go home. Maybe they are going to fight the Englander."

Gunther pulled on Thomas's arm. "No, they're just practicing. There are no Englanders around here, or they would be shooting." Thomas let Gunther pull him ahead a couple of steps, then stopped. Gunther tugged on his shirt, but Thomas leaned back.

"Mutti wouldn't like this. She would tell me to go home right now!"

Gunther let go of Thomas's shirt. "If you want, we could run back, wake up your Mutti, and ask her."

Thomas weighed the choices and decided that waking his mother in the middle of her nap was not a good idea. He had done that once before when his father was napping with her, and he would never do that again!

The soldier started running toward them, waving his gun, and Thomas ran toward the pond with Gunther on his heels, breathing down his neck.

The red cloth didn't work. Lying on the flat cut-stone courtyard in front of the Palais, shading his eyes to eliminate the reflection, Gunther announced that the fish he could see in the clear water ignored the strip of red. He guided Thomas's rod, placing the hook a few millimetres in front of a fish's nose, and the fish swam around it.

"We have to find something else." Gunther stood and looked around. "What do carp eat?"

"Mutti said they eat vegetables. We give pieces of bread to the ducks, and if it sinks, the fish eat it."

Gunther announced the obvious: "There isn't any bread here, and is bread a vegetable?"

Thomas shrugged his shoulders and lay down on his stomach, shading his eyes. "They're eating something off the stone wall." He put his hand in the water and pulled out a handful of green guck. He sat up, crossed his legs, and spread the guck on his palm. A small worm wriggled through the soft green ooze. He washed his hand in the pond and lay down again.

"I think they're eating little worms buried in the yucky green stuff stuck on the stones. But maybe they're eating the green guck."

"Let's put both on our hook and try it!" Gunther reached over the side and came out with both hands full of soft green ooze. Thomas ripped a wider strip of cloth off the bottom of Gunther's shirt and fashioned a bag for the stuff with an opening on the top. Gunther stuffed it full, including two tiny worms, just in case.

Thomas carefully lowered the hook into the water amongst a group of fish a metre from the wall. They immediately gathered around and poked at it with their noses. Gunther watched them, ready to signal Thomas to pull if a fish put the bag in its mouth.

"Scheisse!" Gunther rolled back, turned around and yelled, "Pull!" but the fish was already leaving with the bag and Thomas's fishing line.

"You've got him!" screamed Gunther, "and he's a monster!"

The fish swam lazily across the pond while Thomas tried to turn it toward him, but it didn't seem to notice the fishing line. Thomas pulled as hard as he dared; he had often tangled the line around bushes in a brook and had a good idea of when the line would break. The fish swam slowly in an arc, gradually turning until it faced him.

Gunther ran to a bush at the courtyard's edge and shamelessly cut a large branch with a robust shoot growing out of the big end. He quickly cut it to suit his purpose using his Swiss Army knife. When he returned to the top of the wall where Thomas had led the giant fish, he lowered the branch under the fish's belly and pulled up. The fish kicked and fell forward.

"I need another one." Gunther ran to the bush, and the plant sacrificed another major body part to the fish retrieval.

"I don't think I can lift it out alone." Gunther laid the second stick beside Thomas, who had the fish next to the wall again. "You will need to lift with me."

The apparatus worked perfectly on the first try, and the surprised fish flopped on the flat stones of the courtyard, searching for something to push against. Gunther ran away, then returned in seconds with a piece of decorative sandstone that looked suspiciously like the stones someone had used to build the palace wall. He bashed the fish's head over and over until it straightened, quivered, then relaxed in death.

◇◇◇◇◇◇◇◇◇◇◇◇◇◇◇◇◇◇◇◇◇◇◇◇◇◇◇◇◇◇◇◇◇◇◇

The breathless boys stared at their victim, enjoying the excitement of outsmarting and overpowering such a large fish. They felt like men.

Gunther tried to pick up the fish using the tail and then its head, but it was too heavy, long, and slippery. "We need a pole so we can both carry it," he announced and went toward the Palace gardens. He returned with a rake handle, freshly broken, close to the end where the implement had been. Thomas had a question he decided not to ask.

"We can use our bootlaces to tie it to the pole." Gunther and Thomas sat down, removed the laces from their boots, and then tied the fish to the rake handle, leaving a short piece of grip on each end. They grabbed the handles, lifted, and the fish came up with the rake handle.

"*Scheisse*, that fish is heavy." Gunther put the handle on his shoulder, facing away from the fish.

Thomas lifted his end; it dug into his shoulder, and the fish's tail slapped against his leg.

"Mutti says you shouldn't swear."

"Did I swear?" Gunther laughed.

419

"Yes, you said *Scheisse.*"

"So did you. I won't tell on you if you don't tell on me."

Thomas laughed and followed Gunther to the street.

Gunther stopped at the edge of the field.

"Look…there's a path across the field; if everyone else goes across the field, why not us?" He pulled gently on the broom handle, and Thomas followed him, staggering under the weight and too tired to protest.

Halfway across the field, a whizzing sound passed the two boys, a gun fired, and then a cacophony of whizzes and bangs were everywhere. Thomas immediately connected the whizzes and the sound of guns firing.

He shouted, "Run!" at Gunther, but Gunther was already pulling on the end of the broom handle. They ran less than five metres before Gunther fell, dropped the rake handle, and the falling fish pulled Thomas down.

"They got me!" Gunther screamed, looking at his leg where a hole in his thigh gushed blood.

"Mutti will kill me!" He put his finger in the hole in his pants. "I ruined my pants!"

Thomas took the red tail from Gunther's shirt out of his pocket, bunched it, and pushed it on the wound. The blood slowed.

"That hurts." Gunther tried to pull Thomas's hand away, but Thomas sustained the pressure.

"Losing blood is bad—we have to plug the hole." Thomas noticed blood on the ground under the inside of Gunther's leg and put his head down to look at it. "The bullet went right through—we need another plug."

Thomas removed his coat, then his shirt; he tore it into two pieces and used one to stop the blood pouring out of the inside hole.

◇◇◇◇◇◇◇◇◇◇◇◇◇◇◇◇◇◇◇◇◇◇◇◇◇◇◇◇◇◇◇◇◇◇◇

The sound of gunfire from the direction of the river frightened Barbara into action. She woke, dressed quickly, and searched for Thomas. She remembered he had pestered her to go fishing at the Palais Teich every day since the ice had melted. Then she remembered Gunther hanging around waiting for Thomas to finish his Mittagessen. She looked for his fishing gear on top of his Kleiderschrank—it was gone—and made a very well-educated mother's guess. Lately, he had asked endless questions about carp—what they taste like, whether his mother liked carp meat, where the biggest ones would be. She had told him about the pond at the Palais, something she now regretted.

Shots came from the direction Thomas would have taken, and Barbara panicked. She ran toward the battle, raging with ever more furious intensity. Machine guns, rifles, and then explosions echoed through the streets. People ran to their houses and closed their blackout curtains, but Barbara kept running toward the battle. War had come to Detmold, and Barbara's worst fear was coming true.

She pushed back the memory of two years ago—the bomb had killed Lisa without a hint that it could happen, tearing Barbara's world apart. Only four bombs had landed on Detmold so far in this war, and one of them had hit the house where Lisa celebrated her friend's birthday. Barbara was terrified that she would lose Thomas.

The edge of the field was the edge of the battle, and Barbara stood frozen—Thomas and Gunther lay on the ground halfway across the field. When one of them moved, she charged ahead, ignoring the whizzes.

"Stop firing! Hold your fire!" shouted a voice into a British combat radio.

"Feuer abstellen!" shouted a German sergeant into his radio.

The message passed down the line on both sides, and the immediate silence was deafening.

<hr>

Barbara reached her son, who was bent over Gunther, looking at Gunther's leg. "Thomas...Thomas, are you alright?"

Thomas lifted his head, still holding the cloth plugs on Gunther's leg; Gunther had decided that he would cooperate, and the pain made him feel like a hero. Thomas looked up at his mother. Her eyes were those of a very determined woman. When his mother wore that expression, he knew he was in deep trouble.

"Thank God you're alive," she cried, then held Thomas so tight she hurt him, but he still managed to keep the cloth against Gunther's leg. She looked down when she realized that her son was not reciprocating, and the blood on the grass startled her, but she regained her sense of logic just in time to figure out that Gunther was the one with a hole in his leg.

Barbara gently examined the wounds.

"We've got to get Gunther to a hospital," she announced, sucking in her breath. "Hold those pieces of cloth on Gunther's leg until I figure this out." She recognized the cloth and asked, "Did you ruin your new shirt?" Thomas nodded toward Gunther's missing shirttail. "I used his shirt too!"

Barbara stood up and shouted, "I need some help!" She looked first at one side of the field, then at the other—and heard silence.

She shouted again, in her limited school English and then in German. "A little boy is wounded. Ein Junge ist verwundet. He will die if you don't stop your foolish fighting! Er stirbt wenn sie nicht mit dem blöden Kreigspiel aufhören!"

She shielded her eyes and again looked at both sides of the field.

A German officer appeared, coming out of a house, carrying a dirty white cloth tied to the end of his rifle. He waved it back and forth as he walked toward Barbara. He had only taken three steps when a British soldier stood up from behind a stone wall and walked toward her from the opposite direction, waving an equally dirty piece of white cloth that looked vaguely like underwear.

The German soldier arrived first, looked at Gunther's wounds and waved at his comrades. He shouted, "Schick' mal den Sanitäter!" and waved his arm. Two medics with red cross armbands trotted across the field.

The British officer arrived, looked at Gunther and waved to his side, shouting, "Medic!" very much as the German had.

While the medics trotted across the field—one of the British medics carried a stretcher—the first British soldier said in perfect German, "Das ist ein wunderbarer Fisch!" and pointed at the carp. The German soldier touched the fish and stroked it lovingly. "Ich liebe es zu Angeln. Ich habe noch nie einen solchen Fisch gesehen!"

While the medics discussed Gunther's wounds, agreed on the treatment, and then bound his leg, the Brit and the German officers examined the fish. Barbara waited patiently, watching the medics closely.

Finished, the English soldier offered the stretcher for Gunther and a chocolate bar for the German medic. The man took the chocolate and one end of the stretcher, and an English medic took the other. The German and British officers carried the fish, insisting that Thomas tell them every detail of where and how he and Gunther had caught it.

◇◇

When they reached the edge of the field, the German soldier touched his cap and spoke to Barbara.

"We will wait until you are safe before we begin firing."

"You should stay away from this area until we settle this," said the Brit.

"That is insane!" Barbara pushed the German soldier backward. "Don't you know the war is over?"

He said, "I regret; I must do my job unless I get an official command to surrender." The English soldier shrugged. He touched his hat to indicate the discussion was over and turned to go.

Barbara caught the German's arm and pulled him back. The British lieutenant decided to stay where he was and listen.

"What if the mayor tells you to stop the fighting? I know him, and I'm sure he will do it."

"Perhaps, but a Wehrmacht officer would be better." The soldier, a sergeant, began thinking about it, and the English lieutenant spoke before he could think too much.

"I will guarantee that we will keep you in a camp close to your family, and you can go wherever you want as soon as the war is over. We will feed you three meals a day, but you must put up with English food." He laughed, and the German laughed with a clear tone of relief.

Barbara had heard enough. "I'll get Bürgermeister Keller while you take the boys home." Barbara pointed. "It's only a short walk… Thomas will take you there."

Barbara ran to the Rathaus, the city administration building, and noted a *Kubelwagen* and two guards parked in the square waiting. She guessed that Bürgermeister Hans Keller was in his office with the local Wehrmacht commanding officer.

Barbara didn't slow down to speak with the receptionist. She ran

423

past her, opened the door, and found herself face to face with the Oberst in charge of Detmold's defence. She began to talk, interrupting the men. The German officer closed his mouth and listened.

When Barbara finished, Oberst Humboldt told her to lead him to the British officer. He and the Bürgermeister followed Barbara out the door and into the courtyard, where they boarded the Kubelwagen.

When they arrived at Barbara's house, the English lieutenant was waiting for them in the street. When he spoke perfect German to the oberst, he explained that he had a German father and had lived in Mainz before the war. A dozen British and German soldiers milled around exchanging cigarettes, using bits of one another's language they had picked up. They managed to tell one another about their sweethearts and home and discovered they had a lot in common. The Lieutenant spoke into a radio handset, and a minute later, an American Thunderbolt fighter roared overhead.

"I have fifty pieces of heavy artillery and a flight of twenty Thunderbolts waiting for me to call them." The British lieutenant said it as a fact, not a threat. "Please save your brave men and your beautiful city."

Oberst Humboldt and Hans Keller moved to one side and spoke quietly, and then the oberst pulled out his pistol. He gave it to the lieutenant. Bürgermeister Keller said, "The city is yours."

"The city is yours and ours. We will need your help until the war is over and the German people can take over their country again."

"You are very kind, sir, but we both know the reality."

◇◇◇◇◇◇◇◇◇◇◇◇

Johann began to cry. Home was so close, and yet so far.

"…and Doctor Baumgartner said that Thomas had saved Gunther's life!"

He wiped his eyes, but new tears washed into them. He put the letter down until he got control of them, then tried again.

"Detmold is saved. Mayor Keller and the British soldiers are getting food and clothing to us from England, and Theo is already talking about opening a music school in the Palais. He wants you to teach the violin and play in the theatre as soon as he can get it started again. The British are willing to help.

"Unfortunately, Herr Keller has been a party member and will not be able to remain as Bürgermeister."

Barbara added a postscript.

"The fish fed the whole neighbourhood, and everyone in Detmold is talking about it. A photographer took a picture of it with the boys, and no one can remember anyone catching such a big fish in the Palais Teich."

Chapter Forty

April 1945

No quarter given

They wrote in the old days that it is sweet and fitting to die for one's country. But in modern war, there is nothing sweet nor fitting in your dying. You will die like a dog for no good reason.

Ernest Hemingway

JOHANN'S SHATTERED, DECIMATED JÄGER COMPANY followed Eleventh Panzers Nordland, First Company's new home, northwest to the German border. Johann had inherited a few men from other companies and lost six men in Operation Sonnenwende. He now commanded thirty-four men, a company in name only.

The sheer numbers of the Russian forces crushed the Wehrmacht, destroyed whole divisions, left soldiers searching for another unit or a way home. With nowhere to go, they mingled with refugees, some with rifles, others without weapons. They trudged head down, ashamed, exhausted, many of them wounded. Although they intermingled, refugees and soldiers paid little attention to one another. Their goals differed, and, like defeated soldiers in any army, the losers got no sympathy.

Healthy armour and infantry units took the right-of-way, one way or another, without pity for defenceless people who had nothing.

A woman looked at Johann as though she were going to spit on him. He gave her a wide berth and said to Ian, "They hate us for losing and being on the road."

They walked with the refugees because there was no alternative—apart from the roads, there was only water, mud, land mines, and death. German uniforms and vehicles drew fire from Russian ground-attack aircraft, and the refugees knew it.

Johann abandoned his demag when there was no more Benzin for it, leaving it among the many redundant vehicles littering the fields and roads. Many were undamaged, but without fuel and ammunition, they became nothing more than embarrassing monuments to man's stupidity.

During the defeat at Arnswalde, as in all the lost battles since Stalingrad, if there were no spare tanks or tractors to tow damaged armour to repair facilities, German crews had destroyed their disabled vehicles. Since Unternehmung Sonnenwende, the Wehrmacht had rationed the meagre fuel supply to panther and tiger panzers and their supply vehicles. Explosives had run out, and less useful but battle-worthy tanks, demags, and lastwagen were left for the Russians to use against their previous owners. Germans built excellent equipment; add fuel and go!

Following their victory at Arnswalde, the Russian forces committed themselves to rebuilding their army at Küstrin in preparation for the run to Berlin. Their plan was simple—build the army bigger and better, cross the river, then overwhelm the Seelow Heights with hordes of armour. From there, a few days would take them to Berlin's doorstep.

They could smell Hitler's blood, and Russian officers competed for the right to be the first in Berlin!

Only the Wehrmacht defence lines on the Seelow Heights stood in their way, and the Ninth Army's General Busse wanted to know when to expect them. Johann's First Company was assigned to monitor the Russian buildup at Küstrin and let him know, but they had to get there before the Russians crossed the river.

<hr>

First Jäger Company walked down the twenty-kilometre slope called the Seelow Heights to the Oderbruch Plain, a three-thousand-metre stretch of flat swampy land on the west bank of the Oder River. Three lines of fortification construction cut the slope and the Oderbruch Plain into three parts, each line designed to slow and then stop the Russian advance.

When they reached the German side of the bridges, Johann and his men found the Oder River crossings intact. As soon as night fell, they eliminated four Russian sentries and crossed the railway bridge.

First Jäger Company spent their days monitoring the Russian buildup with the objective of predicting when they would attack. Whenever Johann reported that the attack was imminent, German army engineers would open a reservoir dam upriver, flooding the Oderbruch Plain and buying a few more days to build fortifications. Too early or late wouldn't do.

Johann, Ian, and Väinü hid their men in a wooded area east of the Russian camp on the northeast side of the river. They had a radio, and Johann reported daily to Busse's intelligence office. At the end of the call on the second day, Johann spoke to General Busse himself.

The general said, "We can count on a fight in the next few days, so it's time to get out of there. Over."

"No sir; the Russians won't attack for at least a week; they aren't ready yet. We must stay here until we're sure. You must flood the plain at the right time; only we will know when that is. Don't worry about us…" and then he had a suspicion… "Are you calling to tell me about Hitler's latest idea? Over."

"Yes, and I have a question for you. But first, you should know what our Führer has done. He joined my Ninth Army and the Fourth Panzer Army to make up what Hitler calls the Army Group Vistula, making us his last hope. General Gotthard Heinrici will command Vistula. Someone you know told me you've had some experience with General Gräser, the commander of the Fourth Panzer Army. He will guard my southeastern flank, and I'm interested in your opinion of what he will do. Over."

Johann hesitated and asked himself, "What the hell does it matter now?"

He decided to tell the truth, pushed the transmit button and said, "At the first sign of combat, Gräser will fold. He doesn't know how to fight and withdraw simultaneously, so don't count on him—you're on your own. Over."

"I guess that's clear enough. Now, I want to talk about what you've seen. I have your estimates in front of me, but Hitler says you are exaggerating—there can't be a million men. Are your numbers correct? Over."

Johann didn't hesitate—he could only report what he knew.

"I estimated a million soldiers based on the number of tents and services, the camouflaged holes in the ground, and the sheer numbers of them walking around. They are everywhere—hidden in the forest, in the town, and the woods and fields are full of underground bunkers filled with Russian soldiers. Multiply whatever you see on a photograph by ten. Over."

Johann keyed the mic again before Busse could key his. "About the tanks—we've counted so many tanks and guns we had to check our numbers twice before we believed them. Over." Johann released the microphone and waited. Busse finally keyed his mic.

"How many? And no exaggerations, please. Over."

"It is impossible to find and count every tank and gun—there are too many. But if you are standing, please sit down." Johann gave him a moment, then said, "Three thousand T-34s, a few heavy tanks, and a few 105mm tank destroyers, probably close to four thousand pieces of armour altogether. There are seventeen thousand heavy artillery guns, mostly 88s, which also could be a low number. There is no chance I am exaggerating!" Johann hesitated, then said, "Over."

It took thirty seconds for Busse to answer. When he keyed his microphone, he said, "That many? Are you certain? Over."

"Sir, I've been fighting Russians for four years; I know how to find them, and I know how to count. Over."

Busse clicked his mic and said, "Out." with a finality that did more than end the radio conversation.

◇◇◇◇◇◇◇◇◇◇◇◇◇◇◇◇◇◇◇◇◇◇◇◇◇◇◇◇◇◇

The Germans had built their defences along three lines, the last located twenty-four kilometres from the river, the first at the edge of the Oderbruch Plain, three kilometres from the water.

A few hours later, Johann read the orders he received from Busse, and he laughed—at first a chuckle and then a full-throated laugh that resonated in his belly.

"What's so funny?" Ian made an apparent effort to sound interested.

"Hitler named the last defence line the 'Wotan Line.' Do you know who Wotan is?" Ian shook his head, not interested in the least.

"Hitler loves Wagner's operas, and Wotan is the major god in the four operas of the 'Der Ring des Nibelungen' Cycle."

"So why isn't that a good name?" Väinü leaned against a tree trunk and casually flipped his knife at a tree beside Ian. It struck straight and true, close enough to Ian's head to get his attention. "We need a major god on our side." He didn't blink when Ian pulled the knife out and flipped it back at the tree he was leaning against, fifteen centimetres from his head.

Johann said, without amusement, "All the gods, including Wotan, lived in Valhalla, and in the last scene of the last opera, Valhalla burned to the ground, consuming the gods." Väinü pulled the knife from the tree, balanced it on his fingertips and smiled at Ian.

Johann, frustrated, said, "Enough play. You two aren't good enough to keep doing that."

They grinned stupidly, like little boys asked to stop roughhousing by their mother.

The following day, the First Belarussian Front began to move equipment to the riverbank, and Johann sent Busse's intelligence a report that the attack was hours away. It was time to go; the scouts crossed the railway bridge under cover of darkness.

◇◇◇◇◇◇◇◇◇◇◇◇◇◇◇◇◇◇◇◇◇◇◇◇◇◇◇◇◇◇◇

Busse was not a Hitler fan; "Hold to the last man!" was blasphemy to the General. He read Johann's report and withdrew his men from the first defence line under cover of darkness—a few hours before Russian guns began the most massive bombardment ever witnessed on the Eastern front.

German engineers had opened the dam upriver eight hours earlier, and overnight, water crept over the Oderbruch Plain. When dawn broke, the First Belarussian Front crossed the river to a flooded plain.

Johann's company moved through the woods ahead of the Russians, directing German artillery's fire onto the Soviet forces slogging through the mud and water on the plains below. The combination of water and men and machines slogging through it churned the flat marsh into a nine-square-kilometre mudhole, and Johann lost count at a hundred and fifty tanks and tank destroyers reduced to smoking ruins. Thousands of infantry lay dead and dying in the morass, but still, their comrades advanced, stumbling, falling, driving their tanks over dead or nearly-dead comrades. When darkness mercifully descended, the carnage slowed, and the Russians had taken the evacuated first line of German defences. The cost of the meagre victory was terrible, even when observed from the enemy's winning perspective.

431

"They certainly are like ants, aren't they?" Ian talked as he lay on the ground, watching the slaughter through Johann's binoculars.

Lying next to him, Johann said, "Yes, and we win if we get home before they eat us."

"Why don't they stop? If they waited, the water would go down—can't they see that this is a disaster? Even the Russians can't afford to lose men and tanks at this rate!"

"Because this battle is the last one. They won't need reserves when Hitler is dead, and no matter what we do or how successful we are, they will overwhelm us if they don't stop."

Johann waved at the men carrying the radio equipment, and they followed him further up the high ground. Ian and Väinü walked on both sides of him.

"Do we know whether they have reserves?" Väinü jumped ahead of Johann as they weaved their way through the edge of a forest. Ian walked in Johann's tracks.

"The estimate we sent to headquarters was about a million men, three or four thousand tanks and tank destroyers, and about seventeen thousand pieces of artillery…." Johann caught a branch that Väinü held onto so that it wouldn't slap him in the face... "give or take a hundred thousand men and five hundred tanks. The artillery is probably a close guess." He laughed. "I don't know whether they have reserves, but does it matter?"

Ian took the bent branch from Johann and started to ask another question. Johann saved him the breath.

"If we scored with every shell and bullet, we could defeat them, but if we miss with half of them, they will be in Berlin in a couple of weeks!"

Ian mumbled, "I guess that puts it in perspective," but Johann heard him.

Väinü knew the answer but asked, "So, do we hold to the last man?"

"Hell, no…we run like the devil is behind us when we need to, and we fight like cornered rats when we can delay them."

They found a woods road, and Johann stepped up beside Väinü. Ian skipped up to his other side. The radio crew followed, smoking and talking about women.

<hr>

Two days later, Johann and his scouts, sheltered from view in a forest near the second defence line two kilometres ahead of the Belarussian advance, watched a mob of Russian soldiers fight their way from trench to trench, bunker to bunker. They bulldozed their way forward with no regard for casualties, sometimes shelling their own men if it led to forward progress.

Johann's radio operator tapped him on the shoulder; Johann passed his Zeiss binoculars to Väinü and took the handset. After a short conversation, he handed it back to the radioman.

He spoke to Ian and Väinü, showing the anger that comes from helplessness. "That was Busse's headquarters—Gräser has done it again—the Fourth Panzer Army stood their ground, and the Russians crushed them, exposing our northwestern flank. When the First Belarussian Front finishes here, Busse can't stop them from going around this end of the Wotan line and straight to Berlin." Johann stood up. "General Busse wants us to play the 'hit and run' game; we must delay the Belarussians for as long as we can."

"No fighting to the last man?" Ian put his binoculars in their case. Väinü passed Johann's to him.

"It's going to be bad enough if we fight smart—if we stand and fight, we will last a day or two, and then the Russians will take the autobahn to Berlin. The Americans aren't close yet, meaning Stalin would get most of Germany."

"What are the chances our politicians will negotiate a truce?" Ian kicked a piece of moss.

Johann began to walk. "About the same as we have of killing all the poor bastards coming up that hill!"

◇◇◇◇◇◇◇◇◇◇◇◇◇◇◇◇◇◇◇◇◇◇◇◇◇◇◇◇◇◇◇◇◇◇◇◇◇

The next day, Johann's First Jäger Company led 227's camouflaged panthers through the forest, hidden from the cloud of Russian aircraft flying unopposed over the battlefield. They kept to narrow wood roads, knocking down trees to clear a path when there was none. When they reached the strip of forest Johann had picked for them to lie in wait for the First Belarusians, Klaus positioned his panthers at the edge of the trees but deep enough to hide them from Russian aircraft and the eyes in the open field below. When they moved ahead, they would be in a perfect position to do tremendous damage to anything trying to cross the open ground below them, then escape using the route Johann's scouts had marked through the forest behind them. Klaus planned to move the squadron forward when the Russian tanks were at close range, assuring the fate of those targetted by the first salvo.

The sacrificial probe of Thirty T-34s and ten self-propelled guns appeared, driving up the hill, working their way across open space with nothing but short spring grass for cover, relentlessly closing the distance to the cannon barrels of Klaus's twelve panthers. Having drawn the short straw, they zigged and zagged like nervous rabbits, knowing they were gifts to the Germans in exchange for information about their position and strength. The Russians would adjust the main attack depending on what happened to those rabbits.

Klaus ordered his panthers to wait until the forward tanks were slightly past their position and then direct fire at the Russian armour's exposed sides. At a distance of less than five hundred metres, it would be like shooting deer in a barn. Every panther initially had its exclusive target—one shot, one Russian tank. When the rear tanks died, Klaus counted on the forward tanks stopping and turning their turrets to find and shoot the German panzers that had killed twelve of their buddies, making them vulnerable for a long time. He was counting on two free volleys before the Russians figured it out, and then he planned to be gone when Russian artillery found the range.

The panthers' long gun barrels followed the dark shapes until Klaus said "Fire!" on the radio, and twelve armour-piercing shells parted the screaming air at three times the speed of sound, travelling the five hundred metres to their targets in less than half a second. A dozen T-34s stopped—four of them flaming coffins. The remaining Russian tanks pivoted to face the panthers, completing their turn just in time to meet the next salvo—but the panthers were not their biggest problem.

While Klaus was telling his panthers to shoot, Johann said, "Fire!" triggering artillery hidden in the woods, and a hundred howitzers two thousand meters northwest of him lobbed their big shells. Five seconds later, the field in front of Johann blew upward, a brown and grey wall of earth suspended like a blanket above the Russian tanks. Half of them disappeared in clouds of pulverized mud, and when gravity pulled the mixture back to earth, dead and wounded men littered the field between wrecked tanks.

The panthers and artillery fired until the tank force ceased to exist, and when four T-34 survivors turned, the artillery's 88s destroyed three of them before they had gone fifty metres. Klaus's panzers killed the last moving thing on the field, and Johann told the artillery to stop firing.

The Russian Air Force dominated the airspace over the battleground and were on Klaus's panzers in minutes, so Johann led them deep into the patch of forest before turning them northwest to join the main force. The Eleventh Panzergrenadier had just over a hundred tanks to meet the million-man First Belarussian Army and its thousands of tanks. Johann had no illusions that they could delay the Russians for long, but Klaus's ambush would undoubtedly introduce a measure of hesitation. The destruction of a few dozen Russian tanks and a few hundred Russian men had for sure bought a little time, and the German war was now only about buying time.

Klaus's panther squadron joined the main Eleventh Panzergrenadier force at noon, lining up at the edge of the trees, ready to move forward to begin the attack. Fifty thousand infantry waited, scattered through the forest, anticipating the inevitable battle. A thousand German artillery pieces located somewhere west of them waited for coordinates and orders.

Johann tried not to think of the countless Russian guns set up to cover the Belarussian Front's advance to the Wotan line. His stomach churned; the coming battle would be different from the initial skirmish; the Russians now knew precisely where the Germans waited in the relatively small forest. Thousands of Russian cannons and tanks and hundreds of aircraft were ready for a fight, gleefully anticipating crushing the Germans. Johann tried to imagine the power that would hit them, but his mind would not go there.

He warned Klaus of the imminent barrage, and a few minutes later, the Russian guns opened up. The panthers closed their hatches and locked them, and men wrapped their hands around something solid. The infantry jumped into shallow trenches.

The bombardment began instantaneously, like the crack of a whip. The Russian guns didn't fire any ranging shots to warn the Germans and caught men in the open with their first salvo. Within seconds, direct hits on trenches sent men and their body parts flying through the air. Wood splinters, tree trunks, and flying stones killed as many men as blasts and shrapnel. The steady pounding killed German soldiers at a rate Johann couldn't comprehend.

The trenches he and his men were in offered little protection against howitzers, whose shells fell almost straight down. Johann pointed deeper into the woods and made a running sign with his fingers. Väinü and Ian nodded, and when Johann jumped out of the trench and ran, the world around him exploded in a shower of wood splinters and shrapnel. Zigzagging between the trees, averaging the straightest line he could, he began to outrun the explosions. He slowed when the killing ground was behind him, then stopped to assess the situation. Breathing hard, bent over with his hands on their knees, Väinü and two men stopped beside him.

Johann straightened and looked past them. He asked hopefully, "Is there anyone else?" but the woods from there to the carnage were empty.

Väinü gasped, breathless, "Ian and two men ran with me, but I don't think they made it." The two men with Väinü shook their heads. "The rest of the men stayed in the trenches."

The bombardment intensified, and no other men showed up, so Johann pointed ahead to an opening in the trees. "We will look for Ian and the men later—they may have jumped in a trench." He pointed to an old wood-harvesting road. "We'll need to go in that direction. If any of our panzers survive, they will need an escape route."

They set out at a fast trot. A knot in Johann's stomach and an ache in his heart competed with a feeling of panic. He wasn't sure that any-thing mattered anymore. His sense of reason told him that the tanks' survival was impossible and that death for him was inevitable.

He mumbled, trying to convince himself. "Ian is lucky; it's over for him."

Chapter Forty-one

April 1945

The best and the worst

"Man schlägt jemanden mit der Faust und nicht mit gespreizten Fingern "

(One hits his enemy with his fist, not with his spread fingers)

General Heinz Guderian

"The object of war is not to die for your country but to make the other bastard die for his..."

General George S. Patton

"There's no honourable way to kill, no gentle way to destroy. There is nothing good in war. Except its ending."

Abraham Lincoln

JOHANN SENT VÄINÜ AHEAD to find the perfect spot to ambush their inevitable pursuers while his men marked the escape route. They blazed trees with their knives and hung pieces of cloth on branches—a trail anyone with eyesight could follow. When they returned to the panzers, Russian aircraft had taken over the effort to eradicate the German tank forces.

While they waited, a few hundred metres from the edge of the battle, Johann and Väinü worked on their ambush plan. A few minutes after the explosions stopped and the sound of aircraft engines faded into the east, Johann prepared himself for the worst.

"Let's see what's left of our panzers." Johann dodged between trees, moving as fast as possible without running into something, and Väinü and his men ran close behind. When they reached the carnage that littered the forest floor, it didn't resemble the place they had left thirty minutes ago. Branches and trees covered everything—men buried under trees screamed and pleaded for help; others got to their feet, crawled out of holes and helped their comrades.

Johann and his men, unsure of where to look, searched for 227 and the King Tiger command tank, picking their way past dead and dying infantry without stopping, leaving the uninjured to save those they could. They worked their way between burning tanks, shattered trees and bomb craters until they found 227. The panther, covered with tree branches and splinters, looked whole, perhaps even usable. A spruce tree leaned over the cannon barrel, and a sizeable tree trunk lay on the cupola. Forest trash and dirt covered everything, but essential equipment appeared undamaged.

The tiger command tank beside 227 had taken several direct hits, and a cursory inspection by Väinü found no life inside, so Johann and his men concentrated on 227.

Johann climbed up on the panther's rump, tapped on the cupola hatch with his gun butt, and when Klaus screwed it open, he peeked in the slit under it.

"It's Finke. We'll clean things up so you can get out."

Johann's men removed the debris from the cover so Klaus could raise the hatch, and Johann crouched beside the cupola.

He said, "The command tank took a couple of direct hits; Hauptmann Stricher is dead." He stretched his arm toward the oncoming Russians, crossing the field like Roman Legions. "You're in charge now, Klaus, and there are hundreds of tanks and thousands of infantry over that hill. You can't stop them all, and when you withdraw, I think the Russians will follow whatever tanks you have that can still fight. We set up an ambush about three kilometres from here, along the escape route we've marked for you." Klaus raised his head out of the cupola, and they looked across the field at soldiers who resembled ants. "Unfortunately, I lost my radio, and communication may be a problem."

As Klaus pulled on his intercom mask, he said, "Simon has a portable radio you can have." Johann heard him talk to the radio operator. Klaus took off his mask, turned to Johann and looked at his three men and the chaos around them. "How many men do you have left?" Dead and dying men littered the forest; those who could still walk tried to help those who couldn't.

Johann nodded toward Väinü. "As far as I know…four." Väinü nodded, looked at his feet, kicked a piece of moss and said nothing.

◇◇◇◇◇◇◇◇◇◇◇◇◇◇◇◇◇◇◇◇◇◇◇◇◇◇

The young loader crawled out of 227's rear turret hatch and looked curiously at Johann as he passed the portable radio to him. And then he shouted, almost joyfully, "Mein Gott! Sie sind Johann Finke!"

"Yes, I am. Who are you?" He looked carefully at the young loader's face but didn't recognize him.

"Lucas Schwartz. Maria and Theo took me in, and I slept in your bed at Gartenstrasse 18! Hell, I stared at your picture every night!" Lucas laughed. "Now that I see you, it may have been a picture of someone else."

Johann felt his spirits rise, and it took him a moment to find his voice. Finally, he said, "Lucas Schwartz, yes, my parents told me about you in their letters!" To keep himself from hugging the boy, he asked, "Have you heard anything from them or Barbara?"

"We haven't gotten mail for a month. But everyone was fine when I last heard…"

Klaus interrupted, "We've got a war to fight!" He spoke to his driver through the intercom. "Kristian, open your hatch so you can see, then move ahead until we reach the edge of the woods. Leutnant Finke and his men will keep you from running over anyone. Marcus, swing the turret clockwise so the big tree falls off. We'll clean up the small pieces as Kristian moves the tank ahead."

Johann turned to leave, but Klaus touched his arm and said, "We must slow the Russians a little. My squadron will stay here to cover the withdrawal of the rest of the tanks and the infantry." Johann nodded and jumped down as the engine started with a puff of black smoke.

Panzers moved, testing their tracks, and tank commanders sent Klaus their status reports—most of them were battle-ready. Johann helped Väinü carry a wounded man away from the panzer, then left to find a machine gun.

◇◇◇◇◇◇◇◇◇◇◇◇◇◇◇◇◇◇◇◇◇◇◇◇◇◇

Sixty tanks lined up on both sides of 227, their 75mm guns loaded and ready. Open fields stretched southeast for over two kilometres, with an uninterrupted wall of Russian armour clearly visible on the far side. They formed a continuous, unbroken line on the horizon two thousand metres from Johann, behind clouds of infantry moving toward the German tanks like bugs.

Four kilometres behind Klaus's panzers, hidden under camouflage and untouched by Russian artillery and bombers, hundreds of German artillery pieces opened fire, and the Soviet line disappeared in explosions. The fertile soil that covered the fields spewed upward to form a moving black curtain in front of and among the oncoming Russians, but despite that, they still advanced.

Gradually, scattered T-34s appeared through the maelstrom, and the panthers began to pick them off. They fired as fast as they could load, destroying tank after tank, but others immediately took their place. The infantry advanced, now following the T-34s, like water running down a hill—a flood of sacrifice flowing into holes blown in their ranks by German artillery shells. The tanks took no evasive action but turned thirty degrees to face the panthers. They fired into the German positions, targeting the smashed forest, hoping a panther would be there. The Russian artillery, hampered now by the Luftwaffe, kept up a sporadic barrage, searching for the panzers, but Klaus frequently moved them.

The Russian Air Force, hazed by Luftwaffe fighters, renewed their bombing, now ineffective, as a second wave of Russian tanks and infantry appeared on the southeastern horizon.

Klaus gave the order on the open battle channel for all the tanks and infantry except his squadron to withdraw, and ten kilometres away, Busse's headquarters confirmed without comment.

Loaded with wounded infantry, the panzers followed Johann and his men along a woods road. Healthy men trotted in the gaps between panthers, and what had been a mighty army disappeared in only a few minutes.

Klaus kept his hatch open, his head and shoulders unprotected, a pair of 'donkey ears' binoculars pressed against his face, calling out target ranges to his gunner. Johann pushed the mike button.

"It's time to go, Klaus. Everyone else is safe."

"If we leave now, the Russians will catch the infantry. If you give us a few more minutes, my squadron can stay ahead of the T-34s. They won't catch us unless we want them to...."

Johann hated to agree, but Klaus made sense.

"All right, we'll wait until you're ready. Leave a few rounds of ammunition for the ambush."

Klaus's unit held its ground for another half hour.

A wide, shallow stream flowed through the forest across the path Johann had chosen for the panther's withdrawal, and his men led the squadron across the creek and another five hundred metres past a field of stumps. The clearing was out of sight behind them when they turned right, using the trees for cover. Crushing trees, they circled back to a position where the panzers overlooked the clearing and the only place the tanks chasing them could ford the stream. The range to anything crossing it and driving into the clearing was less than three hundred metres, eliminating the protection of the T-34s' front armour plate. When they entered the clearing, the Russians would have German panzers on their right, exposing the T-34s' soft sides to their guns, and when the survivors of the first salvo turned to face their attackers, the panthers' armour-piercing ammunition would pass through their front plate. The forest prevented their escape to the left, and an attempt to turn around would be suicide.

The panthers would have a clear view of the Russian T-34s as they waded the stream, exposing them until or if they reached the far side of the clearing. The narrow woods road restricted the tanks to a single file, and maneuvering in the clearing presented an additional problem of hundreds of stumps with soft ground between them, adding the danger of hanging up and presenting a stationary target.

Johann and Väinü rode on Klaus's tank, and the only other survivors of Johann's unit climbed on the second panther. Crouched behind the turret so it protected him from the crashing trees, Johann hung onto the edge of Klaus's hatch, and Väinü crouched on the rump with his fingers locked around the rim of the open rear turret hatch. Klaus's panzer crashed through the trees, leaving a path of destruction a blind Russian could follow.

When they reached the stream, following Johann's plan, Klaus drove five hundred metres beyond it before doubling back through the woods in a wide loop. Two-two-seven took a route through the trees that was invisible to tanks crossing the creek.

The panthers were in position and camouflaged when the sound of Russian tanks' diesel engines and crashing trees echoed through the forest. The Russians smelled German blood, and every T-34 commander wanted to be the first to drink it!

Johann said, "It's working, Klaus…they're leaving their scouts and infantry behind—they don't know you're here." He smiled. "Good luck. Väinü and I will leave you to your work."

He slid down the front of the panther to join Väinü and his men, and they ran into the protection of a stand of small trees, well clear of the coming battle.

◇◇◇◇◇◇◇◇◇◇◇◇◇◇◇◇◇◇◇◇◇◇◇◇◇◇◇◇◇◇

All the T-34s had crossed the stream before the panthers fired—Klaus's first shot hit the lead T-34 in the fuel tank, and it exploded in a burst of bent steel and flames. Immediately, the panthers and the only king tiger in the squadron opened up, and the devastation they wrought from such short range was wicked. The first salvo eliminated the nine lead tanks, and when the two at the rear tried to turn back; the second salvo caught them with rumps, fuel tanks and engines exposed. Their carcasses blocked any chance of retreat that their comrades might have had.

The thirteen Russian tanks still moving figured out what was happening while the panthers reloaded for the third salvo. They turned toward their tormentors, hoping sixty degrees of sloped forty-seven-millimetre armour plate would protect them. As the T-34s charged up the hill over stumps and trees, an eighty-eight-mm shell from the tiger's gun penetrated the front armour of the lead Russian. The Russian tanks fired at two hundred metres, and one of their 76 mm shells found the crack under the turret of a panther, sending the top of the tank skyward. Two rounds hit the king tiger, leaving black marks and a groove on the armour plate. The tiger's gun stopped another T-34, and eleven Russian tanks continued the charge, their only chance to save themselves!

As the range diminished, the panthers' armour-piercing shells' effectiveness increased exponentially. Caught in a dilemma where if they turned, the panthers would have the soft sides and rear to shoot at, the Russian tanks had to win or die.

Two T-34s stopped and spun sideways, their bottom skid plates caught on stumps. Men exited the T-34 nearest the panthers and ran

442

for the woods, but the other was swinging its gun when a 75 mm shell passed through the exposed side under the turret and turned the tank into a flaming coffin.

Two Russian tanks turned sideways when a panther shell struck a track, and their crews died when their commander swung the turret rather than abandon the tank. Twenty-one panthers and a king tiger now concentrated their fire on seven T-34s, with tragic results for the Russian crews.

Not one of the thirty Russian tanks survived, and the action cost Klaus one of his panthers and three men.

Johann looked at the devastation, sick to his stomach but elated. He had won again—he was alive—someone else had died. Nothing moved. The disturbing screams of a man caught in a burning T-34 lasted a few seconds, and then the forest was silent except for idling panther engines.

Johann and Väinü climbed on 227, and Johann spoke to Klaus. "You're almost out of ammunition and gas, and we're all exhausted." He turned to Väinü. "We had better find the fuel trucks and somewhere to rest." Väinü consulted the notes and aerial photos in his pack, then raised his head to look at Johann. He swallowed before he spoke, a sure sign of bad news.

"I'm sorry I didn't tell you sooner, Johann, but the time didn't seem right. I found Ian." He shook his head and looked at his feet.

Johann took a breath and looked toward the route out of the forest. "Perhaps he was lucky."

Battle Command headquarters came on the radio that Johann's radioman had strapped to his back. Johann jumped down, took the handset and listened to the instructions. Every tank that could move was to muster at a point ten kilometres to the west. That could only mean Busse expected another attack; it would be his last stand. Klaus received the news a minute later on 227's radio.

Johann shook his head. "I guess we'll be fighting a little more before Abendessen." He climbed up the front armour plate on Panzer 227; Klaus extended his arm to the west and said, "That way?"

Johann confirmed. "Yes, follow the road at the bottom of the hill." Johann turned and sat on the flat steel engine cover with his back against the turret. He said, "Sheisse!" as he banged the butt of his Papa on the steel between his legs, then looked at Väinü, who shrugged his shoulders and lit a cigarette.

The Finn cradled his beloved Russian sniper rifle in his arms, took the burning cigarette out of his mouth, locked his hands, and regarded Johann with something like pity. "Yeah, I thought if anyone would make it, he would."

Johann guided Klaus's squadron to join the remaining Division Nord tanks gathered at a point of woods less than a kilometre from the labyrinth of tunnels and ditches at the end of the Wotan line, where they would take another swipe at the advancing Russians. From there, Väinü had an escape route worked out for the tanks and infantry to the southwest, through a melange of lakes and forests.

<hr>

German artillery pounded the advancing Russians, buying Busse time to set the trap. Artillery scouts gave them their target; the guns fired a few rounds, then moved. They sacrificed firing time but offered Russian artillery and aircraft an elusive target. German aircraft, now out in full force, using the last of their gasoline reserves, strafed and bombed Russian artillery as soon as they fired. The Germans kept up a steady beat of shells and bombs raining down on the Belarusians, who ignored them and kept moving toward their date with destiny in Berlin.

A Russian barrage on the Wotan line, their last obstacle before the Berlin prize, began at five o'clock and lasted forty-five minutes. Camouflaged German tanks waited patiently while thousands of Russian shells dug craters and threw dirt in the air over Hitler's mythical wall. Wehrmacht soldiers, huddled in the safety of bunkers, waited for the inevitable onslaught, knowing it would be their last battle.

Before the barrage ended, Russian tanks and infantry moved ahead, hammered by a German artillery bombardment that crept forward with them, a moving wall of flying dirt, men, and pieces of tanks. When the Russian forces were barely five hundred metres from the trees where the panthers waited, in position to run around the end of the Wotan line, hundreds of hidden and hitherto silent German artillery guns opened fire from the forest on their flank. The Luftwaffe dropped out of a blood-red setting sun, firing their cannons and dropping bombs on the mass of equipment and men.

Johann and his men joined a line of MG-42 machine guns at the edge of the trees, stationed between the waiting German tanks. They fired down on the Russian infantry laid out on the killing fields below them while seventy panthers and fourteen king tigers pummeled the Russian armour. Väinü, firing his Russian sniper rifle, picked off foolish tank commanders who had their heads out of their turrets.

T-34 tanks and tank destroyers burned all over the field, and thousands of Russian infantry died in a German turkey shoot. They had no protection from the fire coming from the woods; too many men were trying to hide behind too few tanks, and the tanks moved too fast.

Johann's Papa was useless at over a hundred metres, so he guided the ammunition belt to where a man fed it into the breech of an MG-42; the gunner fired long bursts into the Russian infantry ranks. When Väinü could find no more commanders to kill, he fired at infantry, trying to choose those who led. One bullet, one man, was Väinü's creed when he held that gun to his shoulder and pulled the trigger.

The Russians finally turned left to get away from the carnage, moving across the field to where the Wotan Line lay at right angles to their path, paying an awful price for exposing their rumps to Klaus's panzers. As the Russian juggernaut approached the Wotan Line, the German defences raked them mercilessly, giving them nowhere to go but straight at them or back down the hill. The Belarussians drove without hesitation through a two-hundred-metre-wide gauntlet of mines, clearing them by sacrificing men and equipment. With thousands of soldiers and hundreds of tanks and guns flooding the fields behind them, there was no way back for the leading forces.

As an inexhaustible flow of men and machines poured into the awful conflagration, panthers, king tigers, and a thousand men with rifles and machine guns ravaged the Russian flank.

The panzers fired until they had only enough fuel and ammunition to get them to safety, then loaded up with wounded and weary infantry and retreated southwest through patches of forest, protected from bombers by the descending cloak of darkness.

Chapter Forty-two

April 1945

We Win!

Surviving is the only glory in war.
Samuel Fuller

Johann, Väinü, and thirty-five exhausted, hungry, orphaned soldiers approached Klaus's panthers, parked on a residential street on the southwest corner of Halbe. Klaus had become the de facto commander of the remaining panzers, and Johann now commanded all that remained of the Ninth Army Jäger Companies.

A few hundred Waffen SS infantry milled around on the street, some gathering around the tanks, others keeping to themselves in small groups. When Johann found 227, the crew sat or leaned on their tank, eating food the Halbe residents had donated to their heroes in the faint hope they would protect them from the Russians. As Johann and Väinü approached, Klaus left the group, climbed inside the tank, and retrieved two PPSh-41 submachine guns. He handed one of them to Lucas, his *Kindersoldat* gunner/loader.

"Expecting a war to break out?" Only Väinü and Johann laughed at Väinü's stupid joke.

"I feel naked without a gun." Klaus patted the side of the magazine. "It's a habit I'll have to break when this is over."

Johann waved toward three service Lastwagen, going from one tank to another, filling them with ammunition and fuel.

"One way or the other, it will all be over soon. I'll bet the pay I will never get that's the last fuel and ammunition we'll see!"

Johann idly watched four Waffen SS soldiers walk across the narrow street to sit on the stone steps of a 19th-century house facing the street opposite Panther 227. The building's design reminded him of Gartenstrasse 18, and his thoughts wandered to Detmold and Barbara.

His attention divided; Johann only vaguely noticed one of the SS soldiers turn his head as though he had heard something. Johann added a few more attention units when the man left the steps and disappeared around the corner of the house. He got Johann's full attention when he returned and shouted to his companions standing near the crew of 227, "Bring the panzerfaust… the cellar is full of Verweigerer—fucking deserters!"

Johann looked at Väinü, who was watching the scene with the same interest, jerked his head toward the soldiers across the street, and Väinü nodded. Klaus tipped his hat, Lucas stepped beside his commander, and the foursome headed off the soldier carrying the anti-tank weapon.

Klaus asked the young soldier in a tone intended to intimidate, "What do you plan to do with that?"

The private looked uneasily toward the man across the street, then at the Waffen SS tank commander. "I'm taking it to my commanding officer."

"We'll go with you."

The nervous soldier led the foursome across the street and behind the house.

The SS officer, a Hauptsturmführer without a company to command, stood at the top of a cellar entrance with a second officer beside him. The nearly horizontal cellar doors lay wide open, and he stared with ghoulish satisfaction into the semi-darkness. When the officer took the panzerfaust from the private, Johann raised the end of his Papa slightly and racked a bullet into the barrel. Väinü followed Johann's lead, and Klaus flipped his safety off; young Lucas did the same.

"You won't be firing that, not on them!" Klaus pointed at the frightened women and Kindersoldaten looking up from the cellar, their faces registering the stoic resignation of a trapped animal. A wise man would have given the panzerfaust back to the private.

Four SS soldiers standing with the officer trained their rifles on the four men who would interfere with the deserters' execution. A murmur rose from the cellar, and then the world became silent. Johann and Väinü, smiling, raised their Papas—the SS soldiers hadn't fired and knew it was too late. They understood what a Papa in the hands of a Jäger soldier could do. Lucas, hardly more than a Kindersoldat himself, waved his gun at the four soldiers, and they lowered their rifles slightly. Johann decided they had no intention of committing suicide by defending their commanding officer.

The officer grinned, accustomed to small challenges to his command. Johann assumed the officer thought he would deal with his men later. He said, "You've got nothing to say about it. These are deserters, and I will lawfully kill them, along with anyone who helps them. It is every German soldier's duty to fight and die for the Führer and the Reich!"

The SS officer raised the anti-tank gun, and Johann was squeezing the trigger when Lucas screamed, shot the officer and held the trigger down until he killed two of the soldiers. The other soldiers only survived because the boy had emptied his magazine. The panzerfaust clattered to the ground, and the other three Papas swung to the two surviving SS soldiers as they threw their guns away and raised their hands.

Brakes squealed; a truck full of fuel barrels stopped beside 227. Johann jerked his head toward the Lastwagen. "We've got this, Klaus. You and Lucas can go back to your tank."

Klaus looked at Johann, then at the dead officer, and then at the dead SS soldiers. He said pleasantly, "Doesn't it warm your heart to see German soldiers so eager to die for the Führer? If only more SS soldiers would demonstrate their loyalty by giving their lives for Hitler..."

Lucas looked at Johann and Viänü, who smiled wickedly and pointed their guns at the soldiers. The soldiers closed their eyes and grimaced, waiting for the end. Johann and the Finn laughed. Lucas and Klaus returned to 227.

During the two hours it took to service the tanks, a dozen Jäger soldiers joined their commander at the house harbouring the deserters. They whispered to one another as they stared at the dead SS officer and his men and the panzerfaust lying between them. When the tanks moved down the street, the Jäger soldiers escorted the two frightened SS soldiers until they were far enough away that Johann was confident they would not return to the cellar.

◇◇◇◇◇◇◇◇◇◇◇◇◇◇◇◇◇◇◇◇◇◇◇◇◇

It was dark when, under heavy fire, Klaus's panzers crossed the Berlin-Dresden autobahn on their way to the Elbe River and an anticipated rendezvous with the Americans. Johann's scouts led the tigers at the centre of the thrust across first, through a storm of artillery fire, and left them to guard the crossing while the Jäger went hunting. It took them fifteen minutes to find the Russian artillery spotters, and almost immediately, the artillery stopped firing.

Johann climbed up to Klaus's cupola, crouched on the flat rump and said, "We should change the crossing point and scatter the tanks. We've put out their eyes, and they are now firing blind, but they are sighted on this spot, and they might get lucky."

"All right, we'll do that!" Klaus spoke into the intercom and ordered his radioman to put him on the battle frequency.

Johann climbed down, and 227 led two panthers across the highway. Russian artillery fired sporadically, with the result Johann expected—shells fell a safe distance from the escaping German tanks.

The tigers and panthers drove down the autobahn, using fuel and valuable ammunition to fight the Russian tanks that appeared. Behind them, they left destroyed and crippled T-34s all along the route. German infantry scurried across and along the road, protected by the panzers. The panthers and tigers took no casualties from the inaccurate shelling and had cleared ten kilometres of the road for the infantry when Klaus took his panthers into the woods. Soldiers who had been separated from command came from all directions to gather around them, and the ragtag army pushed on to Parey on the Elbe River. They planned to surrender to the Americans at Parey—if they would accept them.

◇◇◇◇◇◇◇◇◇◇◇◇◇◇◇◇◇◇◇◇◇◇◇◇◇◇◇◇◇◇◇◇◇◇◇◇◇

In clear weather with a full moon, sixty-four panthers and fourteen king tiger tanks picked their way through the forest, driving along woods roads, monsters moving in and out of black shadows. The sky was beginning to lighten when Johann and Klaus agreed they were far enough from the Russian lines that it was safe to stop. The crews refreshed their panzers' camouflage, then gathered around small fires under a canopy of thick branches. Johann and Viänü made themselves comfortable on their groundsheets with Klaus and Lucas beside them.

Klaus talked while he dug a small hole in the moss with a stick. The digging had no purpose, but Klaus appeared to concentrate on it, speaking as though the conversation were unintended.

"It's been three days since the Americans shook hands with the Russians on the bridge at Torgau. What do you think that means?"

"Yes, it's all over the camp." Johann dug out his last cigarette, its value growing as he contemplated lighting it. "I suppose it means the war is over, but the fighting isn't. Wenck won't quit until the last refugee is across the Elbe, and the Russians won't quit until they have Hitler's head on a pike!"

The cigarette was a gift from Klaus, who had vowed to quit and given Johann half a pack, and this would finish it. As Johann lit the cigarette, Klaus's expression was of a man full of regret.

Lucas said, "I don't understand. If the Americans and Russians met on the Elbe River, why would we still fight? Do we fight the Americans or the Russians?"

Johann sucked on the cigarette, then flicked the ash on the groundsheet. "Torgau is a symbol, and it's a hundred kilometres from Berlin on purpose. The Russians are tearing Berlin apart; they aren't leaving one brick still sitting on another. Those bastards want blood, and they're getting it." He looked at his cigarette as though it tasted terrible, then continued.

"There is a reliable rumour that the Americans and Russians made a deal, and just like the Russians waited for the Germans to destroy Warsaw, the Americans agreed not to cross the Elbe until the Russians levelled Berlin and murdered its citizens. And they will kill as many Germans as it takes to satisfy their vendetta. There is a rumour that thousands who couldn't or wouldn't leave are committing suicide. Just like Warsaw, a million refugees who want to be on the American side of the Elbe are stranded on the Russian side, starving, waiting to be murdered. The meeting in Torgau was for the newspapers. The people in America think the war is over, so the Russians can satisfy their bloodlust without worrying about the naive Americans' interference."

Klaus jammed the end of the stick hard into the hole he had dug with it, trying to push it into the hard earth. He gave up and said, "General Wenck is back and running the Twelfth Army. We are fighting under him now in the Kurmark Regiment. Wenck is determined to keep a corridor open between the Americans at Parey and the Germans escaping from Berlin. The forests are full of refugees from Poland and the parts of

Germany the Russians have overrun, and the Russians are hunting them."
He lifted the stick and jammed it down hard enough to break it. "Wenck
gave me our orders over the battle channel today, and we must help the
Twelfth Army keep the corridor open. Wenck is trying to get as many
refugees across the Elbe to the Americans as he can."

Marcus, the other loader/gunner on 227, asked what every man
there wanted to know, "So, we fight to the last man for refugees…most
of them Poles? Why should we fight for them and not for Berlin?"

Johann's cigarette was burning the tips of his fingers, but he gritted
his teeth and put it between his lips, pulled on it until the burning
tobacco touched them, then spit it on Viänü's groundsheet, and Viänü
crushed it with the butt of his Papa.

Johann locked his fingers in front of his knees. "The Russians
would like that—they wouldn't have to spread their forces out looking
for us—the lambs would come to the slaughter. No, we cannot save
Berlin, the Reich, or the Führer, but we can save women and children
trying to get to safety. I would consider it an honour to fight for a just
cause for a change. Otherwise, I have nothing about my part in this
war that I would want to tell my grandchildren."

⚬⚬⚬⚬⚬⚬⚬⚬⚬⚬⚬⚬⚬⚬⚬⚬⚬⚬⚬⚬⚬⚬⚬⚬⚬⚬⚬⚬⚬⚬⚬⚬

During the following tumultuous days, Johann's Jäger Company located Russian Armour and infantry, planned traps and ambushes, and
Klaus's panzers carried them out. On Mayday, the panzers fought a
sustained battle against Russian artillery and tanks that left 227 and
its comrades desperately short of ammunition. Six of his panthers and
all of the king tigers ran out of gas, leaving eight panthers still able to
fight, but the battle would be brief.

Wenck's Battle Command called and ordered what remained of
the division's armour to Genthin, where they would guard the refugee
corridor at a critical point. When that section collapsed, thousands of
refugees and Ninth Army soldiers would be trapped and at the mercy
of the Russians. Command offered no assurance of fuel or ammunition, only "Viel Glück!" Johann heard Klaus say, "Luck isn't what we
need—luck doesn't kill Russians or put power to our tracks," as he put
down his microphone.

In the dark hours before dawn, Johann was waiting when 227

reached the road north of Genthin near the Elbe-Havel canal bridge. Johann climbed up on the tank to sit beside Klaus, and the driver shut off the engine to save precious fuel.

Johann said, "The Russians are five kilometres east of us and heading down the road as fast as their infantry can walk. Truckloads of infantry are coming behind them."

Klaus asked, "How long before they're here?"

A stream of humanity flowed past the panther—women, children, old and young; wounded, tired soldiers and civilians walking together, talking, and occasionally, laughing. They were only a few hours from the Elbe and the Americans, and the sight of German panzers gave them hope.

"Two hours—no more. They will leave the Landstrasse before the canal bridge and attack us from the south—there is no question they know we're here. There is no high ground, and you won't see them until they are less than a thousand metres from your position. I suggest you scatter your tanks along the edge of the woods fifty metres apart. Back them between the trees as far as you can and still see to shoot."

Klaus spoke into the turret. "Marcus, how much ammunition do we have?"

Johann heard Marcus answer immediately—he didn't have to count it. "We have two rounds of seventy-five and a box of machine-gun ammunition."

"Kristian, fuel?" Klaus asked the driver.

Johann heard, "If they hit our fuel tank, it won't explode."

Klaus repeated, "If they..."

Johann interrupted. "I heard."

Johann didn't speak for what seemed a long time. When he did, it was with a tone of finality.

"You know we should surrender—if we don't, your men will die."

Klaus played with the cupola's latch. Finally, he said, "We are Waffen SS—they will kill us anyway—what do you want to do?"

Johann said, "I'm not going to get home; nothing matters now."

Klaus answered thoughtfully. "We will delay them for as long as possible. Every five minutes we buy will mean safety for another hundred people."

Johann cleared his throat, then said, "We've got a couple of ammunition belts and an MG-42 on the back of your tank. We'll set it up over there." He waved his hand vaguely to a spot on the edge of the woods.

"Johann, it's been a pleasure." Klaus shook Johann's hand.

"Gleichfalls." Johann slid to the ground.

In the morning twilight, a dozen T-34 Russian tanks, a 105 tank destroyer, and hundreds of infantry moved into the open field in front of the panthers, arrogantly exposing themselves to their big guns. Johann had twenty-two men, and Klaus had eight camouflaged panthers waiting for them with only enough gas and ammunition for a brief skirmish. The battle would be short and final.

When the Russians turned and stopped to face the pitiful ragtag band that had once been the pride of Germany, Johann's men had their fingers on their triggers, waiting for orders to fight and die with honour. Russian soldiers gathered behind the T-34s, a thousand metres from the panthers, intimidating the refugees on the road that ran beside the forest in front of Germany's last hope. The refugees ran into the woods, past Klaus's tanks, and disappeared. The Russians held their fire—they had bigger fish in their net and wanted them alive.

Johann felt the turret move under him and watched the gun follow the T-34 in the centre of the approaching line.

The Russians stopped but didn't fire, so the mass of humanity resumed their journey—there was no alternative—refugees crowded behind those who hesitated, poured around them into the field and onto the road in front of the panthers, running if they could, sensing the coming battle.

Klaus pointed for Johann's benefit, then spoke into the turret. "A half-track is coming our way—it's showing a white flag—don't shoot."

Klaus pointed at the half-track halfway across the field, and Johann nodded. Klaus spoke into the intercom. "Leutnant Finke and I are going to meet the Russians. If they do anything aggressive, shoot the tanks!"

Klaus joined Johann, who had slid to the ground ahead of him. Väinü joined them as they approached the half-track.

A man stepped out of the vehicle and saluted. Johann made a half-hearted attempt to return it. The Russian said, "You have no chance. Surrender, or you will force us to kill you!"

The officer sitting in the half-track leaned over and spoke to the translator. When he finished, the translator said, "If you surrender, we will allow you to live and the refugees to pass."

Suddenly filled with inspiration, Johann said, "What you offer is generous, and I would gladly accept, but I must get approval from headquarters. They will answer in an hour."

The translator spoke to the officer; the officer discussed something with him and then nodded his head. The translator turned to Johann and said, "That is agreeable—you have one hour!"

He saluted again, stepped onto the running board and into the seat of the half-track. He was still closing the door when it jerked ahead.

Klaus said to Väinü, "We all heard the translator...but what did the officer actually say?" His tone left no doubt what he thought the officer had said.

Väinü said, "The actual words aren't important. But I can tell you that he will kill every man with a Totenkopf on his uniform, and if Johann and I are lucky, we will go to the gulags."

"What about the refugees?"

"He didn't mention them, but they will go after the refugees as soon as they finish with us. That's who they were chasing when they found us."

Johann said, with a tone meant to end the discussion, "We are not going to surrender—we must buy as much time for the refugees as we can."

Klaus stepped up onto the front armour of 227. As he walked up the slope, he said, "I have no contact with headquarters, but I will send a message on a frequency the Russians listen to—they will think I am negotiating with Wenck, and that could buy us some time."

Johann said, "You are a devious bastard, aren't you?"

Väinü said, "Keep a finger on the trigger; that Russian bastard hasn't got a lot of patience!" He made a rude gesture toward the Russian tanks.

Klaus climbed into his cupola, leaving the hatch open. Johann heard him say, "Simon, tell everyone to wait, then switch to the battle frequency—the one the Russians have. I will talk from here."

Johann heard Klaus's side of the conversation with a fictitious battle headquarters.

"227 to battle, over." He asked for General Wenck and apparently was told he would have to wait for him to return.

An hour later, Klaus called Wenck again and discussed an "honourable" surrender of his panzers. At the end of the conversation, Klaus joined Johann and Väinü, and they walked across the field. The halftrack met them halfway.

The Russian vehicle stopped, and the translator stepped out.

Johann said, "We had to wait for General Wenck, but he finally talked to us. He must check with Berlin because the Führer has ordered all forces to hold to the last man." He smiled at the shocked Russian. "Of course, that is not the choice we will make, but General Wenck must ask. The only condition he requested is that you respect the Geneva Convention."

The translator spoke to the officer, who became more irritated by the second. He said two words to the translator, and the man turned to Johann.

"You have one hour!" The man stepped on the running board and had the door open when the officer shouted at the driver, and the tracks spun. He had just gotten seated when the half-track reached the T-34s and stopped at what Johann decided had to be the command tank.

<hr>

When Johann, Väinü and Klaus reached 227, Klaus climbed through his hatch. Johann and Väinü sat on the flat rump.

"It's working out better than I thought." Klaus sat in his cupola, his "Donkey Ears" on the edge of the turret. "If we can keep them talking until just before dark, we may have the option of running into the woods before they know we're gone."

Johann said, shaking his head, "No, that's not going to happen... Russians aren't stupid. We will have to face the music one way or another before it's too dark to shoot. And we must shoot before they do."

"That would mean that every one of our men would die..."

Johann watched the Russian tanks through his binoculars. "Not necessarily—if we hit them when they least expect it, we may have time to get far enough away that the infantry won't catch us. We could work out a plan that will get at least a few of us out alive!"

"If we give our men even a small chance, they will take it." Klaus spoke into the turret, "Simon, call up the tank commanders and tell them to meet me in the woods behind 227. They must leave every five minutes, one at a time, as though they need to have a piss."

Klaus said to Johann. "I will go first. Follow me in five minutes." He stepped out of the cupola and climbed to the ground.

An hour later, Johann and Klaus returned with a plan agreed upon by everyone. Johann explained it to Väinü.

"The infantry will begin leaving now, a few at a time. I want you to send a man with each group to lead them to the river."

When Väinü nodded, Johann went on.

"When the infantry is clear, the panzers will hit the Russians as hard as they can. The panzer crews will get out while the Russians are still in shock—hopefully, most of them will make it—and then we will run like hell!"

"We? Aren't we leaving with the infantry?" Väinü grinned. He and Johann had the same penchant for being the last to leave.

"We will wait for the survivors from the panzers. They can't walk a straight line outside a steel box, and they can't fight unless they have a cannon!" He grinned, then became serious. "They need us to show them the way to the Elbe."

The bright light of day faded, and Klaus left his cupola to join Johann and Väinü on the road. The small half-track stopped beside them; a man in the back seat handed Klaus a piece of paper and drove off.

When Johann and Klaus arrived at 227, Johann said, "Did you see which tank he went to? The commanding officer is in that tank!" He handed Klaus the piece of paper. "That's the frequency Wenck should use to contact Russian headquarters, but I think it's probably okay if you use it."

Klaus slapped Johann on the back and laughed. "I've already made a note of that. Two tanks to the right of centre."

Johann grinned; he had come to the same conclusion. Klaus climbed into his cupola and held out a piece of paper so the loader could grab it.

When he did, Klaus said, "Marcus, give that to Simon and tell him to dial it on the VHF. I will let him know when to connect."

Klaus leaned over so that his head was just above the gunner. Johann heard him say, "Move the gun two tanks to the right...I want you to sight on the turret of that tank; your second shot will be for the one beside it. Take fifteen minutes to move the gun." He smiled at Johann and winked.

Forty-five minutes passed, and then the light rapidly faded. Two-two-seven sat quiet, engine off, with its gun sighted on the T-34 that the half-track had twice returned to.

Listening on the field radio, Johann heard Klaus say, "General Zhukov?"...a pause, then... "Trakhni tebya voobshche!"

Väinü chuckled. Johann said to his radioman, "Change to the battle frequency," and immediately heard 227 start, then run its engine up to battle power. The radio crackled as Klaus shouted, "Schiess die Sheisser!" on the open battle frequency.

<hr>

Two-two-seven fired—the Russian command tank's turret upended onto a group of soldiers standing beside it. The MG-42 machine gun opened up on the Russian infantry as those sitting and standing behind tanks stood up or left their shelter to see what was happening and suffered the consequences. Klaus's panther fired again; the shell struck the T-34 beside the command tank. At the same instant, a puff of smoke announced that the Russian gunner had fired before he died.

From eight hundred metres, a shell from a 76 mm T-34 could not penetrate the front armour of a healthy panther, but the armour-piercing round struck 227 full on the front armour at a spot that had already taken two direct hits, and the shell exploded inside the panther.

Klaus immediately climbed out of his cupola, turned, twisted on his belly, and his head and arms disappeared into the hatch. Johann ran up the front of the smoking tank and threw himself down opposite Klaus.

"I'm here, Klaus," he said as he put his arms inside the hatch.

"The torsion bar tube is bent upward, and the turret is off its track, jamming Lucas's foot. Try to grab his collar so you can pull with me."

Johann could only get one arm far enough down the hatch to grab Lucas's collar, but he pulled with all the strength he had, leveraging with his other hand on the edge of the hatch.

Lucas screamed, but the combined strength of Klaus and Johann pulled him free. They dragged him onto the back of the now burning tank, beat out the flames on his pants, then pulled him off the rump and put him on his feet, sheltered from whizzing bullets by the panther. He whimpered and tried to stand, but his legs buckled. Väinü, sheltering behind the panther in a kneeling position, fired his Russian sniper rifle—one bullet, one man. A cannon shell bounced off 227's turret and plowed through the trees without exploding.

Johann pulled one of Lucas's arms; Klaus took the other and yelled in his ear, "Run, or we all die!" Johann pointed with his free hand; Lucas worked his legs, then ran.

Johann talked while he ran, "By now, they've figured out that we've run away...let's hope they've had enough of us!"

Viänü appeared with eight men. Explosions echoed through the dark woods as Viänü said, "They are still firing at the panthers. Without their commander, the infantry isn't interested in chasing us."

Johann pulled Lucas's arm, and Klaus ran behind the boy, pushing him if he slowed. They ran through gaps between the trees, avoiding paths or roads until, finally, with darkness hiding the trees, Väinü and his men stopped, and Johann breathlessly announced to Klaus that they could safely rest.

Johann gathered the men around him in the almost total darkness and laid out the route to the Elbe and the Americans. Lucas sat on a patch of moss five metres from the men, his arms folded over his knees. Johann felt sorry for him; the boy had shit his pants.

Klaus left the group and walked over to Lucas. He took the boy to a spruce tree he could use as a backrest and then looked at his wounds. When Lucas stood up, he headed for Johann.

Johann acknowledged Lucas with a smile as the boy said, "I'm sorry, sir; I'm sorry I'm a coward." Lucas waited in tears for Johann's response, and Johann responded as quickly as he could.

"It's alright, son." Then he added, chuckling, "Perhaps you should walk at the back of the line with Klaus."

Before they started walking, the Russian Artillery behind them began firing.

Lucas, nervous and confused, asked, "What are they firing at, sir? Aren't they firing toward the Americans?"

Johann again put his hand on the young soldier's shoulder. "I'd say they're targetting the refugees along the river, and if that's the case, we can't help them." He pointed at a hole in the woods. "Through there... we had better get going."

Explosions roared from the direction that Johann had pointed. A cold rain began to fall, softly at first, then harder.

Johann said, "Ranging shots; the real barrage will start in a few minutes." The parade assembled behind him. A few seconds passed, and the artillery fire increased to a steady pace.

The rain increased with the pounding barrage, and ground fog, combined with darkness, restricted visibility to a few metres. Väinü passed Johann, and Johann followed in his tracks.

They walked for fifteen minutes, putting another five hundred metres between them and the Russian guns while a steady stream of shells screamed over their heads.

<hr>

And then, the sound changed. Artillery shells came from the opposite direction; the sound of them exploding near the Russians mingled with the Russian guns' sharp cracks.

Johann signalled Väinü to stop, then collected the men. When he had accounted for everyone, Johann said, "Those shells are coming from the west...the Elbe. There are no German guns between here and the river, so the only possibility is that the Americans are shooting at the Russians."

Klaus said, "Perhaps we should wait here until we know what's going on."

Johann stepped toward Klaus. "Yes, I agree. While we're waiting, I've got dry socks and boots in my pack. All of my men carry dry socks, and we grease our boots, so let's get you and Lucas some dry feet, or we'll have to carry you. Tell us the size of your feet, and we'll see what we can do."

Lucas sat on a waterproof Zeltbahn that one of the infantrymen had loaned him and removed his boots and socks. The injured foot had swollen slightly, but Johann's spare boots fit him perfectly. When he stood up, he laughed like a little girl who had just opened her favourite Christmas present. When he tried to return the infantryman's groundsheet, the man showed him how to wrap it around his neck like a poncho. He said he had a spare, but Johann didn't see him put it on.

The Russians stopped firing, and seconds later, the scream of shells from the Elbe stopped.

Johann said, "The Americans wouldn't fire warning shots at the Russians unless they could fire accurately...so...they must have observers where they can see the Russian guns." Klaus nodded, but no one said anything, waiting for Johann to go on. The Russian artillery began firing again, and immediately, the Americans returned fire. The Russian guns again ceased firing, and the Americans did the same.

Johann said, "If we can find the American observers, we can surrender to them. They have to follow the woods to get back to the Elbe, or they would have to cross open fields among the refugees—I don't believe they would do that. If I'm right, they have to pass us, so we could spread out and wait. I think we have a good chance of finding them. What do you think?" He looked at Väinü, then Klaus.

Lucas answered, "Wouldn't they try to kill us?"

Johann responded as though Lucas had asked a stupid question. "Yes, of course they would, if they could...so, we will capture them first, then surrender." He touched Lucas's arm. "Don't worry, this is what we do. You and Klaus will wait here, and we'll come back and get you when we've found the Americans."

<h1 style="text-align:center">CHAPTER FORTY-THREE</h1>

APRIL 1945

Home is where the heart is

Gaius Plinius Secundus, Roman naval commander

THE RAIN SLOWED TO AN ANEMIC SPLUTTER, and the Russians began shooting again. The Americans returned fire—the Russians stopped, the Americans did likewise, and the forest was suddenly silent except for water dripping off the trees.

Johann, Väinü and the last eight men from their Jäger companies dispersed to cover as much of the possible return route the American observers would use as they could, concealing themselves in small bushes growing at the bottom of a ridge. Johann slipped into a trance he often used to shorten wait time and, in a dream state, let his mind drift to Barbara and Thomas, and then to the fish. He smiled, then chuckled. Väinü made a slight 'sssh' sound; Johann cut the laugh and tried to return to the present reality. Even though the Elbe was a two-hour walk to the west, Johann considered his chances of getting to Detmold were low. But they were infinitely better than they had been a couple of hours ago, and euphoria overcame the depression Johann's sense of logic tried to impose on him. He wondered if this was the rapture a dying man feels just before death.

An hour later, Johann heard hushed voices in the dark fifty metres in front of him and getting closer. They spoke English in soft, unintelligible tones, but the sound carried in the windless night. Still chatting, they walked between Johann and Väinü, and it was apparent from the conversation and the voices that there were two of them. Johann whistled, jumped, grabbed the rifle from the nearest American, threw it into the bushes and placed the blade of his knife against the man's throat. The surprised victim yelped but didn't struggle. Väinü put his man on the ground, on his back, staring up at the business end of a Nagant sniper rifle. Johann whistled twice, and the other men joined them.

"Shit!" said Väinü's man, "Please don't kill us!" Then, "Fuck, you don't understand English!"

Johann hesitated, trying to understand what the man had said. He decided it didn't matter, took the knife from his prisoner's throat, and tried what little school English he knew. "We will surrender. Okay?"

The American laughed nervously, relieved but hesitant—the situation was preposterous. "It's either that, or you will kill us?"

Johann shook his head and showed his teeth in a broad smile. "No, we don't kill you; we go away. You promise you do not kill us, and we surrender. Okay?"

"Yep! Sounds like a good deal to me!" the young American chuckled uncertainly. Johann sheathed his knife. Väinü took his victim's hand and pulled him to his feet.

Johann said, "We are ten." He held up all his fingers, then pointed to where he had left Klaus and Lucas and raised two fingers. "Two more. I get, you wait."

Johann stretched his arm to surrender his Papa, then reneged and pulled it back. He couldn't think of appropriate English words, so he put his hand on the American's shoulder, nodded, and left to find Lucas and Klaus. When he returned, Väinü and his men were eating American 'K rations.' Everyone shook hands, and Johann offered his gun to the Americans.

The young sergeant waved it away. "No, I don't want your gun until we're at the river. I'm not supposed to be on this side of the river, so if I kill a Russian, there'll be hell to pay." He smiled broadly, like a Cheshire cat. "But you can do whatever you need to as long as you aren't officially my prisoner—understood?"

Johann didn't understand anything other than he should keep his Papa, and he wasn't going to argue about that. He began to think this might work out.

◇◇◇◇◇◇◇◇◇◇◇◇◇◇◇◇◇◇◇◇◇◇◇◇◇◇◇◇◇◇◇◇◇◇◇◇

The night became brighter, the clouds dispersed, and the moon rose. When Johann heard a metallic click, he could see men's shapes and estimated the sound had come from thirty metres ahead, and when he tried to identify the source, moving his head to see between trees and branches, he caught a glimpse of a cigarette's glow. He grabbed the American's arm and pulled him to the ground beside him. The column immediately crouched behind them. Väinü silently worked his way to Johann, and Johann put his mouth against his ear and whispered, "There is something ahead that isn't right. I heard a click, I saw men's shapes, and one of them lit a cigarette. Perhaps you should take a couple of men and see who's there."

Väinü nodded, and the American looked curiously at Johann; Johann put his finger on his lips, and Väinü and his men disappeared. A few minutes later, the Finn returned alone and whispered in Johann's ear.

"Russians... six of them."

Johann put his mouth against the American Sergeant's ear. "Russians." Johann searched for English words. "You talk...say you're American...say you are...friend?"

"I'll try, but I don't speak Russian," the American drawled.

"Väinü can talk Russian. You talk English."

The American yelled, "We are Americans, and we have German prisoners!" Silence. A few seconds later, Väinü shouted a long sentence in Russian, and a Russian voice answered. The Americans began to stand up, and Johann and Väinü pulled them down as Johann said, "Wait. Don't trust Russians."

He barely had the words out when a stream of bullets passed over his head, homing in on the American's shouts.

"That's enough for me!" The American, obviously angry, raised his rifle, and Johann put his hand on the barrel and whispered, "Stay!"

Seconds passed, and then a few short bursts of machine-gun fire echoed through the woods; minutes after that, Väinü's men returned.

"Prisoners?" The American asked expectantly, and Johann translated. Väinü's men looked at one another, shrugged their shoulders and shook their heads. The American exhaled and said, "That's what I thought..." Then quietly, "...Yeah...better that way."

"All okay?" Johann asked. The American smiled and nodded his head. "Yeah, all okay."

The American sergeant stayed behind Johann until they left the woods and walked into a moonlit field covered with refugees and German soldiers waiting to cross the Elbe. Everywhere Johann looked he saw dead, wounded and dying people, some with grotesque wounds. The Russian bombardment had been accurate—Johann deduced that the ones they had met were the returning artillery observers.

Johann said in English, "Shrapnel from Russian shells... very bad!"

The Americans stopped to help a woman whose child was bleeding from a leg wound. Johann put a bootlace tourniquet on her daughter's leg.

They spent the next three hours working their way downhill toward the Elbe, now less than a kilometre away. They rigged pressure bandages and put tourniquets made from their boot laces and rags on stubs of missing or damaged legs and arms until, carrying wounded children with mothers trailing them, they reached the bank of the river without boot laces or shirts.

As Johann walked shoulder-to-shoulder with the American sergeant, Lucas caught up, touched his arm, and Johann stopped. Lucas said, "I want to find my own way home. What should I do?"

Johann's attention followed the American sergeant. A child had taken his hand and pulled him to where her mother lay. The mother tried to get to her feet, but one of her legs wouldn't respond. Johann fought the urge to help and turned to Lucas.

"Pretend you need to pee, and I'll cover for you." As Lucas turned to go, Johann grabbed his arm and spoke into his ear. "Get rid of the uniform as soon as you can; you might get away with saying you are a refugee."

Lucas turned to go, but Johann held his arm and said, "Are you sure about this? The Russians are probably on the other side of the river, and you are still wearing a Wehrmacht uniform. If you don't surrender here, the Americans or the Russians may shoot you if they find you running around on the roads. The safest place for a German soldier right now is in an American prison camp!"

Lucas kicked the ground with his Wehrmacht boot. Johann shrugged. He didn't like the boy's chances, but Lucas had proven he was a man and able to make rational decisions.

"Okay, I see you've made up your mind...let's hope you stink bad enough they won't want you within a hundred metres of them!" He laughed and squeezed Lucas's shoulder so hard the boy winced. "Go upriver before you cross; then head due west and stay in the woods as much as you can. Travel only at night, and for about…" Johann looked at the river, then Lucas… "three hundred kilometres. You should be home in a week." He passed his compass to Lucas and saluted. A surprised Lucas waved a half-hearted attempt.

Johann's group had joined the people on the edge of the river where rubber boats and makeshift rafts, manned illegally by American soldiers and German civilians, shuttled people across. He and the American carried the woman to a rubber boat as it touched the shore. The wounded, the children and their mothers got priority seating. The demand was endless, but everyone made room for the German Leutnant and the American sergeant to wade alongside the boat and deposit the woman inside. Johann picked up the little girl and sat her beside her mother.

The American smiled at the girl. "Can I count on you to take good care of your mother?" Johann translated what he thought the American had said, and the girl nodded. The mother took the sergeant's hand and said, "God bless you" in English. She looked at Johann, halfway between smiling and crying, and he knew what she was saying without words.

Klaus, Johann, and his men gave their weapons to the Americans, who threw them in the river. They sat on the river bank and ate from the Americans' seemingly endless supply of 'K' rations while waiting for daylight.

◇◇◇◇◇◇◇◇◇◇◇◇◇◇◇◇◇◇◇◇◇◇◇◇◇◇◇◇◇◇◇◇◇◇◇◇

When the morning twilight lightened the eastern sky, they worked their way across a twisted railway bridge resting at a forty-five-degree angle, half-on, half-off the pylons. They crawled hand over hand, with the American Sergeant leading the parade.

As soon as they reached hard ground, Johann and his men gathered in a knot, shook hands, slapped one another's back and laughed like adolescents at their first drunken party. The sun threatened to appear on the Berlin side of the river, and as Johann watched its burning edge peek over the ridge between the lakes, he realized his euphoria had not been false—he felt that it would go on forever.

When a jeep pulled up in front of the sergeant, the American spotters exchanged names and addresses with their German charges. A dozen soldiers escorted Johann, Väinü and Klaus to a covered American troop truck, and two boarded it with them, carrying rifles.

The ride was bizarre—as hard as Johann tried, his mind could not give up the sense of imminent battle it had known for four years. During the bumpy, noisy ride, the men said little, each man lost in what felt like a daydream. Except Väinü—he slept.

The countryside rolling past showed little sign of war, and four-and-a-half hours later, the American army truck stopped near Bremen at an American base confiscated from the German Luftwaffe. Two American soldiers led them to a building in a compound reserved for officer prisoners.

An intelligence officer and his secretary asked basic questions from a list, and a young non-com showed them to their steel-framed beds. Johann, Väinü, and Klaus sat down on their thin mattresses facing one another, and Klaus began to laugh.

"We made it!" Klaus slapped Väinü on the back…hard…too hard… but the Finn didn't wince.

"Jawohl!" Johann leaned ahead and shook Klaus's hand, saying, "We win! We're alive, and we are in Germany!"

Väinü shook his head. "I won't win until I am in Finland."

"Will you tell me what you have in Finland?" Johann knew nothing about Väinü's personal life because the Finn had always refused to discuss it when anyone brought it up.

He took a deep breath and said, "Like everyone else, I have parents and a sister. I had a brother until the Russians killed him—I buried him in the mountains. When I get back to Finland, I will take him home."

Johann said, "The war won't be over for me until Hitler is dead, but that won't be long now—Stalin will want his head hanging over the door to the Kremlin as soon as possible. Let's hope you go home soon and Stalin gets his trophy even sooner."

They struggled for a few minutes to find conversation, then gave up. Väinü left the room and was the first to locate the bathroom and showers. He returned more excited than he had been when they crossed the Elbe.

"Hot water! Showers! Let's go!"

Klaus immediately jumped up and followed Väinü. Johann waved goodbye and sat down at a small desk in the corner. A bottle of ink, a pen and a pile of paper sat ready for whoever wanted to use them. Johann slid a sheet onto the table, screwed the top off the ink, dipped the pen and began writing.

A soft knock on the door interrupted Johann before he had the greeting written—a young adjutant came in without waiting, carrying three bundles of clothes piled on his arms. He saluted as well as he could with the load, pointed at the bed nearest the desk and said, "You?" Johann nodded. "Little guy?" He stood beside the second bed, his open hand indicating someone short, and Johann nodded again. He dropped the bundle, put the last one on the remaining bed, saluted smartly and held the position until Johann saluted. The young soldier crossed the room with a grin, stopped at the door, looked at Johann and pinched his nose.

Johann crumpled the letter he had started and began again. The euphoria disappeared as fast as it had come, and his mood crashed so far that he had to fight back the tears. He wrote, *"Liebling,"* and stared at the page. Finally, the words came.

"The war is over for me, and I will be home soon."

He cursed and scratched a line through the sentence, tore up the page and began again.

"Liebling,"

The door opened, and Väinü marched in, wrapped in a towel.

Johann held the pen poised to write. "The bed nearest the door is yours. The clothes are yours too." He wiped the pen on his underwear and stood up. "I've been told I need a shower."

Väinü quickly verified Johann's observation. "Yes, you do. I was going to say something earlier, but you were carrying a gun."

Johann grunted. "Did you find that towel in the shower room?"

"Yes, but you can take this one. Someone will take your clothes while you are in the shower, and I doubt you will see them again. Apparently, a German Wehrmacht uniform is not appropriate here."

Johann met Klaus on the way to the shower. He was carrying a towel and wearing nothing but a stupid grin, and he passed without a greeting. Five minutes later, Johann knew why. He spent fifteen minutes in the shower, and, as advertised, his clothes were gone when he came out; a large fluffy towel was in their place, and, like Klaus, he carried it back to the room.

An hour later, an American lieutenant, his hat under his arm, dressed in pressed pants and a starched shirt, stepped into the room. He saluted, put his hat on a table, and sat on a hard chair—the translator who had followed him into the room stood beside him.

"My name is Lieutenant John Randall. I want each of you to introduce yourself and shake hands with me. We are no longer going to try to kill one another." He shook each man's hand, and they sat on the beds.

"I'm here to tell you what happens next." The suddenly serious look on Lieutenant John Randall's face told Johann it probably wouldn't be good.

Lieutenant Randall looked from one man to another as he spoke.

"First, I want to thank you for escorting our men back to the river. I don't know that they would have made it without you."

All he got was a blank look until the translator spoke. Then Johann said, "I speak a little English, but not much. Speak slow, and I can understand."

Randall acknowledged Johann with a nod and went on. "Johann and Väinü, being Wehrmacht soldiers, will not be interrogated beyond what has already been done. You..." he singled out Klaus... "are Waffen SS, and we're not sure yet what that means. Orders from God are that we should hold you separate from the other prisoners until we sort things out."

Lieutenant Randall smiled while the translator delivered the response.

Klaus nodded slowly.

The lieutenant raised his hand and shook his head when he saw Klaus's reaction. "I spoke with the colonel, and he agreed that, for now, you can stay here, but only on the condition that you speak openly with our interrogators and explain the difference between what you do and what they do. Your future is uncertain until we find out what it means to be in any army with *SS* in its name." He looked at Johann and Väinü.

The translator did his job, and Johann jumped in.

"He does the same things as Wehrmacht soldiers, but he's better at it. I can tell you from experience that there are divisions within the Waffen SS that have done things Christ can't forgive, but the Waffen SS panzer divisions, such as Klaus's, fought like the rest of us and are the best soldiers Germany has. Klaus is the best of those soldiers."

The translator translated, using more words than Johann had used, and Randall nodded. "And you…what did you do?" The lieutenant looked from Väinü to Johann.

Johann answered. "We are hunters, artillery spotters and scouts. We work mostly at night."

The translator explained, but Johann noted that he spoke far too long.

"I understand what your job was, Jäger tells me that, but I have to ask…did you shoot any prisoners?"

Johann shook his head. "No, we didn't shoot prisoners. We took very few prisoners after discovering what happened to them, and we couldn't take survivors and wounded back to headquarters, so we left them where they were. We hit hard without warning and then ran, inflicting as much damage as we could in the shortest time possible. We gave our enemy no opportunity to surrender, and few of them tried."

Randall nodded when he heard the translation.

"Have you ever knowingly shot an unarmed man?"

Johann didn't need the translator.

"I have shot men sleeping in their tent, firing cannons, standing guard in holes, and running away from their burning T-34s… And I have cut men's throats while they slept. They had a gun close to them, if not in their hands, and none of them tried to surrender. If I had hesitated to check whether they had a gun ready to kill me or stopped to ask whether they wanted to surrender, I would have died in my first action."

Johann understood enough that he knew the translator had gotten the spirit right. Lieutenant Randall looked directly at Johann when he spoke. "You are wise to be honest. My report will say that you were a regular soldier, a scout and a spotter. I will say that you acted in the spirit of honourable and legal combat." He turned to the translator. "There is no need to translate." He pivoted back to Johann, "Is there?" Johann shook his head. He opened his mouth to ask whether the pilot of the Mosquito that had killed his twelve-year-old daughter had seen a gun in her hand, but Randall's wagging head convinced him to shut it.

Väinü broke a momentary silence. "So, what's next? How long will I be here? I want to go home, and I'm sure we all feel that way!" Väinü leaned back in his chair while the Lieutenant explained.

"I'm afraid that all we can offer you right now is a stint in Texas. Except for a few unfortunate German soldiers in France, we are taking all the officers to camps in the States, and you will go there until we sort things out here. Germany will have no government for a few years; the Russians are flattening Berlin, and we can only watch. I can't imagine what they will do with Hitler, Himmler and the rest of that scum, and I can't say that I care."

The translator looked at his lieutenant, reluctant to translate. He got no sympathy and did his best to soften the blow by adding, "…the security will be accommodating to those who behave themselves, and the officers will be well treated. Texas is very nice, but it can get pretty hot in the summer. I am from Texas, and…."

"That's enough, corporal; these men don't care how nice Texas is; they want to see their families!"

Klaus asked, "Will we receive mail? Will you deliver letters to our families?"

Johann was happy to hear Klaus ask the question and added, "The German Feldpost isn't working so well right now."

Randall seemed to understand without the interpreter's help.

"Yes, of course, the mail will go through, but I can do better…" He looked at each man in turn. "Give me phone numbers, and I will arrange for you to call home as soon as possible."

◇◇◇◇◇◇◇◇◇◇◇◇◇◇◇◇◇◇◇◇◇◇◇◇◇◇◇◇◇◇◇

At noon the next day, the only sounds of war came from birds mating on the lawn as Lieutenant John Randall escorted Johann to a building with the Stars and Stripes hanging on the flagpole.

472

Randall led him to a small table with a telephone and told him to sit in a chair facing it.

"When it rings, pick up the receiver; your wife and boy will be on the other end." He gestured to the phone and said as he turned to leave, "You have fifteen minutes, more or less. The operator will warn you a minute before your time is up, but she will not cut you off."

The lieutenant closed the door when he left, and seconds later, the phone rang. Johann stared at it for two rings, then carefully picked it up. He said, "Johann Finke here," heard Barbara say, "Oh, Johann, Ich liebe dich," and they both started to cry.

THE END

FROM THE AUTHOR

I hope you enjoyed the book, and I invite you to read the fifth book in the series, *Kindersoldat*. But before you do, I have a favour to ask. Most people pick books by looking at the cover, reading the blurb blurb or summary, and checking the reviews. I write because I love to do it, and feedback from readers like you is what makes it worthwhile. You can help me by writing a review; your ideas will help me become a better writer, and your honest opinion will help others decide whether the book is for them.

My website is: *thesongsofwar.com*
My Facebook address is: *Robert Faulk, Author*
My email address is: *robertfaulk@thesongsofwar.com*.

You can join my newsletter on the website, or by sending me an email. I promise to keep you updated on what I am doing, along with giving you tidbits like chapters I left out of the book, historical context, and bits from new books I am writing.

Kindersoldat

Book Five in *The Songs of War*

Lucas lost his family in the firebombing of Dortmund and his grand-parents in a bombing raid on Mainz. Left with only his music and his girlfriend, he took both to live with his grand-aunt in Detmold. Six months later, Hitler forced Lucas to join his army.

<u>Kindersoldat</u> is the fifth and final book in this series, and the young violinist's story is based on one told to me by a good friend as he lay on a hospital bed, unable to move because of lingering back injuries sustained while escaping from his wounded panzer.

His family gone, thrust into the violent world of a soldier, Lucas began the passage from boy to man, a ten-year process in a man's natur-al development, but jammed into a few months by Hitler's war. Lucas learned to kill men while still officially a child, saw horror and felt terror that destroyed many brave men.

<u>Kindersoldat</u> is the story of a gentle artist's soul thrust into the vio-lent bowels of a *Waffen SS* battle tank, where a tiny mistake could kill him and his comrades. The musician's tender spirit could not survive in a world of cannons and machine guns, enemy tanks and panzer-killing aircraft, so his spirit broke; the child succumbed, and a warrior took its place.

About the Author

Robert Faulk, a Canadian, born on a farm and educated in a small rural school, grew up in a world of hard workers—men and women who farmed the land and harvested the forests and the sea. He studied engineering in university and worked in construction before taking his family to Germany to pursue a career as an opera singer.

Over the next ten years in Europe, Robert met many Europeans willing to share still-fresh memories of the Second World War. Their stories, often traumatic and always deeply personal, expose the most devastating cost of any war—the human cost. Robert captures the spirit of these stories in a series of four books of historical fiction that he calls _The Songs of War._